ROCKY ROAD

OTHER BOOKS BY JOSI S. KILPACK

Her Good Name
Sheep's Clothing
Unsung Lullaby
Daisy

CULINARY MYSTERIES

Lemon Tart	*Pumpkin Roll*
English Trifle	*Banana Split*
Devil's Food Cake	*Tres Leches Cupcakes*
Key Lime Pie	*Baked Alaska*
Blackberry Crumble	*Fortune Cookie* (coming Feb 2014)

Rocky Road recipes

Download a free PDF of all the recipes in this book at
josiskilpack.com or shadowmountain.com

ROCKY ROAD

A CULINARY MYSTERY

Josi S. Kilpack

SHADOW
MOUNTAIN

To Sadie's Test Kitchen:
Annie, Danyelle, Don, Katie, Laree, Lisa, Megan, Sandra, Whit
Couldn't do this without you guys—thank you so very much

Library of Congress Cataloging-in-Publication Data
Kilpack, Josi S., author.
  Rocky Road / Josi S. Kilpack.
     pages cm
  Summary: Sadie Hoffmiller expects the weekend in St. George, Utah, to be uneventful, but when a local doctor disappears she becomes involved in a murder investigation.
  ISBN 978-1-60907-593-4 (paperbound)
  1. Hoffmiller, Sadie (Fictitious character)—Fiction. 2. Cooks—Fiction. 3. Murder—Investigation—Fiction. 4. St. George (Utah), setting. I. Title.
  PS3561.I412R63 2013
  813'.54—dc23   2013022951

Printed in the United States of America
R. R. Donnelley, Crawfordsville, IN

10 9 8 7 6 5 4 3 2

CHAPTER 1

Bittersweet Anniversary

Following the two-month anniversary of Dr. Trenton Hendricks's disappearance during a hiking trip in the Paradise Point area, his wife, Anita Hendricks, has announced a memorial service to be held in his honor on Wednesday, June 22, at 2:00 at the Red Rock Foundation Hall.

Hendricks was last seen on Friday, April 8, when he set out on a backpacking trip, alone. "He is an experienced hiker," his wife said in an article that first ran in the April 13 edition of this paper. "And he often takes to the backcountry to clear his head following a busy work week."

When Hendricks failed to return from the hike, Mrs. Hendricks contacted Search and Rescue. Hendricks's Jeep Grand Cherokee was found at the Chuckwalla Trailhead the following day, but after six full days and thousands of man-hours, the official search was called off. Nothing belonging to Hendricks was discovered during the search. It is presumed that he is deceased. Hikers are asked to be vigilant as they take to the backcountry and report anything they might discover.

The memorial service will be held just two days prior to the Red Rock Cancer Walk, a Breast Cancer Awareness fund-raising event that Hendricks and his business partner, Dr. Jacob Waters, began nine years ago. Though rumored to be canceled this year due to Hendricks's disappearance, the event will take place as it has in previous years. When asked about the decision to continue with the event, Mrs. Hendricks said, "It is what Trenton would have wanted. He was passionate about his work and I take comfort in knowing that while the hole he has left in so many lives will never be filled, he left this world a better place than he found it." In lieu of flowers, it is requested that donations be made to the Red Rock Cancer Fund, which provides free breast cancer screenings to low-income women in Iron and Washington counties and grants to help cover treatment if patients are unable to cover the costs.

Community members are invited to join the fund-raiser this Friday, June 24, at 7:00 p.m. The 12-hour night-walk will begin at 7:30 p.m. and end with a pancake breakfast Saturday morning at 8:00 a.m. Entry fee for the walk is $45 per person. Each participant will receive a T-shirt and a gift bag with contributions from local sponsors.

Sadie finished reading the article and looked up at Caro, her friend of the past year as well as the cousin of Sadie's fiancé, Pete. Sadie had just arrived at the hotel room in St. George, Utah, where she and Caro would stay as part of an extended girls' weekend. If she'd felt she could do so without hurting Caro's feelings, Sadie would likely have stayed home—she'd been gone for most of the month of June—but she loved Caro and didn't know when she'd have another opportunity to spend time with her like this. Despite Caro being at least ten years Sadie's junior—mid-forties to Sadie's late fifties—the two of them got along swimmingly, and Sadie enjoyed Caro's company very much.

Was it Sadie's imagination that Caro had been a little too excited to have her read this article as soon as they got into their room? And did Caro also seem expectantly interested in Sadie's response? "That's too bad about Dr. Hendricks," Sadie said, refolding the newspaper carefully and placing it beside her on the bed.

"It is too bad," Caro said from where she sat facing Sadie on the other double bed. "And weird, right?"

"Weird?" Sadie said, wondering at Caro's pointed interest. "Weird how?"

"He *disappeared* . . . and everyone seems to be assuming he's dead, but there's *no* proof. No one has found his pack, a shoe—nothing."

"Disappearances are always hard to deal with," Sadie said, ignoring what she feared was behind Caro's leading questions. Caro wanted to investigate; Sadie could feel it, but didn't share Caro's anticipation. She'd come to St. George to enjoy a few days with her good friend, not to investigate the disappearance of a man she'd never met.

"He was Tess's doctor, you know, when she found the lump—she said he was really great, and the foundation saved her life. She—and lots of his other patients—are really broken up over his disappearance."

Sadie put her hands in her lap and pondered a few seconds more before speaking. Caro's dark eyes were bright with excitement when Sadie looked up at her again. "Please tell me this isn't why we're here," Sadie said with a somewhat pleading smile. "Please tell me we came to attend some plays and go shopping and be a part of the walkathon with your cousin?"

"Of course that's why we came," Caro said, looking sheepish as she waved away Sadie's concern. "Tess and I have participated in this walkathon every year since she was first diagnosed, and I'm so excited that you're with us this year—you're going to love Tess." She looked at the newspaper lying beside Sadie on the bed. "And I didn't think much about Dr. H's disappearance, either, when Tess first brought me up to speed on it, but the more I read about it and talked with her, the more I thought that since we're here maybe we could, you know, look into things. Here, let me get the other articles for you—Tess gave me a whole stack when I got here Sunday."

Caro hurried to the dresser. Once her back was turned, Sadie let out a breath, trying to figure out how best to communicate that her level of interest in solving a mystery was at an all-time low right now. A glance at the diamond ring on her left hand initiated the familiar zing she felt every time she thought about what it represented. At the age of fifty-eight—after being a widow for more than twenty years and raising her now-adult children on her own—Sadie was engaged. Engaged! *To be married!*

July 26th had been chosen as the big day . . . and it was just over one month away—five weeks from today, in fact. It was probably a good thing that Sadie had plenty to do between now and then, this trip with Caro being one of the things that would fill the days of waiting until Sadie became Mrs. Peter Cunningham. For his part, Pete was right now in Cabo San Lucas enjoying a guys' week of deep sea fishing that offset her girls' weekend of shopping and pedicures. It was silly how much Sadie missed him, but she did. She saw the ring again and felt the zing once more. Would she ever get used to this?

"Sadie?"

Sadie blinked and looked up to meet Caro's bemused expression. "What?"

Caro was sitting on the bed across from Sadie again, holding a stack of papers in both hands—the articles Tess had given her, Sadie assumed. "I asked if Dr. H's disappearance seems strange to *you*. Have you dealt with anything like this in your other cases?"

"Not like this, no." She *had* been involved in a disappearance case before, though, and couldn't help thinking about it now that Caro had brought it up. It had been hard—and frightening at times—and yet the resolution had brought a lot of people peace. But she still didn't want to investigate this one. She wanted to order napkins with her and Pete's names on them and research honeymoon destinations. That the last few years of her life had been filled with a variety of investigations—murders, mostly, but a few others as well—wasn't something she wanted to dwell on right now.

Caro seemed disappointed in Sadie's response. When the two had worked an investigation in New Mexico several months ago, Caro had been a natural: detail-oriented, smart, and uninhibited about sneaking around. But Sadie's head was in a different place now—she had a wedding to plan, a married life to prepare for. And Pete, who had always served as a support system in the other cases she'd found herself involved in, wasn't available for her to bounce ideas off of—he was wrestling marlins and swordfish off the coast of Mexico. No, now was not a good time for Sadie to put on her Sherlock Holmes hat.

"I wonder," Caro said, with boldness coloring her words, "if you and I could look into things while we're here, ya know? Answer some of the as-yet-unanswered questions and figure out what happened to Dr. Hendricks. It could be fun!"

Fun? "Search and Rescue looked for six days, Caro." She thought of the expansive wilderness that surrounded this relatively small city—a bit of an oasis in the midst of magnificent red rock mountains, canyons, and plateaus. Even though this was Sadie's first visit to St. George, she knew about southern Utah's numerous national parks that protected the unique topography of the region. Though Sadie had hoped to go on a hike or two while they were here, it was crazy to think they might be able to find a missing hiker.

"I don't mean we should search the backcountry. I mean, why did he go out by himself, and why hasn't anyone found any of his gear, and what was his personal life like? Professional life? Was anyone angry with him? Did he have debts to hide from?

"St. George isn't a big city, and the people are nice. I bet we could gather a lot of information—find things the police know nothing about and figure out what really happened to Dr. H."

Sadie mentally tamped down the curiosity Caro's questions were stirring. Her own investigative instincts were never very far below the surface, and she repeated Caro's questions in her mind. Instead of giving in to the tingle and pull, however, she shook her head and tried to think of what Pete would say in response to this. "I'm sure the police investigation is exploring all those questions. And you're jumping to some pretty extreme conclusions with no evidence or circumstance. Did Tess ask you to do this?"

"Not really," Caro said, which meant Tess *was* a part of it. She'd gathered all the articles and given them to Caro for a reason. Did Tess know about Caro's foray into investigation work? Did she know about Sadie's?

"I'm happy to share my concerns with Tess, too," Sadie said, still channeling Pete's wisdom. "But if you're thinking of trying to investigate this, you'll have to count me out." She smiled in hopes of softening the impact of those words, though she meant every one of them. "Most people who know my history won't believe this, but I don't go looking for mysteries to solve—especially now. I have a wedding to plan and I'm still recovering from that cruise. I realize that his disappearance is difficult for the people who cared about Dr. Hendricks, but I'm really not interested in pursuing this, Caro. I'm sorry."

Looking at the pile of papers in her lap, Caro bit her lip, her disappointment impossible to ignore. Sadie felt bad shooting down Caro's hopes, but she sincerely meant what she'd said, so she refrained from apologizing again.

"What if . . . ," Caro said just as the silence was becoming awkward. Sadie waited for her to continue, but Caro seemed to be thinking hard about what to say, or, perhaps, whether to say it at all. Caro couldn't know what her delays did for Sadie's curiosity—it was getting more difficult to hold back. What if Dr. Hendricks *did* have a reason to disappear?

"What if *what?*" Sadie asked, still pulling tight on the reins of her interest.

Caro looked up from the articles she seemed to be holding tighter than before and met Sadie's eyes. "What if we already found something?"

CHAPTER 2

W hat did you find?" Sadie said, hating the eagerness in her tone and trying to push it back down again. Her instincts were working against her.

"Here," Caro said, jumping off her bed with the stack of papers in her hands and then sitting next to Sadie a moment later, causing both of them to bounce slightly. "Let me show you." She shuffled through the articles before removing one. She put the other articles—most of them printed off a computer rather than cut from an actual newspaper—beside her on the bed, and then handed the one she still held to Sadie. Sadie quickly read the date—April 19th—and the title, "Physician still missing." Caro pointed to the picture under the title. It showed a gravel parking lot surrounded by brush, a rough two-rail fence, and red sandstone. There were a police Jeep and a silver Jeep Cherokee in the parking area and several people standing around looking official. A small brown building in the center of the circular parking area was likely a restroom.

"That's Dr. H's Cherokee," Caro explained as Sadie's eyes traveled to the caption beneath the photo. "'*Dr. Trenton Hendricks's Jeep Cherokee was located on Tuesday at the Chuckwalla Trailhead, where it is presumed Dr. Hendricks went hiking on April 8.'"* Caro continued, "His wife reported him missing Monday morning and his car was found a day later with his cell phone on the front seat. It had been turned off Friday afternoon."

"Okay," Sadie said, scanning more of the article in hopes of determining why this particular article was significant enough to have caught so much of Caro's attention.

"Now, look at this," Caro said, riffling through the stack of articles she'd set aside. She pulled out a photograph printed from a computer and put it in Sadie's hands. The photo showed two women smiling into a camera, with a red-rock landscape similar to that in the newspaper picture behind them . . . wait, it was more than similar.

Sadie put the photo beside the grainier newspaper photo and looked between them several times. "Is this the same parking lot?" she asked. The angles weren't exactly identical, but there was a trail marker that said "Chuckwalla" in both photos—to the left of the smiling women in one and in the right corner of the shot printed in the newspaper. In both photos, the same two-rail wooden fence enclosed the parking area. The line of mountains on the horizon behind them remained unchanged.

Caro grinned, nodded quickly, and handed Sadie another photo. This one, a landscape photo, showed the same parking lot in the lower corner but was taken from a vantage point farther away. "Look at the cars," Caro said, pointing to the vehicles in the photos. Sadie had to squint—the cars weren't the focal point of the picture and didn't stand out, but she saw a red sedan, a dark-colored truck, and a yellow Hummer. The Hummer was parked in the same place as the Cherokee in the newspaper photo. Caro continued, "No Jeep

Cherokee—despite the fact that this photo was taken on Sunday, April tenth, two days *after* Dr. H left to go hiking."

Sadie looked at the photos again to verify the placement of the vehicles. She noted that there was no date and time stamp on the printed photos, which meant there was no way to prove that the photo had been taken on April tenth. She looked up at Caro, "So you think . . . what?"

"I think something's fishy," Caro said, looking rather pleased with herself as she returned to her bed. They were facing each other again. "He left on Friday. His car *wasn't* there on Sunday, but it *was* there on Tuesday morning. What if something else happened to him and someone put his car in that lot to make it *look* like he disappeared while hiking?"

Sadie chose to play devil's advocate. "What if he hiked somewhere else on Saturday and then went to the Chuckwalla Trailhead after this photo was taken on the tenth?"

Caro shook her head. "He was supposed to have been home on Sunday afternoon."

"Maybe he wanted to take one more short hike Sunday evening."

"And he took his entire sixty-pound frame pack on a quick hike? Sunset is around eight o'clock that time of year—I looked it up. Why take his whole pack if he's planning to be back to the car in a few hours?"

Sadie still felt it was a stretch to be too concerned about this, but she couldn't help asking more questions. "Who's in this photo?" she said, holding up the one of the two women.

"That's Tess's friend Kathryn," Caro said, pointing to the younger woman. "She's a breast cancer survivor like Tess and has gone on a hike every year on the anniversary of her doctor telling her she was cancer free. She doesn't live here in St. George, and she posted the photos on Facebook only a few weeks ago. When this new article came out, Tess made the connection." She waved toward the first article Sadie had read. "When I got into town yesterday, Tess showed me the photos to see what I thought. It's the same parking lot—you can tell, right?—and his car isn't in it."

"But, like I said, that doesn't *prove* anything. There's no *proof* these photos were taken the same Sunday his car should have been there."

"Kathryn talked about the hike before and after on Facebook," Caro said. "That counts for something."

"I'm not saying anyone's a liar, but—"

Caro cut her off. "This photo *proves* there is an inaccuracy in what the police think happened, which is that Dr. H went hiking on Saturday and never came back."

"Yes, okay, that's a good point," Sadie said with a nod. She'd seen in more than one case how a small detail could make all the difference. She felt better knowing that Caro wasn't seeing this as proof that foul play had taken place, just that the police assumptions were incorrect in this one small detail. "Did you take this to the police, then?"

An immediate look of disappointment crossed Caro's face. "Well, no."

Sadie knew she hadn't. If she'd taken this to the police, the gleam in her eye wouldn't be quite so bright. Sadie picked up the other articles and handed them and the photographs back to Caro with an understanding smile. "Then that's the next step."

Caro's shoulders slumped slightly. "I thought you and I could look into it—ya know, see what we could find out on our own."

Sadie reached across the aisle between them and put a hand on Caro's knee in hopes it would make the letdown a little easier. "Caro, this is an active police investigation, and you've found potential evidence. You know we need to take it to the police."

"But, Sadie—," Caro said, sounding a little exasperated. She looked past Sadie for a moment, as though lining up her argument, then made eye contact with her again. "You have a gift. You are so good at this stuff. You change lives and find what no one else can find. I've seen it."

Sadie couldn't help being flattered, but it didn't change her mind. Part of her hesitation was likely because the other investigations she'd found herself in were months apart, giving her more time to recover, whereas her last case—if you could call it that—was just a few weeks ago. "I've also made a lot of messes, too. And this doesn't feel like something my skills would lend themselves to. This is a disappearance in the backcountry—not my forte to say the least, and I don't have any personal investment here—which isn't an aspect I can just make up."

"But if something's happened, isn't that enough for you to become personally invested in it?"

"Not right now, it isn't," Sadie said, not liking how cold she sounded but not sure how else to explain it. "I'm getting married next month. There's been a lot going on. This isn't the right time."

Caro wasn't giving up. Sadie could see it in the set of her brow and the angle of her chin. "I don't know that personal investment and timing is the right way to determine what's right and wrong. In the Bible it says we shouldn't hide our light under a bushel, Sadie. I think God gave you this light and—"

"And sometimes those bushels catch on fire," Sadie said, her voice just a little bit sharper. "Which happened to me just a few weeks ago, and I haven't healed from it yet. I'm sorry. I'm not ready to tackle another case, and this one isn't right for me anyway. We need to take these photos to the police and let them handle it."

Caro looked into her lap, but Sadie—though she was tempted—was not swayed to give in to her feelings of empathy. In the past, she had been guilty of not going to the police when she should have, and so, while she understood Caro's reluctance to do so, it didn't change the facts. When Caro spoke next, her voice was softer, more humble. "Tess had this idea to put together a scrapbook for Dr. H's family, and we could use that as an excuse to talk to people. Ya know—without getting people all suspicious. Maybe he told someone something, or had some secrets that could explain the discrepancy."

Sadie stood her ground. "Caro, the photos are evidence."

Caro nodded her understanding, but Sadie could tell she felt the sting of being excited about doing something only to have Sadie shoot it full of lead. "And," Sadie continued, "it's important information for the police to have. I bet they'll be really grateful to have it—in fact, why don't we take it to them right now?"

Caro looked conflicted. "Now?"

"Absolutely," Sadie said, wanting to validate Caro's hard work in gathering this information. Regardless of Sadie's feelings about the case, she could appreciate Caro's investment and feelings of disappointment. "That article on Sunday shows there's still community interest in this case, and this could be the break the police need to figure out what's happened. Maybe they've found other discrepancies that this will help support. Who knows? I'm so impressed that you and Tess put all of this together." It was difficult not to lecture Caro on the fact that she and Tess should have taken this to the police right away, but she hated those lectures when she was on the receiving end and therefore chose the kinder and gentler route. And a scrapbook? Talk about a flimsy cover story. It would never have worked. She was doing Caro and Tess a favor by stopping this before they embarrassed themselves. "The authorities need to know about this. What time are we meeting Tess tonight? Are we still having dinner with her family?"

Caro still sounded subdued. "Yeah, we're supposed to be at her house at six o'clock."

It was just after four now. "We could run to the police station right now and turn this information in," Sadie said. "Or . . ." She picked up the article with the incriminating photo of the Cherokee and scanned the page. "It says a Sergeant Woodruff is an investigator on the case. We could call him and set up a time to meet with him. That way we would know the information got to the right person."

"You really think that's best? I mean, you don't want to just, I don't know, talk to Dr. H's wife or maybe one of the reporters who've followed the case or . . . someone else who might know something? I think Tess's scrapbook idea could really work—she's already started getting the layout put together."

Sadie took a breath and kept her smile in place. Oh, how well she remembered feeling this way when she was worked up about a new case and people told her to just be still. How ironic that, for once, it was Sadie giving the counsel to do less and pull back. "It's a police matter, Caro. The very best thing we can do is help them do their best work, and this will help them do that. Why don't you call Sergeant Woodruff and ask him what we should do with all this information?"

Caro looked at the articles in her hands again and nodded. "Can I make copies of everything first?" Caro asked, giving Sadie a hopeful look. "Just in case?"

CHAPTER 3

In the end, Sadie agreed to let Caro make copies of the articles, and Caro agreed to call Sergeant Woodruff. The call went to voice mail. When Sergeant Woodruff didn't call them back by five o'clock, Sadie convinced Caro that they should take the original documents into the police department and set up an appointment to speak to someone there the next day. That would allow the officers time to go over the documents.

At the police station, Sadie let Caro be the spokesperson, hoping it would help her be satisfied and keep Sadie's name out of the situation. She didn't look too good on paper these days—at least not to law enforcement.

A desk officer assured them he'd get the documents to the investigator currently in charge of the case and that Caro would be contacted if he felt it was necessary.

"I really have to explain the photos for it to make sense," Caro said as they pushed through the front doors of the station on their way back to her car.

"I'm certain they'll call if they need more information," Sadie said. "You did the right thing."

Caro's blue car seemed to glow in the bright summer sun. Pointing the key fob, she pushed the button to unlock the doors, and the car beeped in confirmation.

"Tess is going to be disappointed," Caro said. "She was really into the idea of looking into this ourselves."

"That's only because she's never dug around in other people's business before. Don't you remember how intense everything got last time?" Sadie hadn't forgotten the overwhelming fear she'd felt when things came to a head. Returning to those moments in her mind made it even more surprising to her that Caro wanted to take on another case.

"Sure I remember." They reached the car and moved to their respective doors. "But it was also exciting."

Sadie gave her a doubtful look as they looked at each other across the top of the car. "So you *don't* remember."

Caro laughed and they both slid into their seats and pulled the doors closed.

Though it was beautiful, the desert region of St. George was hot. The heat trapped in the car, first at the hotel, and again when they went into the police station, was stifling. And so very dry. It was different from Colorado heat, or even the heat in New Mexico where Caro lived. Was there any humidity in the air at all? Sadie immediately turned the air conditioning to high and said a silent prayer of gratitude for Freon.

They headed south toward St. George Boulevard, one of the main east-west streets in the city center. Caro turned right, then merged into the left lane and made the first turn toward the white-domed tower that rose above the city, marking the Mormon Temple in St. George. They planned to tour the grounds and visitors center while they were in town, and Sadie was excited to learn more about it. The bright white building was like a pivot point, as though the entire city had grown from that one plot of land. Maybe it had.

"Tess lives just a few blocks from here," Caro said, noting the way Sadie looked at the temple. "You can see the top of the temple from her house—she and her husband, Paul, were married there."

"It's beautiful," Sadie said, craning her neck as they passed the building. When she faced forward she asked about Caro's children—twin daughters attending two different colleges—and Caro's husband, Rex. It had been so long since she and Caro had had a chance to just catch up. Caro was happy to give an update.

It sounded as though things were on the mend for Caro and her husband; they'd been in a rough patch when Sadie had stayed with them last year. Rex had started coming to the gym with gym-rat Caro in the evenings and they had joined a horseback-riding group made up of other couples who took weekend day trips all over New Mexico. Sadie hadn't even known they liked horses; they didn't own any of their own. Could you rent horses for a weekend like a car or a carpet cleaner? What an odd concept.

In September they were going on an eight-day horseback trip somewhere in Texas.

"We were going to go in July," Caro said, turning onto a residential street. About half of the houses had xeriscaped yards, with limited vegetation, while the other ones had grass. Sadie could only imagine how much water it took to keep the grass green in this climate. Caro continued, "but then *someone* decided to get married and we had to reschedule—luckily we hadn't finalized the travel plans yet."

Sadie couldn't help but grin. She looked at the diamond on her hand again. *Zing.* She forced herself to look away. She had kept herself from thinking about wedding plans for several hours, but now those thoughts began to surface. There was so much to be done, but most of it would need to wait until she was back in Garrison. She could wait a few more days. "So—tell me about Tess," Sadie said aloud, to change the direction of her thoughts. "Other than the fact that she's your cousin—on your mother's side, right?—and had breast cancer." With so much going on, Sadie hadn't asked as many questions as she normally would.

"Well, she came to St. George for college and met Paul, her husband. She has two awesome kids, and she's a big-time scrapbooker. She's really wonderful and high-energy and fun—did I tell you she's only thirty-two?"

"That's so young," Sadie said, heavy with the realization. *How old were her kids when she was diagnosed?* Sadie wondered.

"It is young, too young. Latinas don't have high breast cancer rates to begin with, and our family doesn't have a history of it, so we were all taken by surprise. Tess was only twenty-nine when she found the lump."

"And Dr. Hendricks was her doctor at that time?"

Caro nodded. "He'd delivered Gabby a few years earlier. She didn't have insurance when she found the lump so she went through the foundation."

"And that's what the walk is for on Friday." It was the reason they had come *this* weekend. So much had happened in the last few weeks that Sadie hadn't taken note of all the details Caro must have already told her. She hoped talking about Dr. Hendricks didn't re-whet Caro's interest in pursuing the case.

"Right. They help uninsured women get mammograms and things. Dr. H oversaw her through the whole diagnostic procedure, and then, before they did any treatment, Dr. H helped her freeze some of her eggs so she might be able to have a baby after everything was over—most women are made sterile through the treatments, and Tess wanted more children."

"The foundation paid for all of that?" Sadie said, surprised that such additional costs as egg preservation would be covered.

Caro nodded and glanced at Sadie. "Amazing, huh? Once she's been cancer-free for five years, they'll consider in vitro. Hopefully it will work out and she'll get to be a mother again."

"And she's Mormon?" Sadie asked, assuming as much because Tess had been married in a Mormon temple. Sadie knew that Mormons had pretty much settled the state of Utah after being run out of the cities they built back east.

"Yeah, she converted in college—Paul was born and raised in the Mormon church. He's one of seven kids. Mormons usually have big families."

"I've heard that," Sadie said with a nod. "Is that why Tess wants more? Because of her church?"

"Not necessarily, but I'm sure it's part of it. Being a mom is really important to her and they struggled to get pregnant with Gabby as it was. It was devastating when she realized she might not have the chance to even try again—which makes Dr. H that much more important to her, ya know?"

Sadie nodded. "But she's doing well now? Cancer free?"

"Sure is," Caro said with a tender smile as she made another right-hand turn. "She had reconstruction surgery just six months after her mastectomy and has really done great with her diet and exercise to improve her overall health—I've been really proud of her. I can't imagine going through something like that, especially at her age."

"They've come such a long way with breast cancer research in recent years. When I was Tess's age, it was a death sentence."

"I know," Caro said with a nod. "Early detection makes all the difference—Dr. H and his foundation saved her life. She was only six weeks post-op the first time we did the fund-raising walk, and she just walked the first mile. I finished the rest for her. Last year we walked the whole thing together. This year, we're planning to run-walk it."

"I'm so glad she's doing well," Sadie said, wondering if she could run-walk twelve whole miles. She was in good shape these days. She had taken a page out of Caro's book and realized how important it was to remain strong as she aged, but twelve miles was . . . well, it was *twelve* miles. "I look forward to meeting Tess," Sadie said. She also hoped that her not wanting to investigate Dr. Hendricks's death wouldn't destroy the potential friendship between her and Tess. She wanted very much to like this woman Caro thought so highly of.

Caro began to slow the car down, and then she pulled in front of a modest home, xeriscaped like some of its neighbors, with a bright floral wreath hanging on the front door and a collection in the yard of bikes, scooters, and toys fading in the desert sun. It was six o'clock in the evening, and the temperatures were still in the low nineties.

"Shoot, I'd meant to stop and get a hostess gift," Sadie said as they got out of the car.

"Don't worry about it," Caro said, waving off Sadie's concerns. "Tess's very easy-going."

Easy-going or not, Sadie would still have felt better if she'd had something in hand. Like bubble bath or a nice salami. A friend from Colorado Springs had once given Sadie a box of Swiss chocolates when she'd stayed overnight for a wedding in Garrison. Sadie had told her she was welcome back anytime. Because Sadie didn't carry a purse, her hands felt even more conspicuously empty. She'd lost and replaced so many purses in the last few years that she didn't bother carrying one any more unless she had to. She kept her phone in one pocket and a slim wallet with her ID and a credit card in another, and that was it. But there was nothing to do about a gift for Tess now. The best she could hope for was to learn from this and be more prepared next time.

They knocked on the front door and a girl about six years old opened it a minute later. She had dark hair like Caro's, but lighter skin and hazel eyes, which led Sadie to assume that Tess's husband was Caucasian. The little girl wore a fairy costume, complete with wire-rimmed wings, one of which was bent at the top. The smell of bread came through the doorway, and Sadie took a deep breath—dinner rolls, perhaps? She hadn't felt particularly hungry when they'd left the hotel, but she was suddenly starving. Especially for home-cooked food, which Sadie had enjoyed very little of in recent weeks.

"Hey, there, Gabby," Caro said to the little girl.

"Hi," Gabby said shyly, pulling against the door and looking carefully back and forth at the two women.

"This is my friend Sadie," Caro said, waving a hand in Sadie's direction. "We get to have dinner at your house tonight."

Gabby nodded, looked between them again, and then turned and ran back into the house, calling for her mom. Her wings bounced behind her as she made her retreat.

A woman immediately appeared at the end of the short hallway, drying her hands on a dishcloth and smiling widely as she walked toward them. "Hello!" she said, opening her arms, one hand still holding the dishcloth, and giving Caro a big hug before turning to Sadie with a smile. Her dark hair was cut short in a spiky modern style. Her build was thicker than Caro's, but she had similar curves and dark Latina coloring. She wore a bright pink fitted T-shirt and denim capris, with no shoes but glittery toenails that matched her shirt. "I am *so* glad to meet you, Sadie. Caro has told me *so* much about you and we have *so* much to talk about."

Sadie kept her smile in place and hoped Tess wasn't referring to the investigation Sadie had nipped in the bud.

Tess turned back the way she'd come and waved for them to follow her. "Dinner's just about ready," she said.

She headed down the hallway, obviously expecting Sadie and Caro to follow her, which they did. The house was painted in rich tones of brown and terra-cotta. Above a table in the entryway were the words "Live well. Laugh often. Love much." Knowing Tess's medical history made the words more poignant.

Sadie stayed a step behind Caro as they entered the kitchen, which was located in the center of the house. Tess went to the stove, and Gabby sat at the counter coloring in a coloring book and watching them shyly. Sadie could hear a TV in another room.

"Can we help with anything?" Caro asked.

"Oh, no," Tess said, waving off the suggestion as she put on a pair of oven mitts that had seen better days. The kitchen was cluttered but not uncomfortably so. "Paul's finishing up dinner and I already set the table." Sadie's glance followed the wave of Tess's hand. She saw a perfectly set table and, through the sliding glass door beyond the table, a man bent over what looked like a fire pit built into the back patio.

"Did Paul do one of his Dutch oven dinners?" Caro asked. The excitement in her voice caught Sadie's attention almost as much as the words "Dutch oven" did. Sadie had eaten meals cooked in those large cast-iron pots, though she'd never cooked in them herself. She knew that they had a unique way of capturing the heat produced by coals or charcoal, creating a self-contained "oven." What a fun way to kick off her trip!

"Oh, he's always looking for an excuse," Tess said as she pulled open the oven door. "And as long as he's willing to put up with the heat to do it, I'm always game."

"Mmmmm," Caro said. "I still remember that stew he made last year."

"Wait until you have this, then," Tess said as she removed a pan of rolls—perfectly golden brown—from the oven and set it on the stovetop. This meal was looking better and better. "It's a recipe his dad used to make, but he's changed it up a little and it's so good."

Sadie continued to watch Paul—though she hadn't been formally introduced to him—through the glass as Tess explained his love for Dutch oven cooking and how he was looking to turn it into a side business. Paul straightened, and Sadie hurried to open the door for him. "Thank you," he said. He had the same hazel eyes Sadie had seen on his daughter, and a kind face. "I'm Paul, but my hands are covered with charcoal so I won't make you shake them."

Sadie smiled. "I'm Sadie, Caro's friend. Nice to meet you." She closed the door behind him.

"I think we're ready," he announced to the group.

"Great," Tess said, putting the last of the rolls in a basket lined with a flour sack towel. "Gabby, go get your brother for the prayer."

Gabby did as she was asked and returned with Paul and Tess's son, Ryan, who looked ten or eleven years old. He said a prayer over the food, and then Paul instructed everyone to pick up their plates from the table and come outside to be served. Sadie had to stop herself from being the first in line and graciously let the children go in front of her.

As soon as she stepped outside, the heat was forgotten because of the amazing smells coming from the two Dutch ovens. One had chicken in it and the other a potato casserole. Sadie had to swallow in order to keep her enthusiasm in check. Really, her food obsession was a bit out of hand.

"This is wonderful," Sadie said after Paul slid into his seat at the head of the table. She'd already enjoyed a few bites of both chicken and potatoes, and they were delicious.

Paul grinned his appreciation for the compliment but said nothing, probably because his mouth was full. She waited for him to finish before asking about the recipe, which he said he'd be happy to share. She committed to buy a Dutch oven and make it for Pete. Maybe after they were *married*. *Zing*.

"Oh, I forgot the rolls." Tess jumped up and headed for the kitchen, returning seconds later with the basket of rolls that completed the meal perfectly. She also put a small bowl of what looked like strawberry cream cheese in the center of the table.

"When we got married, Paul's mom gave me a whole cookbook full of her family's favorite recipes, including this one," Tess explained as she returned to her seat. "It's from a restaurant called Maddox in northern Utah—that's where Paul's from. The rolls are especially good with raspberry butter."

Raspberry butter, not strawberry cream cheese.

Sadie was happy to sample a roll. She spread both halves with a generous helping of the raspberry butter. "These are delicious," she said one bite later. "Is it a batter roll?" It was so light it couldn't possibly be from a traditional kneaded dough.

"It *is* a batter roll. They're my go-to roll recipe—so easy to whip up and so good. I'm glad you like them."

"I like everything. Thank you both for your efforts."

"Sadie's a bit of a foodie," Caro explained with a teasing smile in Sadie's direction.

"And a very, very happy one right now," Sadie added, causing the adults to chuckle. She was soon lost in the joys of really excellent home-cooked food.

For the next twenty minutes, the group ate and talked and got to know each other. As soon as dinner was over, the kids disappeared outside with Paul to clean up while the three women cleared the table and stored the leftovers. Tess put the last four rolls into a zippered plastic bag for Sadie and Caro to take to the hotel to eat later. Sadie was overjoyed! Would it be rude to ask for some raspberry butter, too?

The three women worked together like a well-oiled machine. When the kitchen was clean, Tess pulled out a half-gallon of vanilla bean ice cream and asked Caro to get a jar of hot fudge out of the fridge. Paul and the kids weren't ready for dessert yet, so Tess, Caro, and Sadie made only three hot fudge sundaes for themselves.

"So," Tess said with a glint in her eye after they sat around the table again. "Are you ready to discuss the *case*? I have the layout for the scrapbook all worked out and ready to go—now I just need the info to fill it with."

Ol' Dad's Dutch Chicken

Breading:
1½ cups flour
1½ tablespoons cornstarch
2 teaspoons salt
2½ teaspoons paprika
1½ teaspoons sugar
¾ teaspoons red pepper powder
1 teaspoon turmeric
½ teaspoon onion powder
½ teaspoon garlic powder

Combine breading ingredients and coat 18 pieces (approximately 4 pounds) split boneless, skinless chicken breasts.

Brown breaded chicken in skillet in 2 tablespoons vegetable oil. When browned, place chicken in 12-inch Dutch oven. Cover and cook over low heat 2 to 3 hours. Check occasionally; if contents are too dry, the pot is too hot. Do not stir. When chicken is tender, serve as desired. (Chicken may tenderize in pan for approximately 1 hour.)

Slow cooker directions: Place 2 tablespoons vegetable oil in bottom of slow cooker before adding browned chicken. Cook 2 to 4 hours on low heat setting.

Oven directions: Place browned chicken in 9x13-inch pan, cover with foil, and bake 1 hour at 350 degrees.

Makes 18 servings.

Ol' Dad's Dutch Potatoes

1 (10.75-ounce) can condensed cream of celery soup (or any cream soup or homemade white sauce)
8 pounds potatoes, unpeeled and sliced ⅓-inch thick
3 medium onions, finely chopped
2 pounds cheddar cheese, sliced or grated
Salt, to taste
Pepper, to taste
½ (1-ounce) packet ranch dressing mix, blended with 2 tablespoons water (mixture should be thick, like condensed soup)

Spread undiluted soup over bottom of Dutch oven. Fill oven ⅓ full with sliced potatoes. Add a layer of ⅓ of the chopped onions; sprinkle with salt & pepper. Add two more layers of potatoes, onions, salt, and pepper; top with ranch dressing mixture.

Place over low heat about 2 hours, being careful not to let potatoes burn; stir every 30 minutes. If potatoes seem dry, the pot is too hot. If potatoes on bottom of pot burn, do not disturb them—the rest of the potatoes may still be enjoyed without tasting the burned ones.

When potatoes are tender, cover with ½ of the cheese. When cheese is melted, stir potatoes a final time. Just before serving, add remaining cheese; allow cheese to melt and serve this delicious dish.*

Feeds about 18 adults as a side dish.

*When potatoes are tender, serve within 10 minutes or dish will turn mushy.

Note: One-half or one-third of this recipe may be made in a slow cooker. Grease slow cooker before adding ingredients as listed. Cook 2 hours on high heat setting before adding ½ of the cheese, stirring, and then adding additional cheese.

Maddox Rolls

The Maddox Ranch House is located in Perry, Utah.

1 tablespoon active dry yeast or instant yeast
¼ cup warm water
¼ cup sugar
⅓ cup shortening
1 teaspoon salt
¾ cup scalded milk*
½ cup cold water
2 eggs, beaten
3½ cups flour

For regular yeast: In small bowl, sprinkle yeast over warm water; set aside. In separate larger bowl, combine sugar, shortening, and salt; mix well. Add scalded milk, cold water, and beaten eggs; mix about 1 minute, or until well combined. Stir in dissolved yeast. Add flour. Mix four minutes.

For instant yeast: In mixing bowl, combine 2 cups flour,

1 tablespoon yeast, sugar, and salt; mix well. Add shortening, eggs, scalded milk, and ¾ cup hot water; mix 2 minutes. Add remaining 1½ cups flour; mix 2 minutes more. (This is a "batter" roll rather than a "dough" roll. Batter will be soft.)

When ingredients are combined, cover bowl; let batter rise in warm place 45 to 60 minutes, or until doubled in size. Stir batter down. Spoon into greased muffin tins, filling 18 muffin cups about ⅔ full. Cover; let rise an additional 45 to 60 minutes, or until double in size.

Bake at 400 degrees 15 to 20 minutes, or until lightly browned. Makes 18 rolls.

*Evaporated milk may be substituted for scalded milk.

Raspberry Butter

½ cup butter
¼ cup raspberry jam
½ teaspoon vanilla

Mix all ingredients together until smooth. Makes about ¾ cup.

CHAPTER 4

Sadie had almost forgotten about the investigation, and neither she nor Caro answered Tess immediately. Not seeming to notice their hesitation, Tess turned toward Caro and continued. "Remember that list we made of people who could be good sources of information? Well, you'll never guess who's in town and possibly available for an interview. I almost didn't put her on the list because I thought it was such a long shot."

Suddenly the ice cream wasn't quite so delicious. Sadie put down her spoon.

"Uh, who?" Caro asked. Sadie lamented the missed opportunity to let Tess down from the start.

"Lori Hendricks," Tess said. She looked back and forth between Sadie and Caro, her eyes showing that this name should mean something to them. "Dr. H's ex-wife. Nikki's ward is hosting the memorial luncheon and Lori's helping with it."

"Ward?" Sadie couldn't help but ask. "Who's Nikki?"

"Oh, uh, a ward is what we call a Mormon congregation," Tess said.

"Nikki Waters is Dr. Waters's wife," Caro said, turning to

Sadie. "He and Dr. Hendricks were partners at the clinic and the foundation."

"That's sure nice of Nikki's congregation to head up the luncheon," Sadie said.

"Mormons do that kind of thing all the time, and Dr. H was a member of the Church, just not active." Tess leaned closer to Caro and Sadie. "But the fascinating part is that Lori's helping with the luncheon. She'll even be at the church tonight. So I told Nikki we'd love to help set up. It might create an opportunity to talk to Lori, right? And maybe Nikki, too."

"Uh," Caro stalled, shooting a look at Sadie.

Tess continued, still not properly interpreting the lack of response to her enthusiasm. "Lori's son, Joey, was in Ryan's first grade class—that was before Lori and Dr. H divorced—and Lori and I did an art council fund-raiser together. It's that whole foot-in-the-door thing you were talking about, Caro, you know? I'm still friends with her on Facebook and now she's in town. Isn't that great?"

"Well," Caro started. "I'm not—"

"And I told Nikki about the scrapbook idea and she loved it. She's going to talk to Dr. Waters about sharing some of his memories for it."

When neither Sadie nor Caro made any comment, Tess sat back in her chair a little and drew her eyebrows together, finally recognizing that something was wrong. "Why aren't you excited about this?"

"Actually," Caro said slowly, saving Sadie the trouble of bursting Tess's balloon of anticipation. "There's been a bit of a change of plans."

"What do you mean?"

"Well, I talked to Sadie," she motioned toward Sadie, and Sadie tried not to shrink back when Tess turned her confused look in her direction. "And she thought that we should turn the pictures over to the police and let them follow the leads. Ya know, since they're already involved and everything. The pictures are probably evidence."

Probably? Sadie repeated in her mind.

Tess was quiet for a few seconds and put her spoon down on the table. "You mean, you don't want us to look into this on our own like we talked about?"

Caro shifted her weight in her seat and looked at her ice cream. "Well, uh . . ."

"I don't think it's a good idea," Sadie said, attempting a rescue for poor Caro. "It could be considered interfering with a police investigation, which is why we took all the articles and pictures to the police department on the way here, so they can evaluate them and use them toward their own investigation."

"You took them to the police?" Tess lifted her eyebrows and looked back and forth from Sadie to Caro in shock.

"It's a police investigation," Sadie repeated. "And I'm certain they will appreciate you guys helping them out." She smiled in an effort to lighten the mood of the conversation.

When Tess focused on Sadie, her eyes narrowed slightly. "But—I thought this is what you did. You're a PI and everything, right?"

"I had a private investigator business for a while, but I don't do it any more."

"But you solve murders and stuff. Caro told me about what you did in Santa Fe, and then something back east, too, right?"

"Well, yes, but I don't do those things on purpose." That didn't sound right. "I mean, I don't put my nose into things that aren't my business." That was a bald-faced lie. "I mean, well, I believe it's best to help the police figure this out rather than do it ourselves. They know more than we do, and for us to act on this independent of them would be duplicating information and could cause some problems with their case."

"What kinds of *problems*?" Tess asked, accusation and challenge heavy in her voice. The nice bubbly woman Sadie had first met was gone and in her place was a woman who likely wished Sadie had never come to town.

"All kinds of things can go wrong when you're doing an investigation and the police are better trained to deal with those things. We certainly don't want to mess anything up for them."

Silence fell on the table between them and after a few more seconds Tess picked up her spoon and took another bite of her ice cream, staring at her bowl. Her annoyance was palpable, and Sadie felt bad despite knowing she was doing the right thing. At her core, Sadie was a people pleaser—she liked people to be happy. Tess was *not* happy right now.

Despite the awkward mood, Sadie wondered about this list of names Tess had mentioned. Caro hadn't mentioned it. Had they planned to create an *actual* scrapbook? Or just tell people that's what they were doing? What else had they done in preparation for this "case"? But Sadie couldn't allow herself to think about that for very long. It wasn't safe, considering how easily she'd become invested in past cases.

"I'm sorry, Tess," Caro said after several seconds had passed. "I should have thought about turning the pictures over to the police sooner."

"What if they don't do anything with it?" Tess said sharply, looking at Caro—not Sadie. "Dr. H's foundation saved my life and he was the only one who seemed to understand how important it was for me to keep the option of having another baby. He's made that a possibility for me—*he did*. In the two months since he's disappeared, the police have found no leads. Not one. And we did. I owe it to him to find out what it means. I can't believe you two decided that didn't matter without even talking to me about it."

Ouch. "The police haven't found leads they've *shared*," Sadie cut in, though she tried to smile to make up for her rudeness in interrupting. Tess did not smile back as Sadie explained further. "There are things that take place behind the scenes that aren't necessarily made public. And they might be things that your discovery could help with. I understand how strongly you feel about this, Tess, but the police really are the best option for evaluating the photographs. They can do more than we ever could." Even as she said the words, dozens of memories rushed through her mind of times when the police hadn't found the answers Sadie had sniffed out on her own. Caro had said as much back at the hotel, but now Sadie was remembering actual details about things she'd uncovered that no one else had. But with those memories came the reminder that she'd also gotten in the way of police investigations. She'd put herself in danger, and she'd created dangerous situations for other people. This was far more complex than either Caro or Tess realized.

Caro and Tess returned to their ice cream. After a few moments, Tess looked up again. "That's really it, then?" she asked in a tone that seemed casual, but didn't mask her disappointment . . . or frustration. "All that planning for nothing? I never considered that we were wasting our time with the lists and everything." She cast a quick accusatory glance at Sadie, and Sadie looked away again. Her hopes that she and Tess would be friends began to thin.

"I'm sorry," Caro said.

Even the last bite of ice cream couldn't make Sadie feel better about this. What a killjoy she'd turned out to be. *Who else was on that list? Why was Lori Hendricks helping with the memorial luncheon for her ex-husband?*

"So *you* agree with her?" Tess asked Caro as though Sadie weren't sitting right there.

Caro paused a moment, but then she nodded. Sadie would have liked a stronger answer.

"And you guys took all those articles I found to the police? Without even asking me about it? I spent hours gathering those articles. *Hours.* If I'd known you were going to just hand them off, I'd have kept them myself."

"I'm sorry," Caro said. "I should have told you about it before we went to the police. I made copies of the articles, though. I'll bring them over tomorrow."

Tess stood up, pushing back her chair and leaning over the table to gather the bowls. This time she didn't make eye contact with either Caro or Sadie. "Well, I told Nikki I would help set up at the church tonight, and I need to keep my word. You're welcome to come with me if you'd like, but don't feel obligated."

Tess didn't wait for an answer before heading back into the kitchen. The bowls clinked together as she put them in the sink. Sadie and Caro stayed at the table.

"That didn't go as smoothly as I had hoped it would," Sadie said quietly enough that Tess wouldn't overhear.

Caro leaned toward Sadie so she could also keep her voice down.

"Yeah, Tess can get a little intense sometimes, and she felt like this was something she was supposed to do—as in, 'God wanted her to.'"

Oh, boy.

"Couldn't we help her set up tables at the church?" Caro asked a moment later. "It sounds like she told them we'd come—they're counting on us, and maybe it would help Tess feel better about all this."

It was on the tip of Sadie's tongue to ask if Caro's and Tess's real motive for going were to create an opportunity to talk to Dr. Hendricks's ex-wife after all. But Tess hadn't *said* she was going to continue the investigation, and Sadie still wanted Tess's friendship. "I'd be happy to help set up."

"Oh, good," Caro said brightly as she got to her feet, a little too brightly for Sadie's peace of mind. "I'll let Tess know."

Sadie hoped this wouldn't be a decision she'd regret.

CHAPTER 5

Sadie had been inside her town's Mormon church for a couple of weddings and a Scout ceremony once, but it wasn't like this big, new, modern building. Sadie appreciated the light colors and functional design as she followed Tess and Caro into a large room Tess called the cultural hall. It looked like a basketball court to Sadie and, while the roominess was nice, it seemed too informal a location for a luncheon.

A woman in her early forties with shoulder-length auburn hair and an overall soccer-mom quality hurried in their direction. She was slightly overweight but she had an engaging smile and was dressed nicely in white capris and a multicolored top, with matching necklace, earrings, and bracelet. She had magnificent skin, and Sadie suspected regular facials.

"I'm so glad you guys could make it," she said, giving each of them a hug before introducing herself as Nikki Waters. "There's a softball tournament tonight, so some of our helpers didn't show up." She waved toward three people who were rolling a giant rack full of folding chairs through a set of double doors at the far end of the room. "We're so glad you could help." Her bracelet jingled when she gestured with her hands.

"We are, too," Tess said. Sadie hoped she was the only one who could tell the smile was a little forced. "Where do you need us?"

"Well, we need to set up all of those chairs," Nikki said, motioning toward the rack of chairs again. "We need to get some round tables from the closet in the hall, and someone put 'fruit' on the sign-up sheet we sent around on Sunday instead of 'fruit salad,' so we're kind of scrambling in the kitchen to get it all cut up." She turned to Tess. "Didn't you say you wanted to talk to Lori about the scrapbook? She's already working on the fruit."

All three were silent for a few seconds—just long enough for Nikki's expression to turn to confusion. Sadie wondered how much Nikki knew about the motivation behind the scrapbook. One of the first rules of investigation was keeping a tight lip.

"I'd be happy to help with the tables," Caro said, clapping her hands together and interrupting the awkwardness. "Where are they?"

"There's a closet in the hall just through those doors," Nikki said, pointing toward another set of double doors on the opposite side of the room. Sadie noticed that there were no fewer than four sets of doors around the perimeter of the room. And a stage at the front. The possible uses for this room seemed endless—if you didn't mind the basketball court painted on the floor.

Caro headed toward the doors Nikki had pointed out, obviously eager to do something other than continue this conversation.

"I can help with chairs," Tess said a moment later.

Nikki's confusion deepened. "But I thought you wanted to talk to Lori."

"Change of plans," she said, making Sadie think of all the things she needed to do back home in Garrison. If this trip were going to continue to be uncomfortable, maybe she'd just go home. Caro and Tess could do whatever they wanted. But she'd feel bad backing out of the entire weekend, and she worried that Caro and Tess would make a mess if she left them to figure things out on their own. Ugh.

"I'll help Lori, then," Sadie said, eager to escape as Caro had. "Where do I go?"

"Um, through those doors," Nikki said, pointing to another set of double doors. "The kitchen's straight across the hall. You can't miss it."

"Great. Thanks," Sadie said as she headed that direction. She wasn't fast enough to avoid overhearing Nikki whisper, "What do you mean a change of plans? I thought . . ."

As Sadie made her way to the kitchen, she told herself that she was the best choice to help Lori. It would keep Tess or Caro from being unable to help themselves from acting on their agendas. But something prickled in her chest, all the same. This was the ex-wife of Dr. Hendricks—someone who might be more honest about his flaws than most people would be. The information Sadie could learn from a conversation with this woman was impossible to quantify. She hoped she would be able to control herself.

"It would be interfering with an investigation," she muttered under her breath as she saw the open doorway and prepared herself to be strong. *I am not here to investigate. It would be wrong and hypocritical for me to do anything the least bit investigative after I shut Tess's and Caro's ideas down.*

At the door, Sadie took a deep breath.

"Hi," Sadie announced as she entered the kitchen, a big "no agenda" smile on her face. The woman who had to be Lori Hendricks—there wasn't anyone else here—looked up from where she was cutting a honeydew melon. Lori was stocky, with dark red hair—dyed at home, Sadie would bet—and a black bandana tied around her forehead biker style. She wore a yellow T-shirt and black athletic shorts and had green flip-flops on her feet—she cast a sharp contrast with Nikki Waters, though they had both been doctors' wives at one point. "Nikki said you could use an extra set of hands," Sadie said.

"Absolutely," the woman said, smiling back. "There's a cutting board over there—I'll grab you a knife. I'm Lori, by the way."

"Nice to meet you. I'm Sadie," Sadie said. A hundred questions began lining up in her brain as she retrieved the cutting board. Since Lori was helping with the luncheon, did that mean she'd had an amicable relationship with her ex-husband? Why did they get a divorce in the first place? How long had it been since they'd split up? Was Dr. Hendricks a good dad? Did Lori have any idea why his car wasn't where it should have been on the Sunday before it was discovered? Sadie tried like crazy to push the questions away as she washed her hands and dried them with paper towels from the dispenser beside the sink. *Don't give in*, she told herself. *Be strong.*

"I really appreciate the help," Lori said when Sadie came back to the counter. There was a big, grey garbage can between them, and Lori handed Sadie a chef's knife. "I think two great big bowls of the fruit salad would work pretty well—what do you think?" Lori had already filled one large metal bowl a third of the way full.

"Sounds good to me," Sadie said, positioning her cutting board so that it wouldn't slide on the counter. She wished she had an apron, but since Lori wasn't wearing one she assumed there weren't any available. She'd just have to be extra careful. "And then we'll just store it in the fridge overnight?"

"Yeah. I brought stuff to mix up for a dressing, but I thought we should probably wait until tomorrow to add it, don't you think?"

"Makes sense," Sadie said even though, from her experience, she thought it didn't really matter. In fact, letting the flavors of the dressing and the fruit blend overnight could be really good. Still, she wasn't in charge. "What kind of dressing are you making?" Sadie asked.

"I just put together plain yogurt, some maple syrup, and vanilla—nothing fancy."

"Sounds good," Sadie said. "I don't think I've ever had maple syrup in a fruit salad, but I imagine the natural flavors complement each other."

"Exactly," Lori said. "But I can't really take credit. Nikki gave me the recipe several years ago—she's a great cook. I like it 'cause you don't really have to measure anything—just a little of this and that until you like the level of sweet and vanilla. Then mix it all together—easy breezy."

"Simple and delicious are the best kind of recipes," Sadie said as she picked up one of the four cantaloupes laid out on the counter. There were also five honeydew melons and four big watermelons. She hoped there were strawberries somewhere. And maybe mangos, too—mangos were so good in fruit salad.

Sadie sliced the cantaloupe in half, scraped the seeds out of the middle with a big spoon, and lay it cut-side down on the cutting board. Using the knife Lori had given her, she cut off the rind, exposing the orange melon below the surface. She sliced, and then diced the melon and then lifted the handfuls of fruit and dumped them in the bowl. Through every motion, she tried not to think about how to begin a meaningful conversation with this woman. *That is not why I'm here!*

"How did you do that so fast?" Lori asked, interrupting Sadie's thoughts, which was a relief, really. If she could keep her mind occupied, it wouldn't go into auto-pilot investigative mode. Sadie had told Caro earlier that she didn't have a personal investment in this case like she'd had with the others she'd worked on. She was beginning to think she didn't need a personal connection, though. With the kind of experience she had, what was to keep her from becoming invested simply because of the fact that she knew what a resolution would mean to the people who did have a personal investment?

Focus on the fruit!

Lori was holding a wedge of cantaloupe she'd been cutting the fruit from. Sadie smiled—she used to cut melons that way too.

"I cut the rind *off* the fruit instead of cutting the fruit *out of* the rind. It's faster and you get more fruit that way. Want me to show you how?"

Lori nodded, and Sadie used the other half of her cantaloupe to demonstrate the technique. A minute later Lori was cutting the rind off of her own cantaloupe half. "I can't believe how much faster this is."

"A nice trick, huh? I learned it in a cooking class I attended a few years ago. The best part of those classes is when chefs share their tips." She sliced another cantaloupe and scraped the seeds into the garbage can while making a note to be sure the garbage got taken out tonight. No one wanted a pervasive cantaloupe smell to permeate the church building.

"Do you cook a lot?" Lori said.

"As often as I can," Sadie said. "At times it's been a bit of a problem for me."

Lori laughed.

"Do you cook?" Sadie asked.

"Not much," Lori said with a shrug. "I'm a single mom, *and* working, *and* going to school. I'm afraid we eat a lot of bagels."

"Been there," Sadie said with a nod. "I look back now and wonder how I ever did it." She kept to herself the fact that, for her, things like cooking and cleaning were sanity-savers and fulfilling in more than just a role-playing way. But she realized not every woman had the same experience, even when circumstances were similar.

"I wonder *every day* how I'm going to do it," Lori replied as she went back to cutting. After several seconds, she spoke again. "It's not my business, but were you divorced, too? I should have told you—I'm the ex-wife of Dr. Hendricks." She said it as though confessing something that should be said in whispers.

"I was widowed, actually. And I knew who you were," Sadie said, giving Lori a quick smile to alleviate any awkwardness. "I came with Tess—I don't know what her last name is, sorry—to help set up. Tess said that the two of you led an art project when your sons were in a class together a few years ago. First grade, I think."

"Tess Callbury?" Lori said, smiling, and glancing toward the door leading to the hallway. "I haven't seen her in ages. I didn't know she was in Nikki's ward."

It took a beat for Sadie to remember that "ward" was the word for a Mormon congregation. "I don't think she's in this ward," Sadie said, trying to remember what Tess had said earlier. "But she's friends with Nikki, and Nikki needed some extra hands."

"I didn't even know they knew each other—small world," Lori said, still slicing. "I like Tess quite a lot."

"Me, too," Sadie said, even though she wasn't sure what she thought about Tess right now. She'd been warm and wonderful until Sadie shot down the investigation, and then she'd been rather rude. Passive-aggressive maybe? Sadie hated dealing with passive-aggressive people.

"I'm sorry to hear about your husband," Lori said, turning the conversation in an unexpected direction. "That must have been hard. Has it been a long time?" It was a perfect segue into the questions Sadie was trying not to ask and, even though Sadie tried to resist, after holding her breath for a few counts, she just couldn't keep silent.

"Over twenty years. I'm sorry to hear about your ex-husband, too. This has to be a very difficult time for you."

Lori was quiet for a few seconds as she sliced a honeydew in half. "I'm not sure anyone has shared their condolences for me, specifically."

"Really?" Sadie asked, surprised.

"I'm the *ex*-wife," Lori said, as though Sadie had forgotten.

"But you were married to him for . . . how many years?"

"Thirteen," Lori said, a hint of sadness to her voice.

"That's a long time to spend with someone. Of course it's hard when something like this happens to him. Especially when you have children together."

"Do you girls need any help in here?" Nikki interrupted, poking her head in the doorway.

"I think we've got it handled," Lori said with a smile. "But thanks."

"Good deal—I'm on the hunt for tablecloths, then."

She disappeared, and Sadie worried that the interruption had ruined the flow of conversation, but Lori picked it up right where she'd left off, which showed how much she wanted to talk. This wasn't surprising. Most people did want to talk, and for whatever reason, people really seemed to like talking to Sadie. "I know we're divorced and everything, but I can't believe he's really gone."

"How long ago did you two get divorced?"

"Four years next month," Lori said, shaking her head as though surprised to admit it.

"I'm so sorry—divorce is already so hard." Sadie tried to ignore the way her brain was filing away all this information. She finished cutting up the second half of her melon. "How are the kids dealing with this?"

Lori's face fell completely. "Hard. I think it's harder to deal with not knowing than it would be if he'd had an accident or we at least knew what had happened. Joey, especially, is really upset about this memorial service—it's making it all too real for him, I think. My daughter—well, she's fifteen, and this is just one more thing to make life miserable. Is there a worse age for a girl than fifteen?"

"Not that I can think of," Sadie said, remembering both her own experience and that of her daughter, Breanna. Even a mellow "fifteen" was awful.

"But we'll get through it," Lori said, with just enough forced brightness in her voice to sound sincere. "And we need this memorial. As hard as it is to face it, we all need to accept that Trent isn't coming back. I'm really hoping that we can finally start healing now."

Sadie nodded her understanding. "My kids were really little when their dad died. I asked a friend to take pictures at the service and graveside so that as they got older, I could show them and let them see that they were part of saying goodbye to Neil." A bubble of emotion rose in her chest at remembering that time—that day, specifically. The heaviness of the loss had been compounded as her children faced their own mourning, which was spread over years as they continued to grow in their own understanding of what it meant not to have their dad. She blinked quickly and cleared her throat. "Sorry," she said, embarrassed. "Even after all these years, it catches me off guard sometimes." She looked at Lori and attempted to turn the focus back to her. "I hope no one makes you think that you don't have every right to mourn him. Divorced or not, he was a big part of your life, and there will be emotional journeys for you to take through this."

Lori was staring at her, and Sadie realized how presumptuous she must have sounded.

"I'm sorry," she hurried to say, turning back to the fruit. "I don't always know where my boundaries should be. I didn't mean to make you uncomfortable."

"No," Lori said, shaking her head, still looking at Sadie. "No one else seems to think I have any right to be broken-hearted over Trent's death. In fact, one friend of mine told me how lucky I was— that she'd *love* for her ex-husband to disappear." Lori turned back to her cutting board. "I'm not in love with Trent anymore but he was my best friend once upon a time, and even though we didn't end up being right for each other, he was a good man and a terrific dad. I can't believe he won't be at the kids' graduations or weddings . . . I'm not sure how we'll get along financially without his support—he was generous in the divorce. It's been frustrating that people think I should somehow be unaffected by this." She shook her head at the very idea.

"Absolutely," Sadie agreed. Dr. Hendricks was beginning to feel like a real person, and that both frightened and invigorated Sadie. There would be consequences for letting herself feel close to this—to invest in it on a personal level. But Sadie could relate to Lori in several different ways, and those answers that Caro and Tess had so wanted to discover began morphing from vague hopes to important stepping-stones toward healing for Lori and her children. And what about Dr. Hendricks's current wife? His parents? Siblings? Friends? Patients like Tess who credited him with their continued existence? The more she thought about these things—concretely—the more she wondered how she could have so easily shot down the idea of finding solace for these people. That she'd been so confident in her decision not to proceed, however, continued to hold her back. Was she being caught up in feelings and emotions that were unwise to encourage? It could be so difficult to know the right direction at times, and she wasn't sure that she could trust her own decision about what was right.

A silence lagged between them, and Sadie struggled within herself about what to do—and yet, when she opened her mouth, she wasn't the least bit surprised that her question was a leading one.

"Did you guys get along after the divorce?"

"Better than we had for several years of our marriage, in fact."

"Really?" Sadie said, but what she meant was, "Tell me more."

No-Brainer Fruit Salad

10 cups fresh fruit of your choice, such as mangos, strawberries, bananas, and grapes, cut into 1-inch pieces (well-drained canned fruit may be used)
1 cup plain Greek yogurt
2 tablespoons maple syrup (real maple syrup is best)*
½ teaspoon vanilla extract
1 cup chopped nuts (optional)

Place fruit in large mixing bowl. In small bowl, mix yogurt, syrup, and vanilla together. Pour dressing over fruit; toss to coat. May be made the night before.

*Shawn likes a few handfuls of mini marshmallows added because syrup just isn't sweet enough.

Note: Lasts well in the fridge (as long as no bananas are used) for up to five days. (If you use bananas, add them just before serving.)

Note: To slice grapes easily, line up a row of grapes on your cutting board. Get a rectangle-shaped plastic lid and hold it against one end of the grapes, leaving the other end poking out. Use your knife to cut down the middle. Easy-breezy.

CHAPTER 6

It was as though once we knew we didn't *have* to make it work, we both just calmed down and became friends again. It wasn't enough to save our marriage, but it managed to preserve our *relationship*."

"Did he see the kids regularly? You live in Vegas, right?"

Lori nodded, and sliced open another melon. "I moved down there to go to school, and he didn't love it, but he supported me in it all the same—even paid my first year of tuition until I was able to get some scholarships. He was really good about staying involved with the kids and would drive all the way to Vegas when they had school things or sporting events whenever he could. I'm really glad that the kids have so many good memories." She paused a moment and her face fell slightly. "My dad was a bum, and when he died a few years ago, I felt nothing but relief. It's bittersweet but ultimately a good thing that the kids have reason to miss their dad."

"And his new wife—do they get along with her?" Sadie couldn't remember the new wife's name.

"They like Anita. In fact, she invited the kids to stay through the weekend. They've always been involved in the cancer walk for the foundation, and she set aside little jobs for them to do this year, too. I've got class Thursday and Friday, so I'll head home after the luncheon and be back for the walk Friday night. I don't know what their relationship with her will be like in the future, but I'm glad she's kept them a part of things this year. Helping with the luncheon is my way of showing that I'm still here—that I still want to be a part of the Hendricks family, and that I don't consider myself no longer a part of it."

"You are an impressive woman," Sadie said. "I'm not sure many women in your shoes could encourage that relationship like you are."

Lori shrugged but she seemed to appreciate the compliment. "Maybe you just got me at a good moment. I've certainly had my share of blind ones, where I can't see anything but the ugly."

"No one can fault you for that. It's a very complex situation."

They both went back to cutting their fruit, and Sadie noted that they were halfway finished, which meant that Sadie's chance to talk to Dr. Hendricks's ex-wife would be coming to an end. Someone Sadie hadn't met came into the kitchen to get a washcloth and asked if they needed help. Lori assured her that they had things covered.

Sadie cut into the first watermelon and scowled at the juice that immediately began pooling beneath the heavy fruit—she hated cutting watermelon. There was no way around the mess, however, and so it must simply be tolerated. "When did you last talk to him?"

"A few days before he disappeared. He was supposed to have the kids that weekend, but called me to cancel a few days earlier—we had words about it."

"Did he cancel very often?"

"No," Lori said with a shake of her head. "But that was the third time he'd canceled since Christmas, so I was a little bugged about it. *And* he was supposed to take Joey on an overnight hike for a

Scouting thing he needed so he could finish his Second Class, so Joey was really bummed about it, too."

"But then Dr. Hendricks went hiking on his own?" Sadie asked. If he'd planned to go backpacking anyway, why didn't he take his son with him?

"I know, right?" Lori's look said that she questioned Dr. Hendricks's actions but that she wasn't bothered by the inconsistency as much as Sadie was. She shrugged. "Like I said, I'm really hoping this memorial service will help me be able to move forward and make peace with what's happened."

"What do you think *did* happen?" Sadie asked, moving more watermelon to the bowl. She realized too late that they had filled one bowl with cantaloupe and honeydew and the other bowl with watermelon, rather than mixing all three in both bowls. "To Dr. Hendricks, I mean."

"I think he fell." Lori said sadly. She was slicing more slowly than she had been, with thoughtful and ponderous motions. "He'd taken up backpacking a few years ago—he never did that kind of thing when we were married—but I don't think he was as skilled as he thought he was. He'd told me about some canyoneering he'd done by himself, and I made him promise never to do that with the kids. I think he got in over his head on that last hike and either fell or got lost or something. Maybe that's why he canceled with Joey—because he had plans to do something Joey couldn't do with him."

"It seems strange that no one found any of his gear."

"It isn't all that uncommon," Lori said. She started slicing off the rind of her second watermelon. "After Trent disappeared, I spent a lot of time Googling similar situations—wanting to find some reason to believe that he'd come back, you know? There were dozens of cases where nothing was ever found or something was found years afterward. If he hiked into the red rock—which is what he loved—there are all kinds of crevices and slot canyons. That was his favorite thing to explore, and since he didn't tell anyone where he was going, he could have gone anywhere. I really wish they'd found *something*, though. It would be easier for all of us to know for sure what happened to him."

Sadie felt compelled to ask the next question even though it deserved a better foundation than she felt she had time to create. "Have you ever wondered if he just . . . left?" She felt the need to qualify the question. "Remember how in that Julia Roberts movie she faked her own death in order to start over again? What if that's why they never found anything?" Sadie held her breath a little, knowing that question was more pointed than the others.

Lori flicked a guilty look at Sadie and then turned back to the watermelon. She was quiet for several seconds while Sadie finished her section of watermelon and put it in the bowl. Juice continued to drip from the cutting board to the counter and onto the floor. Sadie was itching to get a mop, but she retained her focus. "I'd be lying if I said I hadn't thought about that, but he went to school for twelve years to have this life as a doctor, and he and Anita were really happy together—and I know he loves our kids. Besides that, when I last heard anything about the case, there was no money missing, no activity on his credit cards, and his phone was in his car. How could he disappear without any money? And what would he be running from? Especially so soon after Anita was sick? It just doesn't fit his character."

"Sick?" Sadie asked, startled by new information she hadn't expected to hear. "Anita was sick?"

"She's fine now," Lori explained, looking up. "Didn't you know she was diagnosed with breast cancer last year?"

"No," Sadie said. Had that been in the articles Sadie hadn't read? "That's awful."

"Stage one, I guess. Which meant a lumpectomy and a little chemo was all she needed. She claimed to be cancer free in March, but it's one more reason I can't imagine Trent leaving."

"How had Dr. Hendricks coped with her diagnosis?" Sadie asked. How would it feel to have your wife diagnosed with the disease your foundation was attempting to combat? And yet it didn't sound like it was a serious case, not like Tess's cancer that had resulted in a double mastectomy at the age of twenty-nine.

Sadie thought of the photograph that showed Dr. Hendricks's Cherokee not being at the Chuckwalla Trailhead that Sunday and felt a wave of realization finally wash over her—a realization she'd been trying to ignore since Caro had first showed her those articles. Dr. Hendricks had *not* gone hiking on a Friday afternoon in April and never come back, which is what everyone believed until Tess and Caro made the connection with the photographs. Unless Tess or Kathryn were lying about the date the photos were taken—and Sadie didn't believe they were—there *was* a mystery here. A pretty big one. The answer to why his car wasn't there the Sunday before it was discovered *mattered*.

Sadie felt a rush of adrenaline as she faced those two realizations full on. Tess and Caro must have already felt this, embraced it, and deemed it factual. Sadie was slower on the uptake, but now that Dr. Hendricks was more real to her, and Lori had given her more information, she knew she wouldn't be able to let it go. Maybe she was becoming personally invested after all.

Lori continued speaking, and Sadie tuned in again. What had she asked about before zoning out? Oh, yeah, how had Dr. Hendricks coped with Anita's cancer. "Trent didn't talk to me about it, but

Nikki said it seemed to really impact him—he even started going back to church, which he hadn't done for years. I imagine it must have been really difficult for both of them—Anita pretty much runs the foundation. Having her own diagnosis after watching so many other women through the years must have been surreal, you know?"

Sadie nodded, but was now more focused than she'd been before. "Could he have had debts, or an addiction that he was struggling with?"

Lori shook her head. "He wasn't that kind of guy. He was raised with really high standards and worked hard and smart. There wasn't room in his character for those kinds of things."

If something had happened to Dr. Hendricks, someone could have put his car at the trailhead to make it look like he'd gone camping. If he'd disappeared on purpose, he could have done the same thing for the same reason. Caro had posed these exact scenarios, but Sadie hadn't taken them in. Now it was like rediscovering the possibilities. "What about another woman?"

Lori looked at her quickly, but with boldness. "Not Trent."

Sadie met her eye. "You're so certain?"

Lori went back to the fruit. They were almost finished. "My father was married to someone else when my mom got pregnant, and my mom went on to have two more kids with two more men before she finally settled down with a complete creep who was never faithful to her. It created chaos for all of us that I swore I would never repeat. Trent's reasons for being faithful were different—he was raised religious, and even though he ended up with questions about the theology of the Mormon church, he believed in abstinence and fidelity, which they draw a hard line on. He wouldn't cheat. Besides that, Anita is a *perfect* companion for him. She's domestic and elegant and smart. She helps run the office *and* the foundation *and* the boutique.

She hosts dinner parties for his friends and golfs with their wives. I was never that kind of woman—which I've come to realize is likely the biggest reason why it didn't work for us—but Anita gave him everything he wanted. And she'd just recovered from cancer." She turned to look at Sadie. "I know why you're asking and, like I said, I've wondered the same thing, but every time I go down that road of thought I end up with only one possibility: something happened to him out there in the backcountry. I can't come up with any reason he would leave this life on purpose."

But Sadie had more questions. "Could anyone have wanted him not to come back? Even if he was living a clean life, like you said, maybe he made some enemies along the way." But people who lived clean lives didn't make those kinds of enemies.

Lori shook her head. "Everyone liked Trent. He wasn't the type of guy who had conflicts with people. In fact, this one time we had a property dispute with a neighbor, and after months of back and forth, Trent just signed over the few feet we were arguing about. We had to redo our sprinkler system and our fence line, but he said it just wasn't worth the fight. He and that neighbor ended up being golfing buddies after that. Really, he was a good guy—who overestimated his backcountry skills."

Sadie nodded and went back to her fruit, pondering what she had learned. Lori lived two hours away from Dr. Hendricks and the life he had here. Though they were divorced, they seemed to have a good relationship, and what she saw in his life was likely what everyone else saw, too. Sadie agreed that a substance addiction was an unlikely possibility because it would affect his work a great deal, but there were other types of addictions: pornography or gambling, for example. And despite Lori's assurances of his living a clean life, Sadie had seen too many people with a public persona that was different from who they were behind closed doors. Leaving to pursue that kind of addiction would require money, though, and Lori had said nothing was missing—though she might not be aware of everything.

"Lori!"

Startled, Sadie looked up to see Caro and Tess come through the doorway. Sadie was instantly reminded of how she'd shut down this investigation less than an hour ago. What would Caro and Tess think of her having changed her mind so drastically?

Tess headed toward Lori with a huge smile on her face. "I haven't seen you in forever. Other than Facebook, I mean. How are you?"

"Hey!" Lori said, just as happy to see her old friend. "Let me wash my hands." She moved to the sink, and Tess followed her.

"How'd it go in here?" Caro asked, approaching Sadie as she finished up the last of the watermelon. Sadie's shoes were sticky from the watermelon juice. Where was that mop?

Lori and Tess began chatting by the sinks, and Sadie hoped Lori wouldn't betray the depth of their conversation until she had a chance to explain things to Caro and Tess. "It went well," she said. Sadie threw the last bit of rind in the garbage can. "How about you guys—did you get everything set up?"

"Yep. Looks like you two are just finishing up, too."

Sadie nodded, dicing the last of the watermelon. When she finished, she picked up a huge, drippy, double-handful of the fruit and dumped it into the bowl. "We still need to mix up the dressing, but we're pretty close to being done."

Tess's voice suddenly rose above the conversational tones she and Lori had been using on the other side of the room. "Sadie was asking you about Trent's disappearance?"

Sadie looked up to see three sets of eyes watching her. Caro and Tess looked surprised, but Lori just looked confused, probably because Tess had made such a point of the question. Tess had the slightest smirk on her face as she turned back to Lori. "Did she tell you about the pictures?"

"Tess!" Sadie and Caro said at the same time.

"What?" Tess replied, turning back to Caro with a challenging look. "Sadie's been in here questioning her the whole time." She pointed at Lori for emphasis, and Sadie felt her face heating up in reaction to the accusation.

"Questioning me?" Lori looked at Sadie again.

"I was not questioning her," Sadie explained, glancing back and forth between them. "We were just . . . talking."

"About Dr. H," Tess said accusingly.

"Well, yeah, and other things, but—"

"Wait." Lori put up her hand, looking somewhat cornered. They all went quiet. "What are you talking about?"

"Sadie's an investigator—didn't she tell you that?"

Sadie didn't know what to say. Tess was making it sound like Sadie had been deceptive, which she hadn't been. The conversation had just . . . evolved, of its own accord. Okay, maybe she'd guided it a little bit, but there was so much more to it than that, and she felt cheapened by the way Tess was pouncing on this circumstance without even trying to understand.

"Did she tell you about the photos?" Tess asked again.

"What photos?"

Tess began explaining to Lori all about the photos and her idea about using the scrapbook to get information from people. Sadie couldn't believe the turn this had taken, and she looked at Caro. Caro shrugged. She didn't seem upset about Sadie asking questions—which was good—but she certainly seemed curious and wasn't picking up on how bad Tess was making Sadie look to Lori right now. Sadie looked down at the sticky floor at her feet and tried to think of how to explain what had happened.

"So—we're on the case?" Caro asked. She leaned her hips against the counter, folding her arms over her chest and raising one eyebrow.

"Well," Sadie said, glancing at Tess and Lori on the other side of the room and reflecting on the new questions her conversation with Lori had raised about Dr. Hendricks's disappearance. Even with regret sitting heavy in her chest, pulling back now was impossible and she knew it. After all, she'd gathered so much information, and Tess was now in the process of telling Lori everything. Suddenly, another thought crossed her mind.

"Did you set me up?" Sadie asked, looking at Caro square-on. "Did you know that sending me in here with Lori would end like this?" She hated the idea, but couldn't ignore the possibility that this might be true.

"No," Caro said, and her reply seemed sincere. "I volunteered for the tables because it would keep *me* away from Lori and any temptation to ask her questions—I think Tess did chairs for the same reason. We assumed you weren't going to, either."

She didn't mean to sound accusatory, but Sadie felt the reprimand all the same. Sadie couldn't fault Caro for telling the truth, and yet she still felt manipulated somehow. She glanced at Tess and felt embarrassed all over again because of the way she'd confronted Sadie in front of Lori. Even if Sadie deserved it, there were other ways Tess could have handled it. At the very least, in confronting Sadie like that, she had undermined Sadie's character to Lori— which couldn't be in the best interest of the case.

"You must have learned stuff that changed your mind, right?"

Caro asked with a hopeful tone Sadie didn't like but could totally relate to. She asked herself once again if she really wanted to do this. Did she want to keep dealing with Tess? Did she want to take all the risks inherent to any investigation? Then again, maybe she and Tess would get along better if they were working on this together. And *not* doing anything about what she'd learned had risks, too. Oh, who was she kidding? She was in. All in.

"She did tell me some things that make me think we could try looking a little deeper until Sergeant Woodruff calls us back. But just a little."

"Ri-ight," Caro said, a gleam in her eye. "Just a little."

CHAPTER 7

"Tomorrow, then," Tess said to Lori half an hour later, after the fruit had been properly stored and the dressing mixed together for the next day.

"I'll let you know when I know what time I can meet," Lori said as the four of them came to a stop in a loose circle near the glass front doors of the church. After learning about the photos, she'd wanted to see them for herself. It would have to wait for the next day because Lori needed to get back to her kids, who were with Dr. Hendricks's parents at the hotel where they were staying.

"Perfect," Tess said, giving Lori a hug and then hurrying back down the hall to say good-bye to Nikki. "Call me when you know when you can get away."

"And I need the little girls' room," Caro said, pointing over her shoulder in the direction they'd just come from. "I'll be right back."

Lori and Sadie were left in the foyer of the building, a large open space with a purple floral couch, some matching wingback chairs, and a painting of Jesus on the wall that Sadie had admired when they entered. Seeing His face made Sadie think about what Caro had said about hiding lights under bushels. *Would He approve of what*

I'm doing? she wondered. It was too big a question to expect an answer to, and Sadie had struggled with her faith in such things these last couple of years. Her own mortality had come into question very strongly following a case where one of those bushels had caught on fire, as she'd mentioned to Caro. She looked away from the painting.

Lori began moving toward the front doors—she'd barely made eye contact with Sadie since Tess had announced that Sadie had been questioning her.

"It wasn't my intent to question you," Sadie said to Lori's back. Lori stopped, her hand on the large glass door, and then she turned to face Sadie. Her facial expression was cautious.

"I have to hand it to you—you're very smooth," Lori said as she, too, surveyed the foyer, possibly as an excuse not to meet Sadie's eyes. "I had no idea you were trying to get information out of me."

Sadie felt her face heat up. "When we started talking, that's all it was—talking. Conversation."

"But you had an agenda." Now she did meet Sadie's gaze.

Sadie shifted her weight. Agenda was such a strong word. "I'd already explained to Tess and Caro that this is a police investigation, not something we should pursue. I wasn't trying to get anything from you." Oh, she wasn't explaining this well, and it frustrated her. She wanted the fact that she hadn't entered the kitchen with expectations of gathering information to offer some kind of defense, but maybe she was being unfair in trying to justify herself.

"But you *did* get information from me," Lori reminded her. "And you're an investigator." Her expression was hard, and Sadie continued searching for a way to make this right. There was only one way to earn back this woman's trust—complete honesty. Come what may.

"I *used* to be a private investigator," Sadie said, dropping her shoulders in surrender to the truth. "In recent years, I've helped solve several investigations. Caro and Tess found the discrepancy with the photos before I got into town and came up with a plan to try to figure out why Dr. Hendricks's car wasn't where it should have been. When they told me about it, I told them we couldn't interfere. Then I ended up in the kitchen with you, and you were so kind and open and . . . I guess I got carried away. It began to feel important, not like a story that was so far away from me." It wasn't the first time Sadie had stepped over the line she herself had drawn. She feared it wouldn't be the last.

"So, then, now that you know my 'take' on things, what do you think?" Lori was still guarded, but her expression showed enough interest that Sadie thought she might be thawing a little bit.

"I'm not sure what you mean."

"I told you all about my marriage and what I know of Trent's life and disappearance. Did it change your mind about being willing to investigate?"

"I'd be lying if I said talking to you didn't make me feel more invested, but I still believe the police are the ones who should be finding the answers to the questions I have now. They have access to more information than I do. They see a bigger picture." And yet Sadie also knew that the big picture often distracted people from the small details that could change everything. "But they haven't contacted us yet. Probably tomorrow. Until then, I feel that trying to make some connections *would* be a good thing."

"The police never talked to me other than getting my alibi for that weekend—which was solid if you're thinking I had something to do with Trent's disappearance."

"I don't think that," Sadie said quickly. "The thought never crossed my mind." For half a second, however, she wondered if it should have. Ex-spouses were often brimming with motive. Sadie was careful to keep any hint of those thoughts out of her own facial expression.

Lori relaxed a little more as she regarded Sadie again. "Are you really a widow?"

"I didn't *lie* to you," Sadie said, bristling slightly. "Everything I said was true."

Lori looked away for a few seconds, perhaps to gather her thoughts, and then she folded her arms over her stomach. When she looked back at Sadie it seemed as though she'd made a decision. "The police have told me nothing. Anita doesn't talk to me about the case. Trent's family only talks to me about the kids. Like you said before, I lost someone important, and no one seems to care." She blinked back tears and took another breath before she continued. "Do you have any idea what a relief it was to finally have someone talk to me about this? And then find out that they had an agenda for it?"

"I'm so sorry," Sadie said, wishing she could go back in time and be up front with Lori from the very start of their conversation. "But I meant what I said—you *have* suffered a loss. You deserve the same opportunity to grieve as anyone else does."

Lori looked over her shoulder through the front doors, taking a deep breath that was possibly meant to help her control the emotion she was fighting. It was getting dark outside, and she stared into the twilight. "Even if you did talk to me just to get information—"

"I didn't, I swear I—"

"*Even if you did*," Lori cut in, turning her head quickly to pin Sadie with a look, "it gave me a chance to feel understood and supported in my feelings. I think Tess's scrapbook is a great idea—people will talk to you guys differently than they talk to the police—take it from me. I told you more than I told them because I knew they were looking at me as a suspect, not as a person struggling to make sense of what's happened to a man I loved." She paused to take another breath. "I'm not mad at you."

"Thank you," Sadie said. They were quiet for a moment, looking at each other. Sadie pondered what Lori had just said: "The man I loved." Did she mean to say "once loved"? It was ambiguous, the way she'd said it, and yet nothing else she'd said had hinted at the fact that she might still have those kinds of feelings for her ex-husband. Sadie needed to say something out loud, and she settled on what came naturally to her—offering support. "I'm sorry you have to deal with so much."

"It will help to see those pictures, to be a part of the process to figure out why his car wasn't where it was supposed to be."

"There certainly doesn't seem to be an easy explanation for that—and his canceling with Joey like he did." Sadie wished she could better explain the process of how she'd gained her own interest in this, how talking to Lori and learning more about Dr. Hendricks had made Sadie feel a kind of obligation to find answers. But that wouldn't matter to Lori. It might even be interpreted as further justification of Sadie's "questioning" her.

Tess's and Caro's voices could be heard approaching from the hallway. Sadie was glad to know that she and Lori seemed to be okay with each other and united in their goal to find information, but she didn't love the fact that there were now four people involved in this. That meant a lot of opinions to sort through, a lot of coordination, and the big risk that one person might mess everything up for everyone else. Sadie preferred to be the only one responsible. Then she would be the only person responsible for getting herself in trouble.

"I'd really like to know what happened," Lori said quietly before Tess and Caro joined them.

They all said good-bye again, and Lori promised again to call when she knew what time she'd be available the next day. During the ride back to Tess's house to drop her off, the three women made a plan, just as though they had been together on the case from the beginning. Sadie couldn't read Tess at all. She'd seemed annoyed with Sadie prior to the conversation with Lori, and now she acted rather cocky about the turn of events. Sadie firmly reminded them both that they were only doing this until Sergeant Woodruff got back to them. They agreed so quickly that she doubted they fully understood what it meant to turn things over to the police. On the heels of that thought, however, was the question of whether she herself were ready to do that.

CHAPTER 8

Despite being tired from the long drive that day, Sadie stayed up reading the articles Tess and Caro had collected. Now that the shift in her thinking had occurred, she wanted to become as familiar as possible with the facts about Dr. Hendricks's disappearance. She appreciated Caro's notes and the lines she'd highlighted that made it easier to hone in on what Caro deemed most important. Thank goodness Caro had thought to make copies before they turned over the originals. As she read, Sadie created a timeline of events, starting in December when Anita's cancer was first diagnosed, though it wasn't written about until January. In several articles, a few people were quoted as saying that Dr. Hendricks had seemed withdrawn in the few months prior to his disappearance—but it was easy to tie that directly to Anita's illness.

Too easy?

While Sadie compiled the timeline, she also made a list of questions the timeline raised. After the third mention of "the boutique" in some of the articles, Sadie turned to Caro, who was sitting cross-legged on the bed with her computer in her lap.

"What's the boutique? Lori said something about it, and then it keeps being mentioned—is it part of the foundation?"

"Yeah," Caro said, moving her laptop and stretching her legs out in front of her. "Tess said they opened it a couple of years ago. It has a lot of post-cancer items like surgical bras, prosthetics, and tops that don't go too low."

"What's the name of the boutique?" Sadie asked as she opened a new browser tab on her computer.

"Pink Posy Boutique," Caro said. "Tess wants us to stop in some time this week. In addition to their post-mastectomy stuff, they have a line of fitness clothing she thinks I'll love and then a whole jewelry line with their logo on it—a little pink flower. Part of everything they sell goes back into breast cancer research."

Sadie thanked Caro for the information, and then scanned the website when it loaded. The site was obviously done by a professional, not someone playing around with a design program, and Sadie admired the crisp graphics and user-friendly menus that included a full catalogue, online ordering, links to other breast cancer-specific sites, and an explanation about the company. The history included on the site gelled with what Caro had said. "It says here that they donate seventy-five percent of profits to cancer research," Sadie said, meeting Caro's eye. "I guess the rest goes to operating costs? Or do they base the profit on net rather than gross?"

Caro shrugged. "It's a pretty generous donation, either way."

Sadie nodded and read some more, impressed with how many areas of the breast cancer community the Hendrickses had moved into. One particular jewelry item, the "Pink Posy Pin," was advertised on the sidebar of every page, and Sadie clicked on the graphic to see why it was so popular.

The Pink Posy Pin, designed by Anita Hendricks, is a representation of the hope that Pink Posy Boutique and The Red Rock Cancer Foundation are dedicated to. Made of sterling silver, with enamel inlay and pinch-pin backing, the simple design is meant to remind us that there is always room for hope, even if it begins as a very small seed. Wear it for your sister. Wear it for your friend. Wear it as a tribute to your own journey toward a second chance.

Like a flower that blooms every spring, we can grow hope one petal at a time!

*100% of all proceeds of the Pink Posy Pin goes directly to breast cancer research

One hundred percent? Wow. The Pink Posy Pin seemed to be the boutique's version of the pink ribbon that symbolized breast cancer awareness. Sadie scrolled down to the price and online ordering information and felt her eyebrows raise—$189.00 for a pin that wasn't more than an inch in diameter? Sadie scrolled back up and looked at the pin in greater detail. It was a simple flower made of sterling silver, with a rhinestone center and five pink petals. It was pretty, but $200 seemed like a steep price to Sadie's mind. Maybe it was something advertised that no one actually bought. Or maybe Sadie was being too cynical about the symbolism it represented to women whose lives had been directly affected by breast cancer. With a hundred percent of proceeds going to research, maybe the inflated price was to amplify the charitable value of the piece.

She clicked around the website a little longer and then reviewed what she'd put on the timeline so far, noting that the boutique had been opened a year ago in February. This year they'd introduced a new jewelry item—a Pink Posy Pendant—to celebrate the anniversary. After reading through the website for a few more moments, Sadie went back to the articles and found herself inundated with questions again. Could there have been something else contributing to Dr. Hendricks's emotional state in the months leading up to his disappearance? Had he hiked Chuckwalla before? Some of the articles pointed out that Chuckwalla wasn't the best choice for accessing the backcountry because it was so close to St. George. It was stated over and over again that there hadn't been any activity on his phone or bank accounts since April eighth. She wished she could look at those records herself but knew that wasn't likely.

For her part, Caro was reading some hiking forums that had threads relating to Dr. Hendricks's disappearance. She found that many stories about disappearances—his and others—often unraveled into conspiracy theories ranging from government cover-ups to alien abductions.

"It does seem like the backpacking community—if that's what you call it—is aware of his disappearance," Caro said after laughing about a particularly fervent comment regarding little green men going after hikers who accidentally wandered into their invisible research fields. "Search and Rescue issued an alert about him in May with the understanding that at this point, it will likely be another hiker that discovers his body."

"Can you make a list of all the different people who seem to be commenting on those threads? See if anyone stands out as more interested than others. You can leave out the nut-jobs."

"Ah, but the nut-jobs are so interesting," Caro said. They lapsed into companionable silence again, save for the tapping of keyboards and the scratching of Caro's pen as she made notes on the hotel's notepad.

Sadie found another article about Anita's cancer and copied the link.

"I'm e-mailing a link to Tess about Anita's cancer and the foundation," she said. Because there was no printer in their hotel room, Tess was printing anything they needed at her home.

"Anita's lucky to have been so involved in the early detection community," Caro said, stretching her arms over her head and twisting from side to side. "Tess said Anita didn't even lose her hair because she got what they call 'light chemo.' Other than losing some weight, Tess says you'd never know she even had cancer."

She turned back to her screen to look at the photo of Anita that had run with the article. She was quite thin, but not emaciated like many other cancer patients seemed to be. Nor was she puffy and swollen like others. "It's a real testament to their program, isn't it?" Caro said. "That she caught it so quickly."

"And yet Dr. Hendricks seemed so upset by it." Sadie looked at the picture again. Was Anita still having treatments when this photo was taken? It was dated in February, and Anita had claimed to be cancer free in March.

"Well, it's still cancer and he dealt with a lot of women who aren't nearly so lucky. It would be a tough diagnosis regardless."

"I'm not downplaying the impact of it. I'm just a little surprised that he wasn't interviewed for any of these articles. They all feature Anita, but not a single one has so much as a quote from him."

Caro cocked her head to the side and furrowed her brow. "That is interesting. Maybe it was just too much for him to take." She waved toward the other articles. "A lot of people said he was withdrawn following her diagnosis—maybe that was his way of coping."

"Lori said pretty much the same thing," Sadie confirmed, but she hadn't disposed of the idea that something else could have been going on with Dr. Hendricks behind the scenes. "I wonder if Dr. Waters noticed something, seeing as how they worked together every day. Did Nikki already set up a time for Tess to talk to him about the scrapbook?"

"I don't know," Caro said. She pulled out her phone and started typing in a text. It was after ten o'clock, and Sadie wondered if Tess had already gone to bed. Sadie herself was feeling the ten-hour drive she'd split up between yesterday and today.

Caro's phone chimed. "She says Nikki is still working on it. I guess Dr. Waters has been crazy busy since Dr. Hendricks's disappearance." She put her phone down.

"It will be good to get his perspective," Sadie said before covering a yawn with one hand.

"I guess you haven't heard back from Pete?" Caro asked, referring to the e-mail Sadie had sent to her fiancé. Sadie looked at her ring. *Zing.*

"I'll be really surprised if he even checks his e-mail on the trip." She didn't mention that she hadn't said anything to Pete about Dr. Hendricks or the minor investigations they'd begun to make into his disappearance. She knew it would worry him, and with their limited ability to communicate, he wouldn't be much help to her anyway. So why bother him with details that would simply take away from his trip? It was the first time she'd been on a case and had not had him at least available to her, though. She wasn't sure how she felt about that. Anxious, certainly, not to hear his steadying opinions, but it also made her feel as though she were, in a way, taking on his role. Caro and Tess were now the newbies and Sadie was the one with experience and perspective they didn't have. It was an interesting shift. Sadie hoped she was up to it.

"So—what should we focus on tomorrow?" Caro asked.

"I wonder if Nikki might have the names of other people Tess can talk to—it makes more sense to have Tess do that part since she's the one doing the scrapbook. I'm encouraged by how much we learned from Lori—getting more first-hand accounts of his behavior in the weeks before he disappeared could give us a great deal more information to work with." She paused and then looked at Caro again. "Are you mad that I ended up talking to Lori like I did after telling you guys we shouldn't do this?"

"No. You have good instincts and you follow them—I saw it as confirmation that my interest in pursuing this case wasn't as out of line as I'd started to think it might be."

"Are things going to be okay with Tess, do you think? I was having a hard time reading her."

"I think Tess is just happy to be working the case again. She feels very driven about it, and you being on board probably confirms the pull she already felt." She finished with a yawn. "Are you at a good stopping point? I'm about ready to turn in."

Sadie agreed. Half an hour later, Sadie lay in the darkness staring at the blinking green light of the smoke detector and waiting for her thoughts to stop racing. It hadn't even been three weeks since the Alaskan cruise, and she was worn out from that investigation in more ways than one. And yet, even as part of her protested getting involved in this situation, another part—a primal part that she hadn't even recognized a few years earlier—was hungry for the pending hunt, hoping Sergeant Woodruff never called and that the threads she'd picked at this evening kept going and going and going until she knew exactly what had happened to Dr. Hendricks.

Allowing herself to tap into that part of her mind dispelled any lingering doubt she had about her commitment.

Giving up the final remnants of reticence allowed her brain to commit to the tasks ahead. *Where was Dr. Hendricks?* she wondered as sleep began dominating her senses. *Was he alive? Was he dead? Had he known when he left that he wasn't coming back?*

CHAPTER 9

Despite the late night, Caro was up at 6:30 Wednesday morning and dragged Sadie to the hotel workout room. Caro never missed a workout, and she insisted Sadie would feel better if she'd sweat a little bit. After they'd been at it for an hour, however, Sadie cried for mercy and made a break for it before Caro could get off the Stairmaster and stop her escape. Exhaustion was part of Sadie's reason for stopping before the ninety-minute target Caro was shooting for, but she also wanted to be ready to go the second Lori contacted them with a meeting time. What she would do when Sergeant Woodruff called back was never far from her mind, either.

Sadie was showered and working on her grey-and-silver-streaked hair that required a blow dryer for proper styling these days when a sweaty Caro came back from the gym. They finished getting ready for the day and Sadie checked her e-mail—nothing from Pete. They grabbed a quick breakfast of fruit and yogurt from the hotel and headed to Tess's, arriving just after nine o'clock.

"So glad you guys are here," Tess said after opening the door and heading back toward the kitchen. The house smelled like chocolate and baked goods, and Sadie was immediately hyper-attentive to what might be behind that smell. "I just talked to Lori—she's going to meet us here around ten-thirty. Do you guys want a muffin?" She waved at a cooling rack with three muffins set on it. "I keep a batch of the batter in the fridge and bake up half a dozen every morning—it's a recipe from another northern Utah restaurant Paul's mom loves, called The Greenery."

"They look delicious," Sadie said. The muffins were still warm, and she broke one in half and slathered it with butter from a bowl next to them. Caro took one, too, but skipped the butter, pinching off a bite of muffin instead.

"These are super good," Caro said. "Bran?"

"Technically, they're called Mormon Muffins, but yeah, they have a lot of bran in them. Some people add shredded carrots or zucchini or crushed pineapple, chocolate chips—whatever. We love 'em."

"They are really good," Sadie said after taking a bite. Not too different from her own bran muffin recipes, she would guess, but these were called *Mormon* Muffins. How cool was it to come to Utah and eat something like that?

"That's great that you've already gotten things figured out with Lori," Caro said, reminding Sadie that they weren't here just for food.

"I know. I was so glad she called early. She sounds really excited." Tess was beaming as she waved them toward the kitchen table. She moved to a bowl on the counter that Sadie hadn't noticed but now reminded her of the chocolate she'd smelled upon entering the house. "I'm finishing up a batch of fudge—I remembered that Lori really liked it when I brought it to one of our planning meetings all those years ago and thought it would make a good thank-you gift for her." She stirred the contents a few more times.

"It smells delicious, too," Sadie said, hoping that today would be a day for her and Tess to rebuild their relationship. "What kind is it?"

"Rocky Road," Tess said, still stirring. "I thought it was appropriate, seeing as how we're working on this case full force now."

"Clever," Sadie said.

Tess didn't look at her or comment. Instead she looked at Caro. "Did you read the morning paper?"

"No, why? Is there something in there about Dr. Hendricks?" Caro reached for the paper on one end of the table. Sadie chose to believe that Tess's snub wasn't intentional.

"His obituary," Tess said, lifting the bowl she'd been stirring and holding it up in order to pour the smooth chocolate punctuated with mini marshmallows and nuts into two different aluminum containers. The yogurt and banana Sadie'd had for breakfast suddenly felt paltry. How long would it take the fudge to set up? She took another bite of her muffin and felt better.

Caro pushed the paper over so that she and Sadie could read it together. As Sadie read this final tribute to Dr. Hendricks, she realized that, despite reading all the articles about his disappearance, she didn't know much about him. It was interesting to read his personal history, but it left Sadie wanting more information.

"So Nikki set up a couple people to talk to me at the memorial service," Tess said, putting the bowl in the sink. She turned on the faucet and washed her hands. "She still hasn't talked to Jake, though."

"Jake?" Sadie asked. "Who's Jake again?"

"Dr. Waters," Tess said tightly, as though Sadie should know that. Maybe the earlier snub hadn't been accidental.

"Sadie put together a timeline," Caro said, gesturing toward the laptop bag Sadie had brought in with her. Sadie took the cue and retrieved her laptop. She brought up the timeline, and though Tess came over to give it a cursory look, she didn't spend even five seconds taking in the details before picking up a notebook from the counter and sitting on Caro's other side. "I went over the list of people we could talk to and circled a few of them," she pointed out one of the names to Caro and explained that this woman worked in Dr. Hendricks's office. Tess had already sent her a text message. "Oh, and I finished the scrapbook layout," Tess said. "Come see what you think, Caro." She stood and started heading toward a room to the left of the kitchen.

"Come on, Sadie," Caro said. From the look on her face, Sadie could tell she'd noticed Sadie hadn't been invited. "Let's check it out."

"You go ahead," Sadie said, not wanting to force herself on Tess. "I wanted to work on my notes anyway."

Caro hesitated but then followed Tess into the other room. Sadie opened a new document that would serve as a kind of journal for this process. She did it for every case she worked on—it provided a priceless way for her to review all of her movements. She opened another document to make a to-do list of things that, while journaling her experiences, would come to mind for her to explore. The first thing she put on the to-do list was to do background checks on the key players—Dr. Hendricks and Anita Hendricks for sure, and possibly Lori and Dr. Waters as well. She thought about asking her son, Shawn, for help. He was far more skilled at creating background checks than she was, but he also had a lot going on right now. Pete was *geographically* unavailable, but Shawn felt equally off limits even though he was only a phone call away. Caro's phone started ringing from her purse that she'd slung over the back of one of the kitchen chairs, and Sadie retrieved it for her, then met her halfway as she ran toward it. "Thanks," she said quickly before glancing at the caller ID and putting the phone to her ear.

"Hello? . . . Yes, this is she . . . Yes, I did leave some information at the police station last night. Um, thank you for calling me back."

Sadie remained standing and tried to share a look with Tess as she entered the room, but Tess didn't meet her eye. Judging from Caro's comments, it had to be Sergeant Woodruff, which meant that, according to their agreement, they were now off the case. It was a hard realization to accept, and Sadie felt her energy drop. "Um, actually, ten-thirty is a little early for me to come in," Caro said into the phone. "Yes, I could be there at eleven-thirty." She made a face at Sadie before looking at Tess, who was shaking her head. That seemed to confuse Caro, and she gave her cousin a "what am I supposed to do?" look. Tess shook her head again. When Caro glanced at Sadie again, Sadie gave an even more encouraging smile to make up for Tess's poor advice.

"Okay . . . Yes . . . Thank you . . . I'll be there at eleven-thirty . . . Bye." She hung up the phone and held it out in front of her as though it had betrayed her.

"I'm so glad they're taking it seriously," Sadie said, keeping her tone upbeat. "And they're meeting with you in person as well. That's great."

"That's terrible," Tess said as soon as Sadie finished, causing Sadie's attention to snap in her direction. "They can't just waltz in here and take over."

"Yes, they can," Sadie stated. "They're the police, and this is their job. Like I said from the start, this is an active investigation, and they can do more with it than we can. Making your meeting with the police after we meet with Lori was a great idea. We'll be able to give them even more information by then."

"You're not disappointed?" Caro asked Sadie. "Even just a little bit?"

"I'd be lying if I said I wasn't a little disappointed," Sadie said honestly. "But I still believe they are the best people to have in charge of this. And our efforts get to help with that. It's the best-case scenario." She didn't feel as good about it as she was making it sound, however. Walking away would be hard.

"I respectfully disagree," Tess said. Her tone didn't sound very respectful to Sadie. "We're meeting with Lori in an hour, and I'm not just going to shrug off the interviews I've already set up."

Sadie wondered if this was how Pete felt when he'd tried to be "reasonable" in the past and she'd been caught up in the drama of a situation. "Look, I understand that this is frustrating, and it's not what you expected, but—"

The sound of music from the kitchen area behind them cut her off. Tess hurried to get her phone. "This is Tess. . . . Hi, Lori." Her expression fell, and she turned away from Sadie and Caro, who stood watching her and listening to her side of the conversation. "Oh, really? . . . I see . . . Would you like to set up another time? . . . Oh . . . No, I understand . . . Um, you're welcome . . . Yeah, you, too."

She hung up the phone, looked at it in her hand, then put it back on the counter before turning to face Caro and Sadie. "Lori's not coming."

"Why?" Caro asked before Sadie had a chance to.

"She said she has a school assignment she'd forgotten about that she has to finish up this morning. I tried to set up another time, but she said she couldn't spare even five minutes."

"Maybe we can talk to her at the luncheon," Sadie said, trying to create a plan B. "Once the service is over, she might be less anxious." Assuming it was anxiousness that inspired the change.

"Except I will have talked to the police and we'll be officially off the case," said Caro.

Oh yeah, Sadie thought to herself. "Why would she cancel? She'd seemed so invested last night."

"You don't think it's a school assignment?" Caro asked her.

"I suppose it could be, but it does seem strange. Maybe the police called her before they called you. Or maybe someone else told her not to come."

"Why would they do that?" Tess asked.

"I have no idea, and maybe I'm wrong, but it seems really strange—she wanted to see those photos. She wanted to be a part of finding out why the photos didn't match up."

"Well, then, I'll talk to her about it at the service," Tess said with resolution. "If she's lying about the school assignment, then we'll figure out the real reason."

"Except we'll have already talked to the police," Caro repeated.

Tess lifted her chin. "I don't see why we can't continue working on this regardless of the meeting with police," she said, coming around the counter. "We've already done so much and have a lot more we can do."

Tess's determination caused Sadie's defenses to rise. "This has always been a police matter, and if—"

"That's obviously not what you thought last night when you questioned Lori."

Sadie felt her face grow warm. "I've already explained about last night, and I've said from the start that this is a police investigation."

"And why do we have to do this your way?" Tess challenged as Caro looked back and forth between them. "You're the least interested in what's going on here—you've made that very clear—but we're supposed to just listen to you?"

"I have experience with this kind of thing," Sadie said. "And I know the consequences of pushing farther than you should. The reason you asked for my help in the first place was *because* of my experience."

"Well, I feel like we should keep working on it. I feel that very strongly, and I don't appreciate you trying to dictate everything."

"Okay," Caro said, putting up her hands. "This isn't helping anything." She turned to Tess. "We did agree to stop when the police called us back."

Tess folded her arms over her chest and looked to the side, out the back window. Her expression was tight. Sadie, while sympathetic to the younger woman's position, liked her less than ever.

"We need to focus on what's going on right now, which is that the police want to talk to us. Will you come with me to talk to the police?" Caro asked.

Sadie wasn't sure who she was talking to until she realized Caro was looking at both Sadie and Tess. She wanted all three of them to go?

"I really have no reason to be there," Sadie said. "And I might just make things worse."

"Worse? How?" Caro asked.

Sadie took a breath, noting that Tess was watching her now. She tried to think of how to say this without drawing even more of Tess's censure, but she couldn't come up with anything that would defuse the tension between them. "I have an official record, and it doesn't make me look very good. I worry that if I'm connected to all of this, it might hurt things more than help them."

Caro knew what Sadie was talking about, and she looked embarrassed for putting her on the spot. Sadie caught the briefest look of satisfaction on Tess's face before Tess turned and went into the kitchen, where she set about washing dishes. Caro followed her.

"Will you come with me, Tess?" Caro asked.

"No," Tess said stubbornly. "I think you going to the police at all is a mistake."

Sadie let out a breath, hating everything about this and having no idea how to fix it. She went back to her computer and finished typing in a summary of the case-that-almost-was. She consciously blocked out whatever Tess and Caro were talking about. She felt conflicted and frustrated and suddenly eager to be done with this whole thing, though she knew that was simply a reaction to the negativity. It would be very hard to truly walk away.

"Will *you* please come with me?" Caro asked. Sadie was startled because she hadn't realized that Caro had returned to the table. She glanced past her friend and noted that the kitchen was empty. Where had Tess gone? Caro continued, "I really don't want to go alone, and I'm not worried about you hurting anything—I mean, that won't even matter if we're just turning things over, right?"

Sadie focused on Caro's pleading gaze and remembered that it had been Sadie's idea to take everything to the police in the first place, and it was Sadie who was insisting that this was the right course now that they had responded to that information. With those things in mind, how could she send Caro there alone?

"Sure," Sadie said with a smile.

Caro looked instantly relieved. "Oh, good—thank you. He'd wanted to meet with me around ten-thirty, but I put him off because of our meeting with Lori. Do you think I should call and see about coming in earlier? I kind of don't want to put it off any longer than I have to."

Mormon Muffins

Recipe from The Greenery Restaurant in Ogden, Utah

2 cups boiling water
5 teaspoons baking soda
1 cup shortening
2 cups sugar
4 eggs
1 quart buttermilk
5 cups flour
1 teaspoon salt
4 cups All-Bran cereal
2 cups bran flakes
1 cup walnuts, chopped

Add soda to boiling water and set aside. Whip shortening and sugar until light and fluffy. Add eggs slowly; mix well. Add buttermilk, flour, and salt; mix again. Very slowly add soda water. Gently fold cereals and walnuts into the mix. Spoon ⅛ cup batter into greased muffin tins. Bake 30 minutes at 350 degrees. Cool 5 minutes.

Muffin mix must sit in the refrigerator overnight before baking. Mix will last one week, covered and refrigerated.

Yields 3 dozen muffins.

CHAPTER 10

D espite having agreed to go with Caro, Sadie had hoped that she could wait in the car or the waiting room. But it became obvious during the drive to the police station that Sadie would be accompanying Caro every step of the way. Caro became increasingly nervous the closer they got to the actual interview. Caro had given an official statement to the police after the situation they'd involved themselves in the year before, so she had experience with police interviews, but that made her even more nervous. Sadie did her best to talk down the significance of this meeting, but at the same time she was increasingly anxious, too. Oh, how she hated these interviews.

Would Sergeant Woodruff be the kind, understanding, and gentle type of cop she rarely encountered? Or, instead, would he be the chip-on-his-shoulder, hard-nosed detective who used intimidation and in-your-face declarations to ensure everyone knew who was in charge? A quick glance at Caro's white-knuckle grip on the steering wheel and tight-lipped expression left Sadie praying for the former option. *Please let him be nice.*

For the first time ever, Sadie was disappointed when they were not asked to sit in the waiting area. Instead, they immediately followed a female officer down a short hallway, where she initiated a series of stops and signatures before Caro and Sadie were led into what Sadie knew to be an interrogation room. Rather than a mirror-sided wall that would allow them to be watched, two video cameras were attached to opposite corners of the light grey room. There were two chairs on one side of the table, and no chair on the other side.

"Shouldn't there be a third chair?" Sadie asked the officer who had served as their guide up to this point.

The woman just smiled and waved them to their seats. "Officer Nielson will be with you shortly. Please have a seat."

"Nielson?" Sadie asked quietly once the door had closed and she and Caro were alone. They each pulled back a chair and sat down at the table. Sadie's chair legs weren't even, and the chair wobbled slightly.

"We're meeting with Officer Nielson," Caro confirmed. She looked at the camera set in the corner closest to them and swallowed nervously.

"I thought it was Sergeant Woodruff."

"Nielson is the one who called me back."

How had Sadie not realized that? She, too, eyed the cameras and decided not to talk about it right now. She settled back in her seat and restated in her mind the goal of this meeting: to discuss what they knew without drawing too much interest in themselves.

The doorknob turned, and Sadie took a breath before looking at the area where the face of this Officer Nielson should be if he were of average height. However, once the door opened, the spot she'd focused on was a few feet too high, and she felt her eyes travel lower and lower until they met the blue eyes of a man in a wheelchair. Sadie tried to hide her surprise, but she knew he'd seen it all the same, and she felt her cheeks heat up in embarrassment. He gave her a slight smile of acknowledgment and steered himself into the room with one hand while the other held the door open. It wasn't until he was completely in the room that Sadie realized she should have offered to help. But would that have offended him?

Caro hadn't looked up as Officer Nielson entered the room, and she was slightly startled when she did look up to see him wheeling up to the other side of the table. Sadie noted a thick file resting on his lap and a fanny pack secured around his waist. Just like that, they were suddenly eye to eye, and, except for his unexpected means of arrival, he had the demeanor of any other officer Sadie had encountered. That she felt sorry for him bothered her a lot. She knew he wouldn't want her sympathy, but she also worried that being taken off guard by him had already put her at a disadvantage.

He put the file on the table and a moment later took a bottle of hand sanitizer from his fanny pack. He squirted some into one hand and then rubbed it into both hands. "Don't let the chair intimidate you," he said with a half smile. "I won't hold it against you that I'm twice as fast as you are and have the upper body strength of a god."

Both Sadie and Caro were quiet for a moment and then smiled anxiously at the joke.

He snapped the sanitizer's lid back in place and returned the bottle to the fanny pack. Only then did he extend his hand across the table. He did have incredibly well-muscled arms, and Sadie found herself blushing for the second time since he'd entered the room. When he met her eye, she could swear he knew what thoughts had inspired her reaction, just as he had the first time. Caro and Sadie introduced themselves in turn, and Officer Nielson immediately opened the cover of the file and asked about the photos Caro had indicated in the note she'd left with the articles the day before.

At first, Caro seemed hesitant to answer the questions he asked, but when Sadie didn't jump to answer in her place, she stumbled through the explanation and after a few sentences seemed to find her groove. Sadie was grateful that Officer Nielson did, in fact, seem to be one of those detectives who led with confidence and authority.

He asked about the origins of the photograph of the two women, and he wrote down what Caro told him, letting her know he would need to verify the dates with Kathryn. Caro told him to turn the photo over and see where Tess had written Kathryn's contact information a few days earlier.

He asked good questions that established why Caro and Sadie were there, their connection to Dr. Hendricks, and what they thought the photos meant. Sadie couldn't have been more proud of how Caro handled everything. She was professional and well-spoken.

Officer Nielson opened the file and thumbed through the rest of the papers. "And these other items?"

"We gathered all the information we could about Dr. Hendricks in hopes of figuring out any other discrepancies in the case."

"And did you find any?"

When Sadie and Caro didn't answer immediately, he looked up at them expectantly.

"Maybe not a discrepancy," Caro said. "But there were some strange things that stood out to us after Sadie talked to Lori Hendricks last night." She motioned toward Sadie, turning Officer Nielson's attention to her for the first time. Sadie cringed but tried not to show it on her face.

"Lori Hendricks is Dr. Hendricks's first wife, correct?" the officer queried.

He didn't already know that? Why wouldn't he be familiar with the details of the case? His ignorance seemed to confirm that a call from him hadn't been the catalyst for Lori changing her mind about wanting to see the photos this morning.

"Um, yes," Caro said, possibly thinking the same thing.

"Why don't you tell me about what you learned from Lori Hendricks."

Sadie and Caro were both silent for a beat or two until Officer Nielson raised his eyebrows. Caro looked at Sadie and raised her eyebrows, too. Sadie took a breath before giving a quick recap of events from last night, ending with the fact that Lori Hendricks had cancelled the appointment.

By the time Sadie finished, Officer Nielson was leaning to one side of his wheelchair, with one elbow resting on the arm of the chair and holding up his chin. He held her eyes longer than she wanted him to. It felt too searching, too much as though he were making conclusions about her. She looked away first.

"Are you somehow employed by law enforcement?" he asked her.

"No, sir."

"You use the lingo."

"Well, I, um, have some experience with investigative work."

"But you're not a law enforcement employee?"

"No, sir. I, um, used to be a private investigator." She kept to herself that most of her investigative experience had little to do with the actual business she'd run for less than a year.

He looked at her a few seconds longer, and Sadie knew that as soon as she left this office, he would type her name into his fancy-pants computer and learn everything about her. She didn't know what her official file said, but Pete had described it as "extensive" when she'd pushed him for information. With that in mind, Sadie wondered what she had to lose in this interview. "Can I ask you a question, Officer Nielson?"

"Certainly."

"Is Sergeant Woodruff no longer working the case? We've read all of those articles and your name never came up."

"Sergeant Woodruff was the investigator on the disappearance case, and he was over things until about two weeks ago, when the file was given to me. I've been employed with the department for sixteen years, but about four years ago, I was injured in a search and rescue and was taken off of active duty. I now work here in the station, closing out cases, doing phone work for other investigators, and anything else that doesn't require legs." He smiled to soften the impact of the words, but Sadie felt her sympathy rising again. "I was given this case to close, but it hasn't been a priority—I expected to finish it off by the end of the summer. Until these came in." He tapped the top of the folder. "I've spent the morning reviewing the file, but I'm certainly not yet familiar with the intricacies of the case. I'd like to review it some more and, perhaps, ask you some follow-up questions. Would that be all right with the two of you?"

"Sure," Caro said with a nod.

"Of course," Sadie confirmed.

He put the file back in his lap and pulled back from the table. "Great. I'll be in touch then, if both of you would kindly leave your contact information, including where you're staying while you're here in town, with the officer at the front desk, I would appreciate it."

He reached the door and pulled it open before either of them could do it for him. The same female officer that had escorted them inside was waiting for them outside the door and led them to the front of the station. They retrieved their purses and left their contact information, as Officer Nielson had instructed, and headed through the front doors.

"Well, that was . . . "

Caro didn't finish the sentence, and Sadie wasn't sure she knew how to finish it, either, so she simply agreed. "Yeah."

They got into Caro's car, which was already hot from the morning sun. Caro started the car and turned the AC all the way up. "They're closing the case already. That must mean that they really aren't working on any leads, right? They didn't find anything in their investigation that warranted keeping the case active."

"That's what it sounds like," Sadie said, turning to smile at Caro across the seats. "And giving them this brought it back to life. Well done."

Caro smiled and shifted into reverse, catching Sadie's eye as she looked over the seat to pull out of her parking space. "I'd have never done it without you telling me to. Maybe it will help Tess feel better to know the police are picking things up from here."

Sadie felt mean-spirited toward Tess right now and so she didn't make any comment in regard to wanting Tess to feel better about things. They pulled out of the parking lot without continuing the conversation.

"Now what?" Caro said after pulling out onto 200 East.

"I guess we continue the weekend as we'd originally planned," Sadie said, trying to ignore the letdown of being off the case. "There's those outlet stores, and the tour of the temple visitors' center, and . . ." She wasn't feeling much enthusiasm for those things any more.

"Just walk away?"

"It's in the hands of the police. Our part is done."

Caro slowed down at the stop sign. "What do we do about Tess?"

Sadie's first instinct was to point out that this had never been about Tess, but she stopped herself. Caro was in a difficult position, and Sadie had no desire to make it harder. "I suppose Tess can do whatever she wants. As can you and as can I. I am secure in the fact that the police are taking care of this situation, and I'm not interested in stepping on any of their toes, even if it is hard to walk away. You and Tess will have to make your own decisions."

Caro was silent as she stared out the window. Sadie waited with her, eager for the answer but not wanting to break the train of thought in Caro's mind. "I don't know what to do," she finally said quietly.

"Why don't you drop me off at the hotel? Then you can go to Tess's and decide where to go from there."

"You don't want to come with me?" Caro turned to look at her.

"Tess doesn't like me, Caro," Sadie pointed out, though she hated saying it out loud. "She and I are on opposite ends of the spectrum on this subject. My being there when you decide what to do will only cause additional friction. I've made up my mind—the two of you can make up yours."

Caro didn't like that, and Sadie could see how her friend might feel a bit abandoned by Sadie's refusal to continue on. But in the long run, it was for the best. "And," Sadie said as Caro pulled into the hotel parking lot. "I understand that this weekend was, first and foremost, about you and Tess carrying out an important tradition. Tess and I haven't gotten off to a good start, and I'd rather go home and let you two enjoy the weekend than get in the way of things."

"I'm sure it won't come to that," Caro said, sounding surprised at the consideration. "You don't want to stay?"

"I want to stay if my being here is the best thing, but I don't want to get in the way of you and Tess, and I think I already did that."

Caro pulled up beneath the covered entrance of the hotel. "I don't want—"

"Just keep it in mind," Sadie cut in. "You and I are okay

regardless, okay? Just see what you can work out with Tess in the meantime."

As Sadie headed for their room, she reminded herself that she'd done the right thing by making Caro take those articles to the police. She really had. She really, really, really had. But she couldn't help but wonder about where things would be if she hadn't made Caro take that file in. The police had already wrapped up their investigation—they were done. Nothing Sadie, Caro, and Tess would have done would have interfered with anything. But that was something she would never say out loud to Tess or Caro.

Her phone rang while she was searching for her hotel key from her laptop bag that she'd used today in place of a purse. She looked at the number on her phone, but it wasn't one she recognized, which meant she knew nothing about who was on the other end of the line or how they might change her current course.

"Hello?" She held the phone with one hand and found her hotel key with the other.

"Sadie Hoffmiller?"

"Yes." She slid the key into the lock and pushed open the door.

"This is Officer Nielson. We just spoke a little bit ago about the Dr. Hendricks case."

"Yes?" Sadie said, taking her computer bag from her shoulder and putting it on the floor.

"I wondered if you might be able to come into the station again."

"Um, well, sure, I'll need to call Caro and see if—"

"Just you will be fine," he cut in. "How soon can you be here?"

CHAPTER 11

T hank you for coming in," Officer Nielson said after Sadie sat down across from him. They were in an office rather than an interrogation room this time, and though it had been less than fifteen minutes since Sadie had talked to him on the phone, she'd managed to work up her levels of anxiety to a fever pitch while trying to figure out why he'd called her in.

"I'm not continuing to work on this case," she blurted out, unable to keep the anxiety at bay any longer. "And it wasn't my idea. Not that I'm trying to push blame on anyone else, but I only arrived in St. George yesterday afternoon, and Caro and Tess had developed this whole plan before then. I told them we needed to give the information to the police and we did. The discussion with Lori Hendricks just kind of—"

"You're not in trouble, Mrs. Hoffmiller."

Sadie's mouth was still open, prepared to continue her defense. It took a moment to reset her approach. "What?"

"You're not in trouble," he said again, this time with a bit of a chuckle. "I didn't ask you to come in so that I could reprimand you."

"Oh," Sadie said, sitting back in her seat and trying to remember if she'd come up with any other reasons for this meeting. If she had, they had been sacrificed for the more likely possibility that she was in trouble. Except Officer Nielson said she wasn't. "Then why did you ask me to come back in?"

"Well," he said, opening the file on his desk that she recognized as the one she and Caro had dropped off the day before. "I'm sure you know that when someone types your name into the database, it comes up with an interesting amount of information."

Sadie just nodded, still on edge.

"It says much more than just the fact that you owned your own private investigation business for a time." He met her gaze straight on. She nodded again.

"I attempted to contact Detective Cunningham, who's listed as a contact, but apparently he's preparing to get married and is having a bachelor's type vacation in Mexico—but I guess you knew that." He smiled again, and Sadie felt her cheeks turn pink.

"Congratulations," Officer Nielson said. "According to the police chief in Garrison, Colorado, the date is just a few weeks away."

"Five weeks," Sadie clarified. She glanced quickly at her ring and felt just the whisper of a zing. That was all that could cut through her continued confusion about this conversation.

"I hope the two of you are very happy together—perhaps you'll re-open your investigation business. With his experience and your knack for finding yourself in the middle of a *situation*, you could keep each other on your toes."

He smiled, but Sadie wasn't sure if he were teasing her or not, and she didn't respond to the possible joke. "If I'm not in trouble, why am I here, Officer Nielson?"

"I don't mean to make you uncomfortable," he said, his smile softening but not going away. "So—let's get down to business."

He clasped his hands on his desk and leaned forward on his forearms. "Would you say that you're invested in Dr. Hendricks's disappearance?"

"I'm not sure what you mean. We gave you all the information we had out of respect for the police's interest in this case and not wanting to interfere—that should prove that we aren't still investigating."

"You talked to Lori Hendricks *after* bringing in these documents. I admit I didn't spend a great deal of time researching your history, just took what I read on your profile at face value, but it seems that you usually have a personal interest in the cases you've been involved in. Your neighbor, a co-worker, your son's situation. So I'm wondering if you have a personal interest in this case as well."

Sadie wished she knew why that mattered, but she couldn't figure it out in the moments she was allowed between his question and her answer. She could only think that being honest would be the best choice right now. "If you mean, did I know Dr. Hendricks or any of those people close to him that would give me a personal interest in regard to how I'm affected by the situation, no, I am not somehow connected to this case. If, on the other hand, you mean, am I interested in the outcome of this case and concerned about those people influenced by what that outcome might be, then, yes, I would say I'm personally invested." He nodded and she took that as permission to continue. "I don't know what it says in my profile, but my reasons for being connected to those other situations that my file talks about were about more than just knowing someone involved or my life being directly influenced by the outcome."

"What would you say your involvement was about, then, if not because you were personally affected by the outcome?"

"I think truth is important," Sadie said simply. "And I found that

I could discover important information and help find the answers that might help people." Caro's comment about Sadie having a gift came to mind, but it was a bit embarrassing to think about it that way right now. She wasn't "all that," and she knew it.

"You discovered information the police didn't find, then? Is that what you mean?"

Sadie shifted awkwardly in her chair and took a breath. "Sometimes I have found things the police didn't," she said. "But I realize that I made problems for them sometimes, too, if that's what you're getting at."

"That's not what I'm getting at," he said, his hands still clasped and his eyes still focused on her, which made her feel as though he saw more into what she said than just what she was telling him. It was disconcerting.

"I understand that you still have a lingering threat over you— you were in hiding for a while."

Sadie nodded. She didn't want to talk about that, didn't want to think about it. "It's been a year and a half and nothing has happened. I've chosen to live my life. Hiding was . . . not good for me." The emotional toll of the fear had been worse than facing the threat head on, but his bringing it up made her feel tense. "Is that why you've called me in? Has something been found?" Pete checked on her situation weekly, but he was out of the country right now. Had he somehow put an additional alert on her profile that Officer Nielson had information about?

"No," Officer Nielson said. He sat back in his chair. "But you said something in one of your cases that for some reason Detective Cunningham made certain to include in the notes on your profile. It says that you feel as though God directs you toward these cases and that at times you've felt as though He is leading you toward the resolution."

Sadie felt her cheeks heat up again and looked at her hands in her lap. She didn't remember when she'd said that, but she knew it was before Boston because after what happened in Boston—and the threat that had become paralyzing—her faith had wavered.

"*Do* you believe that?"

Sadie took a breath and looked up. "When I said it, I believed it. Since my situation in Boston, I've . . . been working through some complex feelings." She was about to ask him why this was important enough for him to have called her in when he spoke again.

"Do you believe in God, Mrs. Hoffmiller?"

"Yes—can you tell me why this is important?"

"Do you believe that God embraces truth—that He wants us to find it?"

"Yes, I do, but why are you—"

"Do you believe that God uses people to find that truth?"

"Officer Nielson, I don't mean to offend you, but I'm not entirely comfortable with the direction of this conversation." She'd never talked to a member of law enforcement like this, and it felt pointed and strange.

"I apologize," he said, sitting forward. "I don't mean to make you uncomfortable. I was merely curious because it will likely influence your answer to my request."

"Your request?" Sadie asked. "Forgive me for pointing out that you haven't made a request. I still have no idea why I'm here, unless you simply wanted to satisfy your curiosity about my history."

Officer Nielson smiled. "My request is an unusual one, but I hope you will consider it carefully because it is sincere."

Sadie lifted her eyebrows expectantly.

"As I told you before, I was given Dr. Hendricks's file in order to close it out. The investigation done in the weeks following his disappearance was extensive. I don't want to give the impression that I'm in any way critical of what was done—interviews were conducted, financial records searched, leads followed up on, and so forth. Everything that should have been done was done. But when the work doesn't lead us anywhere, we are left with nothing to explore. Does that make sense?"

Sadie nodded.

"Good. So, then, this morning when I came in, this file of information was waiting for me." He tapped the file. "I read your friend Caro's note, and I looked at the photos, which happened to relate directly to one of the questions left over from the investigation. It was in regard to the Chuckwalla Trailhead—have you been to that trailhead?"

"I haven't," Sadie said.

"It's a popular trail. Runners and climbers, specifically, use it frequently. It's located right off Highway 18, just past a major parkway in St. George, and is mostly a day-use trail. The detectives involved worked hard to find anyone who could verify that Dr. Hendricks's vehicle had been there four full days, as it would be unusual for someone as experienced as he was to start a multi-day hike from a basic trailhead like Chuckwalla. We felt sure that if his vehicle had been there for that long, someone would have seen it, but I believe that actually worked against us. Because of the popularity of the trail, cars come and go all day long, and no one that we talked to noticed his car at all."

"So they didn't remember it being there, but they didn't remember it not being there."

"Exactly," Officer Nielson said with a nod. "Your photos give us the first proof—we'll need to verify it, of course—that his car might not have been there the whole time. It's a fresh lead."

"Does that mean the case has been reopened?"

"I wish it were that easy, but, unfortunately, it isn't. Sergeant Woodruff, who headed up this case, has moved to a new department farther north. Whoever ends up with this case will be starting from scratch, and it will take some time to bring them up to date. While this lead with the photos is interesting, it's not groundbreaking. It doesn't give us cause to automatically suspect something criminal—it simply gives us reason to keep looking at the same dead ends we already have."

Sadie nodded, feeling her excitement rise, even though she still had no idea what this had to do with her.

"You already talked to the ex-wife," Officer Nielson said. "You said she then canceled an appointment with you to see the photos. You're attending the memorial service and the luncheon, and, due to your history, the unique circumstances, and my own intuition, I would like to ask for your help until we have detectives prepared to step in and work this case in an official capacity."

It took a couple of seconds for Sadie to absorb what he had asked. Holy cow! When she spoke, however, she made sure to keep her tone even. "You want me to work on the case?"

"I want you to gather information and relay it back to me. You know the procedures—it's in your profile—you give very detailed notes, you know how police go about things, and according to your profile, you're capable of defending yourself, though I don't expect it will come to that. I am not asking you to put yourself in any compromising positions or act on any leads yourself, but I think your abilities of observation and information collection could be very helpful to us. I'll be working on verifying that photo today, and I'll be meeting with my superiors tomorrow morning about reactivating this investigation. But the memorial service is today. The luncheon is today. I don't want to miss the opportunities those events provide to us, but I can't be a part of them myself, and no one else is up to speed on this case."

"So you want me to work on the case," Sadie said again by way of confirmation. She felt a bubble of excitement begin to grow in her chest. The *police* were asking for her help? They *wanted* her involved? This was new ground for her, and it made her head spin.

"We do," he said with a nod and smile that told her he knew she was excited about this. "We want Tess to keep working on the scrapbook, and we want you to try to figure out why Lori Hendricks canceled her meeting with you. We want you to be our eyes and ears and record keeper of what you see. It will create new information for the detectives to work on once the case is assigned—give them a running start, so to speak. Will you do it?"

"Of course," Sadie said. She cleared her throat, not liking how enthusiastic she'd sounded. "And Caro and Tess, too?"

"Yes, though I would prefer to communicate with you due to the fact that I feel I can talk to you on a more professional level."

Sadie nodded. "And I assume you don't want anyone to know I'm working for you?"

"Well, you're not *working* for me. I'm utilizing you like a reserved officer of sorts—volunteer, unofficial, unpaid."

Untrained. But Sadie didn't say that out loud. Something he'd said earlier came to mind, and she cocked her head to the side. "You said that your intuition was one of the reasons you're doing this. What did you mean by that?"

He paused for a moment, regarding her in that see-too-much way of his before he spoke. "I understand that you're still working

Josi S. Kilpack

through your thoughts in regard to God helping discover truth. For my part, I no longer have doubts about that—though I did at one time." He tapped his palm on the armrest of his wheelchair, indicating that there was a connection between his confidence and his disability. Sadie hoped he would tell her more, but he didn't. "There are times, within my personal and my professional life," he said, "that God leads me somewhere unexpected. When I follow His lead, I always succeed in my goal. Every time."

Sadie felt a strange warmth in her stomach, a kind of embarrassment, but also a pull to believe what he said. He had such confidence.

"When I read your profile," he continued, smiling slyly, "I felt very strongly that you were an important part of this case and that God had led you to it."

Sadie swallowed, that warmth growing as it traveled through her chest and arms, seeming to confirm what he'd said. God wanted her to work this case? Officer Nielson knew it? She was supposed to acknowledge that?

"But I'm not here to preach to you, despite all that God-talk," he waved his hands in the air as though giving her permission to move past the questions he'd planted. "I just need your help with this case for the next few days. I don't want to miss anything, and I believe you're just the net we need to keep anything from getting away from us."

"I'm humbled by the request," Sadie said. "And I am happy to help you with this case. Um, thank you for asking."

"Thank you for accepting," he said, extending his hand across the desk. When they finished shaking on the deal, he pulled his hand back, and then he handed her a business card. "That's my cell phone number—call it any time. I will do my very best to answer your call, any time night or day—and if I don't answer, I will call you back as soon as I can. Call me with anything you might have—questions, updates, whatever you need."

It was a surreal drive back to the hotel, where Sadie sat on the bed and processed the entire conversation again. Unbelievable. Then she hurried to her computer and updated her notes before going through them and revising them, with the understanding that they very well could be part of an official police file. She'd never worked with the police on purpose before—they'd never wanted her. It was a heady mental shift to make.

She lost track of time until Caro let herself into the room. "We're late," she said after the door shut behind her. She went straight to the closet where most of her clothes were hanging. "The memorial service starts in just forty-five minutes. We're still going, right?"

Sadie turned in the desk chair to face Caro. "We're definitely going," she said as she stood up and went toward the dresser. The only skirt she'd brought was a cotton maxi skirt she could pair with a white tunic top and silver ballet flats. It wasn't as dressy as she would normally wear for a memorial service, but she hadn't planned to attend one when she'd packed for the trip. "You will not believe what happened while you were gone. I'll tell you about it while we get ready."

CHAPTER 12

C aro called Tess on their way to the memorial service and explained what had happened with Officer Nielson. Tess was surprised but also excited. Sadie couldn't say she was looking forward to working with Tess. She didn't like to think she held many grudges, but she was certainly hesitant to believe that everything would be good between them simply because they had the green light to continue forward.

They met outside the foundation building, which was located on the first floor of the same building Dr. Hendricks's clinic was in. The first thing Sadie noticed when she saw Tess was the pin she wore on the collar of her purple dress. For one thing, the pastel pink of the pin and eggplant color of the dress didn't match, but Sadie recognized the pin from the Pink Posy Boutique website she'd surfed last night.

"Is that the Posy Pin from the boutique?" Sadie asked as she pulled open the glass doors at the entrance of the building. There was a foyer area with an elevator and a staircase leading to the second floor, where the clinic was. The double glass doors that led into the foundation offices on the first floor were propped open, extending the space for the memorial service into the marble-floored foyer.

A warm smile spread across Tess's face as she touched a finger to the pin. They walked through the doors, and Sadie patted herself on the back for getting a good response. Maybe the relationship between them could be repaired after all. "Isn't it beautiful? Paul got it for me after my three-month-cancer-free check."

"It is beautiful," Caro said, leaning in to see it more closely once they were inside.

"Thanks," Tess said.

"So it's like a badge for survivors?" Sadie asked, following Caro and Tess.

"It's not a *badge*. It's a symbol of support for breast cancer awareness and increased research toward a cure. Anyone who wants to beat cancer wears it to show their desire for change, and all of the money for the pin is donated directly to breast cancer research."

Sadie smiled politely, subdued by the somewhat snippy tone of Tess's response.

"It's lovely," Caro said again. She looked at Sadie. "Maybe we should go to the boutique later and get one for ourselves to show our support."

"Um, I'd love to go to the boutique," Sadie said, sidestepping the fact that she wasn't sure she wanted to spent two hundred dollars on the pin. She felt sure Caro would agree once she knew the price, but she didn't want to bring it up in front of Tess.

"Now, just to clarify," Tess said. "I'll talk to Lori since I'm the one she canceled with this morning, right?"

Sadie had expected to be the one to talk to Lori.

"That's a good idea," Caro said before Sadie could say anything.

Sadie looked away, not wanting to argue with them. She'd just make sure she was close by so she could overhear the discussion and break in if necessary.

They continued across the foyer and into the foundation suite, where four easels held bulletin boards filled with pictures of Dr. Hendricks from his childhood through recent years. Sadie stepped up to the first one, eager to immerse herself in the life of this man who was becoming increasingly interesting to her.

The photos with his children made her especially sad, and she was reminded that, investigation aside, this memorial service was a tribute to a man's life. She wanted to make sure she didn't forget that. The walls of the foyer were covered with plaques of achievement, a billboard of community events, and a wall of photographs taken at various fund-raising events the foundation had sponsored. There were several photos from past Red Rock Cancer walks, most of them featuring Anita, Dr. Hendricks, Dr. Waters, and Nikki.

Caro soon joined Sadie in looking at the photos, while Tess visited with people she knew. They entered the Gathering Room, where the service would be held, about ten minutes before the memorial service was to start. It was a wide room with accordion dividers so the room could be divided into three sections when necessary. Sadie assumed this was where the support groups met that she'd read about on the foundation's website. It was fitting for the memorial service to be held in the foundation offices, but it looked as though it would seat only about a hundred people. Sadie expected more people to attend than that.

An expectant hush was wrapped around the whispers being exchanged between attendees. Sadie scanned the room for Lori. It didn't look as though she and her children had arrived yet. Anita Hendricks—Sadie recognized her from the pictures she'd seen—stood at the front of the room, welcoming people, exchanging quick hugs with acquaintances, and thanking them for coming. Sadie remembered doing the same thing at Neil's funeral even though she'd felt on the brink of collapse with all the emotion she was holding back. It had been such a miserable day, and she felt for Anita and what this was likely costing her. A few feet away from where Anita stood was a large portrait of Dr. Hendricks. It tugged at Sadie's heart that all they had left of this man were pictures.

An older couple Sadie assumed were Dr. Hendricks's parents stood a few feet away from Anita, also exchanging greetings with attendees. Sadie's heart broke for them, too. Though Sadie had struggled through the loss of many people she'd loved during her life, the idea of saying good-bye to one of her children made her chest tighten. Not to know what had happened to take him from them must make that pain even more excruciating.

"How well do you know Anita?" Caro asked Tess after they met back together to find seats.

"She and I talked on the phone a few times when she was helping coordinate my treatment plan, and I've seen her in the clinic when I've gone in for appointments with Dr. H, but I haven't really talked with her. I don't think she knows me."

"What's she like?" Caro asked. "I'm sure people have talked about her reputation and things."

"She's a business woman through and through, so I've heard people say she's a little cold sometimes and no-nonsense, but at the same time she's very generous, too. Nikki gets along with her really well, and I've always trusted Nikki's judgment about people. She said since Dr. H's disappearance, Anita divides her time between the clinic, the foundation, and the boutique to the point where she's putting in fourteen-hour days six days a week. She told Nikki it keeps her from having to go to an empty house." Tess stopped at the head of a row about halfway to the front and turned to look at Caro with sorrowful eyes. "Isn't that sad?"

Sadie and Caro nodded while they moved to the center of the row. Sadie settled into her seat, with Caro on her right and Tess to Caro's right. Without any pockets in her skirt, Sadie'd had to bring her purse, and she stowed it under her chair. She hoped she wouldn't forget it when they left.

Anita had a handkerchief—not tissues—in her hand, and she kept dabbing at the corners of her eyes as she listened to people's comments. She must have chosen waterproof mascara today because her makeup was perfect. Sadie wondered if Anita were counting to ten in her head over and over again, like Sadie had done at Neil's funeral. It had distracted her just enough, and she didn't break down until she got back home and stared at the fourth chair at the dinner table.

Tess turned in her seat to say hi to someone in the row behind them. Sadie focused on the portrait that stood in place of a coffin or urn. She'd seen the head shot before, though it was smaller and grainier in the newspaper articles. Dr. Hendricks had a receding hairline and short hair, nearly shaved, a round face, and a wide smile complete with parentheses lines on either side of his mouth. His teeth were too white to be naturally so. She'd seen photos of him online that had shown a rather non-athletic physique, on the thick side, if not a little bit chubby, but the head shot didn't really show that. He didn't look like Sadie's idea of an outdoorsman, but it was easy to see him as Lori had described: good, kind, hard-working, and without a secret life. She turned to look toward the back of the room, surprised that Lori, or at least her children, weren't part of the informal receiving line. Lori wouldn't have changed her mind about coming to the service, would she?

"There's Dr. Waters, Nikki's husband," Caro whispered, prompting Sadie to turn and look in the direction Caro was nodding. Dr. Waters was an attractive man, tall and lean with hair greying at the temples in that distinguished way men could pull off so well. He wore a grey suit with a blue tie. Nikki walked beside him, with three teenage children following behind.

Sadie watched the family file into the second row. Another man, looking equally prestigious, came in behind them and shook hands with Dr. Waters before sitting a few seats away from the family. Were they colleagues?

Anita came forward to shake hands with Dr. Waters and Nikki across the row of chairs between them. Was it Sadie's imagination that Dr. Waters seemed to stiffen slightly when Anita spoke to him? Nikki Waters, on the other hand, seemed genuinely warm as she hugged Anita over the top of the chairs and shared some consoling thoughts—at least that's what Sadie assumed she was sharing. Unfortunately, Sadie was too far away to overhear. She *was* close enough, however, to notice the Pink Posy Pin on the lapel of Anita's jacket. When Nikki turned her way, Sadie could see that she also was wearing the pin.

Sadie began scanning the room, and from where she sat she could see at least a dozen women with the same pin and a few men who used it as a lapel pin or tie tack. It really did seem to be a thread that was woven into this community. Sadie admired the fact that the foundation had created a way for people to come together in such an important cause. At the same time, however, Sadie was watching Anita Hendricks dab her eyes, and she wondered if the handkerchief were even wet. There was something rote in Anita's movements, though Sadie felt bad for thinking it. Still, it seemed like Anita was a little bit too composed and was trying to cover up her composure.

Tess saw someone at the back of the room and got up to say hello. The two women must not have seen each other in a while. They embraced and then moved to the side so they wouldn't be in the way of people getting to their seats. Sadie scanned the room again—still no Lori—and noted that the seats were filling fast. They should have chosen a larger venue.

"There's Lori," Caro said, elbowing Sadie lightly. Sadie looked over her shoulder and watched as Lori hurried two children to the front row, a teenage girl and a boy the same age as Tess's son. From the obituary Sadie knew their names were Kenzie and Joseph, though the son went by Joey. Lori looked nice in a brick-red dress with matching jacket that was almost as long as her knee-length skirt and nearly the same shade as her hair. Her gold pumps shouldn't have matched, but they did somehow. Perhaps because she also wore a chunky gold necklace. And no Pink Posy Pin.

Lori had a polite but stiff smile on her face as she sat at the far end of the first row. Her children sat on either side of her, but they quickly got up and greeted their grandparents, who hugged them both and smiled through their grief. Anita approached the children as well. There didn't seem to be any strain between them and their stepmother as she hugged each of them in turn. Sadie glanced at Lori and saw that she was looking at her phone. The woman Sadie assumed was Dr. Hendricks's mother approached Lori, and Lori slid her phone into the pocket of her jacket and shook the older woman's hand. Lori smiled, but she didn't stand or talk to her ex-mother-in-law for very long. As soon as Mama Hendricks walked back to the children, Lori checked her phone again.

"Someone looks a little uncomfortable," Caro whispered. Sadie glanced at her and saw that she was watching Lori, too.

Sadie nodded her agreement and considered going over to say

hello to Lori. It would be a reasonable thing for Sadie to do after their talk last night, right? But Tess had already said *she* wanted to talk to Lori. A quick glance found Tess still in deep conversation with the woman she'd been talking to for several minutes now. Sadie hoped Tess would hurry and take advantage of this opportunity. The service would start soon.

"When you said something must have changed Lori's mind about meeting with us," Caro said, "did you think someone could have told her not to come to this? She looks like she's . . . nervous or something."

Sadie shrugged and nodded at the same time. "Something significant has changed since last night. I sure wish I knew what." It was killing her to just sit here and do nothing. Had Tess even noticed Lori's arrival? "Should we go get Tess? She's going to miss her chance to talk to Lori if she doesn't hurry."

"I'll get her," Caro said. She stood up to make her way out of the row they were sitting on at the same time Nikki tapped Lori on the shoulder from behind. Lori turned in her chair and her expression softened as they talked quietly with each other. Nikki seemed concerned about her, but Lori seemed to be insisting that she was fine. Caro and Tess were a few rows from the front of the room when a loud male voice brought them up short.

"Hey, everybody."

Sadie's gaze shifted to a man who'd come to the front of the room. He looked enough like the portrait of Dr. Hendricks for Sadie to assume they were brothers.

"If everyone could please take their seats." He waited until the rustle of people obeying his request began to settle. Tess and Caro slid back into their seats. Tess smoothed her skirt over her thighs.

She leaned in front of Caro and whispered, "Sorry, guys. I guess I didn't see Lori come in."

Sadie smiled her forgiveness but wished she'd taken the chance to talk to Lori herself. Now they would have to try to catch her at the end of the service instead, which narrowed their window and, therefore, their chances of talking to her at all. The Hendricks kids returned to their seats, and Lori pulled her phone halfway out of the wide pocket of her jacket, glanced at it, and returned it to her pocket so she could put her arms around the shoulders of her kids. Was she expecting a call? Now?

Sadie thought back to the idea that someone might have told Lori not to be involved in today's events, which may be the reason for her current mood. But Dr. Hendricks's mother had spoken to her, albeit briefly—and why would anyone tell Lori to stay away when that might mean the kids would stay away with her?

CHAPTER 13

T he man at the front of the room welcomed the guests, introduced himself as Josh, one of Dr. Hendricks's brothers, and explained that he would conduct the service.

"We'll have an opening prayer by my father, Eugene, and then
my brother, Richard Hendricks, will read the obituary," he said.
"After that, Anita and my mother, Ruthie, will speak to us. There
will then be a musical number and a closing prayer." He looked toward the back of the room. "I'm sorry there aren't enough seats for
everyone," he said, prompting the entire audience who did have seats
to look around. There were at least forty people standing against the
walls and in the limited space at the back of the room. The doors
were open, and Sadie could see that the waiting area was also quite
full. "But we're very glad to have you all here in attendance."

"I'm surprised that Anita's giving a talk," Caro said quietly, leaning toward Sadie as Josh Hendricks sat down.

Sadie nodded her agreement. Spouses usually didn't speak, but,
as Tess had said, Anita was a business women. A type A personality,
Sadie assumed. Reliant on logic more than emotion. Sadie wondered
what Anita would think about the discrepancy of Dr. Hendricks's

Cherokee not being at the trailhead when it should have been. In the next moment, Sadie wondered if she already knew. Not to view Anita with some suspicion was just stupid. There was a reason spouses were often the first person of interest in an official police investigation.

Papa Hendricks rose to give an opening prayer. He asked for comfort and compassion and healing for all who were in attendance and for peace to accompany the service. Sadie was glad there was a religious flavor to the service and wondered about what Lori had said about his attending church in the months prior to his disappearance. Had he reconciled with his faith or was he simply seeking solace in light of the brush with mortality Anita's diagnosis created for him?

After the prayer, Dr. Hendricks's brother Richard read the obituary. He also looked a lot like Dr. Hendricks, but a few years older, Sadie guessed. Seeing the resemblance to his brother as he read the tribute was touching. Richard's voice shook with restrained emotion, and a chorus of sniffling began to sound throughout the room. When Richard finished, he shared some brief memories of his brother, including a time when they had shaved a neighbor's cat with their dad's electric razor, and how Dr. Hendricks—Trent, his brother called him—had used Richard's ID to cover up his trouble-making as a young man. The audience chuckled at the stories and Dr. Hendricks became even more real in Sadie's mind.

Sadie looked at Anita and saw that she was still dabbing at her eyes with that handkerchief. Sadie's gaze slid to Lori, seated half a dozen seats away from Anita. Lori was a contrast to Anita in every way. While Anita was dressed in traditional black, Lori was in red with gold shoes. Anita's hair was conservative and elegant, while Lori's was an unnatural color in a punk-like style. The contrast seemed to echo what Lori had said about Anita playing the part of a doctor's wife to perfection, while Lori had never fit that role.

Lori had one arm around the shoulders of each of her children, who were both crying, but she stared straight ahead, not even looking at the speaker behind the podium. Her expression was intent, and very different from last night when she'd had a few emotional moments and spoken with such depth and honesty. While Sadie watched, Lori removed her arm from her daughter's shoulder in order to pull her phone halfway out of her jacket pocket again.

"What's with the phone?" Caro whispered to Sadie. Apparently she was watching Lori, too.

Sadie leaned over to make sure they weren't overheard. "I don't know. She seems really tense, doesn't she?"

"What are you talking about?" Tess whispered from Caro's other side. Sadie suppressed a sigh but refused to dwell on her annoyance as Caro turned to her right and quietly explained their conversation to Tess.

Sadie tried to remember if she'd sensed any apprehension from Lori last night in regard to attending the memorial. She was quite certain, however, that Lori had felt comfortable and confident about being there. Watching her now, however, she seemed to be wrestling with some very intense emotions.

Richard Hendricks sat down, and Anita stood and made her way to the small podium at the front of the room, just to the right of Dr. Hendricks's portrait. Her pencil skirt fit her trim frame perfectly, and her heels—three inches at least—sculpted her calves. If she'd lost weight with her cancer treatments, she'd bought that suit recently—it fit her like a glove. Once she faced the crowd, Anita smiled sweetly. Sadie judged her to be in her thirties. She looked every part the doctor's wife and the grieving widow.

"Trenton would be touched to see so many of you here today," she said with a tremor in her voice. Sadie glanced at Lori, who once again was not looking at the speaker. Instead, she looked from the floor to her children beside her and, now and then, at the portrait of her ex-husband. She showed no emotion but maintained a stoic presence that Sadie sensed was taking a great deal of effort to hold on to.

Sadie looked back at Anita Hendricks when she began speaking again. "One of the things I most admired about Trenton—and he had so many admirable traits—was his ambition."

Ambition? Sadie thought to herself. It seemed an odd lead-in to talk about her husband.

"In fact, you could say that's how we met. Our ambitions aligned, so to speak, and from that first conference forward I knew that he was the man I would spend my life with." She raised the handkerchief to cover her mouth as emotion got the better of her. The sniffling throughout the room doubled. Caro elbowed Sadie and nodded toward Lori.

For the first time, Lori was looking at the speaker but with a look Sadie couldn't quite define. Had Anita said something that upset her? A moment later, she looked back at the floor, and her tension seemed to increase. Sadie could almost feel the heat of it, and she was several yards away from where Lori sat. She discreetly scanned the room and noted that no one else was looking at Lori. Would they have noticed Lori's reaction to Anita's words if they had been watching her?

"I honestly don't know how I will continue on," Anita said, her voice a squeak. She took a breath and put her handkerchief to her chest. "But I know that I must because without Trenton here, I know that it falls to me to carry on this legacy and continue to bless lives the way he has blessed so many." Lori continued to stare at the floor. Sadie couldn't tell if she was holding in emotion or was just . . . angry? Sadie rewound Anita's words in her mind to see if she could determine what it was that had upset Lori. Could it be that Lori did still have feelings for her ex-husband and hearing about Anita's affections was upsetting to her? Lori's inability to control her response now, however, was very different from the way she'd had control of herself the night before. Then again, at one point the night before Lori had mentioned loving Dr. Hendricks, and Sadie had wondered if she meant current feelings or had intended the past tense.

When Sadie tuned back in, Anita was explaining Dr. Hendricks's commitment to his patients and the foundation. The foundation had donated a record amount the previous year, and they hoped to increase that amount at Friday's cancer walk. Anita talked about her own cancer and how frightening it had been but how it strengthened both her and Dr. Hendricks's resolve to fight the disease even more. Something didn't feel right about this message, but it wasn't until Anita was concluding her remarks that Sadie figured out what it was. Sadie'd been to a lot of funerals in her day, and a few memorial services, but this sounded more like a speech than a tribute to her husband's life. There was an arrogance about it that was out of place and a lack of sorrow that was even more unusual.

Sadie glanced around the room, but no one else seemed to share her confusion at Anita's message. Perhaps it was because each of them knew Dr. Hendricks—perhaps he was equally passionate and would appreciate the fervor behind the words. Sadie and Caro might be the only people here who were strangers to him, and maybe that gave them some objectivity. Sadie saw that Lori was now clutching her phone at her side so tightly that her knuckles were white. She continued to stare at the spot of floor in front of her feet, and Sadie felt sure she was forcing herself to remain calm. The speech wasn't necessarily objectionable, it just wasn't . . . appropriate. Lori, however, seemed very upset by it. Barely holding on to her calm.

" . . . And so, thank you," Anita said, hand to chest once more as she scanned the room with a loving gaze. The white handkerchief was a stark contrast to her black suit. "Thank you for being a part of Trenton's life and for honoring all that he has done with the time he had. I am touched by your love for him and thank you all for this remembrance of the man I love."

She sat down and Caro leaned over to Sadie. "Not a word about his two children sitting in the audience?"

Sadie hadn't noted that, but she knew Caro was right. Was that why Lori was so upset? A quick glance confirmed that Lori was still solid as a statue, clutching her phone and staring at the floor.

Dr. Hendricks's mother, Ruth, stood to speak. In contrast to his widow's, Dr. Hendricks's mother's tribute was heart-wrenching and deeply personal. Sadie had to get a tissue from the pack she always kept in her purse when, with tears streaming down her soft cheeks, the doctor's mother talked about the father he was to his children. Mrs. Hendricks spoke directly to her grandchildren, reminding them of how much their father loved them, how proud he had been of them, and how sorry she was that they had to face such a tragedy. She talked about him watching over them from heaven and reminded them that this life is only part of the journey each of them was making.

Looking up at her ex-mother-in-law, Lori finally melted, her tears overflowing as she wiped frantically at her eyes. Nikki handed her a tissue over the seats between them, and Lori smiled a weak thank-you. Nikki squeezed her arm before sitting back in her chair. Sadie shifted her gaze to Anita, who continued to dab at her eyes in the same cadence Sadie had noticed when she first walked in.

There wasn't a dry eye in the room by the time Mrs. Hendricks declared her final devotion for her son. After she sat down, a male quartet stood and sang a hymn Sadie didn't recognize. The beautiful harmony and tender lyrics had Sadie reaching into her purse for another tissue. By the end of the song, Lori was composed, though her face was splotchy from emotion. Her son's head was now resting on her lap, and her arm was around her daughter. Both of the children were still crying but had calmed some. It was hard for Sadie to look at. She had sat through her husband's funeral, and had tried to comfort her children, even though they were so young they had only a limited understanding of what was happening. Was that all that Lori's behavior signified? An extreme reaction to what was happening today? Could reality have hit her so hard that she lost all the confidence she'd had the evening before? Tess did say Lori could be high-strung. Still, it just didn't feel right, and the more Sadie watched her, the less right it felt.

CHAPTER 14

A closing prayer was offered by someone Sadie didn't take note of, and then the memorial attendees either rose to their feet or turned to talk with those sitting next to them. "Beautiful service," Sadie heard one woman say. "Poor Anita," said another. Sadie agreed with both sentiments, but her eyes were on Lori, who was on her feet a moment after the "Amen."

"I'm going to talk to Lori," Tess announced. Sadie was annoyed that even though she'd missed her first opportunity, she still considered herself in charge. *Teamwork stinks,* she thought.

"I'll go with you," Caro said, and she began following Tess out of the row. A woman sitting behind them called Tess's name, and Tess turned toward her.

"How are you? It's been ages, hasn't it? How are you doing?"

Sadie muffled an exaggerated sigh at the delay as she watched Lori move toward the door with her children. She'd gone the long way around, skipping the family and friends who were congregating at the front of the room. Sadie looked back and forth between Lori, Tess, the woman Tess was still talking to, and the door Lori was heading toward. Lori was leaving. Now. Sadie tried to take comfort in the thought that Lori would still be at the luncheon, but somehow she didn't feel very sure of that.

If Tess weren't going to make talking to Lori a priority, Sadie would. But Tess was blocking one end of the row, and on the other end, an elderly couple were taking their time as the woman looked through her purse. Sadie was trapped. A middle-aged couple stopped Lori near the back of the room, which bought Sadie a little more time. Judging from the polite but tense smile on Lori's face, however, it wouldn't be a very long delay if Lori had anything to do with it. She'd kept a hand on one shoulder of each of her children as though to make sure they didn't leave her side. Was she afraid of someone?

Sadie had to step up her game plan if she were going to intercept Lori before the couple ended their conversation with her. She adjusted her purse strap on her shoulder and moved a chair in order to step into the row behind them, but she still couldn't get out of either end. She moved another chair and then another, making a path to the back of the room as quickly as she could, but she didn't move as unobtrusively as she would have liked. Luckily, Caro was following behind her and replacing the chairs as soon as she got around them—she must have felt the same urgency Sadie did. Despite her attempts to hurry, by the time Sadie reached a row with a clear way out, Lori was gone, and the couple she'd been talking to had engaged someone else in discussion.

Sadie hurried out of the room, scanning the foyer on her way to the front doors. She was just pushing them open when she saw that Lori was already on the sidewalk in front of the building. She was being detained by yet another older woman, who had her hand on Lori's arm. Thank goodness these St. George people were so determined to talk to her. The woman seemed to be sharing her condolences, and, although Lori was being polite, she was turned toward the parking lot, likely counting the seconds before she could continue to her car. Sadie used the opportunity to plan how she would approach Lori when this woman was finished.

Suddenly, Caro stepped in front of Sadie and pushed through the doors, causing Sadie to step to the side to get out of her way. Caro pulled her phone from her pocket and put it to her ear as she walked toward Lori. Sadie had no idea what Caro was doing. Caro accidentally bumped into Lori from the side, pushing her into the woman she was talking to. *What on earth . . . ?*

"Oh, I'm sorry," Caro said, grabbing Lori's arm as if to help her maintain her balance. If Sadie hadn't been trying to figure out what Caro was doing, she might never have noticed how Caro's hand slid into the wide pocket of Lori's jacket and emerged with Lori's phone. Sadie felt her eyebrows go up in surprise, and then she quickly schooled her expression so no one would notice. She glanced around quickly, relieved that no one else was paying any attention to Caro's hijinks. Lori looked quickly over her shoulder to see who had bumped into her, but Caro was already a few steps away. Lori turned back to the woman she didn't want to be talking to. The kids looked toward Caro longer than Lori did, but then they, too, turned back to their mother and the other woman.

The woman talking to Lori had barely stopped for a breath. Caro kept walking, pressing the stolen phone to her side, and then turned sharply to the left. She cast Sadie a quick look before disappearing around the corner of the building and nodding in Lori's direction as if to say, "You're up." It took Sadie a split second to move forward again, just as Lori finished her conversation with the woman. The woman headed toward the parking lot, and Lori moved toward the street as fast as her heels would allow. The parking lot had been nearly full when Sadie, Caro, and Tess had arrived, and Lori must have had to park farther away. But luck was on Sadie's side in catching up with Lori—she'd worn flats.

"Lori!" Sadie called when Lori reached the sidewalk that ran parallel to the street. She tried to ignore the heat that assaulted her when she stepped out of the shaded entryway of the building, but it took her off guard all the same. Lori looked over her shoulder to see who had called to her, but she didn't slow down when she saw Sadie. In fact, she may have even sped up. She urged her kids to hurry ahead of her.

"Lori!" Sadie called again, and she broke into a jog when she also reached the sidewalk, her sandals sounding like gunshots as they slapped the hot pavement with each step. She caught up to Lori in just a few steps and grabbed her arm as gently but firmly as she could. Lori turned toward her, an expression of frustration on her face. "What's wrong?" Sadie asked, a bit breathlessly. The kids stopped a few feet away, looking confused and unsure of whether to continue or not. There was no time to beat around the bush. "Why are you in such a hurry to leave? Are you still going to the luncheon?"

"I can't stay. I've got a family emergency," Lori said quickly, pressing her keys into her daughter's hand. "Go start the car, Kenzie. I'll be right there." Her daughter looked at them both before hurrying to a dark blue sedan parked a few car lengths ahead. Joey followed her.

"What's happened?" Sadie asked, choosing boldness over the possibility of not getting a straight answer if she tried to dance around things. "You seemed to want to be involved last night, and now you're leaving as fast as you can. What made you change your mind?"

Lori looked toward her kids, who were punching a code into the keypad on the driver's side door. "I told you. I have a family emergency."

"This morning you said it was a school assignment. What's going on?"

Lori looked back at her, and for a moment she looked as though she might say something. Her eyebrows pinched together and she took a deep breath, but then she looked past Sadie's shoulder. Sadie heard the sounds of clicking heels coming toward them, and she looked over her shoulder, too. Caro was approaching them. *Really bad timing, Caro*, she thought to herself. *Really, really bad.*

"Lori?" Caro said sweetly, holding Lori's cell phone out to her as she approached. "Is this your phone? It was on the floor by your chair."

Lori's hand went quickly to her jacket pocket, and her eyes widened in surprise as she stepped past Sadie and snatched the phone from Caro's hand. If she recognized Caro as the woman who had stumbled into her a few minutes earlier, she didn't show it. She looked at the phone for a second before returning it to her pocket and then kept her hand in her pocket as though to make sure the phone didn't disappear again. Sadie was impressed by Caro's skills— she'd never seen Caro put on such an act before, but she wished Caro had waited a few more minutes to return the phone. Sadie hadn't had much time to talk to Lori.

"I'm glad I caught you," Caro said.

"Yeah," Lori said, still seeming a little confused. "Me, too. Uh, thank you."

"You're welcome," Caro said innocently. She looked back and forth between Lori and Sadie. "Everything okay?"

"Fine," Lori said, attempting a tight smile. "But I really need to go, and I think you should just . . . stop everything you're doing. I . . . uh, just don't feel good about what you guys are doing."

"Did someone talk to you? Did someone tell you not to be involved?"

Lori straightened, and Sadie knew she'd pushed too hard. "Just leave me alone," Lori snapped, taking a backward step toward the car.

"Can't I help you?" Sadie asked, quickly softening her tone even though she feared she was out of luck.

"You can back off," Lori retorted, out of patience. "And, no, you can't help me. I need to take care of my kids right now and I need to get home—that's it." She turned on her heel and marched toward her car, her golden shoes beating a tempo on the concrete. Sadie didn't try to stop her again. She and Caro stayed on the sidewalk, watching as Lori pulled out of her parking spot and disappeared down the street. She had been one of the first people to leave the service. Did the children's grandparents know they'd already left? Did they know the kids wouldn't be at the luncheon?

Sadie turned to Caro, who had a smug look of accomplishment on her face that killed any thought Sadie had about reprimanding her earlier interruption.

"What *was* that whole pickpocket thing?" Sadie asked.

"I read this detective book where the sleuth did that kind of thing all the time," Caro said, turning back toward the building. "I've been practicing on Rex all summer—he finds it hilarious, as long as I don't take cash out of his wallet after I lift it."

Sadie hurried to keep up with Caro's quick steps and didn't get a chance to comment before Caro spoke again.

"I think I found a place we can talk inside—it's so hot out here." They went back inside the building, and Caro led Sadie toward the far end of the foyer. None of the mourners had congregated there, even though people didn't seem to be in a hurry to leave.

Caro looked around to make sure they weren't being overheard, and then she pulled her cell phone from her purse. "Lori seemed to be really intent on her phone, so I figured she was expecting a call or a text or something, right? I took pictures of her call logs." She tapped the camera icon, and a picture filled the screen. "Maybe whoever she was waiting to hear from called her earlier or something. If someone did warn her about meeting with us, maybe we can figure out who it was based on when they called her."

"Brilliant," Sadie said as she leaned forward and squinted to see the photo better. It was a very clear picture. Caro's phone had a nice camera.

Most of the numbers on the call log had names assigned to them, such as "Grandma H" and "Carol W." Two calls on the log that weren't assigned as contacts in Lori's phone, however, took place not long before Lori had called Tess to cancel the meeting. Both numbers had the 435 prefix.

"Is 435 the area code for Vegas?" Caro asked.

"No, Vegas is 702—435 is a Utah area code. Northern and southern I think, not central." Sadie had become a bit of an expert on area codes during a previous case. It was a nice little super-power to have for moments like this.

"These numbers are from this area, then, not from Vegas."

"And that first number was an incoming call?"

"Yep. And after that she made a call to this second one. I checked her text messages, too." Caro used her finger to move to another photo on her phone. All of the numbers on her texting log were assigned, and Caro scrolled through more pictures that showed the conversations Lori had had with her friends—she hadn't missed a thing. A conversation with Nikki was about Lori not being able to help with the luncheon.

Nikki: Is everything okay?

Lori: School stuff, and I don't want to deal with Anita.

Nikki: I understand. Hang in there.

"Lori didn't seem to have an issue with Anita when we talked last night," Sadie commented.

"Weren't the kids going to stay with Anita after the luncheon?" Caro asked.

Sadie nodded. "Go back to the call log." Caro scrolled back to the screen Sadie wanted to see. Sadie looked at the numbers and noted that the incoming call had lasted about six minutes. Within a minute of hanging up, Lori had called the other unknown number. That call had lasted only twenty-one seconds. Was it unreasonable to assume that the first call had prompted the second? And just a few minutes after that call, Lori had called Tess to tell her she wasn't able to meet that morning after all.

The familiar energy of the hunt made Sadie's elbows tingle. If she could find answers to the increasing number of questions, where might this investigation end up? To have all her actions sanctioned by the police department—well, within reason—made it even more interesting. "Which one do you want to call?" Sadie asked as she shifted her purse to dig out her own phone, eager to act on this lead. She considered calling Officer Nielson before moving forward, but he hadn't given her a timeline on when she was supposed to give him updates. She would rather contact him when she had a significant amount of information rather than giving it to him in bits and pieces.

"Either one," Caro said.

Sadie looked at Caro long enough to see the wide smile on her face. She was loving this.

"Why don't I take the incoming call and you can call the other one?" Caro said.

"Okay," Sadie said as she punched the outgoing number into her phone and turned toward the glass doors, staring down the street where Lori Hendricks had disappeared a few minutes earlier. *What are you hiding, Lori?* Sadie wondered as the phone rang on the other end of the line.

CHAPTER 15

S adie heard three rings before the line clicked and a recording came on. *"You've reached the office of Attorney Kyle Edger. Please leave a message, and we'll get back to you as soon as possible."*

Sadie hung up. She called it back and listened to the message again. It wouldn't do any good to leave a message at this point. She didn't know enough to ask reasonable questions, and an attorney would tell her very little anyway. At best, she'd get just one chance to ask any questions at all, so she had to be smart about the questions she asked. Why would Lori have called an attorney right after receiving that inbound phone call? Wondering what type of law Kyle Edger practiced, Sadie opened up an internet window on her phone and entered his name.

The firm—she wasn't sure it could be called a firm if it were just one attorney—didn't have its own website. She eventually found the name on a listing resource for southern Utah attorneys.

"Contract and patent law?" she whispered. Why on earth would Lori need to contact a patent attorney?

"Pine Valley."

Sadie hadn't heard Caro approach. She looked up with what

must have been a questioning expression that prompted Caro to explain.

"The call Lori received was from the Pine Valley Motel located in a little town about forty-five minutes away." She nodded toward Sadie's phone. "Who was your number for?"

"An attorney," Sadie said. "It just went to voice mail. How long did Lori's call to that number last again?"

Caro scrolled through her phone and showed Sadie the picture with the duration of the two calls. Twenty-one seconds. "I can't imagine she spoke to anyone for that short a time," Sadie said while redialing the number. This time she counted off the seconds it took for the short message to play. She hung up when the beep sounded and met Caro's eyes. "Eight seconds. She must have left a message, but not a lengthy one."

Caro nodded her agreement.

"What about that incoming call? Do you know who called Lori from the motel?"

"No," Caro said with a frown. "And the girl who was working this morning is off for the day—but I did find out that the call was made from the front desk phone rather than one of the rooms. Those would have shown up with a different number. So the front desk girl very likely knows who made that call—it's not a large motel. I went ahead and booked us a room for tonight so that we could talk to the front desk girl in the morning."

It took Sadie a moment to realize what Caro had said. "You booked us a room?"

"Sure, isn't that what you would have done? I remember you telling me once that face-to-face conversations were always more effective than over the phone, and it's a small town—I bet we can figure out who made that call if we're there to talk to people, don't you think?"

The sound of approaching footsteps interrupted their discussion, and they turned to see Tess hurrying toward them. "I can't find Lori anywhere," she said, sounding annoyed. She looked out the front windows. "Maybe she already went to the church for the luncheon."

"She's not going to the luncheon," Sadie said. "But I caught her before she left."

"I was going to talk to her."

"But you didn't." Sadie wasn't concerned with tiptoeing around Tess right now. If Sadie hadn't acted like she had, none of them would have talked to Lori before she left.

Tess huffed and looked at Caro. "I thought we had an agreement."

Caro shrugged. "She was leaving, Tess, and you were talking."

"I happen to know a lot of these people—some of us went through treatment together."

"I know, but we needed to talk to Lori."

Tess let out a breath and looked around as though counting to ten in her head. "So, what did she say?"

"She said she's going back to Vegas right now," Sadie answered, keeping her voice level. "Only this time she said she had a family emergency. She didn't say much and seemed really anxious to leave."

"Did you ask her more questions? Did you tell her the police were involved?"

"Telling her the police are involved didn't seem important, and she didn't stick around for many questions. But then Caro got her—"

"I'd have asked her more questions," Tess cut in. "And she'd have answered me."

"You were not there," Sadie snapped. She paused and took a breath before casting a look at Caro. She didn't like to lose her cool like this, but Tess was pushing all of her buttons. "I'll wait for you in the car—tell her about the photos you took of Lori's call logs."

It was a few minutes before Caro joined Sadie in the car. She'd been waiting long enough that the air conditioner had restored normal temperatures to the car's interior, and Sadie had cooled down along with the air around her. "I'm sorry for spouting off like that," she said to Caro. She wanted to justify her actions, but she knew that would make things uncomfortable for Caro. Tess was still Caro's cousin and her good friend.

"It's okay. She wasn't listening to you anyway."

"Did you talk to her, then? Did she soften up?"

Caro nodded and put on her seat belt while Sadie shifted the car into reverse. "She understands."

Sadie waited for more information, but when Caro didn't offer any, Sadie didn't push. She would do her best to stay out of Tess's way from here on—hopefully Tess would do the same for her.

They arrived at the church a few minutes later. There were already a dozen cars in the parking lot, and they hurried inside. Nikki sent them both to the kitchen, where everything was being prepped for the buffet. While they were on their way to the kitchen, Tess came in, but she didn't follow them. It was just as well.

A woman who was already in the kitchen introduced herself as Jean. Sadie introduced herself and wondered if maybe Jean had known Dr. Hendricks. If so, perhaps she would end up giving Sadie information like Lori had in this very kitchen the night before. Unfortunately, Jean said she'd never met the man and turned out to be not much of a talker. After half a dozen attempts to start a conversation and getting only one-word answers, Sadie gave up and went about her work. There were aprons today, and Sadie chose a purple one with "Stand for the Right" embroidered on the front—she felt she could use the motivation. The apron Caro ended up with was bright yellow with bumblebees all over it. Yellow had never been Sadie's color, but it looked great on Caro. After a few minutes, Nikki came in and asked Caro to help serve.

By the time Caro came back a few minutes later, Sadie had become familiar with the kitchen and where the different dishes of food were set up. "They'll be saying a blessing on the food in about five minutes, and Nikki wants two pans of funeral potatoes. Can you get that?"

"I'm on it," Sadie said.

Caro smiled and went back to the gym. Jean was mixing the fruit salad and made no move to help Sadie follow Nikki's direction, so Sadie was on her own. She didn't know what funeral potatoes were, but she'd seen four foil-covered 9x13-inch pans in one of the ovens.

"Are these funeral potatoes?" Sadie asked after opening the door of one of the ovens.

Jean looked over her shoulder long enough to nod once before going back to her stirring. Sadie felt it was a bit inappropriate to call the casserole "funeral potatoes," especially since this wasn't actually a funeral, but, like the term "cultural hall," it didn't seem to bother anyone else. Must be a Mormon thing. She put on a mismatched pair of oven mitts she found in a drawer and removed the first pan and set it on top of the stove. The oven was only keeping the pans warm, so it wasn't too hot. The potatoes smelled delicious, but when she peeked under the foil it just looked like hash brown casserole to her. Was that crushed cornflakes on top? Sadie removed the other pan from the oven and took the foil from both pans. One seemed to be made with shredded potatoes and one with diced. They smelled wonderful.

A woman came in with two cakes—one with chocolate frosting

in a 9x13-inch pan and the other in a clear pie dish. On the second dessert, Sadie could see a layer of crust, then one of cream cheese, with strawberries on top. She made a mental note to get herself a piece of that one if she had the chance—amid all the back and forth to the police station, there hadn't been any time for lunch today. In Sadie's prior community involvement there always seemed to be an unwritten rule that helpers were entitled to a sampling of whatever was being served, as long as they were discreet about it. Sadie was the pinnacle of discreet. Well, most of the time.

"Should I just set these here?" the woman asked, indicating a portion of counter where other desserts had been laid out.

"That would be great," Sadie said with a smile.

The woman set down the desserts and then pulled a stack of papers out of her pocket. "The last time Lillian made the Strawberry Pretzel Pie everyone wanted the recipe, so she sent some copies with it this time. I'll just set them right here so anyone who asks about it can help themselves."

Sadie thanked her, and the women disappeared. Sadie looked at the stack of recipes. What a brilliant idea to bring the recipe already printed up. Some women were so efficient. If the dessert tasted half as good as it looked, Sadie couldn't wait to give it a try. Right now, however, she needed to get the potatoes out there. She'd be sure to grab the recipe later. Jean had moved on to mixing the other fruit salad, content to take her time and focus on just that one thing. No matter. Sadie had this.

Sadie took the pans to the serving table in the gym, a little bothered by the cheap plastic tablecloths on the serving table. She could see crayon marks on the tabletop underneath. Fabric would look much better, but then if people were serving themselves—which she assumed they were since the food was set up on both sides of the table—it could be rather messy. She didn't think even Mormons had someone who specifically served as the congregational laundress.

There were nearly forty people in the room when she laid the serving spoons beside the pans. She noticed Tess talking to Dr. Hendricks's parents near the double doors that had been propped open. Despite her conflicted feelings toward the younger woman, Sadie hoped Tess had success with her part of the plan. Sadie went back to the kitchen for the first bowl of fruit salad just as someone stepped forward to say a prayer. The third prayer of the day, she noted.

For the next forty minutes, Sadie stayed busy changing full pans for empty ones and cleaning up spills people made on the table while serving themselves at the buffet. Caro and Nikki were in and out quite a bit as well. Tess kept her distance, staying mostly in the gym. Sadie saw her talking to a variety of different people.

During a lull in serving, Sadie sneaked a portion of funeral potatoes when one of the pans came back with just enough for one serving left in the corner. It was delicious, and she would swear it hadn't been made with canned soup like many hash brown casseroles were. She tried to discuss the topic with Jean and ask her if everyone used the same recipe or made their own version, but even something with the name of funeral potatoes couldn't interest the woman in conversation. Instead, Jean washed dishes, slowly and methodically, seemingly lost in her own thoughts. In Sadie's mind, Jean got points for serving, but not for being fun to work with.

Jean had to leave at 4:15. Sadie didn't miss her when she left. The luncheon activity had died down, and Sadie's thoughts were moving forward. To Pine Valley. To learning who had called Lori and changed everything.

The tap of high heels on linoleum pulled her from her thoughts, and Sadie turned with a soapy bowl in hand to find Anita Hendricks coming toward her across the kitchen.

"Oh, hi," Sadie said, tightening her grip on the bowl as her earlier opinions of this woman leapt to the forefront of her mind. Sadie had to remind herself that since she'd never actually met Anita, it wasn't fair to make judgments about her character, but the campaign-style speech at the service couldn't be ignored, either.

"Hi," Anita said with a warm smile. She took a few more steps into the room and twisted the wedding ring on her left hand with the thin fingers of her other hand. The ring was lovely, with a large princess-cut diamond in the center and several smaller diamonds in graduated sizes spreading from the center stone on both sides. Sadie wondered if Anita would take it off now that the memorial service was over, or if, like Sadie had when Neil died, she would find her hand uncomfortable without it and wear it a few years longer.

"I wanted to personally thank you for your help this afternoon. The whole thing has been just lovely." She waved toward the gym and then put her hand out to shake Sadie's. Sadie hurried to put the bowl back in the sink and dried her hands on her apron as she crossed the distance between them. She tried to read Anita's tone of voice or the words she had just spoken, but she couldn't find anything dubious. Anita had a firm handshake, something else Sadie couldn't criticize.

"I can't take much credit," Sadie said. "All I did was keep cold things cold and hot things hot."

"Well, I know it takes a lot of people to pull off something like this, and it was very kind of you to be a part of it. I'm not a member of your church, and yet you have all been so thoughtful. I really do appreciate it."

"Oh, I'm not a member of this church, either. I came into town for your foundation's cancer walk this weekend, but a friend of mine was involved in this, so I tagged along."

Anita smiled a little wider and cocked her head slightly to the side. "Then I owe you even more thanks for supporting us through this wonderful meal *and* for being a part of the fund-raising events this weekend. Thank you very much."

"Oh, you're welcome," Sadie said, slightly embarrassed by the level of this woman's praise. "But it's the least I can do. I'm very sorry for your loss."

Anita's smile fell slightly, and though her expression remained kind, sadness crept into her hazel eyes. The sorrow seemed sincere, which had Sadie reevaluating her earlier thoughts. Maybe Anita simply didn't know how to cope with such an emotional circumstance and was doing the best she could. "Thank you," Anita said quietly, twisting her ring again. "I appreciate your condolences. It's been a very difficult time, but I've been lucky to have such wonderful support from friends and family and even strangers like yourself."

Sadie nodded while dozens of questions came to her mind—each one completely inappropriate to ask at a memorial luncheon.

"I look forward to seeing you at the walk on Friday. Be sure to stop by and say hello when you get there."

There would be something like a thousand people at the walk, but Anita Hendricks was inviting Sadie to say hi to her? She probably said that to everyone, but an invitation was an invitation. "Maybe I will."

"I hope you do," Anita said, turning toward the door. "You're obviously a generous person. Thank you again for sharing that with so many people."

Sadie thanked her for the compliment despite feeling it was a little bit over the top—all Sadie had done was help in the kitchen.

As Anita left the room, Sadie lamented that she hadn't worked that conversation very well. She hadn't learned a single thing. A moment later, she shrugged it off and headed toward the gym to see if there were more dishes to clear from the buffet table.

As she crossed the hallway between the kitchen and the gym, she heard Anita's voice and looked to her right, where Anita and another woman were talking. Sadie was beginning to turn her head back when a movement farther down the hall, in the shadows past the foyer, caught her eye. She couldn't very well come to a stop in the middle of the hallway, so she continued to the gym and grabbed an empty potato dish and a nearly empty bowl of fruit salad. She hurried back to the kitchen, slowing her step as she entered the hall-way between the rooms and trying to hide the fact that she was trying to get a better look past where Anita and the other woman continued to visit. A man stood in the shadows . . . No, Dr. *Waters* stood in the shadows farther down the hall, where the lights hadn't been turned on. He wasn't necessarily hiding, but he did seem to be making himself inconspicuous, which for Sadie made him that much *more* conspicuous. He was watching Anita, and when she turned her head in his direction, perhaps seeing him out of the corner of her eye as Sadie had, she gave an almost imperceptible nod without inter-rupting her conversation.

When Sadie reached the kitchen, she quickly deposited the empty dishes and scanned the room for another excuse to cross the hall. Yes, a third crossing might look suspicious, but she'd been go-ing back and forth during the entire luncheon, so someone would be hard-pressed to make a case out of it.

There were two more desserts left on the counter and she grabbed the first one—the strawberry-topped cream-cheese creation she'd had her eye on earlier. It had already been sliced, so it was the perfect excuse to enter the hall again.

With the pie dish in hand, she made another trek across the hall, coming to a stop when she saw the woman Anita had been talking to enter the gym just steps ahead of Sadie. With a quick turn of her head, Sadie saw Anita moving toward the section of hallway where Dr. Waters had stood moments earlier. She couldn't see him anywhere. Was he waiting for Anita farther down the hall?

Funeral Potatoes

White sauce:
2 tablespoons butter
2 tablespoons flour
2 cups milk
½ teaspoon salt, or to taste
½ teaspoon pepper, or to taste
2 teaspoons chicken bouillon
1 (8-ounce) container sour cream

Casserole:
1 (32-ounce) bag frozen hash brown potatoes, cubed or shredded
1 to 2 cups sharp cheddar cheese, shredded
¼ cup French's fried onions, crushed
2 cups cornflakes, crushed
¼ cup butter

Preheat oven to 375 degrees.

To make white sauce, melt butter in sauté pan. Add flour and mix until a thick paste forms. Add milk and whisk constantly until sauce thickens. Add bouillon, salt and pepper, and sour cream, and mix well. Remove from heat.

Put potatoes in very large bowl. Add cheese and mix together. Add white sauce mixture and stir until combined. Add onions and mix well.

Spread potato mixture into 9x13-inch pan or casserole dish.

Melt butter and combine with cornflake crumbs. Sprinkle buttered crumbs on top of potato mixture.*

Bake until melty and bubbly, about 40 to 60 minutes. If cornflakes begin to brown too quickly, cover with foil.

Feeds 2-16, depending on how much they love it.

*Use less cornflake/butter mixture if desired. If using pre-crushed cornflakes in a canister, use about 1 cup. But it's best to crush the cornflakes yourself and not worry about the pre-crushed ones. You get a better texture.

Note: For easy white-sauce preparation, mix equal amounts of butter and flour. Drop by tablespoons on wax paper, freeze, and remove to an airtight container. Keep frozen. To make white sauce, put frozen base in a frying pan, using 1 tablespoonful per cup of milk.

CHAPTER 16

Sadie was turning in the direction in which Anita had disappeared when Nikki Waters suddenly appeared in front of her. "I was just coming to see if we had any more desserts."

Sadie blinked at Nikki, who smiled back, oblivious to the direction Sadie's thoughts were following.

"There's another cake on the counter," Sadie said, pointing over her shoulder toward the kitchen.

"Wonderful," Nikki said, stepping around Sadie. Sadie looked back down the hall, then in every direction to make sure no one was watching as she turned and, dessert still in hand, hurried after Anita Hendricks.

Sadie glanced over her shoulder as she crossed the foyer, but no one was watching. She proceeded more slowly once she was in the darkened hallway on the other side of the well-lit space, looking and listening carefully as she moved forward. There were recessed doorways on both sides of the hallway that seemed to curve around the building, but this part of the building hadn't been used for the service, so the lights had not been turned on. The only light came from small eye-level windows in the doors on the right side of the hall—the rooms on the other side of those doors must have windows that allowed natural light to shine through. She looked over her shoulder as the curve of the hall blocked the foyer from sight. Good. No one from that side would have reason to wonder what she was doing. She stopped quickly when she heard the murmur of voices ahead. She couldn't be too covert in her approach because if they saw her they'd question her stealth, but neither did she want to interrupt their conversation by making her appearance too intrusive if she could help it.

Sadie kept a cautious pace as she moved forward, only to find after a few steps that the murmur of voices was now behind her. Looking right and left she stopped, turned, and began heading back the way she'd come, listening closely. She turned her head to the right when the voices seemed to be at their loudest—though she still couldn't hear actual words—and realized that the voices were coming from one of the rooms with the recessed doors. Sadie knew she'd be seen if she tried to look through the window set into the door, so she ducked beneath the glass and stepped closer to the door in order to try to overhear what was being said.

Apparently Mormons used high-quality doors because all she could hear was the buzzing murmur of words. She could tell that the voices weren't raised, and she could make out one masculine voice and one feminine. It had to be Anita and Dr. Waters. But what could they be talking about right now? Alone . . . in an empty room . . . in a dark hallway in a church?

Tess had said Dr. Waters was on the board of the foundation—was that what they were discussing? He also worked in the clinic that Anita managed. Maybe they were talking about work. But that didn't explain why they were hiding in order to have this discussion. Sadie leaned closer, wishing she'd brought a glass from the kitchen so she could better overhear what was being said on the other side of the door. Was it worth going back to the kitchen to find one? She leaned a bit closer in case she could pick something up through the door. She didn't want to risk going back to the kitchen and missing her opportunity.

BAM!

The force of the door hitting Sadie in the head sent her reeling backward. By reflex, her hands went up and out, sending the dessert soaring through the air. She tried to keep her balance, but in the middle of the hallway she lost the fight and fell hard on her backside, sending a jolt of pain all the way up her spine, where it met the pain in her head and left her completely stunned and unable to breathe for several seconds.

"Are you all right?" a man said to her left. Her ears were ringing, and the walls were spinning, but she immediately tried to stand, embarrassed to be in such an unlady-like position. As the man helped her to her feet, she realized that it was Dr. Waters. *Biscuits.* A few feet away from her was a mass of cream cheese, strawberries, and bits of crust beside a clear pie dish turned upside down in the middle of the hallway. *Double biscuits.*

"What were you doing outside the door?"

Sadie blinked a few times in order to focus on the fact that Anita was standing in front of her and regarding her with a questioning look that Sadie completely deserved. Sadie felt her face heat up, which she swore made the pain in her head worse. "I, uh, was looking for a, uh, restroom," Sadie said, willing her brain to stop spinning within her skull.

"You mean *that* restroom?" Anita pointed past Sadie's shoulder. Sadie turned her head enough to see the very clearly marked sign for the women's restroom on the other side of the hall. Pain shot through her neck with the movement. "With a cake?" Anita added.

Sadie looked at the ruined dessert again and searched her scrambled brain for an explanation. When nothing presented itself, she looked back at Anita. The kindness Sadie had seen when Anita had thanked her for her help a few minutes earlier had disappeared so completely that Sadie doubted it had ever been there. Now Anita was suspicious and appraising.

"You were listening at the door," Anita accused.

Sadie wondered how this had happened. How had she not heard them coming closer to the door? And the dessert was ruined.

"It's okay, Anita," Dr. Waters said, giving Anita a pointed look. "I wanted to share my condolences with you in private, but what's most important here is that this woman is all right." He turned to look at Sadie again, and he moved her head slightly to look at the spot just above her right ear that was surely swelling by now. "I don't think you have a concussion, but you should get some ice for that."

"I should," Sadie said, latching onto the escape he'd handed her. "And I need to clean up the mess I made. Thank you for your help."

"Can I help you to the kitchen?" Dr. Waters said.

"Your wife is in the kitchen." She shouldn't have said that—there was accusation in it. Sadie blamed her head trauma. She had communicated that she knew Dr. Waters and Anita Hendricks were trying to meet without anyone's knowledge.

For a few beats no one spoke, then Dr. Waters smiled, but the smile didn't reach his eyes. "Even better—she can help."

"No, no, I can do it," Sadie said, turning toward the kitchen in a hurry to get away without making eye contact with either of them. "Thank you, though."

She walked as fast as she could, but every step hurt her back and her head. Had she ruptured a disk or cracked her skull? She could hear Anita and Dr. Waters whispering as soon as she was several feet away, but she didn't slow down. For one thing, it took all of her focus to walk in a straight line.

"What happened?" Caro exclaimed when Sadie entered the kitchen several seconds later with one hand on her head and the other hand reaching for the counter for support.

"I need some ice for my head," Sadie said, glancing around the room to see who else was there. Thankfully, it was only Caro and a woman who'd been helping here and there whose name Sadie couldn't remember at the moment. "And Tylenol . . . and I dropped a cheesecake down the hall. There were strawberries on top. I'm worried about the carpet."

Caro hurried toward her, and the other woman grabbed a rag from the sink. "I'll get the strawberries off the carpet," she said as she headed for the doorway.

"I'm so sorry," Sadie said after her, earning a sympathetic smile from the woman before she disappeared.

"Are you okay?" Caro asked.

Sadie tried to nod, but the throbbing pain made her want to cry. She moved her hand and Caro leaned closer to look at Sadie's head. She made a hissing sound between her teeth. "That's quite a bump," she said. She crossed the room to the freezer. "What happened?"

Sadie heard someone come in, and she looked toward the door. Tess crossed the threshold, looking in Caro's direction but not seeming to see Sadie.

"Wasn't Sadie supposed to clear the table? There's empty dishes everywhere."

Caro nodded toward Sadie while she pulled out a partial bag of ice from the freezer. "Sadie hit her head. Tess, will you get her a chair?"

Tess gave Sadie a momentary look of sympathy and confusion as she left the room. Sadie continued to lean against the counter with her hand to her head, even though it didn't help the pain. It was even more frustrating to realize that she'd been discovered and physically injured, and she hadn't even learned what it was Dr. Waters and Anita had been talking about. She *had* determined they were together and that they didn't want to be overheard, but that information didn't feel equal to the price she'd paid for it. She felt sure Officer Nielson would not be impressed.

"Is everything okay?"

Sadie looked at the doorway. Nikki was standing there this time, taking in the scene.

"I hit my head," Sadie said again. She hated being fussed over and looking at Nikki filled her with conflict. Should she tell her about the private meeting between Dr. Waters and Anita? She looked away and closed her eyes again, hoping darkness would help her throbbing head. Her stomach felt queasy. "Caro, do you have that ice?"

"I'm working on it," Caro said from beside the sink, where she was chopping at something. "I think this ice has been here for years."

"Run it under hot water for a few seconds," Sadie offered. "It'll break up the cubes better."

"Oh, good thinking." Caro turned on the faucet.

"Here's a chair," Tess said as she reentered the room.

"Thank you," Sadie said. She opened her eyes and stepped aside as Tess put the folding metal chair next to the counter against which

Sadie had been leaning. She was grateful to sit, but she winced as the position seemed to exacerbate her back pain. She didn't mean to be picky, but surely there was something with a cushion in the building.

Tess and Nikki stood there as though they were unsure what to do. "Could someone get me some Tylenol?" Sadie asked. "There's some in my purse over there." She waved toward the back wall, and after a moment's hesitation Tess headed that way. Sadie looked at Nikki again and attempted a smile. "I'm okay, really."

Sadie looked past Nikki's shoulder, straightening slightly when she saw Anita Hendricks standing in the hallway outside the kitchen door. Anita watched Sadie with a decidedly unhappy expression on her face. Nikki said that as long as Sadie was okay, she'd put the last of the desserts out. She crossed to the counter and picked up the last dish—something with raisins in it, which was probably why it was the last dessert standing.

Sadie continued to hold Anita's gaze, and she felt her heart rate speed up, which increased the ache in her head. Anita knew Sadie had been listening at the door, but Sadie knew Anita had been talking to Dr. Waters about something she didn't want anyone to overhear. They both held something over the other. What would they do about it?

"I'll be right back to see how you're doing," Nikki said, turning toward Sadie with the raisin dessert in hand. "And I'll see if my husband can come in and take a look at that."

Sadie looked away from Anita to look at Nikki instead. "I'm fine, thank you." Caro came over with ice wrapped in a dish towel, and Nikki headed toward the door. Sadie looked at Anita again in time to see her expression instantly repaired. "Oh, hi, Anita," Nikki said. "Can I help you with anything?"

"No. Thank you, though," Anita said with that soft, kind tone she'd used when she'd thanked Sadie. "Do you guys need any help in here?"

"No, no, no," Nikki said, shaking her head and continuing across the hallway. "I don't want you to lift a finger—this is our gift to you. It sure was a lovely service, wasn't it? How are you holding up?" Anita didn't make eye contact with Sadie again but turned to follow Nikki back into the gym.

Sadie held the ice to her head as she continued to stare at the double doors Nikki and Anita had disappeared through. Tess put two extra-strength Tylenol tablets in Sadie's hand, and Sadie thanked her. Though nothing had been said, she had felt the threat behind Anita's stare. She suppressed a shudder. Who was Anita Hendricks, really—the cold woman Sadie had seen three times now, or the kind woman who'd thanked her for helping with the luncheon? And what, exactly, was she talking to Dr. Waters about behind closed doors?

Strawberry Pretzel Pie

2 cups finely crushed pretzel sticks (about 8 ounces before crushing)*
¾ cup melted butter
3 tablespoons sugar
8 ounces cream cheese
1 cup sugar
8 ounces Cool Whip
1 (6-ounce) package strawberry gelatin
2 cups boiling water
2 (10-ounce) packages frozen strawberries, sliced, with sugar, partially thawed**

Mix the first three ingredients together and press in bottom of greased 9x13-inch pan. Bake 8 minutes at 350 degrees for a metal pan, or 325 degrees for a glass pan. Allow to cool completely.

While crust is cooling, beat together 1 cup sugar and cream cheese until smooth. Fold in Cool Whip. Spread over pretzels, being careful to cover entire crust (or gelatin will make pretzel layer soggy).

Mix gelatin and water until gelatin is dissolved. Add strawberries. Stir until well combined, then set aside for 10 minutes (only 10, or gelatin will start to stick to the bowl) to allow gelatin to thicken slightly. Pour gelatin mixture over cream cheese mixture. Chill until set, about 3 hours.

*If pretzels aren't crushed finely enough, crust may be hard to chew.

**One 16-ounce container of fresh strawberries may be used as a substitute for two 10-ounce packages frozen strawberries.

CHAPTER 17

Sadie was useless for the remainder of the luncheon, which, thankfully, was nearly over. The Tylenol had taken the edge off the pain, but it hadn't gone away completely, and even with the ice, the contusion on the side of her head looked like a golf ball beneath her skin.

With everyone else busy with things Sadie couldn't do, she asked Tess for Lori's number.

"What for?"

"I want to call her," Sadie said, holding Tess's gaze. She was tired of Tess, and she didn't back down until Tess finally gave her the number.

Sadie called Lori, but she didn't answer, which was frustrating. Sadie didn't want to go to Pine Valley, and with her head killing her, it seemed much better to simply tell Lori she knew she'd received a call and demand answers from her. She called again. When Lori still didn't answer, Sadie didn't leave a message, and she threw her phone back into her purse. She'd tried. The kitchen was deemed restored to its original condition a few minutes later, and Sadie, Caro, and Tess gathered their things together.

"So," Caro said as they approached the car, which was parked in the rare patch of shade. It still wasn't cool, but every little bit helped. Caro turned toward Sadie. "Are we still going to Pine Valley? Are you sure you don't want to get your head checked?"

"I'll be fine," Sadie said, even though the last thing she wanted to do was drive to a different hotel. She mostly wanted to sleep, but tomorrow she would have wished she'd gone to Pine Valley.

"You're both going?" Tess asked.

"You're welcome to come, too," Caro said. "I just didn't know if you could get away."

Tess let out an exaggerated breath and turned to Caro. "I thought you were going to help me work on the scrapbook," she said. "That's what we'd talked about earlier."

Probably while Sadie was talking to Officer Nielson.

"But that was before we knew about Pine Valley," Caro said, sounding conflicted.

"I could really use the help," Tess said. "I have a dozen interviews to translate into the scrapbook—it'll take all night if I have to do it alone."

Sadie decided to make it easy for Caro, who was obviously feeling caught in the middle. "I can go to Pine Valley on my own, Caro," she said. "You can stay here and work on the scrapbook." If she were honest with herself, however, she'd admit she was a little frustrated that Caro was trying so hard to placate Tess. How could she help Caro see that she really ought to decide what *she* wanted to do?

"Great," Tess said, smiling at Caro before turning to Sadie. "So—what happened? How did you hit your head like that?" her words sounded surprisingly sympathetic.

Sadie tried to minimize the more embarrassing aspects of the situation, but there was only so much she could leave out when relating why she'd put herself in a situation that resulted in being knocked over by a door.

"Dr. Waters said he was sharing his condolences?" Caro asked when Sadie finished. Tess looked more surprised at the information than Caro did. Probably because she knew these people and, more importantly, she knew Nikki. Sadie watched Tess process the information.

"That's what he said," Sadie confirmed. "But they work together all the time, right? Why arrange for such a private conversation?"

"They had to be . . . talking about something they didn't want anyone else to know about," Caro said, but she and Sadie shared a look that communicated the other possibility they didn't want to say out loud.

"Nikki and Dr. Waters have a good marriage," Tess cut in, saying the very thing they were avoiding. "They go to church and everything, and Anita—my gosh, she just memorialized her husband."

"Church attendance doesn't explain away the possibility, and we have to look at everything that doesn't line up," Sadie insisted. "And their going off alone doesn't line up the way I would like it to—there has to be a reason." She decided not to tell them about the silent exchange of thought she'd had with Anita when she'd looked at Sadie from the hallway. Better to let Tess ponder on one part of this before adding more to her plate.

"I'm sure it was nothing," Tess said. "You're taking it completely out of context."

Sadie let out a breath. "No one is jumping to any conclusions. You asked me how I hit my head, and I told you." Because of Tess's reaction, she also didn't mention Dr. Waters's reaction when Sadie had mentioned his wife being in the kitchen. He obviously did not want her to know. She wondered if he were stressing out right now, thinking Sadie was going to tell Nikki what she'd seen.

"Well, I'd like to get on my way to Pine Valley," Sadie said when no one else broke the silence. She looked at Caro. "I can take you back to the hotel, and then you'll have your car." She looked back and forth between the two of them. "I'm sure I don't need to tell you that we shouldn't talk to anyone about what I saw—like Tess said, we don't know the context of that meeting."

"Of course," Caro said, nodding her agreement. Tess nodded, too, but she didn't say anything out loud.

They said their good-byes, and Sadie and Caro headed to the hotel. They were both silent for quite a while. "I'd rather be going to Pine Valley," Caro said.

"Then come to Pine Valley," Sadie said evenly.

"But Tess wants me to help with the scrapbook."

"Then help with the scrapbook."

"She's kind of driving me crazy," Caro said quietly.

Right? Out loud Sadie said nothing.

"I don't like being in the middle."

Sadie considered her options before she replied. "You're the one putting yourself there."

Caro turned quickly to look at her. "Me? I'm trying to keep everything good between the three of us—I'm the common link and I don't want to push anyone away. You're my friend, and she's my cousin—and my friend as well. I came here to support her on the walk but everything's gotten so crazy."

"Yes, we're both your friends, but that doesn't mean we're the ones putting you in the middle." She kept her voice kind, hoping that Caro would know she wasn't angry with her. "You are a grown woman, and you can make your own choices." Sadie turned onto Bluff Street.

"You make it sound so easy." Sadie liked the annoyance in Caro's tone.

"It is easy—maybe not comfortable, but it's easy. Decide what you want to do and do it. If Tess freaks out, she freaks out. If I freak out . . . well, I won't freak out." She turned enough to smile in Caro's direction before facing forward again. Caro didn't answer.

Bluff Street ran along the west side of the downtown area of St. George and parallel to a large mesa that stretched toward the blue sky. Caro told Sadie that an airport used to be on top of the mesa but it had been moved to a nearby town. Their hotel was coming up on the right—it didn't butt up against the mesa like the businesses on the left side of the street—and was landscaped with palm trees and a bridge that ran over a gurgling stream between the parking lot and the hotel. They'd done a great job of creating an "oasis" feel in this town—Sadie wished she were enjoying it more than she actually was.

She pulled into the parking lot. She and Caro both remained silent as they headed to their room. Entering the room seemed to finish the conversation about Caro deciding for herself what she wanted to do. Sadie was glad. She'd made her point—the rest was up to Caro.

"Do you think there's something romantic between Anita and Dr. Waters?" Caro finally asked. "You were there—did it have that kind of feel to you?"

Sadie pondered on the question, then shrugged. "I could hear them talking the whole time, so I don't think they sneaked away for some kind of tryst or anything like that. But there's something up between them. If you could have seen the look on Anita's face when she realized I'd been at the door . . . And then, later, she stood outside the kitchen doorway and watched me when you were getting ice. Those aren't the actions of a woman who isn't worried about what I might have overheard."

Caro kicked off her shoes and reached around to unzip her dress. Sadie pulled open a drawer and tried to decide what to take to Pine Valley and what to leave in St. George. "Remember how Dr. H had been going to church these last few months?" Caro continued. "If he knew his wife was cheating on him, he might be in search of some kind of comfort."

"And it might be a reason to leave this life behind and start over somewhere else," Sadie offered.

Caro nodded as she shimmied out of her dress.

"It could also be a motive for someone to murder him," Sadie said—and even she was surprised that she'd jumped to such an extreme conclusion so quickly. Could she blame that on the head trauma, too?

Caro looked quickly at Sadie with her eyebrows raised. "You really think so?"

"In my experience, secrets can change everything. It must have been really important for Anita and Dr. Waters to talk in private to-day—at a church, with their families close by. Why? What was *that* important to take such a risk for?" Sadie's thoughts were still lining up. "And with the way Nikki greeted her in the hall after that, Anita knows I didn't tell Nikki what had happened."

"Right," Caro said, though she sounded unsure of why that was important. Sadie wasn't sure she could explain it. She was just say-ing what came to mind—and was glad her brain was still thinking despite its constant pounding.

Fifteen minutes later, after Caro called to change the reservation into Sadie's name, they parted ways in the hotel parking lot. Sadie was going to Pine Valley to pursue the mysterious call that had changed Lori's mind about meeting with them, and Caro was going to do whatever it was Tess wanted her to do. Caro didn't say again that she wanted to go with Sadie, and Sadie didn't tell her she should. They simply wished each other luck and went their separate ways.

CHAPTER 18

※

Sadie pulled back onto Bluff Street after typing Pine Valley Motel into her GPS as her destination.

"Stay on Bluff Street Highway 18 for twenty-six miles."

Bluff Street would take her right to Pine Valley? How convenient.

She drove past businesses, parks, and residential streets for a few miles before the buildings started to spread out and the landscape became more natural. She stopped at a light and read the name of the street: Snow Canyon Parkway. Officer Nielson had said something about a parkway and the Chuckwalla Trailhead where Dr. Hendricks had been parked. The light turned green, and in less than a mile, there was a sign indicating that Chuckwalla was coming up on the left. Sadie changed lanes, and when another sign indicated the entry to the trailhead, she turned left into the gravel parking area that looked familiar because of all the photos Sadie had seen of the area.

There were six vehicles parked in the lot on this Wednesday afternoon. While Sadie circled the restroom set in the middle of the roundabout, a couple on bikes came over the rise. Sadie parked and got out of the car, walking to the edge of the fence to get a better view. From where she stood, she could see numerous homes and condominiums to the left—within half a mile of the trail that disappeared around a small mesa. To the right was a sheer rock wall where, despite the 90 degree temperatures, a couple of rock climbers were making chalk marks on the already heavily marked wall. They must be tourists desperate for a climb. Sadie imagined locals knew better than to attempt a climb in this heat.

She spent a few more minutes walking around the parking area. She observed the traffic on Highway 18 only a few yards away and watched as another car arrived and the biking couple secured their equipment and pulled out. It was a busy trailhead, just as Officer Nielson had told her. While she didn't know enough about it to verify that it wasn't used by hikers for more than day hikes, she could see why it would be less attractive to a more adventurous hiker like Dr. Hendricks. She pulled out her phone and called Officer Nielson, realizing she should report what had happened this morning.

He answered on the third ring, and she didn't waste time with small talk. Instead, she told him about the phone logs they'd gotten off of Lori's phone and how she'd told them to leave the case alone. She also told him about Anita and Dr. Waters.

"You're on your way to Pine Valley now?" Officer Nielson asked when she finished.

"Yes, I should be there in about an hour."

"Well, good luck, and thanks for the update. I'll put it in my report and present it with the photos in the morning."

"Great," Sadie said, surprised but not complaining that he wasn't giving her more instruction or guidance. "I'll talk to you tomorrow. Good luck with the presentation."

"Thanks. Take care."

Though the tiny hamlet of Pine Valley was only thirty-five miles from St. George, it was reached by a two-lane highway that went through several small towns, requiring her to slow down every so often in order to obey the posted speed limits. For almost ten miles, Sadie was stuck behind a slow-moving truck that never broke fifty miles an hour. With her head throbbing she didn't dare pass on the winding road.

The landscape changed from red rock in St. George to more arid land covered with sagebrush and cedar trees and dotted with outcroppings of black lava rock. In the town of Central, her GPS instructed her to turn right, but she wouldn't have missed it due to the signs pointing her toward Pine Valley. Once on that road, the cedar trees grew more dense and the road more winding. After several miles of seeing not a house or barn or any other signs of civilization, she turned a corner and a beautiful valley surrounded by pine-covered mountains opened up below her. The view was breathtaking.

The road came to a T-intersection lined with houses and a pretty white church on the right. Following the instructions from her GPS, Sadie turned left and took in the quaint homes and log cabins along both sides of the road. After almost a mile, the GPS told her that her destination was on the right. A moment later, she spotted the sign for a restaurant—the Brandin' Iron—and, next to it, the Pine Valley Motel. Across the street was the Pine Valley Lodge—a two-motel town? Impressive.

Though she wanted to check in and collapse into bed as soon as she pulled into the motel parking lot, Sadie forced herself to remain dedicated to her reason for being there in the first place. She wrote down the license plate number of every other car parked there—all four of them—to give to Officer Nielson, just in case. She found herself wondering what Pete was doing right now. What would he think of her working with the police on this case? She made a note to e-mail him about it tonight, even though she was pretty sure he wouldn't see it until he got back next Monday. She glanced at her ring but was too exhausted to feel the zing she usually experienced when her thoughts turned to her sweetheart.

Sadie forced herself to focus on the task at hand. The car Sadie had seen Lori drive away after the memorial service wasn't one of the vehicles in the lot. That moved the possibility that Lori was meeting someone here farther down Sadie's list of considerations.

The fireplace in the foyer of the motel might just be for looks since it was still 78 degrees at eight o'clock in the evening. Two couches, a coffee table with an assortment of magazines, a breakfast room off to the right, and a single computer set up on a small table around the corner from the reception desk made up the rest of the décor. Oh, and a huge chandelier made entirely out of antlers in the middle of the room.

"Good evening," the desk attendant said as Sadie approached the counter.

"I have a reservation for Sadie Hoffmiller."

The girl handed Sadie some paperwork to sign and then gave her a regular metal key attached to a leathery key chain with the motel's logo burned into it. "Breakfast is right here in the lobby from seven to ten in the morning. Have a nice evening."

Sadie was on her way to the room before she realized she should have asked the girl some questions. But she knew this girl wasn't the one who had been working when the call was made, and Sadie couldn't think of what else she might have to offer.

Sadie's phone chimed a text message as she made her way down the hall, but she waited until she was in her room before she checked it.

Caro: I'm on my way. Just leaving St. George.

Sadie raised her eyebrows and immediately called Caro back. She didn't have the patience for texting right now and didn't want to tempt Caro to text her back while driving.

"You're coming to Pine Valley?" Sadie asked when Caro answered.

"Tess and I had a good talk, and she finally realized that this isn't about her."

Sadie raised her eyebrows again. "Well done." She'd love to have overheard that conversation.

"Thanks," Caro said. "I guess I do have something to add to all of this other than my pickpocketing skills."

"You have a lot to add," Sadie assured her. "I'd have left Tess on the side of the road a long time ago if it weren't for you."

Caro laughed, but then seemed embarrassed that she had. "Enough about that. Any tips I need on finding this place?"

"Well, there are only three businesses in town, so once you get here you won't have a hard time finding it. Make sure you turn left at the T-intersection with the white church on the side."

They finished the call a minute later. Sadie hung up the phone with a smile on her face and moved her overnight bag to the bed closest to the bathroom. There was a nightstand between the two beds and a dresser across from them upon which sat the TV Sadie wouldn't be turning on. While waiting for Caro to arrive, she decided to look into Anita Hendricks, who had now risen to the top of the list of people she wanted to know more about.

Over the course of the next thirty minutes, Sadie learned that Anita was originally from Atlanta. She'd done an internship in college with the American Heart Association, the first of half a dozen charity organizations she'd been employed with since then. It was easy to track her evolution through the different events she'd coordinated over the last fifteen years and, setting her suspicion aside, Sadie had to admit that Anita was certainly a go-getter, with a passion for charity work.

Sadie wondered what had prompted her to make cancer her focus. Had she lost a family member or in some other way been directly affected by the disease in the past? In all the information Sadie ferreted out, including company bios and a few articles where Anita was quoted for one reason or another, Sadie never could discern a solid motivation. Anita never talked about her childhood, family, or personal mission. Instead, anything she said was about the focus of the organization she was representing. When Anita's timeline intersected with the Red Rock Cancer Foundation, Sadie shifted her focus to looking at the foundation as a whole, rather than at Anita specifically. She read up on the foundation's public mission and history and then dug into databases for the bones of the organizational structure.

Sadie located the registered articles of incorporation pretty easily and was able to verify the start date, board members, and federal approval for the nonprofit status. Everything looked good until Sadie realized there was no mention of the boutique within the document. It often took some time for the public domains to reflect updates to public records like this, but the boutique had been in operation for nearly two years. If a change to the articles had been made, those changes should have been reflected in the information available to the public. Sadie made a note to see if the oversight was due to a backlog of Utah nonprofit updates being posted. Writing the note, however, gave her another idea, and she started a new entity search. This time, she looked specifically for the Pink Posy Boutique. Her head was killing her, but she wanted to wait up for Caro, and the hunt for information took her thoughts away from the pain. A little bit, anyway.

When the search found a match with a company registered in Washington County, Utah, Sadie assumed she'd simply misunderstood and that the boutique was its own nonprofit organization, rather than an appendage of the Red Rock Cancer Foundation. She sat up straighter, however, when she realized that, while the boutique was registered as a separate entity, it was not a nonprofit. Instead, it was a Limited Liability Company—a business model under no umbrella of charity.

Sadie went back to the boutique's website and read every word of the "About Us" pages to confirm whether or not it said specifically that the boutique was part of the Red Rock Cancer Foundation, a nonprofit company. It did. Sadie went back to the official website listing entity information and dug as far as it would take her—which wasn't very far because this was a private business and therefore protected from the public scrutiny nonprofits were subject to. Jacob Waters's name wasn't mentioned anywhere on the boutique paperwork. Anita Hendricks was listed as the owner of the company, with Trenton Hendricks as vice president.

Sadie's phone rang and she glanced at the caller ID. It was Caro.

"Hey," Sadie said into the phone, distracted by what she'd just discovered and still trying to wrap her head around the fact that the boutique was a *for*-profit company. Someone was making money.

"It was tricky to find one motel in such a sprawling metropolis, but I think I made it. What room are you in?"

"I'm in room six," Sadie said, standing up to stretch her increasingly sore back. Was it too soon to take more Tylenol? "I've found something I want to show you."

"Okay. I'll be right there."

Once Caro reached the room, Sadie ushered her into the desk chair Sadie had been sitting in minutes earlier. Sadie filled her in on what she'd found, letting her read the nonprofit assurance on the boutique's website for herself before changing to the website that listed the boutique as an LLC.

"What does that mean?" Caro asked.

"It means the boutique is a for-profit company. It makes money."

"That it donates to cancer research, right?"

Sadie looked over Caro's shoulder and read the registration information again. "It's not required to. It's a regular business like any other clothing store without any tax exemptions or scrutiny of its books to prove its donations."

Sadie went on to explain the general points of a limited liability company versus a corporation and, specifically, a 501c tax exemption approval from the federal government. When she'd had her own private investigation business in Garrison, Colorado, she'd become familiar with business entities and the like while investigating a fraud case. She hadn't expected it would come in very handy once she finished that case, and soon after that she had closed her business. But knowledge was power, and it was validating to have this bit of knowledge on hand right now. "If they *are* giving money to cancer research, the boutique should be a nonprofit to protect them from the tax liabilities of running a traditional company. To use an LLC as an entity to raise money makes no sense at all—the whole point of a limited liability is that there is someone carrying that liability and that person is usually the one making money. *And* being an LLC keeps their financial information private, whereas an IRS-registered nonprofit is required to make their tax returns public."

"So no one is verifying that the money raised by the boutique goes toward research?" Caro summarized.

"Nope. It doesn't mean that the boutique *isn't* making the donations, but it's a really strange way for them to organize it, and the fact that Anita Hendricks has been involved in this type of industry for so long makes this even stranger—she knows how to set up and run a nonprofit, so why didn't she do that with the boutique?" Sadie leaned forward and with her pen tapped the screen of her laptop, right where it said that the boutique was a nonprofit.

"But . . . if they say they're a nonprofit and they're not, that's fraud," Caro said. "Wouldn't the IRS have figured this out? Or the police?"

"If there were an investigation going on with that, why would Officer Nielson be closing the case?"

"Good point."

Sadie waved Caro out of the chair, explaining she needed to look up something else on the computer. Caro complied, taking Sadie's place standing behind the chair while Sadie Googled watch groups who reported on charity organizations. Once she found a credible watch-group website, she did a search for the Red Rock Cancer Foundation and found good ratings.

"The boutique wouldn't be there, though, would it?" Caro pointed out when Sadie typed the name of the boutique into the search bar. "It's not a charity organization."

"True." Sadie did a few more searches, but she couldn't find anything that showed these watch groups had any idea what the boutique was doing. Maybe because the boutique was in such a small area, it had flown under the radar, or perhaps it was new enough that people weren't aware of the discrepancy. Everyone Sadie had talked to in southern Utah seemed to take the foundation and, by default, the boutique at their word.

At the bottom of the screen, Sadie found a "contact us" link. She clicked on it and was taken to a comment form she didn't hesitate to fill with the basics of what she'd just discovered, requesting they contact her for additional details. The chance that they would contact her tonight was zero. The chance that they would contact her tomorrow wasn't much better, and the fact that the boutique wasn't a charity organization might put her concerns outside of their sphere altogether—but who else could she talk to?

Officer Nielson came to mind, and she bit her lip while she considered it, argued with herself about it, and eventually decided she had to share what she knew. Feeling territorial in regard to things she learned wasn't a new feeling, but she had to consciously remind herself that this case was different from any other case she'd worked before. She was working with the police this time, and she'd given her word to turn over anything she discovered to them. Even if it were difficult to do.

"Caro, could you get my phone out of my purse? I'd better tell Officer Nielson about this."

Caro crossed to the bed and retrieved Sadie's phone for her. Sadie wanted to call Officer Nielson before she talked herself out of it. He didn't answer, so she left a brief message about what they'd uncovered and asked him to call her for more details. She also told him it could wait for the next morning.

She and Caro spent another half hour digging into anything they could think of for dirt on the boutique, but all they found were glowing reviews from customers and several comments about how good it felt to shop for a cause. There wasn't a single complaint registered with the Better Business Bureau.

Sadie did find a series of articles focused on fraudulent cancer foundations. She was shocked to learn that in the past year over 1,400 foundations in the United States were supposedly raising money for cancer. Of those 1,400, it was estimated that well over 1,200 were donating less than sixty percent of their profits. Some were completely fraudulent in their claims and admitted to donating only manpower for events rather than actual money.

From what Sadie read, she could see that there were millions of dollars unaccounted for in the breast cancer fund-raising market. Instead of raising money for research, most "Pink" merchandise didn't raise a penny for anyone other than the business owner who cashed in on the altruistic appeal of their products. Sadie would never look at the pink coffee mugs and chef's knives sold every October the same way again. Was there an arm of the government that oversaw the 1,200 companies that weren't getting good ratings? Would watch groups come to a small town in the Utah desert to sniff out possible misrepresentations?

It was Sadie's throbbing head that finally sent her to bed. She and Caro both felt encouraged but exhausted. Sadie took two more Tylenol and tried to find a position for her head on the pillow that didn't make the pain worse. She wished Pete were available to talk to—she could use his expertise. And his advice.

Soon they had turned off the lights, and the hum of the air conditioning unit provided the backdrop of what Sadie hoped would be a good night's sleep. "If we're right," she said, "and there was some shady stuff going on with the foundation, Dr. Hendricks had a reason to leave town."

"I thought about that," Caro said. "But it's Anita who owns the boutique."

"He's on the paperwork, too, and he has a medical license to lose."

"A medical license he gave up if, in fact, he disappeared to escape what they'd done."

"Good point," Sadie said. "Running would save him the public embarrassment, though. People go to great lengths to preserve their reputations."

After a stretch of silence, Caro spoke again. "I was thinking about that phone call from the motel to Lori."

"Yeah?" Sadie asked, pushing aside the other thoughts so she could be on the same page Caro was.

"It seems like most of the people who could have upset her that much were at the service—like in-laws or old friends or someone like that. But I didn't pick up any specific tension between her and anyone there."

"Except Anita," Sadie said.

"Right, but I can't imagine that Anita called her from Pine Valley the morning of the memorial service."

Another good point. "True."

"And Lori kept checking her phone, which I thought might have meant she was waiting for the attorney to call her back. But then I wondered if it could be something else. Or someone else."

"Like who?" Sadie said, but an itch of an idea had started tickling her chest.

"Well, if I had to disappear for some reason, the people it would be the very hardest for me not to have contact with would be my kids."

"Right," Sadie agreed as the itch got stronger.

"But if my kids were young, whoever was taking care of them would be the next hardest person to cut ties with."

Sadie considered that, really considered it, and finally scratched that growing itch. "You think Dr. Hendricks may have called Lori from this motel?"

"I know it's a long shot, and I'm probably just really tired, but it did cross my mind. And now that we've determined a couple of possible reasons for him to leave, it feels more possible. A call from him would certainly send Lori into a tailspin, don't you think? And if he were asking for help to come out of hiding, wouldn't contacting an attorney be a reasonable thing to ask her to help him with?"

Sadie picked up the train of thought. "And the mother of your children would want to go about things in a way that had the least impact on the children. What I mean is, Lori wouldn't go to the newspapers. She'd want to protect her kids." Sadie's battered mind was racing. "An attorney could help with that, especially if Dr. Hendricks were to think he's coming back to criminal charges."

"In fact, he might want an attorney with him when he turned himself in."

"Except that Kyle Edger is a contract and patent attorney, not criminal."

"Maybe he's a friend of Dr. H and could give him a recommendation," Caro suggested.

"You're very good at this, you know," Sadie said into the dark.

"Well, thank you," Caro answered, obviously pleased by the compliment. "I guess we'll find out tomorrow if any of these ideas turn out to be worth anything."

CHAPTER 19

The next morning, Sadie woke up with Caro's theory thick in her brain. Her head still hurt, but not nearly the way it had the night before. The swelling had gone down, but the bruising was worse. Thankfully, between Caro and herself they were able to cover it enough that she didn't think anyone else would notice it. Their work here felt more important than ever, which is why Sadie frowned when Officer Nielson hadn't called them back before they shut the door to their room behind them. It was after eight o'clock in the morning and Sadie hoped to have heard from him by now.

"The gal we want to talk to is Candace," Caro said as they headed toward the lobby. The smell of waffles made Sadie's stomach growl. She hadn't had dinner the night before, and she couldn't remember when she had last skipped a meal because there were too many other thoughts distracting her from the need for sustenance. They turned the corner into the lobby and approached the front desk, where a woman was plinking away at a computer keyboard. She looked up when they approached and smiled.

"Good morning," the woman said in precisely the way Sadie would expect a morning desk clerk at a hotel to respond to a guest.

"Good morning," Sadie and Caro said in unison. They looked at each other and Sadie ducked her chin, turning the interview over to Caro. After all, Caro was the one who'd initially called Pine Valley.

"Hi," Caro said, glancing down at the gold name tag on the woman's shirt. "You're Candace?"

"Yes, ma'am. May I help you?"

"Well, I think so," Caro said. "Someone called a friend of mine from the front desk phone yesterday, and I'm trying to figure out who that someone was. Were you working yesterday morning?"

The openness of the woman's expression closed in a flash, and Sadie tensed slightly in response. "I will not give out information about our guests."

"Oh," Caro said, blinking in surprise. "I'm not going to get you in trouble or anything. I just really need to know who made that call."

"Joanna called me after you talked to her yesterday, and I re-minded her of our policy not to talk about our guests. Is there some-thing else I can help you with?"

"Oh, um . . ." Caro swallowed.

"So it was a *guest?*" Sadie cut in. "Whoever used the phone was staying here?"

Candace paused long enough to give Sadie confidence to move forward. "I understand why you would want to protect the identity of someone staying at the motel, but if he weren't staying at the motel . . ." She'd slipped in the "he," hoping Candace would confirm that detail, but Candace was more closed than ever.

"Can I help you with anything else? I am not at liberty to talk about the phone call yesterday."

Sadie put a bit more clip into her voice to better match Candace's tone. "I appreciate your determination to protect their privacy, but this is really important and I promise we're not trying to get anyone in trouble—them or you."

The woman regarded her for a few seconds, and Sadie's hopes began to build until the woman spoke again and dashed those hopes on the rocks. "You can leave a message for him, and then he can contact you if he wants to."

Him? Sadie felt a tingle go all the way to her toes, and she noticed Caro straighten as she, too, picked up the detail. Did the fact that this woman would take a message mean he came in regularly? "Do you know when he'll be in next?" Sadie asked casually, not wanting to betray how much this woman had said without meaning to.

"You can leave a message for him," the woman said, this time with feigned sweetness that wasn't all that sweet.

"This is kind of urgent," Sadie said. She had to shake off some of her seeming neutrality so she'd have a solid motivation to continue her questions. She decided to proceed the way she would if she had some kind of proof that the "him" they were talking about was in fact Dr. Hendricks. It was a heady thought. "I think he's in trouble and I'm trying to help him. Will he be coming in today?"

Candace wasn't thawed. "I said you can leave him a message. That's all I can do to help you."

Sadie considered grabbing the woman by the collar to prove how serious she was, but that only worked in the movies. Not that Sadie had actually tried it herself. Instead, she nodded and asked to borrow a paper and pen, which the woman handed her. She wrote a quick note explaining she would like to talk to him and wrote down her number. She knew that this option was not likely to succeed if this man were trying to be stealthy about something.

Sadie thanked Candace, and she and Caro went to the breakfast area, where they sat across from one another at one of the three small Formica-topped tables.

"If he's been hiding for months, won't the note just make him run?" Caro asked.

The thought had crossed Sadie's mind, but she'd dismissed it in favor of the possibility that he *might* call her. Hearing Caro verbalize the potential failure of this plan, however, made it seem much more likely that he wouldn't call. But Sadie couldn't ask for the note back. "I don't know," Sadie said with a shake of her head. "But even without the note, this Candace woman would certainly tell him we were looking for him, which would chase him away as well as the note would. I wonder why she's so protective of him."

Caro shrugged, and a moment later, her phone rang. She fished it out of her purse, then said "Tess" before lifting it to her ear. She stood and headed toward the front doors.

Sadie's stomach growled, and she decided now was as good a time as any to make herself some waffles. Maybe food would help her figure out what to do next. Other than sitting here in the lobby all day hoping this mysterious caller would return, she couldn't think of any other options.

There was still a minute and a half left on the timer for her rotating waffle machine when a young couple came into the lobby. They set about getting cereal and fruit, making eyes at each other and stealing kisses every chance they got. By the time the cooker announced the waffle was done, Sadie had pegged the couple as newlyweds. Sadie's own engagement ring caught her eye and she felt her cheeks heat up. *Zing.*

While she put butter into each perfect square of her waffle, the young woman came up beside her to spread peanut butter on the toast that had just popped up from the toaster.

"Hi," Sadie said.

"Hi," the young woman said back.

"Beautiful day, isn't it?"

"Sure is," the girl said, smiling even wider as she looked out the window at the bright summer morning. The valley was a beautiful sight, full of sunshine, surrounded by pine-tree-covered hills, and with a calm serenity that made you want to hike or fish or simply lie in the middle of a meadow and soak it all in.

"I guess every morning is beautiful around here, though," Sadie continued.

"Probably," the young woman said. She began to turn away but then seemed to realize that Sadie wasn't finished talking.

"Were you here yesterday?" Sadie asked, trying to ease into this but not feeling particularly smooth.

"Yep, been here since Tuesday." She leaned in a bit conspiratorially. "We got married on Monday—this is our honeymoon." Her cheeks reddened, and Sadie offered her sincere congratulations. The new groom came up behind his new wife and snaked an arm around her waist. Sadie felt sure if she hadn't been here he'd have nuzzled the girl's neck. As it was, Sadie was glad he restrained himself. Otherwise she'd have been blushing, too.

"Did you happen to see that guy who came in yesterday morning—I think he used the phone or something?" She reached for the syrup but poured it very slowly. She was so hungry at this point it felt as though her stomach were eating itself, but it would just have to wait.

"The kind of scruffy one?"

The girl's easy answer startled Sadie, and she dripped some syrup on the counter. Sadie looked up at her. "Yeah, do you know who he was?"

"Why would we know that?" the groom answered for her, but his tone was kind.

"Um, I don't know, I just wondered about him. Do you remember what time you saw him?"

"You must have seen him, too, right?" the groom asked rather than answering her question.

"Well, I thought so, but I couldn't remember what time it was." Not that she could think of why the time would be important.

"Is the time important?" the groom echoed her internal question. He regarded her a bit closer. "I don't remember seeing you here."

"Uh . . ."

Caro pushed through the front doors, giving Sadie an excuse to make her escape. She smiled genuinely at the young couple. "Congratulations on your wedding. Have a great day."

They both watched her more than she was entirely comfortable with, but she pretended not to notice as she took her plate back to the table. She wasn't having a great morning so far.

"That looks good," Caro said, nodding toward Sadie's waffle. "I'm going to get one and then I'll give you Tess's update."

Sadie nodded and used the time it took Caro to fix her plate—only half a waffle—to try to renew her confidence while she filled her belly. The waffle was okay, but it was obviously from a mix and was too sweet—more like cake. She missed her own buttermilk waffle recipe and wondered wistfully how long it would be until her life got back to normal enough that she'd be cooking her own favorites again.

"How are things going with Tess?" she asked when Caro sat down.

Caro smiled, genuinely excited to impart the news. "She talked to both of Dr. Hendricks's parents at the luncheon *and* got an extensive interview with Dr. Waters's medical assistant last night, too."

Sadie was glad to hear one of them was having success. "Has she discovered anything significant from these interviews?"

"Yeah. Dr. H called his mother a few days before he disappeared and left a voice mail telling her that he loved her."

"And that was unusual?"

"I get the impression that there had been a lot of strain between him and his parents. It seems like it was improving in the last few years, but the fact that his mom was so touched by the message seems to mean that it didn't happen on a regular basis, right?"

"Or that she focused on it because it was the last communication she'd had with him," Sadie pointed out.

"I guess that's true," Caro said, though she didn't seem to like Sadie's answer. "I saw you talking to that couple—did they know anything?"

Sadie imparted what she'd learned without telling Caro how she'd bungled the conversation. Caro listened with wide eyes, and then she leaned forward. "It has to be him, right? It's got to be Dr. H."

"We don't know enough to be even close to certain of that," Sadie said. "All we really know is a scruffy man was here, and Candace let a man use the phone. We don't even know that it's the same man."

"But it *seems* like it is," Caro pointed out.

"That's not enough," Sadie said.

Voices caught their attention and they looked toward the front desk. A young woman with a lip ring and jet-black hair that hung in her face was talking to Candace about needing to order more glass cleaner. Sadie noted the spray bottle in the girl's hand and the rag sticking out of the back pocket of the girl's impossibly tight jeans. "I like the kind that foams up on the glass, not just the blue-colored ammonia."

"I'll put it on the list," Candace said, not sounding particularly friendly. Maybe she wasn't very nice to anyone.

"Thanks," the Goth girl said before turning and heading back toward the hallway of guest rooms. Before she disappeared around the corner, Sadie noticed that her charcoal-colored T-shirt had the lodge's logo on the back. Sadie turned to look at Caro. "Housekeeping?" Sadie suggested. Caro nodded.

"We might have another shot," Sadie responded. She glanced at Candace to make sure she wasn't somehow overhearing their conversation. If she were, she might put a stop to any attempts they made to have a conversation with Goth Girl. But she was bent over some paperwork.

Sadie gave Caro a quick nod and took one last bite of her waffle before standing up. She kept her gait unhurried and her expression a picture of innocent intention as they followed Goth Girl. She and Caro took turns casting quick looks at Candace. When she turned toward the back office, they smiled at each other and picked up their pace, slowing once they cleared the corner of the hallway.

A housekeeping cart stood against the wall about halfway down the hallway, across from an open doorway into one of the guest rooms. They approached slowly, then stopped when Goth Girl came out of the room. She had headphones in her ears and bobbed her head along to the music.

"Hi," Sadie said when they were within a few feet of the girl. Caro was half a step behind her. The young housekeeper looked up at them and plucked the earphone out of one ear.

"Hi, can I help you with somethin'?" the girl asked.

"I hope so," Sadie said, willing Candace to stay at her desk and hoping that the third time would be the charm in her approaches for the day. She didn't know of any other way to address this than straight on, even though that hadn't worked yet. She took a breath and laid it out there. "Yesterday a man made a call from the lobby phone and I'm trying to find him."

The girl scrunched up her nose. "I'm just housekeeping, so I don't deal with the guests much."

"I don't think he was a guest. The call was made around 9:30 in the morning and lasted several minutes. Maybe you saw him come in around that time and use the phone?"

"I didn't see anyone use the phone," Goth Girl said, shaking her head. "But you must be talking about Wednesday Man, right?"

Waffle Mania Waffles

2¼ cups flour
4 teaspoons baking powder
¾ teaspoon salt
1½ tablespoons sugar
2 eggs
2¼ cups milk*
¾ cup salad oil

Sift together dry ingredients. Combine remaining ingredients; mix well. Just before baking, add flour mixture, beating only till moistened. Batter will be thin. Cook in preheated, greased waffle iron until golden brown.
Makes 4 4-square waffles.

*Substitute up to ½ of the milk with buttermilk for a tangy buttermilk waffle.

Note: Our family's favorite way to eat these: fried diced Spam, whipping cream, and syrup over the top. Yum.

CHAPTER 20

"Wednesday Man?" Sadie and Caro said at the same time. Sadie wondered if the same rush of energy was coursing through Caro's veins.

"Yeah," Goth Girl said, swishing her black-dyed bangs to the side, even though they fell back into exactly the same position. "He comes in on Wednesdays to use the computer."

Multiple Wednesdays? "Do you know his real name?" Sadie asked.

Goth Girl shook her head. "As far as I know he's never talked with anyone, which is why we call him Wednesday Man."

"What does he use the computer for?"

She shrugged. "I'm not looking over his shoulder or anything. Besides, I only see him if I'm cleaning the lobby and he's here at the same time."

"Did you see him here yesterday?" Sadie asked.

"I said hi to him when he came in like I always do—customer service, ya know. He just nods and stuff."

"You don't know if he used the front desk phone yesterday?" Sadie asked.

Caro pulled out her cell phone and started toggling for something.

Goth Girl shook her head. "I was almost done vacuuming the lobby when he came in, and then the people in room four checked out, so I got to work on their room. So do you know him or something?"

Sadie quickly made up a cover story. "We're trying to determine if he's a friend of ours."

Goth Girl smiled somewhat conspiratorially and leaned closer to them. "I bet he has some tragically mysterious past, right? Like, the love of his life killed herself on their wedding day or he suffered a mental breakdown after his family burned to death in a fire."

This girl was cute—lip ring notwithstanding—but a little creepy. Then again, she couldn't be more than nineteen years old and had no idea how truly tragic both of those scenarios were in real life.

"We're really not sure," Sadie said. "Um, how long has he been coming in on Wednesdays?"

Goth Girl shrugged her skinny shoulders. "I only came home from school a month ago, and I know he was coming in before then, but I don't know for how long. You should ask Candace at the front desk—she's the one who kind of gave him the name Wednesday Man, and she'd know if he used the phone yesterday."

Yeah, Candace was a problem.

"Did he look like this guy?" Caro said, turning both Sadie and Goth Girl's attention to the phone she held up. The screen showed Dr. Hendricks's picture, the same one that had been front and center at his memorial service yesterday.

"No," the girl said, shaking her head. "Wednesday Man looks kinda homeless. Scraggy beard. Camo jacket and pants. Real skinny. Tragic-like, ya know?"

Dr. Hendricks losing weight and growing a beard in the course of the last two months wasn't unlikely, and Sadie had to take a deep breath and consciously calm herself down. It was growing more and more possible that Wednesday Man was Dr. Hendricks. She forced herself to remain focused on this conversation. She could consider reacting emotionally to all of this when she'd gotten everything she could from this girl.

"He's not a guest, then?" Sadie asked to make sure she was clear. Goth Girl shook her head.

"Does he live around here?" Caro asked.

Goth Girl shrugged. "I guess, since he walks here every week, but he must not have internet wherever he's staying, right?"

"And you don't see him around town or anything?" Sadie asked. There was a good possibility that this was the only somewhat public computer in town. She really wished someone had looked over his shoulder a little more so they could know exactly what he'd been doing online.

Goth Girl shook her head again. "I've only ever seen him here on Wednesday mornings. I noticed he's always showered and stuff. He's not stinky or anything."

"Have you ever seen him talk to anyone?"

Again the girl shook her head. "Candace has talked to him. See, the computer's supposed to just be for guests, ya know. But he was so pathetic and sad and stuff that she told him it was okay as long as there weren't any guests needing to use it. Oh, and I heard he does some cleanup work at the lodge, so maybe Robert knows him better." She nodded toward the front of the motel, reminding Sadie of the business she'd seen across the street.

"Lodge? There are two motels here?" Caro asked.

"Well, it has camping cabins, but mostly it's a store and a little café. Robert Moore owns it, and I heard he gave Wednesday Man some work in exchange for food and stuff."

A door down the hall opened, and they all looked to see an

older couple coming out of the room. He held a bag over each shoulder and dragged a wheeled suitcase, while she carried only her purse. Sadie could imagine that she had offered to carry some of the load, and he had insisted that he had it taken care of. They were cute in a different way from the newlywed couple.

Goth Girl moved her cart closer to the wall so the older couple could pass by. Caro and Sadie stepped to the side as well and nodded their farewells. "Step ahead of me, Mother," the older man said. "I don't want to slow you up."

Adorable.

Sadie turned back to Goth Girl and asked a few more questions, trying to eke out any bit of information the girl might not realize she had. Finally Goth Girl lifted both shoulders and gave Sadie a sympathetic look. "I've got to get back to work," she said. She was already moving toward the housekeeping cart.

"Thanks for your help," Sadie said as the girl started gathering towels and washcloths and stacking them on the top of the cart.

"No problem." The girl pulled shampoo and conditioner packets from the box on top of the cart. She turned toward the room and put her earphone back in.

Sadie and Caro looked at each other with giddy smiles. "The day is looking up," Sadie said as they headed toward their room. She suddenly stopped and turned back toward the lobby, saying, "But I'm going to finish that waffle before we head to the store."

CHAPTER 21

A s it turned out, there was no need to hurry. The store across the street didn't open until ten-thirty, and it was barely nine o'clock. Sadie decided to update her notes while they waited. She was up to three pages of information when Officer Nielson finally called her. During the two rings she let pass before answering it, she considered how much she should tell him about this morning's discoveries. Did he want possibilities and supposition or just solid leads?

She answered his call before she'd made a decision. "Good morning," she said into the phone.

"Good morning," he repeated. "I've just pulled up the Red Rock Cancer Foundation's articles—tell me exactly what you found."

They discussed the different entities, and he asked detailed questions that she answered as best she could. "That's certainly something that requires more attention," Officer Nielson said when they finished up. "I'm heading into the admin meeting regarding the re-opening of Dr. Hendricks's case and will include this information—I'll be sure to let you know how it goes, but I'm guessing that by this afternoon we'll have new detectives on this case."

Sadie knew that, to him, that was good news. For her, it was a little more difficult to face. She wasn't ready to let go of this case, and because of that, when he didn't ask her if she'd discovered anything else since leaving the message last night, she didn't volunteer it. "I'll look forward to the update," Sadie said.

"Until then," he said before ending the call. Sadie appreciated that he wasn't long-winded—it gave her less time to second-guess herself while he was still on the line.

"You didn't tell him about Dr. H," Caro pointed out when Sadie put her phone down.

"I'll tell him when we know for sure."

"How do you decide what to tell the police and what not to tell them?" Caro asked, sounding genuinely curious.

There was no good answer to that question. "Um, I'm not sure. It's kind of a case-by-case thing."

Sadie checked her e-mail, hoping for something from Pete, but she was disappointed. She could really use his guidance right now. Rather than dwelling on that, she turned her attention back to her notes.

It felt like hours until the time on her computer showed 10:20. She and Caro were waiting when a middle-aged man unlocked the front door from inside and welcomed them. On a grease board set just inside the small store was a Monday through Friday lunch special listed in fluorescent pink marker. Today was Fresh Mex Thursday, and the special was Barbacoa Pork Salad. Sounded delicious.

To the left of the shelves that were filled with one or two options for everything from canned soup to antifreeze was a small lunch counter with napkins, flatware, and a soda fountain. Sadie assumed that when it got closer to lunchtime, that's where the "special" would be made available. She hoped they would still be in town for lunch. Little places like this intrigued her.

"Can I help you ladies find anything?" the man asked, reminding Sadie that he was still there.

She and Caro shared a look and then faced him. "Actually, yes," Sadie said. She wished she had some of her business cards from when she had her investigation company. They would be the perfect offering for her to make right now. "My name's Sadie, and this is my friend Caro. We're trying to learn more about a gentleman known around town as Wednesday Man, and we were told that you might know more about him."

She held her breath, anticipating the same hesitation she'd encountered with Candace. To her surprise, however, his expression remained open.

"You know him?" he asked, heading toward the counter at the back of the small store. They followed him.

"He might be a friend of ours," Sadie said.

"Seems like a good enough guy. I let him do odd jobs in exchange for some food. I'm Robert, by the way." He reached the counter and moved behind it before extending his hand and shaking theirs. "Can't say I know more about him than anyone else in town does, though. He's pretty tight-lipped."

"What kind of odd jobs does he do?" Caro asked.

"Janitorial stuff," the clerk said, looking back and forth at them as he sat on a stool next to the cash register with his arms crossed over his chest. "Seems pretty down on his luck."

"How long has he been working for you?"

"Well, I wouldn't call it working for me," Robert said with a smile. "But it's been a couple of months."

"And you never see this man other than on Wednesdays?" Sadie asked.

"Just at church a few times, but nothing consistent."

"He goes to your church?" Sadie asked, remembering what Tess had said about Dr. Hendricks's having attended church before he disappeared. The look she shared with Caro confirmed that they were thinking the same thing. "Here in Pine Valley?"

"Have you gals not taken a tour of the Pine Valley Chapel? It's one of the main attractions in Pine Valley. The architect was a ship-builder and basically built the church like an inverted boat. It's more than a hundred fifty years old and still tight as a drum."

"Is it a Mormon church, then?" Sadie asked, feeling bad for sticking to the main topic but needing to make sure she had a clear understanding.

"Oh, yeah, the Mormon church." Robert seemed a little embarrassed to have automatically assumed they knew that. "I'm in the bishopric—that's the clergy—so I sit at the front of the chapel. I've seen him slip in a few times, always after the meeting started. He sits on the very back row, if there's room, or stands against the wall. Then leaves during the closing song. I tried to catch him once, but I think it scared him off. When he showed up to work the next week I told him I wouldn't do that again but I hoped he'd come back. He did, which I was glad to see."

Sadie made eye contact with Caro and knew she was thinking the same thing Sadie was: Wednesday Man *had* to be Dr. Hendricks. He was here, hiding out, living this odd life as a transient of some kind. Why? What had motivated him to create this elaborate hoax?

"He didn't come in yesterday, though," Robert said, causing both Caro and Sadie to look back at him.

"He didn't?" Caro repeated.

Robert shook his head. "First time in two months that he wasn't waiting for me when I opened."

Caro's phone rang. "Sorry," she said as she hurried to send the call to voice mail.

"We'd really like to talk to him—do you know where he's staying?"

"I think he's camping up Lloyd Canyon."

"Camping?" Sadie repeated. "The housekeeper at the motel thought he might be staying somewhere with a shower. Said he was always clean."

"He could be staying in one of the cabins, but you'd think someone who could afford a cabin could afford food." Robert paused and made a face. "I hope he isn't squatting up there. I'd hate to see him in trouble with the law, but that's something I couldn't keep to myself."

Sadie appreciated the warning not to tell this man something he would feel morally bound to report. Could Dr. Hendricks have somehow rented a cabin without the police tracking the payment? Maybe he'd disguised the payment as something else in his financial records. But if he'd planned all of this well enough to have hidden the plans, why hadn't he accounted for the fact that he would need food? Frustration over the growing number of questions began creeping in until Sadie remembered that this could be *Dr. Hendricks!* She and Caro may very well have found him. The rising questions were insignificant compared to the impact of what they had pieced together this morning.

"Showered or not, he struck me as someone camping out. He always has the same clothes on."

Goth Girl had said that, too.

"Why do you think he's camping in—what did you call it?—Lloyd Canyon?"

"We talked about him in a church meeting once, people trying to figure out who he was and if he needed any help. A man at church who lives on Lloyd Canyon Road said he'd seen him around—just walking, not causing any trouble—so I figured he must be staying up there."

Caro's phone rang a second time, and she quickly declined the call and apologized again. "I'll turn it off, sorry."

"He didn't tell you his name?" Sadie asked. "Didn't make small talk or indicate why he was here?"

Robert shook his head. "I tried once or twice to talk to him, but he wasn't open to it, and I worried about scaring him off, so I didn't push. You said he might be a friend of yours?" His curiosity was setting in. Unfortunately, Sadie didn't feel ready to give him too much information.

Robert seemed to sense her hesitation, and he smiled good-naturedly. "I'm not trying to be pushy. I just hope he's okay. I worried when he didn't come in yesterday."

"Can you direct us toward Lloyd Canyon?"

"Sure," Robert said, pointing over his shoulder. "Opposite end of town, past the church. You really should stop in for a tour when you have a few minutes. Fascinating history, that church."

CHAPTER 22

They took Caro's car to Lloyd Canyon, expecting a mountain road with cabins hidden in the trees. What they found instead was more like a neighborhood, though most of the houses were cabin designs. The lots weren't large, and some of them had fenced yards. Numerous roads led off of Lloyd Canyon Road, but they didn't go very far from town and looped back to the main street every time.

"If he's hiding in a cabin, it would be one of those," Sadie said as they passed a private driveway with a "No trespassing" sign and a winding driveway that disappeared into the trees before revealing the cabin it led to. "These other cabins are too close together for him to effectively hide—people would know right where he was."

Caro agreed and then slowed down as they reached the top of Lloyd Canyon Road where a chain-link gate barred the road. A large and impossible to ignore "Private Property" sign was front and center on the gate. They both looked at it for a few seconds before Sadie suggested they drive through all the other streets and make note of the other private driveways. She pulled a notebook and pen from her purse so she could draw a rough map and indicate the roads that led to cabins that were not so easily seen from the roads.

They made a second pass of Lloyd Canyon Road and all the streets that looped off of it, noting the private drives and getting a feel for the differences between the cabins. Some of them had carefully tended flower gardens, cars parked in the driveways, and other details that seemed to say that the owners lived there at least in the summertime, or maybe all year-round. Others had limited landscaping, empty carports, and an overall vacant feel about them that communicated only occasional use.

"Maybe he *is* camping out," Caro suggested after they discussed how impossible it would be for him to stay in one of these empty cabins without the neighbors noticing him. In a town like this, it seemed likely that if one person knew where this mystery man lived, the entire town would know by sundown. And yet, neither Robert nor Goth Girl knew where he was staying. Though they were both aware of him and interested in why he might be here, they hadn't launched any kind of campaign to find out. Maybe people camped out in the mountains on a regular basis. Maybe this town was better than most about keeping out of people's business.

"How would he be showered every time Goth Girl saw him if he were just camping out?" Caro asked. "Maybe Candace lets him shower at the motel. Maybe she's sweet on him, and that's why she wouldn't tell us anything."

"Maybe," Sadie said, but that seemed unlikely. Why wouldn't Goth Girl know if he were showering at the motel she cleaned every day?

They'd reached the top of Lloyd Canyon Road again and the gate that barred them from the road that continued on the other side.

"The forbidden is always more interesting," Caro said, looking at the gate, then pointing. "It's not locked."

Sadie looked more closely and saw what Caro saw. Rather than a lock keeping the gate closed, there was only a chain wrapped around the gate and the fence on the other side of it. How forbidden could it be if there were no reason to bother with a lock?

They both got out of the car to inspect the chain and then looked through the gate to the road that extended beyond it. The road turned to dirt on the other side of the gate but they could see where it branched off in a few different directions.

"There must be cabins not used as full-time residences, don't you think?" Sadie asked.

Caro nodded. "It would be a pain to undo the chain every time you came and went if you were here every day. We should check it out."

"But of course," Sadie said, with a smile at her friend, who smiled back.

Caro moved her car to the side so it wouldn't be in the way of the road. Sadie glanced around, worried that a neighbor was going to come out and tell them to skedaddle, but no one did before Caro rejoined her. Sadie unwrapped the chain and swung the gate open just enough for them to step around it, then she re-wrapped the chain and hoped they wouldn't need a quick getaway.

The first road was on the left. They followed it a hundred feet or so before the trees cleared to show a huge log cabin with a green metal roof. Caro whistled under her breath. "How would it be to have this as your second home?"

"I can't imagine," Sadie said, though she'd always thought the idea of a second home sounded like a lot of work. People she knew who owned cabins spent most of their visits doing maintenance. Her friend Janet's cabin had flooded once—they didn't know until they visited months later and ended up having to gut the entire building due to mold. It had never smelled right after that.

They walked around the impressive building and peeked in the windows. From one of the windows on the main level they could see the blinking red light of an alarm system. It didn't seem likely that he'd be staying in a cabin where the owners cared enough to have an alarm system to keep people out. Back on the road, they were heading toward the next private driveway when something farther ahead caught Sadie's eye. "See that oil drum," she said, pointing it out to Caro and squinting to try to read what was written on it. She could swear the word started with an E, and the idea made the hair on the back of her neck prickle. "Can you read it?" she asked even as she hurried toward it.

"Oh, my gosh," Caro said a few moments later, and then she broke into a run. Sadie jogged behind her, but Caro had come to a stop and turned to face her before she'd caught up. "It says Edger."

"As in Kyle Edger?" Sadie asked as she finally got close enough to clearly see the name welded into the oil drum. The hair on the back of her neck stood up straight now. The attorney Lori had called yesterday just happened to have a cabin in Pine Valley?

"Either this cabin belongs to Kyle Edger," Caro said, putting her hands on her hips, "or this is the most ridiculous coincidence ever."

Sadie had stopped believing in coincidences a long time ago. Even with that thought, however, a shiver washed through her as she remembered Officer Nielson's words about his belief that she was *supposed* to be a part of this case. And Caro had pointed out Sadie's gifts. They all seemed to be indicating the same thing: Sadie being involved in this case wasn't a coincidence, either.

CHAPTER 23

S adie looked down the private dirt road flanked by cedars and ponderosa pines and tried to absorb the implications of this discovery. She wished she'd taken the time to learn more about the attorney Lori Hendricks had contacted after receiving that phone call from the Pine Valley Motel.

"He must have let Dr. H stay here, right?" Caro suggested.

"Why would he do that?" Sadie said. "It's got to be some kind of violation of his oaths or something." She considered it further. "And why would he agree to let Dr. Hendricks stay here but not take into account the fact that he'd need food?"

"Excellent point." Caro started moving down the road. Sadie hurried a few steps and caught her arm.

"Wait," she said, thinking fast. "We can't just walk in on him."

"Why not?" Caro said with a questioning look. "We certainly can't put this off—what if he finds out we're asking about him? He used the motel's phone and didn't go to the store, which means he's broken his routine. Who knows what he's planning to do now? We can't put it off."

She was right, but to go in without a plan was impetuous. "We need to know what our goals are before we rush in."

"To see if he's there," Caro said, sounding annoyed with Sadie's delays. "Or verify that he *has* been—he might have already taken off."

"Maybe we should call Officer Nielson first."

Caro's eyebrows went up in surprise, but she wasn't the only one who hadn't expected Sadie to say such a thing. It wasn't like Sadie to miss an opportunity, but she knew Pete wouldn't go barreling in like this. But would he give Dr. Hendricks a chance to get away?

Sadie pulled her phone out of her pocket, convinced that calling Officer Nielson was the right choice and that she'd better do it now before she talked herself out it. But there was no service. She held her phone up and turned in a circle, but couldn't get even one bar to show up.

"Look," Caro said as she took a few steps closer to Sadie. "If you're nervous about us going up there on our own, you don't need to be." She patted her purse.

Sadie looked at the purse and then into Caro's knowing smile. "What do you mean?"

"I mean that I have a paranoid husband who never lets me go on long road trips without having some protection."

Sadie blinked and looked at Caro's purse again. "A gun?"

"And a Taser."

"A gun *and* a Taser?" Sadie repeated too loudly.

Caro shushed her, and Sadie nodded her understanding and lowered her voice. "Where did he think you were going?"

"He's a safety guy," Caro said with a slight shrug. "I think it's kind of cute that he worries about me."

"And sends you with a gun? He must not know how many people have their own guns turned on them?"

Caro gave Sadie an exasperated look. "I have a concealed carry, so I'd better stick with the gun. Why don't you take the Taser?"

"As though I know how to use a Taser," Sadie said. "Why am I just *now* learning that you're a walking ballistics team?"

"Seriously, you need to calm down." Caro reached into her purse and removed what looked like a small electric razor. "Here's the 'on' button. You switch it to 'on' and then, to activate it, you just press this end against whoever you need to disable. It's not hard."

It didn't seem like it would be hard to accidentally tase herself, either, but Sadie didn't want to further annoy her partner, so she took the device and turned it in her hand. "I can't believe you have a Taser," she said under her breath as she put it in the front pocket of her capris, which now bulged most unattractively.

"I don't have a Taser anymore—you do. I've got Penelope." She patted her purse again and began walking toward the private driveway again.

"You named your gun Penelope," Sadie said, hurrying to catch up.

"What—you don't like it?" Caro said, giving Sadie a teasing smile.

Sadie shook her head and began scoping both sides of the road even though she didn't know what she was looking for. "This road hasn't been graded in a while," Sadie pointed out, changing the subject away from Caro's weaponry. The road leading to Sadie's brother's cabin was graded at least three times a year, which made her wonder when this road had last been attended to.

"Maybe the Edgers don't use it very often," Caro said.

"Maybe it's one more way to keep people away."

They walked almost half a mile before the trees parted to reveal a simple A-frame cabin set behind a roundabout driveway carved out of the natural brush and grasses that were green with summertime. A door was set in the center of the building, with a window on each side and another window near the top. A type of lean-to was built onto one side and covered with aluminum siding. There was nothing outside of the cabin but a hammock tied between two of the many trees surrounding the small clearing. The area looked completely deserted.

Sadie pulled Caro behind the tree line. "Let's approach from the side," she said. "We don't want to make ourselves vulnerable." Now that Caro had opened the subject of guns, Sadie wondered if Dr. Hendricks might have one. She put her hand over the Taser in her pocket, feeling better about having it than she had earlier.

"I'll go left. You go right," Caro said.

Sadie didn't love the idea of splitting up, but they could cover more ground than they would if they stayed together, so she nodded. "We'll meet at the cabin—don't hide so well that I can't see you."

"Agreed." Caro moved left while Sadie moved right, carefully scanning the area ahead of her as she did so. Other than the rustle of leaves in the aspens around them and the sound of birds, she didn't hear anything. Sadie reached the cabin first and approached the front door carefully, watching the curtain-drawn windows and listening to the crunch of pea gravel beneath her feet.

The first of the front steps creaked eerily beneath her foot, causing her to pause before remembering she wasn't trying to sneak up on anyone. The second step creaked as well, but she didn't pause that time. She crossed the small porch and looked at the spider webs in the corner that testified to the fact that this door wasn't used much. Still, she took a breath before she raised her hand and knocked three times. The sound echoed within the cabin, and though she antici-pated the vibration of footsteps, there didn't seem to be any move-ment inside.

She knocked again and waited, but the seemingly empty cabin swallowed her attempts to rouse an occupant. Sadie turned and headed back down the steps to where Caro was waiting. "Keep a look out here, okay? I'm going to check the back."

Caro gave a thumbs-up sign while Sadie moved toward the lean-to portion of the building. There had to be a back door.

She rounded the corner and felt a creeping vulnerability about being out of Caro's line of sight. There was a door in the lean-to section of the cabin. Sadie lifted her hand to knock, but because her other knock hadn't been answered, she felt it was probably a waste of time. She tried the doorknob, but it didn't turn beneath her hand. Locks no longer kept Sadie out of most places, but no sooner had she felt the arrogance of her lock-picking skill than she also remembered that she'd left her lock picks in Colorado. Perhaps she'd thought that if she left them home, she wouldn't encounter a reason to need them on this "girls' weekend" she'd planned with Caro, which was supposed to be full of theater performances, shop-ping, awesome food, and some good Samaritan work. Ha!

She walked around the back of the cabin and discovered a huge deck, twenty feet by twenty feet, covered with flattened piles of au-tumn leaves that hadn't been cleaned up since fall and then had likely been snowed on. She climbed the few steps and came to a stop when she heard something that was out of place. It was not the sound of birds or wind in the trees like she'd heard before. Rather, what caught her attention was the lack of sound. When had it be-come so quiet?

A twig snapped, and she turned around quickly, scanning the

trees for what had made the noise. "Hello?" she called and then listened quietly for an answer, either in words or in movement.

As a few more seconds passed, she heard nothing. Then, out of the corner of her eye, she saw movement. She turned enough to see what at first glance looked like trees and brush. An instant later, she realized she was seeing camouflage pants and her gaze traveled upward until she saw a pair of blue eyes peering at her from behind a cluster of brush that almost hid him completely. *Him.* Wednesday Man.

"Dr. Hendricks?" she asked, her voice shaky with fear that she couldn't choke down. What if it weren't Dr. Hendricks? What if it were some crazy mountain man? Where was Caro?

The figure in the trees suddenly disappeared, crashing through the brush as he beat a quick retreat from the cabin. Despite the questions and the fear, it took Sadie .3 seconds to take pursuit.

CHAPTER 24

Sadie ran down the three steps and headlong into the trees those pants had disappeared into mere moments earlier. There was no way she could catch him, and she guessed he knew that, but she gave it her very best effort.

"Dr. Hendricks!" she called out, dodging tree branches and jumping over a clump of brush after several yards of pursuit. He hadn't run up a path, just into the bushes, and it was slow going trying to navigate the natural hazards of the route he'd chosen. It was also uphill, which helped nothing.

"My. Name. Is. Sadie. Hoff. Miller," she said, gasping for air after running several yards. She wasn't in bad shape, but she wasn't conditioned for anything like this. "I. Just. Want. To. Talk. To. You."

She continued several more yards up the incline before coming to a stop, her chest heaving, at a small clearing that leveled off a little bit. She tried to control her breathing enough to listen for movement. He could have taken off in any direction. Or he could have stopped and was watching her this very minute from another cluster of brush—there was plenty of it to hide behind. A rustling to her left caused her to stare in that direction, and a chill ran across her shoulders. This man had gone to great lengths to hide for the last two months—how determined was he to remain in hiding? How vulnerable had she made herself by running after him into the forest?

Sadie looked back the way she'd come. She couldn't even see the cabin from where she stood, though she knew it wasn't far. If not for the incline of the hill, she wouldn't know how to get back to it, and she suddenly felt as though that was exactly what she should do—get back to the cabin and go to the motel, where she and Caro would regroup, talk to Officer Nielson, and make a new plan. Had Caro heard her calling after Dr. Hendricks? What would she do if she came looking for Sadie and couldn't find her?

Sadie heard the shifting of branches, and she jumped around to face the slope of the hill—exactly where she needed to go to return to the cabin. Her heart rate sped up, but she took a deep breath and told herself not to freak out. *Take the situation in stride and let things unfold,* she thought. There was no indication in anything she had learned about Dr. Hendricks that he was prone to violence. Then again, she knew how desperate people could become and felt her muscles tensing as though preparing for an attack.

"I'm not alone," she said, turning quickly and looking all around her but seeing only trees and brush. She was still breathing hard, but she wasn't gasping anymore. It made it easier to listen when her ragged breaths weren't drowning out all other sounds. "And I'm not here to hurt you." It seemed ridiculous to even say that. She, not he, was the vulnerable one right now, but she took comfort again in knowing she had the Taser. There was something about being out in the open like this—it was reminiscent of another incident that nearly cost her her life—that made her very grateful that Caro had insisted she take the weapon. And Caro wasn't far away. Double coverage—triple if you counted her self-defense skills. "I just want to talk, Dr. Hendricks. That's all."

She turned again, listening for more movement that would indicate where he could be. At what point did she go back to the cabin? At what point would Caro come looking for her? She still didn't hear any birds but only the eerie silence that compounded her growing fear.

She tried to moisten her dry mouth and then took a breath. "I know you called Lori yesterday morning before the memorial. Did you tell her not to go to the luncheon?"

No response.

He could be a mile away by now, which would mean she was talking to no one. She paused a few more seconds, then faced down the hill and took a single step toward the cabin.

"Lori told you?"

His voice startled her, and her mouth instantly became dry again. He was here! *Dr. Hendricks* was *right* here. Deep breath. "She canceled a meeting we'd planned on, and I didn't believe her reasons. I managed to get a hold of her phone and found the motel's number—she doesn't know I know." She was suddenly grateful that Lori hadn't answered her calls yesterday.

"Who else knows I'm here?"

"No one who wants to get you in trouble."

"Do the police know?"

"No," Sadie said, also grateful she hadn't said anything to Officer Nielson this morning so that she could give an honest answer.

His voice was coming from down the hill, between her and the cabin, but she still couldn't see him. He had to be close by, but she couldn't tell exactly where his voice was coming from.

"Who are you?"

"My name is Sadie Hoffmiller. I'm a private investigator."

"Who are you working for? Who's trying to find me?"

"Everyone's been trying to find you."

"How did you find out I was here?"

That was too long a story to tell, but Sadie decided to tell part of it, hoping to build a trusting relationship with him. "A friend found a photo that proved you hadn't been at the Chuckwalla Trailhead the Sunday before your car was found there. I traced the phone call you made to Lori to the motel and then asked around town."

He was quiet for a few more seconds. "Why are you looking for me?"

The question brought to mind Sadie's investment in all of this, something that was becoming increasingly complex for Sadie to identify. She focused on why finding him was important to *everyone*, not just her. "You have two children who love you, Dr. Hendricks. And hundreds of patients who credit you with delivering their children or saving their lives. You must have a very good reason for leaving a life that seemed to be going so well."

He didn't respond right away, and she waited, counting slowly in her head. She'd reached twenty-three before he spoke again. "Not everything is as it seems," he said. Sadie thought about the suspicions she had about his wife and Dr. Waters. She thought about the boutique's appearance of being a charitable organization.

"I know that," Sadie said. "I would like to help you."

"How can *you* help me?"

Sadie considered that the question. "Until I know why you left, I can't answer that, but I can promise you my support regardless of what type of help I can provide."

He was quiet again.

For nearly a minute, Sadie waited for him to speak. "Dr. Hendricks? Are you still there?"

Nothing.

"Dr. Hendricks, your parents and children think you're dead. Certainly there's a better—"

"My death would have been easier for everyone," he cut in.

Sadie heard him move before she saw him, but a moment later she blinked at the man standing just ten feet away from her. He'd been crouching behind a shrub she didn't think was big enough to hide him, but it obviously was. In keeping with the description from Robert and Goth Girl, he wore camo pants and a black T-shirt that hung loosely on his skinny frame. His hair was shaggy, but not too long. His grey-streaked beard covered the entire lower half of his face and his neck. If Sadie had the photograph of Dr. Hendricks from the memorial service and held it beside this man, she'd be hard pressed to make an ID. He held her gaze. Silence hung between them, and Sadie wondered what was going through his head at that moment.

He let out a heavy breath. "I knew I should have killed myself when I had the chance."

CHAPTER 25

The two of them looked at each other across the clearing for several seconds until Sadie realized that any time she let slip away would equate to information she did not get.

"Were you suicidal when you left? Was that your intent?"

He looked at the ground and shoved his hands deep into the pockets of his pants. They were a few sizes too big. "Ironically, when I left I thought I was on the hub of getting my life back, but then it fell apart and I . . ." He looked up and regarded her with suspicion. "Who sent you to find me? Who hired you?"

The sound of a voice calling Sadie's name farther down the hill caused them to look toward the cabin. "Who's that?" Dr. Hendricks said as his hands came out of his pockets. He was suddenly as tense as a cheetah and ready to run.

"My friend," Sadie said, feeling bad about the panic Caro must be feeling right now. How long had Sadie been gone? Five minutes? "I told you I wasn't alone."

"Sadie?" the voice called.

Dr. Hendricks moved toward the trees on the left side of the clearing.

"Wait," Sadie said, putting her hand out. "I'll keep her there."

Dr. Hendricks looked down the mountain at the source of the voice, then back at Sadie. "I disappeared once. I can disappear again."

She could tell he meant it. "Don't do that," Sadie said, walking toward Caro's voice. She put her hands to the sides of her mouth and yelled. "I'm coming down in just a minute, Caro—everything's fine."

"Sadie?" came a reply. It sounded closer. "Are you okay? What's happened?"

"Wait for me right there," Sadie yelled. "I'm coming. Sorry. Don't come up."

Caro was quiet for a moment, and Sadie hoped that meant she sensed Sadie's earnestness. "Okay!"

Sadie was relieved to have Caro's cooperation. She turned to look at Dr. Hendricks. He had moved even farther into the trees during Sadie's exchange with Caro. He looked ready to bolt at any moment.

"Please talk to me, Dr. Hendricks. Help me understand what's happened so I can help you." He looked toward Caro's voice, obviously nervous about her being there.

"I'll send her away," Sadie said.

"If she knows I'm here, she'll go to the police."

"She won't," Sadie said. "I promise. You can trust her. She doesn't even have to know I found you." Sadie noted that he wasn't interested in working with the police. She would need to present herself as neutral. "Dr. Hendricks," Sadie said, "surely you realize that if I can find you, the police can, too. Please let me help you use the limited time you have left."

"Why should I trust you?"

"Because you know what the right thing is to do, and your cover is blown. You're on borrowed time."

He shoved his hands into his pockets and let out a breath. "I don't know what to do," he said quietly.

Sadie's mind was in hyper-drive thinking of possible solutions. "Let me come back in half an hour. Alone. I'll . . . I'll bring you something to eat—you didn't work yesterday so you must be hungry."

He looked up at her, and she could see that the mention of food had changed his level of suspicion. "Alone?" he asked.

"I promise."

"I'll know if you lie to me, and I'll disappear."

"That's the last thing I want," Sadie said, but she knew she'd find a way to bring Caro with her all the same. And she would still have the Taser.

"No cops."

"Of course not," Sadie said, deciding in that moment that she wouldn't tell Officer Nielson about finding Dr. Hendricks until after she'd talked with him. "All I want to do is help you, Dr. Hendricks."

He didn't answer, and she feared he was planning another escape. "Please, Dr. Hendricks. You obviously had reasons to leave, and I know that a man of your education and commitment to his children would not have made this choice lightly. Please help me understand, and then maybe I can help you, too."

"Why would you help me?" His eyes darted toward where Caro was waiting at the base of the hill. He looked back at Sadie. "You haven't even told me who hired you."

"No one hired me. I'm involved in this because I have encountered people who care about you a great deal, and they want answers."

"They know I'm here?"

Sadie hesitated. "No one knows you're *here* but me." Sadie looked back down the hill. At some point, Caro would come looking for her again. If Sadie had been the one who was waiting, she'd have already been on her way up the hill. "Please let me come back alone and talk to you."

"Did Anita hire you?"

His comment seemed to indicate that Anita was somehow responsible for whatever circumstances had driven him to leave his life behind. "I promise you that Anita has nothing to do with my being here, and no one hired me."

"Sadie?" Caro called again. "Are you okay?" Her voice was closer than it had been before.

"I've got to go," Sadie said, stepping toward the cabin. "I'll be back as soon as I can."

He paused but then quickly nodded. She would have loved more reassurance, but she felt he was giving her all the benefit of the doubt he possibly could.

Sadie started moving down the hill. "Thank you," she said over her shoulder. "I'll bring lunch."

Sadie didn't look back to see if he disappeared back into the trees. She needed all her focus as she lurched her way down the hillside, trying not to fall on her face. She was amazed that she'd run *up* this hill. The power of adrenaline.

She encountered Caro halfway between the clearing and the cabin.

Caro opened her mouth to say something, but Sadie put a quick finger to her lips. Caro became silent and fell in step with Sadie, glancing over her shoulder only once as if hoping to see what it was that had kept Sadie from coming down the hill sooner.

Once they reached the cabin, Sadie broke into a jog, eager to get far enough away to tell Caro what had happened, get lunch, and come back as quickly as possible.

Sadie was out of breath by the time they reached the gate. Caro was barely winded. They fumbled with the chain until they were able to get through the gate, and then put it back in place.

When they were in the car, Sadie leaned back against the seat and tried to take a deep breath to reset her heart rate to normal.

"You found him, didn't you?" Caro asked as she backed the car out of the spot where she'd parked thirty minutes earlier.

"I did," Sadie said, opening her eyes and staring out the windshield. "I'm sorry I couldn't let you come up. He's like a scared kid, and he almost bolted when he heard you."

"I didn't know," Caro apologized.

"It's okay," Sadie said. "And it worked out. He's letting me come back, but I need to get him some lunch first."

"Lunch?"

"He didn't get any food from the store yesterday. He's got to be starving. He said I can come back if I come alone, and he seems open to telling me what caused him to leave in the first place."

"Alone?" Caro obviously didn't approve. They took Lloyd Canyon Road back to Main Street. At that point, Sadie's phone chimed to alert her that she'd received a voice mail. A second chime told her that she'd received two voice mails. Apparently the cell service stopped at Main Street.

"I think you can hide in the backseat when we go back," Sadie said as she picked up her phone to check the calls. Officer Nielson was the first one. Shoot. The second call was from Lori. Sadie swallowed, unsure what to tell either of them. "I'm glad to have the time to think about what to ask him."

Caro nodded. "Isn't there something I can do?" she asked.

Sadie frowned and tried to think of something. "I don't know—what do you think? We still need background information on people, but you'd have to stay at the motel to work on that."

"I don't like the idea of you going to the cabin alone."

"I don't, either, but he seemed pretty harmless—and I felt a lot better having the Taser with me."

"Still, I'd rather be in the backseat than at the motel worried sick."

Sadie nodded. "Let's head straight to the store, then. I noticed a sign that said it was Fresh Mex Thursday—sounds like just the thing."

They pulled up to the store, and Caro opted to stay in the car and call Tess back. She'd turned off her phone earlier after Tess had called. "I'd better see what she needed," Caro said.

"Okay," Sadie agreed, shutting the passenger door behind her. Robert was behind the counter when she entered. He asked if they'd found Wednesday Man, and Sadie told him that they were still looking. "Is the lunch special ready yet?" Sadie asked, even though she could see the "Now Serving" sign above the counter.

"Sure is, how many would you like."

"Three," Sadie said, thinking of her, Caro, and Dr. Hendricks.

"Three?" Robert repeated with his eyebrows lifted.

Oops. "Well, how big are they? I'm so hungry I could eat two, depending on the size."

He laughed. "They're a pretty good size—I can't imagine you could eat two."

"Okay, then just two—one for my friend and one for me."

"Sounds good," he said, heading toward the counter and calling for someone named Pam.

The bell on the front door of the store signaled the arrival of a customer. Sadie turned to give whoever it was a "hello" smile only to see Caro standing inside the door, her face pale as she stared at Sadie. Without saying a word, she motioned Sadie outside and then turned and went back outside.

What could have happened?

"Robert, I'll be right back."

"Okay—the salads will be ready in a jiffy."

Sadie hurried out of the store. Caro was already back in her car, and Sadie quickly slid into the passenger seat. "What's wrong?" she asked, truly concerned for her friend.

"It's from Tess," Caro said, as she lifted her phone and turned it to face Sadie. Sadie looked at the screen. A text message? When she read it, she felt the blood drain out of her face.

Anita Hendricks is dead!!! Call me ASAP

CHAPTER 26

One beat. Two beats. Three.

It took that long for Sadie to process what she'd read. She looked into Caro's face. "Oh, my gosh, what happened?"

"I don't know—I haven't called Tess yet. I turned my phone on and saw that I'd missed three calls from her. Then I checked my text messages."

"Call her back," Sadie said, gesturing toward the phone. Her chest was on fire. Anita was dead? How? When?

Caro put the phone on speaker a split second before Tess answered.

"Caro?" Tess almost screamed. Sadie and Caro shared a look.

"What happened?" Caro asked.

"Where have you been? I've been trying to reach you for an hour!"

"I had my phone off. What happened?"

"She's dead, Caro. I just . . . Oh, my gosh, it's so awful. A lady from the office found her." Tess's emotion turned to full-blown tears, and Sadie could pick up only a few words here and there: "fall" and "when she went to the house" and "blood everywhere."

Caro attempted to calm Tess down, assuring her that it was okay and reminding her to breathe. Finally, Tess was able to get a hold of herself. "When are you coming back?" she said when she was breathing regularly enough to form comprehensible sentences. Caro looked at Sadie.

"Do you *need* us to come back?"

"I really need you to help me with this. I don't know what to do."

"I don't think you need to *do* anything," Caro said. "Just try to calm down. I know this is really scary . . ." She continued to speak calmly, but Tess was too worked up to even listen. Meanwhile, Sadie picked up her phone from the console between the seats and called her voice mail.

"Sadie, this is Officer Nielson. There's been a development. Please call me as soon as possible."

Sadie frowned as she considered what she should tell him. What *could* she tell him? Where did her loyalty lie, first and foremost? She was pondering her options when the next voice mail played.

"Sadie? This is Lori Hendricks. I'm sorry I didn't return your call yesterday, but I just talked to Tess, and she said you're looking for Trent and . . . uh, I really need to talk to him. Please call me back at . . ."

Sadie listened to the entire message, then repeated it and listened again, her frustration with Tess growing. Tess had felt like a liability from the start. Why would she tell Lori they were looking for Dr. Hendricks? Sadie had specifically told her not to talk to anyone.

Sadie hung up her phone while Caro was still speaking to Tess— almost arguing with her now. She needed more time to process what had happened before she decided what to do about it. She let herself out of the car. The salads were probably ready by now.

Sadie tried to act normal as Robert told her about Café Rio, a restaurant chain that had started in St. George—these salads were a knock-off version of their creation. On any other day, Sadie would be very interested in this story. Today she could barely listen. When the salads were ready, she paid for them and thanked Robert for his help.

When she returned to the car, Caro was still on the phone with Tess. Sadie had decided what to do about the calls she had received. She wasn't going to call Officer Nielson until she'd heard what Dr. Hendricks had to tell her—Tess had talked to Lori, and Sadie saw how complicated things could become if information was shared prematurely. As for Lori, Sadie would ask Officer Nielson what to do about that.

Caro finally said she'd call Tess back in just a minute. When she hung up, she stared at the phone. "She is completely freaking out."

Sadie forced herself not to vent about Tess's blabbermouth and kept her attention on Anita's death. It still felt so unreal. "Did she tell you what happened?"

Caro pulled out of the parking lot of the store and crossed the street to the motel. "No one knows what happened—Anita didn't show up for work, and so someone went to the house to check on her. They think she fell and hit her head or something, but no details have been released—Tess only knows what people are saying."

"I can't believe she's dead," Sadie said as Caro pulled to a stop.

"I know, and the timing is . . . scary."

They looked at each other, and Sadie knew what Caro meant. Was it a coincidence that Anita Hendricks died a day after their investigation began? The idea made Sadie sick. It reminded her of other times she'd felt responsible for terrible things that had happened. "What do we do?" Caro said.

"Dr. Hendricks is waiting on me," Sadie said, turning to face her friend. "Could you stay here and see what you can find out about everything? Anita's death, for sure, but we also need more information on Kyle Edger."

"And send you back to the cabin alone?"

"You'll know where I am, and I don't see how we have time to waste in either arena right now. Tess told Lori we were looking for him, and Lori left me a message—she wants me to help her talk to him."

Caro blinked. "Tess *told* her?" Sadie felt slightly smug about Caro's reaction. It told her she wasn't the only one who saw that Tess was out of line. It also fueled Sadie's frustration.

"We can't tell Tess anything else, especially now that Anita's death has her worked up. She's obviously talking to people—who knows who else she's told things to."

"I'll talk to her," Caro said. "I'm sure she just didn't realize the importance of keeping stuff quiet."

Except that we told her to keep it to herself, Sadie thought. But she didn't say it out loud. "Regardless, we can't risk that again—don't tell her anything about what we've done today."

"Okay," Caro said. She looked at Sadie once she'd parked the car. "You really think going to meet with Dr. Hendricks on your own is a good idea?"

"I'll drive right up to the cabin, and I've got your Taser." She patted her front pocket.

"If you're not back in forty-five minutes, I'm calling the police."

"An hour, just in case."

"Okay, one hour, but not a minute longer. There are big things happening right now, Sadie—we can't be taking chances."

Sadie nodded in agreement and opened the car door. "It's almost checkout time," she said. "Will you get us another night here so that we can stay a little longer?"

"Yeah," Caro said as she turned off the ignition. Before Sadie stepped out of the car, Caro said, "Tess wants me to come back to St. George."

"*Me,*" not "*us.*" "Oh," Sadie muttered, unsure of what else to say for fear it would come across badly.

"Should I?"

"I guess it's up to you," Sadie said, although she hated the fact that Tess had even asked this of Caro. "I understand if you want to, though. I'm not sure there's anything you can do here that you can't do there."

"Except make sure you're okay and that you come back when you're supposed to."

"I can call you when I'm finished."

Caro bit her lip and looked out the windshield. "I'm not sure what kind of help I will be to Tess in St. George, but this stuff is so new for her."

Sadie felt a tiny bit of sympathy for Tess as she remembered how intense feelings could be in the face of such incomprehensible events. "I'll call you as soon as I have cell coverage after I finish with Dr. Hendricks. If you're halfway to St. George by the time that happens, I'll understand."

Caro nodded and got out of the car. Holding the plastic bag with the barbacoa salads in one hand and her phone in the other, Sadie gave Caro an awkward hug. She got out of the car and then had to put the salads down again while she took her car keys from her pocket. It wasn't nearly as hot as it had been the morning before in St. George, but it was still very toasty.

"Be safe," Caro said as Sadie got into her own car.

"I will," Sadie said. "I'll call you in an hour."

She pulled onto Lloyd Canyon Road a minute later and thought about her top priority right now—it was time to get Dr. Hendricks's side of the story. Sadie was more than ready to hear it.

CHAPTER 27

A s Sadie's car approached the cabin, only her eager anxiety kept her from being overcome by the smell of the two barbacoa pork salads on her passenger seat. The heady aroma from the sweetness of the slow-cooked pork and the still-warm tortilla was almost enough to distract her from thinking about what had happened and what might happen next. After unwinding the chain on the gate, she drove through and then chained it back up again. She began the slow, careful drive down the private lane that led to Kyle Edger's cabin.

The sun was high in the sky, but the trees had created large patches of shade that Sadie appreciated when she let herself out of the car. It wasn't the temperature that was causing Sadie to sweat— it was her nerves. How would she tell Dr. Hendricks about Anita? The thought made Sadie's blood pool in her toes.

With what Dr. Hendricks had said earlier—and what Sadie had seen of Anita the day before—Sadie couldn't begin to guess what her death might mean to Dr. Hendricks right now. Not knowing how to anticipate his reaction, she had no idea how she would handle it. If she told him about Anita, she may not get any more information about why he'd left. Was that a reason to put off telling him his wife was dead? What was her goal for this meeting, anyway? Yes, she wanted to know why he'd left in the first place, and she did want to help him if she could, but what were the ramifications of all of that? Maybe she should have told Officer Nielson she was coming here.

Not being certain of her purpose made Sadie's chest feel tight, but she continued walking toward the cabin. She wished she had cell coverage—for peace of mind, if nothing else.

Dr. Hendricks hadn't specified where they would meet, but because she'd encountered him behind the cabin before, that was the direction she headed. She waited for nearly thirty seconds and was turning back toward the front of the cabin when she heard movement to her left. She whipped around, the plastic bag with the salads hitting her in the hip. Dr. Hendricks stood only a few yards away.

"I didn't mean to scare you," he said, but his eyes were on the bag she held.

Sadie attempted a smile. "You didn't . . . much."

He didn't smile, but she wasn't sure if she'd know if he did because his facial hair was so thick. She would never again underestimate the importance of diligent beard trimming. "Can we meet back here?" he said, pointing a thumb over his shoulder. "I try to stay away from the cabin as much as possible." He nodded at the bag, and Sadie wondered if he could smell that sweet pork. "Is that lunch?"

Sadie lifted the bag. "It's Fresh Mex Thursday at the lodge. These are barbacoa pork salads. I hope they're as good as they smell."

She fully expected him to return her smile, but he looked from her to the bag, seemingly uncertain.

"You have to take a bite of everything first," he said.

"You think I *poisoned* them or something?" She wondered why he would care—he had admitted to being suicidal—but she wouldn't ask. He might misinterpret the question as a threat, and that wouldn't help.

He didn't say anything.

Sadie looked at the cabin. Why would he avoid it? Surely there was a table inside that would be lovely to sit at. But she looked at him and nodded. "I'll follow you."

He turned, and they walked away from the cabin until they came across a path that was darkened by shade from the thick pine trees lining both sides. The path turned uphill, and Sadie trudged behind the doctor for at least five full minutes, her anxiety rising along with the elevation. "How far are we going?" she asked. Caro expected her to call in fifty minutes.

"Not much farther," he said over his shoulder. A minute later, he left the trail and began walking through the brush. Sadie hesitated, and after a few yards he stopped and looked back.

"I'm getting a little uncomfortable with how far we're getting from the cabin." If they left the path, would she be able to find her way back?

"I have a kind of campsite up here," he said, coming toward her and putting his hand out for the bag of salads. They'd gotten heavy, and she was happy to hand them over. She was also glad to see that he'd softened a little bit and didn't seem quite so suspicious of her. She chose to believe the change had nothing to do with the fact that she was far enough away now that no one would hear her scream. "And it's not safe to stay close to the cabin," he added.

Safe? Sadie looked around. She couldn't imagine that the cabin was less safe than this. When she looked at Dr. Hendricks again, she realized her protests wouldn't make him change his plan. If she wanted to talk to him, she would need to do it on his terms. She didn't feel threatened, and she still had the Taser in her pocket, but all the same she said a little prayer as she stepped off the path.

She picked her way through the brush with cautious steps, wishing she'd worn long pants. They went over a rise and began a gradual descent into an area that was rockier than the woods they'd been walking through. Just before they rounded an outcropping of rock and walked into a small clearing, Sadie could smell remnants of a campfire. There wasn't a fire in the rock-lined pit, but Sadie guessed he'd made one last night or perhaps this morning. There were two small cooking pans resting upside down on a flat-topped stone, and the red frame backpack Sadie'd read about in the newspaper articles was leaning against a cedar tree. Dr. Hendricks led her to the shaded portion of the clearing just past the fire pit.

"Are you leaving?" Sadie said, pointing to the bulging pack. Other than the pans, there wasn't anything laying out—not a tent, a jacket, a tarp—nothing.

"I'm always ready to go, just in case."

"Just in case what?"

"Just in case someone like you shows up and I have to disappear again."

Sadie understood the meaning behind his words. She didn't have him captured. Things were still very much in his court. And yet he'd brought her here. Why? She also wondered about her objectives again. Did she expect him to come back to St. George with her after they talked?

"Have you been here all this time?"

"Most of it." He put the bag of salads on the flat stone that already held his two pans.

Sadie moved toward the rock, and Dr. Hendricks stepped back. As he watched from a distance, Sadie removed the aluminum containers from the bag and bent back the edges around the card-board lids. She pulled out the plastic cup of dressing and looked up at the doctor. "Do you want to dress your own?"

He shook his head, and Sadie poured dressing over both meals. She always dressed her own salad—that way she knew she had the perfect amount for her particular taste. Maybe he wasn't as picky after living up here for two months.

Assuming he still wanted her to taste both of them, she took a bite of the first salad and then a bite of the second one. It really was delicious—the tangy dressing complemented the sweetness of the pork. The beans and rice at the bottom created a really good blend of texture and flavor. "These are really good," she said after swallowing the second bite.

He made no move to take one of the salads, so she took another bite of each one. "I could do this all day," she said with a smile. "I assure you that I haven't spent the last few years in Australia working up an immunity to iocane powder."

He didn't smile or make a move toward the salads.

"It's from *The Princess Bride*," she said. He showed no recollection of the movie. Sad. "Anyway, which one do you want?"

"I don't care," he said, but he sounded less suspicious, maybe even a tiny bit embarrassed about being so cautious. Sadie picked up one of the containers and handed it to him, along with a plastic fork still in its wrapper. Then she picked up the other salad and looked around for somewhere to sit.

Sadie didn't like eating from her lap, but she had no choice, so she settled herself on a log. He sat on another log that looked as though it had recently been moved to this part of the clearing. Sadie guessed that she was his first visitor. She mixed the salad components together a little more before taking another bite. It was so good. "You don't stay in the cabin?" she asked.

He shook his head and poked at his salad—he hadn't yet taken a bite. Maybe he was waiting for her to finish hers without frothing at the mouth or something. "I've gone in a few nights when it was raining, but I sleep better out here."

"It's a little different from your home in St. George."

"It's better," he said without hesitation, meeting her eyes quickly before returning to his salad. He finally speared a piece of lettuce. "I love it out here."

Sadie took another bite and carefully chose her first question. She suddenly wished she'd thought to bring something to drink, but it hadn't even crossed her mind. Focus. "Why did you leave?"

"What are you going to do with what I tell you?" he asked quickly, as though he'd been waiting for the chance to ask the question.

She liked the fact that he seemed prepared to tell her something if she could offer him some reassurance. "I can promise you that I'm not trying to get you in trouble, and I don't stand to gain anything personally, regardless of your answer. Right now, I just want to *understand*, and then I want to work with you on what the next step for you should be. As I said earlier, if they decide to look, I'm not the only one who will be able to find you." *Especially now that your wife is dead*, she thought. Gosh, how was he going to react to that? She felt terrible for not telling him yet, but she still felt it was the best course.

Dr. Hendricks took his first bite and chewed it very slowly. When he swallowed it, he looked up at her. "I'm giving you far more trust than I'm comfortable with."

"As am I," Sadie said. "What brought you here?"

"Would you believe me if I said God did?"

"Maybe, but I'd need some explanation." The dressing was unbelievable. She refused to be seduced by the impending food-fog.

He took another, bigger, bite, and Sadie took great pleasure in the way he savored it. She'd made a good choice to bring food. Dr. Hendricks began, "You said earlier that I left what seemed to be a really good life. Six months ago, I thought so, too—I thought I had accomplished more than most men did in their lives. I thought I had given back and made the world a better place. And then a brick fell out of that castle in the sky, and then another, and another, and another . . ." He went back to stirring his salad.

"So you ran from it?" Sadie prodded.

"When I left, I thought I was working on a solution." He paused to spear another bite with his fork. "I'd contacted an attorney, and I was supposed to meet him at his cabin that Friday night—somewhere no one would see us." He waved in the direction of the cabin owned by Kyle Edger.

"Why such subterfuge?"

"I'd lose everything if my wife found out what I was doing."

"So, was this attorney a divorce attorney?" she asked, as though she knew nothing about Kyle Edger. Not telling him what she already knew would help her gauge his honesty.

"He mostly did contract law, but he agreed to help me."

"With a divorce?"

"With staying out of prison."

Sadie frowned, sincerely confused by his answer. She'd assumed Dr. Hendricks had gone to Edger for advice on the business, not about something criminal. "What had you done that you needed to be protected from prison for?"

Dr. Hendricks let out a heavy breath and took another bite before looking up at Sadie again. "Do you know my wife?"

Sadie squirmed internally. But she still felt that she didn't know enough of what was going on to tell him about Anita. It would derail this conversation. She felt guilty, but suppressed it. "I've met her," she finally said.

"And I'll bet she was charming and gracious and eloquent, right?"

"She was at first. But then I crossed her and glimpsed another side of her."

"Crossed her how?" Dr. Hendricks asked, an eager quality entering his voice. He held the fork in his hand, anticipating her answer.

Sadie briefly explained how she'd attempted to overhear Anita's private conversation with Dr. Waters. As she spoke, Dr. Hendricks stared at his food, and Sadie noted how very unlike a doctor he seemed. Not just in his appearance, but in his lack of confidence and in his mannerisms. He was slumped forward, his spine rounded and his shoulders pulled in as he stared at the ground instead of at her.

"Ah, Jake," he finally said. It took a moment for Sadie to remember that Jacob was Dr. Waters's first name. Dr. Hendricks didn't sound angry. Just sad. For whom?

"Is there something between Anita and Dr. Waters?"

He shrugged his shoulders and continued eating, with his eyes trained on the lettuce and beans. "I wondered if there could be, before I left, but I never knew for sure. I hope Jake's smarter than that."

"But you think your wife would cheat on you with your business partner?"

"If it helped her get something she wanted that she couldn't get from me? Absolutely."

"Is that why you left?"

"That was part of it, sure. But Anita is . . . false, about everything. Her feelings, her success—our success. Who she cares about and why, assuming she cares about anyone at all. She manipulates and charms her way to the top of everything she does, but it's all a house of cards."

"Like the boutique misrepresenting itself as a charity?"

He glanced at her, and then he nodded and took another bite.

"That was her idea?"

"I didn't even know about it until six months ago."

"Forgive me for being so direct, but how could you not know? You're listed as the vice president of the LLC."

"Aye, there's the rub." He nodded slowly and thoughtfully, stirring his salad. "Ever since Anita took over the management of the clinic and the foundation, I sign whatever she puts in front of me. I know I'm an idiot for doing it, but I didn't think I had any reason to question her—she was my wife and so much better at the business side of things than I was."

"So you're saying she tricked you into signing the papers?"

"She tricked me into a lot of things."

"Like what?" Sadie asked. She was growing weary of the cryptic comments, but she sensed it was Dr. Hendricks's way of warming up to disclosing more information.

He snorted at her question and then sat up and put his salad on the ground. Sadie bit back a warning about dirt or bugs—he could at least put it on the table rock. Maybe she should hand him one of the cardboard lids. But the intent expression on his face kept her silent—the salad was the least of his worries.

He fixed her with a piercing look. "Obviously, you already know a lot. How much do you know?"

He was testing her to see if she trusted him enough to share what she knew. Surprisingly, she did. "I know about the boutique misrepresenting itself. I know that there's something between Dr. Waters and Anita, although I'm not sure what, and I'm hesitant to jump to any conclusions. I know you called Lori yesterday, and she ran for Vegas as soon as she could because of it. I know she called Kyle Edger after she called you, and now I know that Kyle Edger was helping you with, as you put it, keeping you out of prison." She paused, and then she continued. "And apparently he's letting you stay at the cabin."

He looked confused.

"What?" Sadie hated the fact that she didn't know something he expected her to know.

"Kyle died of a brain aneurysm a few days before I left."

Sadie couldn't hide the shock on her face, and Dr. Hendricks continued before she could manage a response. "I thought it was strange that he didn't reply to my last e-mail—I sent it the day before we were supposed to meet. When I got up here, I still had no idea what had happened to him."

Sadie waited for him to continue and then gave him a prompt. "Why did Lori call him, then?"

"I asked her to try to get my file from his office or his wife or something—some way to prove that I'd been meeting with him. I thought maybe he kept notes on what we talked about, even though I asked him to keep it on the down low."

Sadie looked at him for a few seconds. "I don't understand. You didn't know he was dead when you left, but you stayed here anyway? For two months? Why not find proof of your meetings right after you learned about his death?"

"I just . . . I couldn't go back." He stirred his salad. "I was supposed to meet him here, and he didn't show up. When I learned what happened, I . . . I just couldn't go back to that life. It was the last straw, and it broke me."

"Maybe you could start at the beginning for me," Sadie said

when she realized that the bits and pieces weren't adding up the way she needed them to.

Dr. Hendricks was quiet for a moment, and then he reached into the pocket of his T-shirt. Sadie tensed, immediately thinking of the Taser in her own pocket, but then she relaxed when she saw that the piece of paper he took out was a well-worn picture of his kids. He propped it on the ground so he could look at it while he explained what had caused him to run away from a life that, on the surface, looked nearly perfect.

Café Rio-Style Barbacoa Pork

4 lb. pork roast (picnic roast works best)
2 tablespoons brown sugar
1½ teaspoons cayenne pepper
2 teaspoons cumin
1 teaspoon salt
1 (12-ounce) can Coca-Cola (not diet)
1 cup chicken broth
2 cloves garlic, minced
1 onion, chopped
1 cup brown sugar (more to taste, if desired)

The night before, in a small bowl combine 2 tablespoons brown sugar, cayenne pepper, cumin, and salt. Mix with a fork until blended well. Rub mixture over pork roast. Spray slow cooker with cooking spray, or line with a liner; add rubbed roast. Cook overnight on low heat setting.

The next morning, pour Coke, chicken broth, garlic, and onion into slow cooker with pork. Continue to cook on low. One hour before serving, shred roast, and remove any pieces of fat. Add 1 cup brown sugar. Mix well.

Use tongs to remove shredded pork from cooker. Serve over

salad or rice, or serve burrito-style with toppings, such as lettuce, tomatoes, rice, sour cream, cheese, etc.

Makes 8 servings.

Note: May be made on serving day: Follow directions as indicated but cook 3 hours on high heat setting before adding cola, broth, garlic, and onion. Cook 2 additional hours on high. Shred pork, and add additional brown sugar. If there are a lot of juices after first cooking segment, chicken broth may be omitted.

Cilantro Lime Rice

1 cup uncooked long-grain rice
1 teaspoon butter or margarine
2 cloves garlic, minced
1 teaspoon freshly squeezed lime juice*
1 (15-ounce) can chicken broth

Sauce:
1 tablespoon freshly squeezed lime juice
2 teaspoons sugar
3 tablespoons fresh chopped cilantro

In saucepan, combine rice, butter, garlic, 1 teaspoon lime juice, and chicken broth. Bring to a boil over high heat. Cover, reduce heat to low, and cook 15 to 20 minutes over low heat, until rice is tender. Remove from heat. In small bowl, combine 1 tablespoon lime juice, sugar, and cilantro to make sauce. Pour over hot cooked rice, mixing as rice is fluffed.

Makes 2 cups.

*Though fresh limes are always best, bottled lime juice works if it's what you have on hand.

Note: This recipe works well in a rice cooker.

Tomatillo Dressing

3 medium tomatillos, husked and washed, but not peeled
   (leave whole or cut in quarters)
1½ tablespoons (½ packet) buttermilk ranch dressing
¼ bunch cilantro, chopped
2 cloves garlic, minced or pressed
⅛ to ¼ cup lime juice, or to taste*
¾ cup buttermilk
½ cup mayonnaise
1 teaspoon sugar
½ teaspoon seasoned salt
½ teaspoon cumin

Mix all ingredients in blender until well blended. Chill and serve over salad. Store leftovers in refrigerator.

Makes 2½ cups.

*Fresh lime juice is always best, but bottled lime juice will work in a pinch.

CHAPTER 28

D r. Hendricks took a breath before he spoke. "When I met Anita, Jake and I were looking for someone to take over the foundation—we'd started it as a community service thing, but it had gotten so big and was taking so much of our time. We both had families, and our practice was growing. We just didn't feel like we had time for it, and so we wanted to merge it with a bigger organization or bring on someone to run it for us, but that meant growing it to be able to pay for that kind of overhead. It was kind of a 'fish or cut bait' situation, and we were leaning toward cutting bait. Anita was what made us decide to keep fishing."

Sadie remembered from her research that Anita had begun work for the foundation as an assistant director, but he'd just said he "met" her before that, which didn't seem to fit. Sadie filed that question away, not wanting to interrupt his flow. "I've looked into Anita's history," she said. "She has an impressive track record with other charity organizations."

"Yes, she does," Dr. Hendricks agreed. He picked his salad up again and continued eating as if it hadn't just been on the ground. Sadie forced herself not to think about it. "Her dream was to be the director of a nonprofit, and, at the time, my dream was *not* to be the director any longer. We hired her as an assistant director, but it didn't take long for her to take on the director position. She was a force to be reckoned with, and she turned everything around. I was able to focus on my work, and she was doing exactly what she'd always wanted to do."

"Did she become the director before the two of you got married?"

"Just a few months before. She'd been working for us almost a year and a half when she got the promotion."

"And when did the two of you become romantically involved?"

"After she'd been working there for a while. I'd been divorced for a year by that point, and—"

Sadie couldn't let him lie to her. "You already told me you 'met' her somewhere, and she mentioned a conference in her tribute at the memorial service, so I'm assuming there's more to the story than you simply choosing her resumé out of all the other applicants and her just turning out to be such a rock star—which seems to be the story everyone believes."

His shoulders slumped slightly, and Sadie prepared herself to hear something she'd find disappointing. But at least it would be the truth. "Okay, we met at a conference about a year before she came to work for the foundation."

Their initial meeting, then, was somehow scandalous enough that they had hidden it—which meant it wasn't a purely professional interaction. This change fit easily into the basic timeline Sadie had developed Tuesday night.

"You were still married when the two of you met."

"It's not something I'm proud of."

"And it's something you worked hard to keep quiet," Sadie said, recalling what Lori had told her Tuesday night about Dr. Hendricks's

Josi S. Kilpack

unquestionable fidelity. It was hard to keep her judgments to herself, but it was imperative that she do so. "Lori doesn't even suspect anything." At least Sadie didn't think she did. She remembered Lori's expression as she watched Anita give her comments at the memorial service. Had she figured it out?

Dr. Hendricks continued. "We worked hard to make sure no one found out—it would have ruined me. But I was very vulnerable when we met, and she took advantage of that."

"Is that truly a fair reflection of what happened?" Sadie couldn't keep herself from saying it—as much as she wanted to remain neutral.

He looked back at the dirt, and Sadie hoped she hadn't pushed him back behind his wall of reserve. "No, I should have been a better man, a better husband."

Sadie accepted his comment and moved the conversation forward. "It sounds like you and Anita had a good marriage, though, for quite a while. What changed six months ago?"

He stirred his salad. "Last November, I agreed to be interviewed for a research paper one of my patients was doing on cancer foundations for a college course. I knew so little about how the foundation was operating that I decided to familiarize myself with the details so I wouldn't sound like an idiot.

"In the process of the research, I discovered that the boutique *wasn't* part of the nonprofit and that in the previous two years, the foundation had donated less than ten cents of every dollar to actual research. The dollar amounts we donated were going up, but our percentages were going down. The other ninety percent had gone to salaries and overhead." He met Sadie's eyes. "I didn't even know I was *making* a salary from the foundation—I thought the time I spent on it was a donation, but apparently I'd made just under a hundred thousand dollars a year, and Anita and Dr. Waters had made the same amount. I also learned the boutique was making money—good money—none of which was going to research as claimed."

Sadie lifted her eyebrows. "You didn't know any of that?"

He shook his head. "Doctors aren't particularly known for their business sense. Anita has run the clinic, our household, *and* the foundation for the last four years. I sign whatever papers she asks me to sign. I was just relieved that I didn't have to worry about it. But when I tried to talk to her about my concerns last fall, she patted me on the head and explained it away. But I was nervous about what I'd learned. I did some more digging and learned things I didn't know I didn't know—for instance, if members of the board of a nonprofit make less than a hundred thousand dollars a year, it doesn't need to be reported—each of us made $96,000, and we'd been making that amount for three years."

Sadie did the math. Three years with three salaries of almost a hundred grand was nearly a million dollars. In salaries. Not research.

"That didn't count what we paid Anita's assistant, the receptionist, building expenses, printing, marketing, and a dozen other expenses that were *approved* for nonprofits but seemed extremely inflated beyond our needs. I learned that the foundation had loaned Anita the start-up capital for the boutique—and that the profits were substantial but were not paying back the loan. She's funneled nearly three and a half million dollars away from the foundation in one way or another over the last four years."

"Where did it go?"

"I didn't figure that part out before Anita discovered what I was doing. She tried to explain it away, but when she realized she couldn't, she reminded me that it was my name on everything. She said that if I really wanted to make a big deal about this, it would take me down, and she would do everything in her power to help me sink."

Sadie raised her eyebrows, imagining what it would feel like to hear your spouse issue that kind of threat. Dr. Hendricks continued. "Remember how I said that her dream was to be the director of a nonprofit?"

Sadie nodded.

"I had no idea that my role in her life had everything to do with that goal and nothing to do with me."

"Why *was* being a director her ultimate goal?" Sadie asked. It was a question she'd asked before and found no answer for. "Why a nonprofit foundation?"

"Everyone loves a philanthropist. Everyone admires someone who's making the world a better place, and all her work on other foundations had taught her how to get rich doing it. She got power, admiration, fame, respect, and money. Who doesn't want that?"

Sadie didn't, but she knew there were plenty of people who did. "So after the two of you had it out, then what? You said you wanted a divorce?"

He nodded. "She threatened to destroy me if I pursued it—divorce was not in her ten-year plan for the foundation. She threatened to charge me with abuse, which would destroy my professional reputation, and then she'd take me for everything I had. She'd tell Lori the truth about how we met, which would threaten my relationship with her and, ultimately, my kids—Lori has a heightened sense of morality that, even though we were split up, would—"

"I'm not sure expecting fidelity is 'a heightened sense of morality,'" Sadie cut in. "I think most spouses expect it—you said yourself that Anita's flirting with Dr. Waters put you over the edge."

"I didn't mean it like that," he hurried to correct himself. "I just mean that even with us being divorced, she wouldn't take it well, and I couldn't afford to put anything else in the way of my relationship with the kids."

"And so you did nothing about the fraud you'd discovered?"

"I prayed," he said with a soft smile and an even softer tone. "For the first time in years. I begged for help to know how to get out of this. I stopped signing the paperwork she gave me—that's when I noticed her laughing more at Jake's jokes, touching his arm a little longer than usual, asking for his help with things. I tried to learn more about the intricacies she'd built into the foundation, but she limited my access. She changed passwords on all our accounts, on the foundation's computers—even the alarm system for the foundation suites. I was effectively locked out of my own life, and I couldn't figure out how to get back in without exposing her and, in the process, myself."

"And then she was diagnosed with cancer?" Sadie wanted to make sure he didn't jump too far ahead on the timeline. From what Sadie had read, Anita was diagnosed at the start of the year.

He shook his head. "She didn't have cancer, what she *had* was a really great marketing tool and one more way to *own* me. How would the community react to my leaving my wife right after her diagnosis?"

Once again, Sadie's eyebrows went up. "How could she fake cancer?"

"She's smart. She handles all the billing and records at our clinic. She went to an oncologist in Vegas that I've never heard of—or at least she said she did. She said she didn't want to use the local doctors because of conflict of interest. Who, other than me, is going to investigate and make sure she's telling the truth? And if I can prove she's making it up, then what? I expose her, and me, and risk everything all over again?" He shook his head. "And, from what

I understand, the foundation took in as much in donations in the first quarter of this year as we did in the first *three* quarters of last year—due to her campaign to use her own situation as proof of how important early detection is. The woman's a genius."

"And you didn't tell anyone the truth?" She tried to keep the censure out of her voice, but knew she wasn't very good at that. What about the ethics of his medical practice? How could he not expose Anita for what she was? Surely some agency somewhere could help him. There had to be more options than just to stay or to leave.

"I alerted different watch groups. I notified the Better Business Bureau—I did everything I could do anonymously to try to get some attention on the foundation. I never heard back from anyone. I fell into a depression—I was barely getting through the work day, and I could feel myself slipping in my work, in my ability to focus, in everything. Which I think was also part of her plan."

"How so?" Sadie asked, wondering why, if he'd sent these alerts, nothing had shown online.

"In March, she made me a proposal."

"For divorce?"

"Eventually, yes. In the meantime, I was to remain as the head of the foundation, but I had to guarantee a personal loan to build a stand-alone cancer facility that she would run. I was to bankroll the enterprise, support her publicly, and endorse the growing services that this facility would offer. In exchange, she agreed that after the facility was up and running and financially stable, she would grant me a divorce based on 'irreconcilable differences.' She would not slander me or interfere with my medical license in any way. She would agree to a reasonable divorce settlement and do everything in her power to keep my relationship with Lori and the kids intact. She couched it as an offer I couldn't refuse."

"So you refused it by leaving?" When Sadie had first met Dr. Hendricks a few hours earlier, he'd said he should have killed himself when he had the chance. But he'd thought he was meeting Kyle Edger at that point. When had suicide felt like a reasonable way out?

"After Anita's proposal, I contacted Kyle Edger. I couldn't retain him because Anita had tight reins on the finances, and she couldn't know what I was doing. But Kyle was willing to help me figure out what my options were. He told me he would do some searching to verify my information. When I realized Anita was tracking my phone calls, I started communicating with him via a new e-mail address I used only on public computers, like at the library or Internet cafés.

"A few days before I went on that backpacking trip, I got an e-mail about meeting him at the cabin. He'd found something he wanted me to see—and he felt we needed to talk in person. I left Friday and came here—well, to the cabin. I waited all night and then all day Saturday for him to join me. By Sunday morning I didn't know what to think, but I went to the motel and used their computer to check my e-mail. There were no new messages, so I called his home and found out about the aneurysm and that his funeral would be held on Monday. When the woman on the phone asked me who I was, I hung up."

Sadie wanted to ask more questions, but she was worried about interrupting him. Twenty seconds later, she was rewarded for her patience.

"Mentally and emotionally, I just crumbled when I heard what had happened to Kyle—I couldn't live in my life for another day. I couldn't *endorse* Anita when I knew what she was doing, and I couldn't stop her on my own without being pulled down with her. And now the one person who could help me was out of the picture."

Sadie watched him, thinking about what he was telling her. "You planned to kill yourself."

He looked back at the picture of his children on the ground. "I figured if I made it look like an accident, maybe it wouldn't hurt my kids so much. So I drove back to the Chuckwalla Trailhead Sunday evening. It was the third spot I checked—the other ones had cars in the parking lots. I left my phone on the seat, put on my pack, and headed up the trail. I walked for hours in the dark, trying to come to terms with the life I was leaving and what a fool I had been to let it come to this. I finally hiked up to a place where I was certain a fall would kill me, and . . ." His voice trailed off, and everything was silent, except for the wind in the trees.

"You changed your mind," Sadie finally said softly. He looked at her from across the fire pit, holding her gaze. "You found some hope, and you changed your mind."

He nodded. "It took me four days to hike back here, using a compass and map I'd packed when I thought I was bringing Joey with me that weekend. It rained that first night, which I realized would wipe out any trail I left behind. I figured that the cabin was a place where I could plan my next step and weigh my options."

"And did you come up with a plan?" It had been two months. What else could he have been doing?

"Not yet, but I've felt more peace than I have in a really long time. I've come to realize just how depressed I was—I slept for most of those first two weeks. It took time for me to be able to think clearly, and even now that I'm feeling better, this life up here is so . . . free. I'm not accountable to anyone, and the longer I'm away, the less important any of the foundation garbage feels."

"But your kids," Sadie said, unable to wrap her head around that part. How could he abandon his children?

"If I'd stayed, I'd have had to either go along with Anita's plan or expose her and take the fall. It's *my* name on everything, not hers. I'd lose everything—and it's hard to imagine that my kids wouldn't be a part of that loss, and they didn't deserve that any more than I did."

Sadie wanted to argue with that, but could she honestly do so? She could imagine the future he had seen. He could lose his medical license. He could come under federal investigation that might lead to prison or huge fines. He could become an example of a do-gooder gone bad, and Anita would cry to reporters, saying how she was defrauded, and move to another state somewhere to, most likely, try again. And yet, Sadie pictured his children's heartache at the memorial service, and that hurt her own heart. He had chosen *not* to take his life, and that meant he had to figure out how to move forward. His children would have to come to terms with this one way or another, and hiding up here was saving them from nothing and creating a different type of trauma.

"You said you contacted watch groups and nothing came of it—how? How could the investigation into your disappearance not show the truth—even if it's your name on the chopping block, why don't the police know about this stuff?"

Dr. Hendricks shrugged. "I keep thinking they're going to figure it out, that something will come to the surface during their investigation of me—every week when I go to the motel, I look up any new information about my case, but I've seen nothing. I've both dreaded them figuring it out and hoped for it—I know I can't live like this forever."

"You've been watching the case," Sadie summed up from his comment.

Dr. Hendricks nodded. "I go in once a week and search for new articles, follow threads about me on hiking forums, monitor the watch groups, and try to keep up with my kids."

"With your kids? How?"

"I created a fake Facebook profile, and my daughter friended me. She thinks I'm a girl named Emily and that I go to another school. I never comment or dialogue, just read about what's going on with her."

"And she has no idea it's you?"

He shook his head.

"What prompted you to call Lori yesterday?"

Dr. Hendricks paused for a few seconds, and then he looked up. "Kenzie posted that she was staying with Anita after the service. The idea of my kids staying with her terrified me, and I realized that with the memorial, the case was likely closed, or at least pushed to the side."

"Did you talk to Lori about turning yourself in?" Sadie said, trying to get a sense of what his plan was.

"I didn't say it like that, but I asked her to contact Edger's office about finding proof that I'd been working with him, which I hoped would buy me some credibility. And I told her to keep the kids away from Anita, to get back to Vegas, and stay there until I contacted her again."

Sadie thought back to how Lori kept checking her phone at the service and then her message that morning about her need to talk to Dr. Hendricks. Sadie imagined Lori going out of her head, knowing he was alive but having no additional information. "Lori left me a message on my phone this morning. She wants to talk to you."

"She went back to Vegas like I told her to, though? Right?" Dr. Hendricks asked.

"She didn't even stay after the service long enough to say

good-bye to anyone. Judging by her message, I think she's been wait-ing for you to call her back since she talked to you that first time."

"I don't know what to tell her when I haven't decided what to do yet," he said, and then he looked up at Sadie. "How was . . . the service?" He looked embarrassed to have asked and stared at the ground. "I hope my family can forgive me."

"It was a nice service, but very sad." What a strange conver-sation this was. "Your brother read your obituary and your mother gave a beautiful tribute." She wasn't sitting close enough to him to know if this caused him pain, but she imagined he was thinking of the people who loved him. She wondered how he would ever truly explain all of this to them. "Anita spoke, too," Sadie said. He gave her a wary glance. "It was my first clue that something wasn't right. It sounded like a campaign speech."

"Leave it to Anita to use my funeral as a stepping-stone." He took a deep breath and let it out, returning his salad to the ground. He looked up at Sadie and rested his forearms on his knees. "So— you said you could help me before I told you all of this. Do you still think you can?"

It was Sadie's turn to look down at her salad. She'd nearly for-gotten about it while she considered what Dr. Hendricks had told her. Was it trustworthy information? Could she believe what he'd said? If it hadn't been for the little things she'd uncovered already, she'd have been less certain, but his information fit what she already knew. It made sense of things that hadn't made sense before. After a few contemplative seconds, she looked up at him. "I think so."

"How?" he asked eagerly—perhaps desperately.

She would need Officer Nielson's help with this, but she felt comfortable sharing some possibilities she thought the police would support. "Well, I can follow up with Kyle Edger's office or family."

She said she would do it, but she'd already decided to turn that over to Officer Nielson. The police would be much more effective with legal documentation than she would. "Second . . . well, I'm not sure what else we can do unless you're willing to come out of hiding and tell your side of things." She needed to tell him about Anita, but was this the right moment? She still worried about what she might miss if he stopped talking now.

He looked at the ground again. "There's something that could help with that part."

"Oh?" Sadie said, her ears pricked to hear more.

"I'm the only one who knows Anita didn't really have cancer, so I made copies of her medical record before she falsified it and found some other documentation that proves it was all made up. I included notes about when I made certain discoveries, when I contacted Kyle, and things like that. I saved everything on a USB drive I hid at the office after finding Anita going through my things one day. I didn't think I'd need it when I left for that weekend, so it's probably still there." He looked up at Sadie. "After talking to Lori yesterday and considering that I might have to come out of hiding soon, I thought about asking her to get it since it would prove that Anita wasn't what she seemed, but . . ."

Lori wasn't here. Sadie was. "You want me to get it?"

"It's in a back room of the clinic, somewhere no one will find it unless they know where to look. I don't know how you'd get it."

"I can get it," Sadie said with complete confidence. "Are you willing to turn yourself in if you have the USB with you when you do?"

He paused, but then he nodded. "Like you said—if you can find me, someone else will, too." The tone of his voice and the heaviness of his expression showed his terror at that thought.

"Turning yourself in, with verification of Anita's fraud, will help you."

She watched his glance move to the faces of his children in the photo again, and she hurried to give him more incentive to turn himself in. "I know things will be hard, and I know that the future is scary, but I promise you that there are many people who will rejoice in your return, who will support you and love you and help you through this."

He continued looking at the picture. "What if I end up taking the fall for everything? What if my greatest fears are realized?"

Sadie had no reassurance for that. "In a sense, you lost everything when you came here, but you're okay and stronger than you were when you arrived. That should give you confidence to take another uncertain path. And I just don't see how you can wait any longer. If you don't take an active role, your passiveness could work against you."

He paused. "Yeah, I feel that, too."

"Where's this USB drive?"

He explained that it was hidden on an old ultrasound machine. She repeated everything he told her regarding its location, wishing she had a pen to write it down. When they were finished, Sadie knew she couldn't wait any longer to tell him about Anita. From what he'd said about her, however, Sadie thought that perhaps this information would help him with the choice he had to make. "There's one more thing you need to know before you go back. I hope you'll understand why I didn't tell you sooner."

He didn't ask what it was. He just looked at her expectantly, almost bracingly, as though he feared he'd be unable to handle one more thing.

"Anita's dead."

CHAPTER 29

D r. Hendricks didn't feel much like talking after Sadie broke the news about Anita's death, which helped Sadie feel justified in not telling him sooner. He asked for details, and she told him what she knew, which wasn't much.

She found it difficult to read his reaction. He was shocked, certainly, but she couldn't tell if he were happy or sad, relieved or discouraged. Maybe all of those feelings.

"I *have* to go back now, don't I?" he said after a particularly long pause. Sadie watched him as he stared at nothing. A gust of wind blew through the trees around them, ruffling his hair and feeling like confirmation of what he'd said. He lifted his head. "I have to."

"Yeah," Sadie said softly. "I think you do. We can go right now, see what we can find about why Edger wanted to meet with you, get the USB, and go to the police."

He shook his head quickly. "I won't go without an attorney accompanying me. And I need that USB in hand." He sounded determined.

"Forgive me for being concerned, but what's to keep you from running if I leave you here?"

"I need that USB, and I just told you everything. I have no money and nowhere else to go."

It wasn't as much assurance as she would like. "Are you still contemplating suicide?"

"I'd have done that a long time ago if I still thought it was the best option. With Anita gone . . . everything's different." Was there a hint of hope in his voice? Sadie both hated that and understood it. He met her eyes again. "Will you still help me?"

"Of course. But we need to have a plan. What if we go to St. George and get the USB, then call and get you an attorney to meet us at the police station?"

He was shaking his head before she'd finished. "I'm not going back there without the USB."

He still didn't trust her. Sadie scrambled for another idea. "Okay, you stay at the motel, and I'll go to St. George and get the USB—you can call Lori with an update. I'll come back and get you. We'll go to the police together, and you can call an attorney on the way. I'll bring you a listing of attorneys in the area. By the time we reach the police station, you'll have representation, evidence, and support."

"What if they throw me in jail?" He sounded anxious again, but he was obviously considering her suggestions.

"For what? I don't think they can charge you with anything right now, and if you're the person revealing the fraud of the foundation, it seems to me that they'll listen to you in a different way."

He raised his hands to his head and took a deep breath. "Nothing will be the same," he moaned. "How will I live my life?"

"You'll find a way to make it work," Sadie said, on the verge of annoyance. His last comment sounded selfish. "You'll admit your mistakes, help people see the truth, and start a new part of your life with your children at your side."

He nodded and then lifted his head and squared his shoulders. "I want to stay here one more night. You can get the USB and come back in the morning with a list of attorneys."

"I think we would both feel more comfortable if you'd agree to stay at the motel."

"I want to stay up here one more night. I have a lot of thoughts to get organized."

Sadie paused until he looked up and met her eyes. "Forgive me pointing out the obvious, but you've run away before."

"I'll be here," he said, spreading his hands as if to show her he had nothing up his sleeve. "It's time to finish this, and I accept that—if I didn't trust you I wouldn't have been here when you came back. I'm ready to turn myself in—when I have that USB—but I am staying here until then."

"What about Lori? She's waiting for you to call her. You could come down the mountain with me long enough to use my cell phone."

He let out a breath and scrubbed a hand through his overgrown beard. "I-I can't leave," he said in an anxious tone. "I'm not ready."

"She deserves to know what's going on. You brought her into this when you called her yesterday. She's got to be out of her head with stress and worry—she was grieving for you just like everyone else."

He nodded his head and then looked at her. "Can you call her for me?"

Sadie hated that. She hated that more people would know where he was, hated the loss of control it created. She would already be telling Officer Nielson—now Lori, too? And yet, like she'd said, Lori deserved answers.

Sadie didn't see how further argument would change his mind, so, although she wasn't happy about it, she nodded her acceptance of his terms and agreed to call Lori. She would try to tell Lori as little as she could. To Dr. Hendricks, she said, "How about I plan to be here at eight o'clock tomorrow morning?"

"I don't have a watch, but I'll stay close to the cabin in the morning."

"I'll bring you a good breakfast." Would she be able to hold off Officer Nielson for that long? She did not give her word lightly, but she feared that at some point her part in this would be taken over by the police, and she'd end up trying to explain herself to everyone.

CHAPTER 30

Sadie panicked when she got into her car and realized she was five minutes past the deadline Caro had given her. She drove as quickly as she could from the cabin, through the gate, and down Lloyd Canyon Road. As soon as she had two bars of service on her phone, she pulled over and texted.

> *Sadie:* I'm out. You didn't call Nielson did you?

> *Caro:* No. I gave you an extra 15 cause I know you talk a lot sometimes. Candlelight vigil for Anita tonight @ 8:00 @ clinic/foundation building. They think Anita's death was an accident.

Sadie tapped the phone on her chin, wondering how this might play into the events of the evening. The foundation was in the same building as the clinic that she needed to get into. She pulled back onto the road and headed toward the motel, thinking of Caro and Tess, Officer Nielson and Lori. It was all a little overwhelming, and she felt somewhat paralyzed, not knowing what to do about everything and what order she should do it in.

Tonight's room was paid for—she double-checked to make sure

Caro had taken care of the reservation—but she had work to do in St. George. There was no telling where she'd be sleeping tonight, so she packed up everything and tried to prioritize what needed to be done.

Before packing up her laptop, Sadie Googled "Woman dies in St. George." The search didn't come up with anything specific regarding Anita. She thought about other possibilities and then Googled the website for the St. George newspaper, *The Spectrum*. On the front page was a headline that said, "Woman found dead in Bloomington Hills." Sadie clicked on it and read the short article.

Police were called to a home in Bloomington Hills this morning after the body of a deceased woman was discovered. The initial call was made by a co-worker, who said the woman hadn't answered her phone or showed up for work that day. The woman's identity is not being disclosed at this time pending notification of family. More information will be reported as it becomes available.

Sadie sat back in the chair, read the article again, and wondered who discovered the body? How soon would more information be available? Sadie didn't know what kind of enemies Anita might have had, but from what Dr. Hendricks had said, she might have made a few. Perhaps someone else had figured out what she'd been doing with the foundation. But who would be so personally affected by that to kill her?

Sadie couldn't help but reflect on Anita's tête-à-tête with Dr. Waters. He was kind of the last man standing now with regard to the foundation. Sadie had told Officer Nielson about the secret meeting at the church—had he looked into it? Her eyes went to her phone, and she knew she needed to call Officer Nielson now even though it made her stomach churn. So much had happened since they'd last spoken. What would Anita's death and the discovery of Dr. Hendricks do for Sadie's involvement in this case? Would the stakes be so high that they would take her off the case completely? Surely the investigation into Anita's death had quickly re-opened Dr. Hendricks's case without all the red tape Officer Nielson had been attempting to cut through.

Sadie groaned out loud at her own indecisiveness. She picked up her phone and went to her contact list. She stared at Officer Nielson's number and then dialed it before she talked herself out of it. Why was it always so hard to call him?

"Detective Nielson," he said after the second ring. He sounded like he was in a hurry, which was fine with Sadie. She had no desire to prolong this discussion.

"Sadie Hoffmiller," Sadie said. "I got your voice mail about 'developments.' I assume it's in regard to Anita Hendricks—I just read about it on *The Spectrum*'s website."

"It's quite a development."

"All I read was that a co-worker alerted the police—what happened?"

"We're still looking into possibilities, but it looks as though she'd had some wine after the service yesterday and at some point fell and hit her head."

"Do you believe it was accidental then?"

There was a pause. Sadie waited him out. "We're looking into every possibility," Officer Nielson finally said. "It's certainly a turn we didn't expect—I'd like to speak with you in person about some angles we're looking into. Are you available this afternoon?"

Sadie glanced at the clock on her computer—it was almost one-thirty. "I could come in around three."

"I have some time around then. I'll expect you at three o'clock."

"See you then."

When she hung up, Sadie felt as though she'd held her breath throughout the phone call. She'd managed not to give anything away about Dr. Hendricks or to alienate Officer Nielson, either, but she wasn't sure she felt very proud of that. Working against the police wasn't her goal, but finding the truth was. As long as that was still her goal, they were still working together, right?

She had an hour and a half before she needed to be at the St. George police department. She still needed to return Lori's call and . . . she scrambled for anything else that could put off that inevitable discussion. Kyle Edger! Whew, she had a bit more time to prepare for the call to Dr. Hendricks's ex-wife.

She opened a new browser window and spent a few minutes looking up information on Kyle Edger that would confirm the information Dr. Hendricks had given her. It didn't take long to verify Kyle Edger's death, although the cause wasn't stated in his obituary. She looked for verification of his working situation at the time of his death, but she could find only a P.O. Box to go along with the phone number she already had for his office. He must have worked from home following his retirement.

Once Sadie had found everything she could about Kyle Edger, the only thing she had left to do was call Lori and hope she'd make the right decisions about what to tell her and what not to tell her. She had Dr. Hendricks's blessing, which she appreciated, but she still didn't know what to say.

Lori answered on the second ring.

"Hi, Lori, it's Sadie."

"Good," Lori said, sounding relieved. "Is he with you? Can I talk to him?"

"He's not with me," Sadie said.

"But you know where he is, right? I need to talk to him."

Sadie didn't like the franticness in Lori's voice. "You know, there's a lot happening right now, Lori, and—"

"Where is he?"

"Um, well, he's dealing with a lot right now. I've just told him about Anita, and we're working together to get things ready for him to come out of hiding."

What Sadie had told her seemed to diffuse Lori's panic. "He's coming back?" she said.

"Yes," Sadie confirmed. "Tomorrow morning. I know this must be overwhelming for you, but if you could just be patient one more day. He wants to make all of this right, Lori, and he feels terrible for all the pain he's caused everyone." Sadie was actually exaggerating that a little bit. As she reflected on it, she wasn't sure that Dr. Hendricks had come to terms with the impact of his choices. But he would once he comprehended the scope of things. Right now, he seemed to be so immersed in his own experience that he hadn't yet faced up to the things his loved ones had gone through.

"Tomorrow morning," Lori repeated.

"I know you've already waited so long, but can you wait one more day?"

"He's coming back," Lori repeated. Was she crying? Sadie wished she were talking to Lori in person. "Does he know about Anita?" She was definitely crying.

"He does," Sadie said, even though she'd already told her that. "Are you okay?"

"Of course," Lori said. "I'm just so . . . relieved that he's okay."

"He's okay," Sadie said sympathetically.

"Good," Lori said. She sniffled and then took a deep breath as though she were trying to calm herself.

They ended the phone call, and Sadie hoped she'd handled it the right way. It was so hard to know. It felt good to have talked to Lori, though, and set her mind at ease a bit.

CHAPTER 31

Sadie was early for her appointment with Officer Nielson. She was allowed to keep her purse, and by the time another officer showed her back to Officer Nielson's office, she had written two pages of notes about what had happened so far today. It was almost three-fifteen, and the office was empty, which gave Sadie time to inspect the family photo on the officer's desk before the door opened. Sadie straightened and hurried back to her chair as Officer Nielson wheeled into the room no more slowly than a man walking would have.

"Thanks for coming in," Officer Nielson said as he rolled up to his desk. "And I'm sorry for being late—it's been an intense day around here."

"I can imagine," Sadie said, wondering what he had brought her in for. He'd been a bit cryptic on the phone. To her surprise he immediately launched into an explanation of what they'd learned regarding Anita's death. " . . . Everything points toward her having had a few glasses of wine and tripping on the leg of a chair. She had a fair amount of alcohol in her system, and it could easily have thrown off her balance."

"It's a pretty tragic coincidence for her to die on the evening of her husband's memorial service."

He nodded and sat back in his chair. "We're looking into all the possibilities, and we hate coincidences, so you can rest assured that we're looking into every angle."

Sadie nodded and then paused before saying, "I assume that, since it was an unattended death, there will be an autopsy."

Officer Nielson nodded.

"Would it be possible to make a request for them to look for any scarring or other indicators that she had had cancer?"

Her question obviously surprised him, but it wasn't his facial expression that told her so . . . Rather, it was the change in energy, a kind of toughness, around him. "You question that she had cancer?"

"Dr. Hendricks said she faked it."

"What do you mean, 'Dr. Hendricks *said?*'"

"Oh, yeah, I found him."

There was a beat of silence, and even the well-schooled Officer Nielson couldn't hide his surprise. "You found who?"

"Dr. Hendricks."

Officer Nielson started and sat up straight in his chair. "You *found* him? Alive?"

Sadie nodded, but she realized she was saying too much too soon, and she put up her hand. "You can't go barreling up there—he'll run again."

"Up where?" Officer Nielson said, unable to contain his excitement.

"Um, I need some reassurances before I continue."

"What kind of reassurances?"

Sadie took a breath. "It wasn't easy for him to talk to me," she said, even though it hadn't been particularly hard for him, either, once he decided to trust her. "And he's very worried about coming back—he's afraid he'll face charges for running away."

"As far as I know, he hasn't broken any laws, but we'll certainly want to talk to him, especially in regard to Anita's death."

The way he said it made it sound like Dr. Hendricks might be considered a suspect in Anita's death, and Sadie hurried to dispute that. "He doesn't have a car or anything—he couldn't have come back to St. George last night." The last thing she wanted was for him to come back and face an interrogation.

"Where is he, Pine Valley?"

"You can't go up there," Sadie said again, feeling a bit frantic. "I've made arrangements with him and this needs to be done my way."

Officer Nielson didn't like that—Sadie could tell by the way his jaw tightened. He quickly went back to that blank expression she'd seen on the face of so many detectives over the years.

"I'll tell you what I know, but only if you promise to stay with the commitments I've already made to him." There was a pleading tone in her voice she couldn't hide.

"That depends on what those commitments are, Mrs. Hoffmiller. Surely you can see that I can't agree to something I'm unaware of. This is extremely delicate."

"I couldn't agree more," Sadie confirmed. "He's promised to turn himself in first thing tomorrow morning."

"Why then?"

Sadie explained about the USB drive and the information from Kyle Edger that would help prove Dr. Hendricks's story. Officer Nielson listened and took notes and, to his credit, didn't insist on a path other than the one she'd already established. He asked some questions, but he seemed to be careful not to word them in such a way that it would sound as though he were questioning her. She appreciated that. When she finished her explanation, he said his department would take care of the Kyle Edger portion of things.

"We can also retrieve the USB."

"Um, can I let you know if I need your help with that? I'd like to try for that one on my own."

He paused a moment. "Why?"

Sadie wasn't sure how to respond to that. "I just feel like I should do that part—he trusted me in telling me where it was." And she didn't want to turn everything over to the police.

"I'm sure you understand it would take a search warrant for us to retrieve it. I would need to get that this afternoon in order for you to meet your deadline with Dr. Hendricks in the morning."

Neither of them mentioned that she didn't need a search warrant. They sat in silence for several seconds, and Sadie was certain he wanted to know her thoughts as much as she wanted to know his.

Officer Nielson wrote something down, nodding as though he accepted this course. Sadie was certain, though, that he wasn't thrilled about it. "Do you have investigative plans for this afternoon other than retrieving the USB?"

Sadie shook her head.

"We'll talk about the meeting with Dr. Hendricks after you get the USB. In the meantime, I'd like to ask you to steer clear of Jacob Waters."

"Why?"

"Because we haven't spoken to him yet—he's coming in later this evening. I want a fresh interview with him."

Sadie nodded. She hadn't planned on talking to him. Didn't

plan on talking to anyone, really, other than Caro. Sadie remembered her conversation with Lori and shared that with him. "I don't know if you've spoken to her, but it might be a good idea to check in with her—I didn't know how much to tell her, but she knows Dr. Hendricks is planning to turn himself in tomorrow morning. If you're going to talk to her, tonight might be a good time. I sensed that she was hungry for more information."

Officer Nielson scribbled another note on his notepad. His phone rang, and he checked it and then returned it to his belt. "I'm afraid I'm out of time," he said to Sadie. "Please call me with any other significant information." Officer Nielson paused and looked at Sadie. "Things are happening quickly, and if we're to continue working together, I need your word that you will inform me as soon as anything new develops." There was a heaviness to his words and an almost distrust of her that she didn't like but didn't know how to fix. She'd come on very strong in this meeting, and he could very well have pulled her off the case completely. That he hadn't was a compliment to her, but she felt uncomfortable all the same.

"You have my word," Sadie said.

He extended his hand across the table between them and she looked at it for a moment before she took it. "I very much appreciate your help with this, Mrs. Hoffmiller. I had limited options when you first came to me, and, though the department's interest in this case is now renewed and I'm getting the support necessary, we couldn't have gotten here without you."

"Thank you," Sadie said, feeling a bit embarrassed at the praise so quickly after she'd regretted having to curb her approach.

She left the department around four o'clock and checked her text messages as soon as she exited the building into the summer heat. It felt as though the red rock surrounding the town were heat coils pulsing into the valley.

There was a missed call from Caro and then a text message sent shortly thereafter.

Call me—something's up.

CHAPTER 32

When Sadie called Caro, she immediately suggested they meet somewhere. They agreed to meet in five minutes at Frostop, a burger place on St. George Boulevard not far from Tess's house. Caro gave no indication as to the reason for the meeting, and her tone was suspiciously light.

Caro was already there by the time Sadie arrived at the fifties-style diner—not a commercialized, retro-looking fifties style, but an authentic style that hadn't been updated since the actual 1950s. It smelled like French fries, pickles, and hamburgers. Caro was easy to find because only a few of the orange-seated booths were occupied. Sadie slid into the seat opposite her. On the chrome-trimmed, Formica-topped table between them was a huge basket of orange-colored fries—sweet potato, Sadie assumed—and a dipping sauce that looked like Thousand Island dressing. Sadie was instantly concerned. Ordering this type of food was very un-Caro-like behavior.

"You okay?" Sadie asked.

Caro looked up at her and swallowed before taking a swig of her drink, which looked suspiciously like soda. Caro never drank soda—she said it deteriorated muscle tissue and ate away your stomach lining.

"You're totally not okay," Sadie said, nodding toward the drink as Caro put it down. "What's wrong?" She reached over for a fry even though she was still full from lunch. She dipped the fry in the sauce that wasn't Thousand Island dressing. Yum. There was mayo and ketchup in it, but also something tangy. It was really good.

"These are sweet potato fries—they have some nutritional benefits, so I haven't completely lost my mind," Caro replied. She pointed to the dressing. "This is called 'fries sauce'—it's a Utah thing."

"Well, then they get points for a self-explanatory title *and* deliciousness. I think I could drink it. Now, what's going on?"

"Well, you heard Tess freaking out this morning, right?"

"Right," Sadie said. She ate another fry with the fries sauce.

"Well, she wasn't much better when I got to St. George—she was cleaning her house like a madwoman."

"Okay . . . ," Sadie said, wondering where this was going.

"And she was on the phone and on Facebook all day long with friends and things, people wanting to talk about what each of them knew—it's a pretty close community down here."

"Right," Sadie said, still waiting to hear why this was important.

"But there was one person she didn't talk to."

Sadie raised her eyebrows expectantly but said nothing.

"Nikki," Caro said. "Everyone else was calling and e-mailing and texting, but Nikki never did. Tess called her once and sent her a few texts, and she didn't respond, which had Tess really worried. So about an hour ago, she called Nikki again—and as soon as Nikki answered Nikki must have told her to go into another room because Tess looked at me and disappeared into the bedroom. I tried to listen in but I couldn't hear anything but mumbling through the door. They talked for almost ten minutes."

"Did you find out what they talked about?" Sadie asked.

"No. When Tess came out, she wouldn't talk to me about it. She just said Nikki was upset, and then she got really intense and made me promise not to tell you."

"Me?"

"You're the investigator—she didn't want you to know that she'd talked to Nikki."

"Why not?"

Caro shrugged and ate another fry. "I don't know. That's what has me so worried. I promised her I wouldn't tell you." A pained expression crossed her face. "But I knew I had to."

"You definitely did," Sadie said. "But without context, I don't know what to do with it." She could take it to the police, but what would they do with it?

"Maybe you could talk to her," Caro suggested.

"Tess?"

"No," Caro said quickly. "Then she'd know I told you, and I don't think she'd give much up to you anyway. She's still not really over everything."

Oh, brother. "So you think I should talk to Nikki?"

"I know you don't have much to go on, but something's up with her, don't you think? Why else would Tess be so secretive? She and Nikki are good friends, and I get the feeling that Tess feels like she's protecting Nikki somehow."

Sadie considered that for a few seconds, and then her eyes snapped up to meet Caro's. "Did she tell Nikki about Anita and Dr. Waters?"

"I don't know," Caro said, making a face. "We told her not to."

"But that might not mean much. If they're good friends, Tess might feel some kind of obligation to tell Nikki. And we know she told Lori that we found Dr. Hendricks."

Caro nodded and ate another fry. Sadie did, too, needing an excuse to continue pondering. If Tess did tell Nikki about the meeting Sadie interrupted at the church yesterday, what would Nikki do that made Tess feel like she needed to protect her friend? Sadie backed up a step and put herself in Nikki's position. If someone came to Sadie and told her that her husband had been closeted with another woman, what would Sadie do? She would talk to her husband. She looked at the ring on her hand and smiled slightly at the zing she felt before getting back to the task at hand. Focus. But why would Tess feel protective because of a conversation Nikki had with her husband? The next thing Sadie might do would be to talk to the woman her husband had been closeted with. Sadie's hand paused halfway to her mouth and a drop of fries sauce fell onto the table as the idea took full shape in her mind. What if Nikki talked to Anita?

"What?" Caro asked, reminding Sadie that she wasn't alone. Sadie quickly ate the fry and then explained her train of thought. Caro's eyes widened as she acknowledged the plausibility of Sadie's theory.

"That would also explain why Tess was so hyper about everything this morning. If she'd told Nikki about Anita and Dr. Waters, and then Anita ends up dead . . . Oh, gosh."

"I need you to go back to Tess and see if you can find out if she told Nikki and, if so, when? Do whatever you can to find out what she's hiding. I'll go see Nikki—do you know where she lives?" It occurred to Sadie that going to Nikki's might help her get into the clinic as well—she could really use a "two birds with one stone" turn of events right now.

Caro reached into her purse and pulled out a Post-it note that she handed to Sadie. It contained an address, hastily written. "I found it, just in case."

"Well done," Sadie said with a sincere smile. She reached across the table and gave Caro's hand a squeeze, knowing this was hard for her, feeling that she had betrayed Tess. "Let me know what you find out, and I'll do the same."

It wasn't until Sadie was three blocks away that she realized she hadn't told Caro about her meeting with Dr. Hendricks. The case was picking up so much speed that even something as important as that had somehow taken a backseat to this new information.

Fry Sauce

¼ cup mayonnaise
¼ cup ketchup
1 teaspoon red wine vinegar
Dash salt

For spicy fry sauce, add:
¼ teaspoon onion powder
⅛ teaspoon cayenne pepper
⅛ teaspoon black pepper

Mix all the ingredients together. Makes ½ cup.

CHAPTER 33

The Waters's house was located on the back side of a little hill on the east side of town that Sadie had seen when she'd entered the city. For some reason, she had assumed that hill was the eastern edge of the city, but according to the directions of the GPS on her phone, the hill hid a large part of the city from the view of those on the west side. The farther up she went, the bigger the houses got, until she ended up on one of the topmost streets of the neighborhood. It was filled with some of the largest houses she'd seen in the city so far. She found the Waters house easily enough—even in ritzy neighborhoods like this one, not many people had the letter "W" inlaid with pavers into their driveway.

She parked at the curb and headed up the sidewalk, taking in the large, two-level home that could probably serve as a small hotel. How many children did the Waterses have? Sadie had seen three at the memorial service, but maybe there were more who hadn't been there. The red Jeep Wrangler in the driveway was not parked straight, and the smell of baking was heavy in the summer air as Sadie got closer to the front door. Sadie could relate to the idea of baking when you were under stress, but she couldn't imagine baking when the stress resulted from murdering your husband's lover. Hopefully she was wrong to even think about that. Every meeting she'd had with Nikki Waters had been positive. She seemed like a genuinely kindhearted woman. But even the kindest of people had a breaking point. Still, Sadie hoped—really hoped—that Nikki would prove Sadie's worst suspicions wrong. Her hope was so strong she could taste it.

Sadie knocked on the door, and a few seconds later, a teenage girl answered. Sadie recognized her from the memorial service the day before. Was it really only yesterday?

"Hi," the girl said brightly. She had long blonde hair pulled back into a ponytail and wore shorts with a T-shirt that said, "This little light of mine . . ." across the front. A lanyard with a set of keys hung around her neck. Sadie was guessing the Jeep in the driveway belonged to her. There was some heavy metal music playing toward the back of the house, which made Sadie worry that Nikki might not be home.

"Hi. Is your mom here?"

"Sure. Come on in."

Sadie hesitated, but the girl pulled the door wide open and then called for her mom over her shoulder before turning back with a smile. "She's in the kitchen, but she's not in the best mood—she's kind of having a bad day."

Sadie followed the girl as she led her into the hallway to the kitchen. The back of the girl's shirt said, "I'm gunna let it shine!" reminding Sadie of Caro's lecture on using her gifts rather than hiding them under a bushel. Somehow Sadie didn't think Caro had foreseen Sadie using her gifts to interrogate Nikki. But as she made her way toward the back of the house, Sadie realized that she felt good about what she'd accomplished so far. She had become invested in the people involved in this case. Lori, her children, Dr. Hendricks. Even Anita. And Nikki, too. She knew what hiding from the truth could do to people, and she felt good about the role she'd played in trying to bring the truth to light. She was grateful for this moment of reflection—it helped prepare her for anything ugly that might yet lie ahead of her.

The smell of what Sadie guessed were cookies became stronger, as did the volume of the music as they proceeded to the kitchen.

"She's just down there," the girl said, jumping to the bottom step of a flight of stairs that led to the upper level of the house.

"Um, have you guys had dinner yet?" Sadie asked before the girl continued up the stairs. It wasn't quite dinner time, but Sadie would feel much better if there weren't kids in the house when she confronted Nikki.

"Nah," the girl said good-naturedly. "But we had lots of cookies 'til Mom freaked out and banned us from the kitchen." She didn't seem bothered by the ban or by saying such things about her mother to a complete stranger.

"Well, I stopped at this delightful burger place this afternoon called Frostop—have you ever been there before?"

"Um, yeah, I've been to Frostop."

"They had the most delicious dipping sauce—they called it 'fries sauce.' Have you ever tried it?"

The girl looked a bit confused, but she nodded. "Yeah, I've had fry sauce."

Fry or fries? "Then you know how amazing it is!" Sadie pulled her purse off her shoulder and found her wallet. She removed a twenty-dollar bill. "Why don't you and your brothers and sisters go get something at Frostop for dinner, since your mom is so busy with the cookies."

The girl still looked confused. "Only Bailey's here—Kevin's at a friend's."

"Well, you and Bailey can drown yourselves in the fries sauce, then." Still smiling, Sadie held out the money.

The girl looked at the money, and then she shrugged and took it. "Sweet—thanks. But it's called *fry* sauce, not fries sauce."

"Oh, well, now I know." Sadie smiled. "I'll tell your mom dinner is taken care of."

"Okay," the girl said, skipping up the stairs. A moment later she was calling for Bailey.

Sadie took a breath and went into the kitchen.

There were large pink bakery boxes laid out on the dining room table. Two of them were closed and one was open, with what looked like three layers of cookies, separated by parchment paper, inside. Nikki wasn't just baking—she was baking for an army, and apparently she'd done this before. Otherwise, she wouldn't know about the convenience of using bakery boxes, and there would have been fifty paper plates piled with cookies instead. Paper plates were good when taking a dozen cookies to a friend—ridiculous when you were baking hundreds.

The countertops were littered with all kinds of baking paraphernalia, so it took a moment for Sadie to find Nikki, who was backing away from the oven with a hot pan of cookies. Sadie waited until Nikki put the pan on the marble countertop—she should use a trivet or hot pad, Sadie thought—before she said hello loud enough to be heard over the music. Startled, Nikki blinked, her face blank for half a second before she managed a weak smile. Her hair, so perfectly coiffed yesterday, was pulled up in a bumpy ponytail on top of her head, and she wasn't wearing any makeup. Her pink apron, complete with the pink posy logo on the front, covered a white T-shirt and black-and-red-striped pajama pants. Brown leather slippers covered Nikki's feet. By all appearances, she'd had an "undone" kind of day.

"Hi," Nikki said loudly. She moved to the thin stereo mounted underneath one of the upper cabinets and turned down the sound. Before she could find something else to say, Sadie complimented her on the cookies. "Chocolate chocolate chip?"

"Um, sort of. Oatmeal chocolate chocolate chip, I guess. I call them Dream Cookies."

"What are they for? Do you cater or something?"

"I said I'd make some for the vigil tonight. It was the least I could do."

Sadie looked at the cookies in a new light. They were for the vigil? Were they also a way to cover her crimes?

Nikki nervously picked up a spatula on the counter and began moving the cookies to a cooling rack. She really hadn't let them cool on the pan long enough, and, although the first one survived the transfer all right, the second one she removed from the tray broke apart. "I'm really busy right now," Nikki said between cookies, waving her hand toward the dining room table. The fourth cookie crumbled as well. Nikki didn't seem to notice or to care.

"Looks like you could use an extra set of hands," Sadie said. Nikki looked up at her but didn't smile.

A teenage voice called from the hallway. "We're going."

Nikki stepped toward the hallway. "What?" she called—but the front door slammed.

"I gave them some money to go to Frostop. Have you tried their fry sauce? It's incredible."

Nikki blinked at her. "You gave my kids money?"

Sadie kept her tone light and conversational. "I knew you hadn't been able to make dinner, and I didn't think you wanted them here when you and I had this discussion. I know you want to avoid it, but you know in your heart you shouldn't."

Nikki blinked again and Sadie knew she was repeating in her mind what Sadie had just said. Nikki went back to her cookies. "I don't know what you're talking about."

Sadie didn't know what she was talking about, either, and she searched for a way to get Nikki to fill in the numerous blanks. "I owe you an apology," Sadie said as she arrived at what she hoped was the right way to lead into this conversation Nikki didn't want to have.

Nikki looked up. "An apology? For what?"

"Something happened yesterday that I should have told you about. I'm sorry that I didn't."

Nikki tensed and looked away. She went back to transferring cookies and said nothing.

"See, when we were at the memorial service, I saw Anita and your husband go off—"

"I already know, okay," Nikki said quickly and sharply, obviously not wanting to hear it again and yet confirming that Tess had been a blabbermouth. "I don't want to talk about it."

"I understand," Sadie said. "But I think we need to."

Nikki stared at the counter and took a breath. She looked at Sadie. "Look, I don't mean to be rude, but this really isn't any of your business, and I would appreciate it if you would please go."

"Did you talk to your husband about it?" Sadie pushed. If she had, it might have given him some motive, too. More motive than he already had if in fact there was something going on between him and Anita.

"You really need to leave," Nikki said with what sounded like the last of her polite patience. She gripped the edge of the counter with one hand and her knuckles turned white.

"Or did you talk to Anita instead?"

Nikki's head snapped up to meet Sadie's gaze. She held it for a few seconds, with fear in her eyes before they narrowed slightly. She pointed the hand with the spatula toward the front of the house. "Get out of my house."

"Did you go to Anita's house last night, Nikki?" Sadie pushed further. "Did you confront her?"

"Get out!" Nikki yelled. "Get out now!"

"I'm not leaving," Sadie countered, crossing her arms over her chest. "Not until you tell me what happened. You went there, didn't you? You went there to confront her about the meeting she had with your husband at the memorial service. Tess told you about it, and you couldn't help yourself." She could tell by the varying expressions on Nikki's face that she was on the right track. "It makes perfect sense that you would go there, Nikki. I'd do exactly the same thing in your position. Any woman would. How did she react? What happened?"

"I didn't kill her," Nikki said quickly, and then she realized what she'd said and clamped her mouth shut. Tears began forming in her eyes. "I . . . I . . . ." She looked around the kitchen as though she were trying to find an escape. Her glance landed on the boxes of cookies she'd been working on all day, and she closed her eyes, a single tear leaking out of one eye, which she quickly brushed away. "She said I was being ridiculous—as though it didn't even matter if . . ."

Now they could get somewhere. "But you didn't believe her."

"She's beautiful and smart and successful. She spends more time with my husband than I do and helps run his business." Nikki opened her eyes and looked down at the apron she wore and the slippers on her feet. "I've had six kids. I don't understand anything about how to run the foundation or the clinic, even though Jake has asked me for years to get involved, and . . . and it wouldn't be the first time she . . ."

Sadie lifted her eyebrows. "The first time Anita went after a married man? You know about Dr. Hendricks and Anita, then."

Nikki's mouth dropped open in surprise.

"You thought you were the only who knew that?" Sadie asked, trying to play it cool, even though she was making it up one word at a time. Nikki had thrown it out there as a way to defend herself, but Sadie had caught the curve ball and thrown it right back. It was imperative that she stay on her feet for the rest of this inning. "Come on—he and Lori are having problems, and six months later this beautiful woman comes to work for him. Six months after that, they're dating, and six months after *that*, they get married? It's like a script for covering up an affair and making it all appear normal and natural. How did you find out?"

"Jake swore me to secrecy a couple of years ago, and even he wasn't certain. When I learned about Jake and Anita going off like that, I just . . . I just knew." She blinked quickly and looked out the window to the backyard that had actual grass in it. "My family is everything to me, and to think that . . . "

"So—your husband and Anita *were* having a relationship?" Sadie said, saddened that the worst-case scenario could have been the truth. "He confirmed it?"

Nikki scratched at something on the counter. "I haven't talked to him yet."

Sadie blinked, mentally backing up in the conversation. "Then how can you be so sure they were having an affair? Anita denied it, right?"

"They went off together at the luncheon."

"Is that your only evidence?" Sadie asked.

"Isn't that enough?" Nikki responded. "And then other things made more sense. I thought she was calling him all the time because Trent wasn't there for her to bounce things off of and that Jake avoided her because he didn't really like her—he'd said that to me plenty of times before—but now I realize it was all an act, all part of the game they were playing." She raised a hand to her mouth and looked out the window again as more tears came.

"Nikki," Sadie said, keeping her voice soft and even and calm. Dr. Hendricks suspected an affair as well, or the potential for one, but he didn't think it had reached that point before he left. Sadie had learned the hard way to focus on facts, and that's what she needed Nikki to do now. "Those are guesses, assumptions made based on the worst possible fear a woman can have with regard to her husband. I'm the one who found them in the classroom, and, other than working so hard to be private, there was nothing . . . *romantic* in their actions. The whole time I was listening at the door, they were talking—no silences that could have indicated . . . something else." She felt her cheeks heating up slightly.

Nikki turned back to Sadie and wiped at her face with the hand she'd been holding to her mouth. "But why would they do that? They work together every day—why would they need to hide like that?"

"There could be a hundred different reasons. And the phone calls Anita made *could* have been to ask questions she would normally ask Dr. Hendricks, like you said. Dr. Waters avoiding her *could* have everything to do with him not liking her very much." She paused as she thought of something else. "Since Dr. Hendricks's disappearance, things have been really hard for your husband, haven't they?"

Nikki nodded slowly. "For all of us, but especially him. He's tried to coordinate with other doctors in the area, but we're a small community, and there are only so many appointment slots. He hates having to send people to Cedar or Vegas, and he's so worried about the practice going under if he can't keep up with payments and things. He's working fourteen-hour days, and he's on call almost every single night and trying to juggle Trent's patients and his own."

"I bet you miss him a lot," Sadie said sympathetically. "Even as a doctor's wife, who understands the sacrifices, this isn't what you expected."

"Not even close," Nikki said, wiping quickly at a tear and sniffling. "I don't talk to him about stuff with the kids because he's just so overwhelmed, and I'm doing everything at home. That sounds so selfish—it's been way harder for him, I know, but I've had to kind of put all my focus here at home and let him do what he needs to do with the clinic. And then this."

A clearer picture was opening in Sadie's mind. "No wonder you're feeling so anxious about your relationship—no one falls in love and gets married so that they can live separate lives. And then you hear about them meeting up at the church. I am not the least bit surprised that it felt as though they *must* have been having an affair—if that were true it would make sense of everything else and explain the distance in your relationship."

Nikki stiffened. "You think I want to believe my husband cheated on me?"

"Not at all, but things aren't great between you—maybe sort of like they weren't great between Trent and Lori before the divorce— and maybe you resent the time he's been spending with Anita, the way she can get his attention when she asks for his help, and then you heard—third person, remember—that they were found together.

Can you see how circumstances have you primed to believe the worst?"

Nikki swallowed, staring at Sadie as her words sank in.

"What happened at Anita's house last night, Nikki?"

Nikki seemed almost to be in a trance when she started talking. "She denied it. I told her I needed her to tell me the truth, and she told me to leave, that I was crazy."

"Did the two of you argue about it?"

"I kept demanding that she tell me the truth, and she finally yelled at me to get out of her house and go back to my husband that . . . loved me. I-I thought she was mocking me."

"Did you leave?" She held her breath, waiting for the answer, praying that Anita was alive and well when Nikki left the house.

Nikki nodded, and Sadie could breathe again.

"You're sure."

"I'm sure," Nikki said, nodding again. Sadie searched her face for any duplicity or falseness, but the sincerity of a woman who just realized there might be fresh hope in her marriage was all that was reflected back at her. *Please let that hope not be wasted*, Sadie thought. Nikki's chin trembled. "I don't know what happened after I left. She had a glass of wine when I got there. Maybe she *was* drinking heavily—the police said they think it was an accident." There was a pleading quality to her voice. "But my fingerprints might be in the house—on the door, on the glass of water she offered me. I accepted it because I needed something to hold on to. They'll think I did something. They'll know I was there."

"You need to tell all of this to the police."

Nikki went even paler. "I'd have to tell them my suspicions about Jake."

"Nikki, you're a woman of faith, are you not?"

She nodded.

"Then have faith in yourself and your family and your husband. Not faith that everything is fine and that *appearing* perfect means everything *is*, but faith that whatever lies ahead can be faced together. That's what marital vows are about—that in times of difficulty you will remember the promises you made and find a way to soldier through. Beyond that, God tells us to be honest and helpful and good. You need to talk to the police about what happened last night—only then will *you* be able to move forward and will *they* be able to find out what happened to Anita."

"You sound as though you don't think she fell."

Sadie paused for a moment, but she'd thrown caution to the wind so many times that she couldn't think of why to hold back now. "I don't."

"You think someone . . . killed her."

Sadie nodded and watched Nikki carefully. "I do."

Sadie wanted to ask if Nikki's husband had been home last night, but she felt certain that would close the conversation. Nikki going to the police would automatically open that line of questioning, and the police already had an interview with Dr. Waters. Sadie hoped he didn't have anything to do with Anita's death. Relief over Nikki's innocence had transferred her thoughts to Nikki's husband. Nikki closed her eyes slowly and dropped her chin.

"The sooner the better," Sadie said. "It shows you're interested in doing the right thing."

"There really isn't a better way, is there?" Nikki's eyes filled with tears again, and Sadie's heart ached. Nikki Waters was used to being respected, even admired, and to find a chink in that armor of belief, one that was so potentially heart-wrenching, was a very difficult thing to face. Sadie could understand that, and she was glad that, despite all of the difficulty, Nikki had accepted that going to the police was necessary.

Sadie crossed the kitchen and put her arms around the younger woman's shoulders. Nikki fell into her embrace, sobbing with the enormity of what was happening and perhaps some relief for the hope Sadie had given her. Sadie held her for nearly a minute before pulling back. "One more thing," she said with a motherly smile. "Do you happen to know how I can get into the clinic?"

Dream Cookies

½ cup shortening
½ cup butter, softened
¾ cup granulated sugar
¾ cup packed brown sugar
½ teaspoon baking powder
¼ teaspoon baking soda
¼ teaspoon salt
2 eggs
1 teaspoon vanilla
1⅓ cups all-purpose flour
⅓ cup unsweetened cocoa powder
2½ cups rolled oats
1 cup semisweet chocolate chips*
1 cup white chocolate chips
1 cup chopped macadamia nuts or pecans

Preheat oven to 350 degrees. Lightly grease baking sheet; set aside.

In large bowl, beat shortening and butter together with electric mixer 30 seconds at medium to high speed. Add granulated sugar, brown sugar, baking powder, baking soda, and salt. Beat until combined, occasionally scraping sides of bowl.

Beat in eggs and vanilla until combined. Beat in flour and cocoa powder. Stir in oats, chocolate chips, white chocolate chips, and nuts.

Drop by heaping tablespoons or 1-inch scoop 3 inches apart on prepared baking sheet. Flatten dough slightly. Bake 12 to 14 minutes or until just set. Let stand 1 minute on baking sheet. Remove to cooling rack.

Makes 4 dozen.

*Dried cranberries are a good substitute for chocolate chips.

Note: For a flatter, chewier cookie, increase baking powder and baking soda to 1 teaspoon each.

Note: For a less-is-more version of this cookie, cut back to 1¾ cups oats and ½ cup nuts.

CHAPTER 34

Nikki confirmed that she had a key to the clinic, and Sadie tried to keep from showing her excitement as Nikki wiped at the last of the tears on her cheeks. "Why do you need to get into the clinic?"

Proceed carefully, Sadie thought to herself. "Dr. Hendricks hid some information in the clinic before his disappearance. I need to get it to the police so they can review it." It was a pretty good non-lie, if Sadie said so herself. Unfortunately, Nikki didn't buy it completely.

Nikki sniffed and took a breath. "If the police need it, why don't *they* get it?"

Excellent question. "Didn't Tess tell you we're working with the police?"

"She said *you* were, but she was kind of funny about it."

Sadie stiffened slightly. "Funny? Funny how? Like she didn't believe me?"

Nikki shrugged and smiled awkwardly. Sadie took a breath. "I *am* working with the police. Things are happening really fast, and there's no time for a search warrant. Can you help me get into the clinic?"

"Um, I don't know. I probably need to talk to Jake about it."

"Nikki," Sadie said calmly, "I know this is a weird request, and you've had a really intense day, but please, I need to get into the clinic. I promise you that I am retrieving one thing, that it has nothing to do with patient confidentiality, and when your husband learns what it is, he'll be glad I got it. But I need to get it now, before the vigil. As soon as possible."

Nikki held Sadie's gaze for a few more seconds, and then she finally nodded. "I'll have to get the alarm code from someone who works in the office. They change it every few months, and I usually don't have any reason to know it."

"But you can get it?" Sadie asked, trying not to look too relieved.

Nikki searched Sadie's face for a long time, weighing this decision carefully. Sadie tried to breathe normally, but she was well aware of the fact that if Nikki said no, Sadie was in a pickle. She thought back to what Officer Nielson had said about God wanting her to work on this case. Now she would see whether or not that was true. Half a dozen things she'd uncovered in this case pointed to His hand, but this one felt different. More important in a way. Or maybe it was just that the timing was becoming more crucial. "Let me call the office manager," Nikki said. Sadie began to breathe normally, although she tried to hide her relief. "And I've got to change my clothes if we're going to the clinic."

Sadie raised her eyebrows at the idea of Nikki coming with her, but Nikki simply returned the look, daring Sadie to complain. Sadie wasn't about to do that. Instead, she smiled. "I'll box up the rest of the cookies while you get changed."

When they arrived at the building that housed the clinic and the foundation offices almost twenty minutes later, Sadie furtively looked around to see if anyone was watching them. They stopped at the foundation offices first to drop off the cookies at the front counter. There was no one to receive them yet, but neither Nikki nor Sadie wanted to be seen right now. Sadie wanted to keep a low profile, and Nikki kept saying she hadn't left the house without makeup in years. Nikki scribbled a note on the back of a flier, saying the cookies were from her.

Sadie was relieved the clinic was on a different level, and she cast another cautious look around as they headed up the stairs to the second floor. Nikki turned the key in the lock of the big glass doors with her husband's and Dr. Hendricks's names on them. As soon as she pulled the doors open, an intermittent beeping could be heard from inside the office. Nikki hurried toward the reception area, and Sadie followed her. When they reached a keypad, Nikki punched in the four-number code the office manager had given her. There was a final beep before the alarm went silent, and Sadie's heartbeat slowed down as well.

"Now what?" Nikki asked.

"Can you point me toward the x-ray room?"

"It's down this hall," Nikki said, pointing straight ahead, "the last door on your left." She looked nervous, and Sadie prayed that Nikki could hang on a little longer. She was so close.

"Wait for me here," she said. "I'll be right back."

Nikki nodded, and Sadie headed down the hallway. She didn't want to turn on any lights, but the hallway grew darker and darker the farther she got from the reception area, and she finally had no choice. The x-ray room had a big sign on the door, making it impossible to miss. Sadie let herself in and flipped on the light switch. The fluorescent lights flickered overhead, causing Sadie to squint as the bright white light reflected on the equally bright white walls. She scanned the walls lined with cabinets and equipment and wished she didn't feel so overwhelmed by it.

"Mindray," she said to herself, repeating the brand name of the piece of equipment Dr. Hendricks had told her to look for. It sounded loud in the empty room. She walked toward the far corner where Dr. Hendricks had told her they stored unused equipment in an alcove behind a curtain. She drew the curtain back to reveal several wheeled cart-looking pieces of equipment tightly pressed together. Dr. Hendricks had been gone for two months, and although he had assured her it would be here, what if it weren't?

Without any further delay, she pulled on the first piece of equipment, wheeling it out of the dark corner and into the light so that she could find out if this were the Mindray machine. What if there were more than one?

She soon found the manufacturer's name—Voluson—and pushed the machine aside. She pulled out a second one, and, while she tried to find the name of the manufacturer, she knocked a probe or paddle-type thing to the floor. It clattered like a hundred cans of beans spilled in a grocery store aisle and sent her pulse skyrocketing. She hurried to pick it up and tried to store the thing more securely before determining that this machine wasn't a Mindray, either. She pushed it aside a bit more carefully. The wheels of the third piece of equipment were locked, and she wasted nearly a minute trying to figure out how to make it move, only to find it also wasn't the Mindray machine. How many different pieces of unused equipment did they have?

She was wheeling the fourth machine out of the corner that was more than half-empty now when she thought she heard something. She froze for a count of five, waiting to hear the sound again. When she heard nothing, she continued pulling the equipment to the middle of the floor, where she saw, clear as day, the Mindray name on the front of it. Bless them for making it easy to read. Now—to find the USB. She walked around the machine first to visually orient herself with it. Dr. Hendricks had said that the drive was taped underneath, which had seemed like enough information at the time. Now that she was looking at the machine, however, she realized that "underneath" could mean that it was under the main console, or the part that opened in the middle, or underneath the wheeled assembly at the bottom. There were far more "underneaths" than she'd expected there would be.

She heard a footstep in the hall, and she looked at the door, expecting to see Nikki telling her to hurry. Instead, a confused and startled Dr. Waters stood in the doorway. They stared at each other, both of them searching for something to say. Dr. Waters found his words before Sadie did. "What the . . . Who are you? What are you doing in here?"

Sadie straightened and swallowed, looking past him for Nikki— she knew he was here, right? She hadn't left the clinic, had she? "Um, I'm, well, I'm looking for something." She wanted to ask why *he* was there, but it was his office, after all, so there could be any number of legitimate reasons.

"How the heck did you get in here?"

Sadie put up her hands, still waiting for Nikki to make an appearance and remembering that the police didn't want her talking to Dr. Waters. "I can assure you, Dr. Waters, that my intentions are honorable, and that if you could just—"

"Wait," he said as a flash of recognition crossed his face. "I know you." He didn't say how he knew her, but he didn't need to. They both remembered their encounter at the church the day before.

Sadie held his gaze and gave him a single nod, confirming who she was without either of them having to point it out.

"What are you doing here?" His voice was different this time. Not angry so much as concerned. It made it easier for her to tell him the truth.

"I'm looking for evidence against Anita Hendricks's fraud with the foundation and the boutique."

He stared at her, and his mouth opened, but he said nothing for a few seconds. He looked around and said, "In the x-ray room?"

"Dr. Hendricks said it was hidden on a piece of Mindray equipment." She waved toward the machine she'd been inspecting. "I'm assuming he meant this one."

"He *said?*"

Shoot! Sadie watched the realization dawn in his eyes. Dr. Waters took a step toward her. "He's alive?"

"Dr. Waters," she said, putting out one hand with the palm facing him. She tried not to show her distress at letting the truth slip out. "I need your word that you will keep this to yourself until tomorrow morning. There are things at play here that are extremely volatile." As soon as she said it, though, she knew she had to return to Dr. Hendricks at the cabin tonight. There was no way all these secrets could keep until tomorrow.

"But Trent's alive?" Dr. Waters said. He paused, pushed a hand through his hair, and used a word Sadie hadn't expected from a Mormon man. "He left on *purpose?*" He sounded furious.

Sadie didn't know what else to say, and she crouched down and started feeling around the nooks and crannies of the machine in search of the USB. The sooner she could find it, the sooner she could get out of here and work out the details of bringing Dr. Hendricks in as soon as possible. She started pulling at knobs, and opening things up. Why on earth hadn't she asked him exactly where he'd hidden it on the machine?

"What kind of proof are you looking for to prove the fraud?" Dr. Waters asked.

Sadie looked at him, and then she went back to her search. "Well, I don't know exactly. But before he left, Dr. Hendricks stored certain documents that he felt proved Anita was behind fraudulent activities with the foundation." She met his eyes and realized that he hadn't been surprised by hearing what Sadie was looking for. "I assume you must know about it or you would have asked me about the fraud rather than what kind of proof there was."

"Anita said everyone makes money when you put yourself on the line for a nonprofit like we did."

Sadie realized that while Dr. Hendricks claimed not to even know he was earning a salary from the foundation, Dr. Waters would have to have known. The two men never talked about it? "That's what I was talking to her about yesterday at the church," he added.

Sadie looked at him long enough to see his sincerity. She wondered again where Nikki was. He continued. "The accountant sent me a copy of the taxes—I guess he'd always sent a copy to Trent, and without him here he sent it to me instead. I didn't have a chance to look at it until yesterday, right before the service, but my brain was on fire after I saw the numbers. So little is being donated." The last words sounded painful for him to utter.

"What did she say?"

"She tried to explain it away, and all her words made sense, but there was something about the way she said it—intense and kind of annoyed that I would question her—that made it impossible for me to take it at face value. She promised to explain it to me in more detail later, but we never had the chance."

Was that true? Sadie asked herself. Couldn't he have gone to her house later that night, after Nikki had been there, and demanded a better explanation? "When were you going to have that discussion?" Sadie asked in an even voice.

"We didn't set a time," Dr. Waters said, pushing his hands into his pockets. "After the service, I had two hours of appointments and then got called in for a delivery. I had planned to talk to her about it in more detail today, but . . ."

Sadie let the words disappear while she continued feeling around the machine and trying not to think about what would happen if she didn't find the USB. What if Anita had found it already? What if it didn't exist and Dr. Hendricks was hitchhiking to Mexico? Sadie placed her head against the main console to reach underneath. She finally felt something that wasn't metal. Instead, it felt like something wrapped in plastic, or . . . duct tape. She probed with her fingers until she found the end of it, and then she picked at an edge until she loosened a corner of the tape. She pulled at it, and a minute later, she stood up with a bright yellow USB drive in her hands. Bits of adhesive stuck to it, but a cap covered the actual connector, protecting it from the stickiness. She looked up at Dr. Waters with a triumphant grin, only to notice how pale he'd become. He looked from the USB drive to Sadie's face.

"That has proof?" he asked softly. "Proof of everything she did?"

"I assume so," Sadie said as she stood up, her back screaming at her for hunching over so long. "Dr. Hendricks refused to come back without it. Can I ask you something else?" She took a few steps toward the doctor. Nikki hadn't yet shown herself, and Sadie was beginning to suspect one of two things. First, she had seen her husband come in, and she had panicked and hid, or, second, she had killed Anita and was on the run. Somehow, Sadie didn't believe the latter possibility, and she wondered if Nikki weren't hidden somewhere listening to all of this, still unsure of what to think of her husband.

For the sake of time, Sadie chose not to beat around the bush. "Did you have an affair with Anita Hendricks?"

Dr. Waters was visibly startled, and his eyes widened in what Sadie hoped was true surprise. "What?"

"Dr. Hendricks thinks you may have. Apparently Anita has a history of borrowing other women's husbands, but you already know that. I'm concerned at how she may have used you in her ploys for profit and power."

"Trent thinks I would do that?"

"He noticed certain things before he left—advances, I suppose you could say."

Dr. Waters looked past her and focused on the wall behind her head. Sadie tried to scratch some of the tape residue off of the device, the only outward sign she made of how uncomfortable this discussion was. Maybe she shouldn't have brought it up.

"Anita—I don't even know what to call it—is it 'came on to me'? 'Hit on me'? These things aren't a part of my life—I don't even know how to label them." He met Sadie's eyes again. "I did nothing to invite any such thing, and I did nothing to reciprocate what she did. It added an entirely new layer to working with her these last months, but I can assure you—and Trent—that I *never* acted inappropriately with Anita."

"But you met with her behind closed doors after the memorial," Sadie pointed out. "That could be . . . misinterpreted."

"Yes, it could," Dr. Waters said, nodding. "Or if someone overheard that things with the foundation weren't on the up and up, it could be even worse. I didn't want anyone to know what I was asking Anita about, and I didn't feel that there was any time to waste in confronting her about it." His words were clipped, and Sadie liked his tone.

"You didn't seem to want your wife to know about it," Sadie added. "When I told you she was in the kitchen, you became even more uncomfortable."

He shook his head slightly and looked past Sadie's shoulder. "Perhaps you can't appreciate what the last two months have been like for my wife as I have tried to carry on with this practice. Issues with the foundation were just one more part of what had become a miserable situation. I didn't want to worry Nikki any more than I could tell she already was."

A movement behind the doctor startled Sadie for a moment, but then she realized it was Nikki Waters. Nikki's eyes were red, but there was relief on her face as she reached out and touched her husband's arm. He turned quickly in alarm.

Sadie couldn't see his face, but she could imagine the surprised expression Nikki was looking at right then. For her part, Nikki smiled slightly and put her hands on either side of his face. Sadie felt awkward and turned to the side. She focused on removing the tape residue from the USB with her fingernail, allowing them a private moment—but she couldn't spare much more than that. They spoke in hushed whispers for a few seconds, and then Sadie glanced over her shoulder to see the two of them embracing. She tried to swallow the lump in her throat. Over the last few years, she'd seen more than one marriage torn apart by someone who didn't belong in it. She was relieved to know that whatever rebuilding the Waterses had ahead of them, infidelity wouldn't be an obstacle. They had a lot of good to fight for.

Sadie cleared her throat, reminding them that she was still

there. They moved apart, both of them trying to recover from the emotional moment, their hands joined as they stood side by side.

"I need to be going," Sadie said, holding up the USB to remind them why she was there. They stepped aside, and she moved toward the door. "Thank you for your help," she said to Nikki. "Do you still want me to drop you off at the police station?"

"Police station?" Dr. Waters repeated, looking down at his wife.

"Jake," Nikki said after taking a breath. "I need to tell you something."

"Oh, wait," Sadie cut in with feigned innocence. "Don't you have a meeting with the police as well, Dr. Waters? Perhaps the two of you could go together?" She smiled sweetly, and they both looked at Sadie and then at each other as she moved into the hallway and quick-stepped toward the entrance. Once she was out of the suite, she dialed Caro's number. Caro picked up on the second ring.

"I've got the USB," Sadie said, taking the stairs quickly. "Are you at the hotel?"

Chapter 35

Yeah," Caro said.

"I'm going to back up the USB on my computer, and I need a list of attorneys that Dr. Hendricks can choose from. Could you work on that?"

"Sure. And then you're going back to Pine Valley?"

"I think it would be better for everyone if Dr. Hendricks turns himself in tonight."

"I agree," Caro said. "The sooner all of this is over with, the better. I'm going with you to Pine Valley. You know that, right?"

Sadie hadn't even considered that—she was so used to being on her own for things—but she liked the idea of Caro coming with her. She'd been part of this case from the beginning, and she'd given Sadie the support and the distance she needed at every turn. Sadie reached the landing of the stairs that led to the first floor of the building and turned to go down the final flight. "I would love to have us go together," Sadie said.

"Oh, good," Caro said, sounding relieved.

The sound of voices caught Sadie's attention, and she looked up just as a young boy ran past the stairs and out the front doors. She paused and then hurried down the remaining steps to follow him. She could swear it was Joey Hendricks walking along the low wall surrounding the flower beds in front of the building. But weren't Lori and the kids in Las Vegas?

She turned to look in the direction he'd run from and recognized Dr. Hendricks's mother talking to someone on the other side of the glass doors of the foundation suite. Lori's daughter stood beside her grandmother, looking a little lost, or perhaps, like everyone else did, overwhelmed.

"Sadie?"

She'd forgotten she still had Caro on the phone. "Sorry, Caro. I guess Lori's in town. It took me off guard."

"She came for the vigil?"

"I guess so," Sadie said, looking around for Lori. "Or . . . at least her kids are here." Lori's daughter, Kenzie, looked up and saw Sadie. Sadie smiled but Kenzie just looked away. Did she recognize Sadie as the one who chased Lori down after the service yesterday? "I'm going to see if I can find her really quick."

"Okay. I'll work on that list of attorneys and see you when you get here."

"Good deal," Sadie said before ending the call and heading toward the foundation office. She pulled open the big glass doors and smiled when Mrs. Hendricks and the woman she'd been talking to—Anita's personal assistant, Sadie believed—looked over at her. Two men came around the corner just then, carrying a large folding table and catching the personal assistant's attention.

"Right out front would be great," the woman said. "I'll go find a tablecloth." Sadie stepped back to hold the doors open for the men and turned to see Joey Hendricks hurrying to open the other set.

They thanked her, and Sadie nodded her acknowledgment. After they were through the door, she stepped back into the office.

"Mrs. Hendricks," Sadie said as she approached, ignoring Kenzie's wary glance. She put out her hand, which Mrs. Hendricks took in a light handshake. "My name's Sadie. I'm so sorry for this tragedy."

Mrs. Hendricks gave a soft smile and a nod. She had the same slightly dazed look Kenzie—and many others—had right now. "Thank you," she said.

"Certainly. How are you all doing?" She smiled at Kenzie, who smiled in return, perhaps only because she had good manners.

"We're doing all right," Mrs. Hendricks said, putting her arm around Kenzie's shoulder. "Thank goodness for family during hard times."

The comment reminded Sadie of the fact that at this moment Mrs. Hendricks still thought her son was dead. Sadie knew better, and yet she couldn't tell her. Not yet. It was a painful secret to keep, even if she knew she had no choice. But it would be for only a little longer. Sadie looked at Kenzie again and felt the same feeling tenfold. *Your dad isn't dead!* she wanted to tell them. *You'll be seeing your son in just a few more hours!* Sadie had to shake herself out of those thoughts.

"Is Lori here?" she said, looking past them and around the office. Nikki's pink bakery boxes were still on the front counter where they'd left them, and Sadie could hear voices coming from the direction the assistant had just gone.

"Kenzie, go see if Melanie needs any help with those tablecloths," Mrs. Hendricks said, drawing Sadie's attention back to her. Kenzie did as her grandmother told her to, and Mrs. Hendricks turned to Sadie with that same soft smile. "Lori's talking to the

ROCKY ROAD

police right now," Mrs. Hendricks said, looking concerned. "But of course we told the children she was working on an assignment for school—I didn't want them to worry."

"Of course," Sadie agreed, relieved that Officer Nielson had taken her concerns about Lori so seriously. Had Lori come to St. George to meet with Officer Nielson, leaving the kids with their grandparents? If so, Officer Nielson must have worked fast. It had been barely two hours since Sadie had sat across from him and suggested he talk to Lori. Lori must have left Las Vegas as soon as he called, which he must have done as soon as Sadie left. Realizing that Mrs. Hendricks was watching her, Sadie turned to focus on the older woman's face and opened her mouth to make some ordinary comment. As she looked at this woman, however, she was momentarily overwhelmed by what Mrs. Hendricks would experience in just a few hours. How would it feel for her to learn that her son was alive? Would the pain of his staying away be rectified by his return? Surprising them both, Sadie gave the woman a big hug, blinking back her own tears as the woman returned it.

When she pulled back, Mrs. Hendricks looked only mildly surprised. "I wish you the very best as things move forward," Sadie said with absolute sincerity. She held both of the woman's hands in hers and gave them a squeeze. "The people in your life are lucky to have you."

She turned away from Mrs. Hendricks's startled expression and didn't look back as she hurried toward her car, more eager than ever to help put these relationships back together.

CHAPTER 36

Within fifteen minutes, Caro and Sadie were heading north on Bluff Street, which would become Highway 18 once they passed the Snow Canyon Parkway. Sadie had downloaded the documents from the USB onto her laptop, and Caro had written down the names of three different attorneys in St. George. Sadie left a message with Officer Nielson, telling him that she was on her way to Pine Valley and asking him to call when he could. She wanted to explain her reasons for going to Dr. Hendricks now instead of waiting till morning. She also wanted to tell him about what had happened with Dr. Waters, so he wouldn't think she'd ignored his request that she stay away from him. Sadie's stomach was full of butterflies. What if Dr. Hendricks refused to turn himself in? What if her trust that he would stay at the cabin tonight had been misplaced and he was gone for good?

As they drove, Sadie updated Caro on her meeting with Nikki and Dr. Waters. Caro had tried to talk to Tess, but Tess had insisted that she hadn't talked to Nikki and finally claimed she had something to do and hung up the phone. Caro was obviously hurt by

Tess's behavior, but she didn't seem to want to say any more about it, so Sadie let it be.

The drive went quickly, and the sun was just setting when they turned the corner into Pine Valley. Knowing what the view would look like this time didn't make it any less impressive. Sadie's breath caught in her throat as the sunset reflected orange and gold off the windows of the cabins and the lake to the east, which Sadie hadn't noticed before. "It's really pretty up here, isn't it?" Caro said as they began to descend into the valley. "You see all this and realize why the Mormons came to this state in the first place."

Sadie nodded. "I heard once that their prophet told them that they would come to the desert and make it blossom like a rose. They did a remarkable job of taking him at his word."

Caro nodded, but, despite attempts to distract herself, her expression was still tight.

"You know, every person finds himself through some kind of journey. Those pioneers had to overcome some big obstacles to get here. You and I have had to overcome hard things, too, and Tess is no different."

Sadie's words seemed to cause Caro to swallow some emotion, but she looked out the window and didn't answer.

"Situations like this bring out both our strengths and our weaknesses. Give her a little time to figure out which of those things she faced when something happened that she never imagined."

"I'm so disappointed in her," Caro finally breathed. "Which seems like such a silly thought to waste time on with everything else that's going on, but I can't shake it."

"You love her," Sadie said. "That makes it ten times heavier than everything else right now. Tomorrow, or the next day, when the truth is out and you've both had time to reflect on things, you can talk it out and then decide where to go from here."

Caro nodded, but Sadie noted how she quickly wiped her eyes. Sadie slowed down at the turnoff and turned right, passing the bright white church she hadn't been able to tour yet. They drove up Lloyd Canyon Road in silence. As Sadie came to a stop at the gate and shifted into park, Caro asked, "Are we going to drive up?"

"I feel better when the car's closer," Sadie said. Caro agreed, and they worked together to unchain the fence, open it and drive though, then close and rechain it again. The butterflies in Sadie's stomach weren't getting any calmer as they bumped down the road that led to Edger's cabin. Sadie tried her hardest to avoid the worst of the pot holes, but her anxiety was growing.

"Who's here?" Caro asked.

Sadie looked up from the road and was surprised to see a car parked in front of the cabin. Her eyebrows were furrowed as they approached the cabin, and then a wave of heat washed over her as she recognized the dark blue sedan. "That's Lori's car."

Caro inhaled sharply. "Oh, my gosh, you're right. What's she doing here? I thought she was talking to the police."

"So did I." Sadie pulled up beside the car, her mind racing with possible reasons Lori would be here. Had Dr. Hendricks called her? Why? How else would she know to come here? Sadie leaned over the steering wheel and scanned the tree line and the cabin. The shadows created by the setting sun were growing heavy, making it harder to see into the trees. "Lori really wanted to talk to him, but I didn't tell her where he was."

"How would she know he was here?"

"I don't know," Sadie said. "But she was either invited or she wasn't—and either way, I don't like it."

"What do we do?"

Sadie continued staring into the trees as she thought out loud. "Maybe she finished talking to Nielson and then came up here without telling Dr. Hendricks's mother. Maybe saying she was talking to the police was just a cover all along. Maybe Dr. Hendricks contacted her after I talked to him this afternoon. Either way, this feels . . . funny. As of one-thirty this afternoon, she was asking me where he was, which meant she didn't know."

Sadie took a breath and then turned back to Caro. When she'd talked to Dr. Hendricks earlier, she'd wondered if Lori had pieced together that Dr. Hendricks and Anita hadn't originally met the way they had told everyone they had. Could that be playing into *this*? "I want you to go to the motel and see if you can find out if Dr. Hendricks used their phone this afternoon—I think it's the only phone in town he could access without breaking into someone's house. Then I want you to call Officer Nielson." She reached into the backseat for her purse and produced the card he'd given her earlier. "Call his number, but if he doesn't answer, call the police station and insist that you talk to him. Tell him what's going on, and ask him what we should do—ask if he met with Lori this afternoon."

"And what are you going to do?"

"I'm going to try to find out what Lori's doing here."

CHAPTER 37

Caro didn't like leaving Sadie, but she was anxious to do what Sadie asked after Sadie reminded her that sunset led to twilight quickly in the mountains. They needed to act fast. Sadie assured Caro that she had the Taser in her pocket, and she took to the tree line as Caro got into the driver's seat and headed back to town.

The shadows were already darker than they had been when they'd first arrived at the cabin. If Dr. Hendricks knew Lori was coming, they would likely be at the campsite where he'd taken Sadie that afternoon. If Lori had taken Dr. Hendricks by surprise, however, she could be anywhere. It seemed wisest to try to determine why Lori was here before Sadie decided what to do about it.

Motivated by her plan, Sadie headed toward the path, scanning the area and walking on the balls of her feet to keep from making noise that would give her away. She reached the path and looked toward the cabin, standing completely still to listen for telltale sounds. She wanted Lori to be on the back deck or something, jostling the door or trying the windows. She heard nothing but the wind and the rustle of impending nightfall through the trees. Goose bumps broke out on her arms, and she took a deep breath to push down her rising fear. She turned onto the path, and two steps later she caught the faintest smell of campfire smoke on the breeze.

Without knowing it, Dr. Hendricks was leading Lori right to him. Unless he wasn't trying to hide.

Sadie picked up her pace, but she could go only so fast if she hoped to remain silent. She scanned the trail ahead of her and stopped every few steps to listen. The thicker trees made the twilight darker than ever, and even though she wished for a flashlight, she wouldn't have used it even if she had one. The smell of campfire became stronger, and she had a moment of optimism when she reached the place on the path where Dr. Hendricks had cut into the shrubs. Lori might have stayed on the path. Sadie had to step more carefully once she left the trail, but she was also trying to hurry. It was a difficult compromise to execute.

As she moved farther and farther from the trail, Sadie wished she'd paid more attention to how far off the path Dr. Hendricks's campsite had been. All she could do was follow the smell of smoke.

She was several yards off the path when she saw the large rocks that protected his campsite. She picked up her pace, hoping she'd reached him before Lori had, only to be brought up short by the sound of voices. She crouched as low to the ground as her quads would allow and continued forward, faster this time. She was not as concerned now about being overheard—if they were talking, they might not be as likely to hear any noise she made.

"Lori, please," Sadie heard Dr. Hendricks say as she reached the last bit of rock that separated her from his campsite. She knew exactly where she was now, but she didn't know if this was the only way to approach the clearing. "I'm so sorry," Dr. Hendricks continued.

"So it *is* true?" Lori asked, her voice heavy with emotion. "You cheated on me with *her?* Then you lied to me—to everyone—for all these years?"

Lori *had* put the pieces together. Sadie's feelings of sympathy kept her from interrupting—didn't Lori deserve an explanation? It might be good for Dr. Hendricks to hear firsthand the impact his choices had made on the people in his life. Sadie felt a little sheepish for being so concerned about Lori finding him. She wanted closure—was that so bad?

"Lori, you have to believe me when I tell you *she* seduced *me.* I still don't know how it happened. But between the problems you and I were having and her . . . determination to get her hands on the foundation—I don't know that any man could have resisted her advances. And I tried, so help me, I did."

"That's not what she said happened."

Sadie stiffened. *Lori had talked to Anita about the affair? When?*

"She said you were the one who came on to *her,* that you told her how miserable your marriage was, that you would do anything to go back and undo the whole thing if you could."

"You talked to her?" Dr. Hendricks asked, equally surprised. "When?"

"She said that marrying me got your parents off your back, that you knew it was a mistake almost immediately but couldn't stand the idea of telling your parents."

"When did you talk to Anita, Lori?" Dr. Hendricks asked her. "You hadn't talked to her before I called you yesterday, so when did the two of you talk about this?"

"I went to her house," Lori's voice was rising at the same rate as Sadie's heart rate. *When had she gone to Anita's house?* "I asked her point blank how the two of you met, and she didn't even hesitate to tell me—it was at that conference in Atlanta. I remembered it—something was different when you came home, but you have always assured me, and I have always believed that you would never—"

"Wait a minute," Dr. Hendricks cut in. "You went to see Anita last night? She was alive?"

"She told me about the two of you having drinks together and then going to your room." Lori's voice was definitely shaking with emotion. Sadie covered her mouth so she wouldn't let a sympathetic noise escape. "And then you two hatched this plan for her to come work for the foundation after our divorce and make it look like you'd fallen in love after working together. And the whole time you were—"

"It wasn't like that. *I* didn't have a plan. I wasn't acting out some scheme. It was all Anita—you have to believe me. I—"

"You cheated on me! While I was home trying to figure out how to save our marriage, you were with her, breaking all the promises we'd made to each other—all the promises we made to God that I thought meant something to you."

"I'm so sorry, Lori. If I could go back and do things differently, I would." There was silence except for Lori's crying. Sadie mentally egged on the conversation, wanting them to get back to discussing Lori's visit last night. Nikki had been there, too. So which of them had gone to see Anita first? Could they have gone together? Had Nikki lied to Sadie, or had Lori arrived after Nikki left?

"Nothing you say can change what's happened," Lori said, with a flatness in her tone that gave Sadie chills. "And you can't undo what happened last night any more than I can."

"Lori," Dr. Hendricks continued after several seconds had passed. He began asking the very questions that were spinning through Sadie's mind. "What happened when you went to see Anita last night?"

Lori began to sob, and even though Sadie couldn't see her, she imagined Lori sitting on the ground, arms pulling her knees to her chest as she rocked back and forth. "She told me everything, and she loved every second of it. Then she just shrugged and said, 'Not that it matters anymore.' She turned her back on me like none of it was even worth feeling sorry about. I looked at the house you'd traded us in for, the life you'd started after leaving me and the kids behind, and I ran after her. She bolted for the front door, and that's when . . . "

"When what?" Dr. Hendricks asked, urgency in his voice. "What happened?"

"She looked back at me, and she must have tripped," Lori said, her voice softer now so that Sadie had to lean around the rock slightly in order to hear her. "She fell and hit her head on this metal table. I . . . I didn't know what . . . It wasn't my fault." There was fear in her voice.

"What happened after she hit her head, Lori? This is important. What happened?"

"She started shaking, like she was having convulsions, and then she just stopped."

"How long did it take for her to stop shaking?"

Sadie was surprised by the analytical question, but then again, he was a doctor.

"I don't know. Not very long."

Dr. Hendricks's voice was tender when he spoke again. "It wasn't your fault. She hit her head and died instantly. Probably didn't feel a thing."

"But if I hadn't been chasing her, then—"

"She'd treated you like garbage, and she treated me like garbage, and she made a mess out of my life that is going to take a really long time to put back together. It is not your fault she's dead—in fact, I should be thanking you."

Sadie frowned—she didn't like that sentiment one bit. As horrible a person as she may have been, Anita Hendricks's death should not be viewed as a blessing. But maybe Dr. Hendricks was trying to pacify Lori or talk her down from the emotional ledge she was poised on.

"Now put down the gun so we can really talk about this."

Gun?

CHAPTER 38

A firearm changed everything—Lori had come up here *armed?* Lori's voice was shaking. "You can't come back, Trent. It would have been easier for everyone if you'd just died out here. We've all mourned you already, and if you come back, you'll just bring chaos with you." There was a finality in her tone, a kind of acceptance of what she saw as the only option.

Holy cow! Sadie felt the outline of the Taser in her pocket. Could she really use it? On Lori? She hated to even think about it, but she carefully slid the device out of her pocket. She turned it on and was startled at the slight vibration it now made in her hand.

Needing a better view of what was happening on the other side of the rock, Sadie crouched down and moved slowly toward the edge, her back against the rock as she moved quietly and held the Taser as far away from herself as she could—she could only imagine what would happen if she accidentally tased herself right now. When she was still hidden, but close enough to get a view, she turned around and peered into the campsite. Another rock blocked her view of Dr. Hendricks, but she could see Lori standing on one side of the table rock, with her back to Sadie. Her hair looked unnaturally bright in the light of the campfire, and her feet were planted with her arms out straight, her hands holding a small handgun that was pointed directly at Dr. Hendricks.

"Lori," Dr. Hendricks pleaded.

"Just stop it. I can't see my kids hurt by this anymore. They think you're dead, and if they find out you left them all this time, it will mess them up even more."

"You're not doing this for the kids," Dr. Hendricks accused. "You're doing this because you're angry, and unlike what happened with Anita, *this* will be a cold-blooded murder. You can't live with that."

"I can't live with *you* in our lives again! I can't see you and talk to you and pretend I don't hate everything about you, everything you've done. I can't do that for one more day, especially now that I know who you really are. Now that I know the lies you've told me. What else have you lied to me about, Trent? What's real and what isn't?"

Her voice was getting louder, and her emotion was changing quickly to anger, pure and simple. Sadie was running out of time to intercede. She could feel Lori's rage building in the air, as thick as the smoke coming from the fire.

"I'm not here to kill you. I'm here to make sure you never come back. You already left, so make it stick. Don't come back."

Sadie was somewhat relieved, but not completely. There was still a gun pointed at Dr. Hendricks. Lori was still emotionally compromised, and she'd still been at Anita's house the night before. Maybe it was an accident like she said, but maybe it wasn't.

"Lori, I have to come back. I have to make things right with the foundation and everything Anita's done. I know you're upset, but—"

"You're not listening to me!" Lori shouted. "You can't ever make this right with the kids, and that's all I care about. Get out of here! Go away and don't come back!"

The time to act had come. Sadie stood up, her leg muscles screaming from the prolonged crouch. She took a breath and moved out from behind the rock. Lori's back was to her, but Dr. Hendricks quickly glanced at her. His beard hid any change in his expression, and his gaze quickly flicked back to Lori. "Uh, where are the kids, Lori?"

Sadie knew he was trying to distract her from Sadie's approach, and she applauded his quick thinking. When Lori answered, Sadie took a step, hoping Lori's words would cover any sound Sadie might make. "They're with your parents—who also think you're dead. Did you ever think about what that felt like for all of us? And what it feels like now to know that you *chose* to stay away? You *chose* to make us all feel awful."

"I told you, Anita had been stealing all this—"

"I don't care what Anita did! I care what *you* did!"

Sadie took another step.

"People know I'm here. Even if I did disappear again, someone would find me. The kids would know, and then they'd learn that you're the reason I had to stay away. You can't do *that* to the kids!"

"As if you care about the kids!" Sadie took another step, keeping to the shadows. But the closer she got to Lori, the fewer shadows there were to hide in. She still held the Taser out in front of her, but to use it she'd have to get close to Lori, and she wasn't sure she could do that without being detected. If she could get within four or five feet, she could do a roundhouse and kick Lori's legs out from under her. Dr. Hendricks would be on his own in getting out of the way should the gun go off, but if Sadie could make a surprise attack, there was a good chance any shot Lori pulled off would go awry.

Once Lori was down, Sadie and Dr. Hendricks could hold her until the police showed up. She could use the Taser if she had to, but she hoped she'd be able to avoid it. "You've let them believe you were dead for two *months*, Trent." Sadie took another step.

Sadie was about ten feet behind Lori now. She remained crouched over, trying to keep out of Lori's peripheral vision. Her quads were burning like the St. George summer sun. "We've been mourning and going over regrets and holding you up on this pedestal, and all this time you were here. Letting us believe those things."

"I was suicidal when I left, Lori. I was going to kill myself, and then I couldn't bring myself to do it—because of you and the kids."

Sadie took another step, but this time Lori heard her and turned around. Sadie squatted to the ground, dropped the Taser, and placed her hands in the dirt. She swung her leg forward and brought it back to her body in a long, consistent arc. Her foot caught Lori right where she planned, between her ankle and her calf. Lori screamed before falling to the dirt with a thud.

Sadie expected Dr. Hendricks to jump forward and restrain Lori. Instead, he shot past them, heading for the trail. Sadie looked in his direction and then back toward a disoriented Lori, who was trying to get to her feet. The gun was a few feet away from her, and Sadie lunged for it at the same time Lori did. They reached it simultaneously, and Lori screamed again, elbowing Sadie hard in the chest as she tried to get Sadie's hand off the barrel. Sadie twisted the gun in an attempt to wrench it out of Lori's hand, but Lori was stronger and her stakes were higher. She hit Sadie again, but this time Sadie lifted her elbow quick enough to snap Lori in the jaw. She kneed Lori in the side and finally got her feet underneath her and wrenched the gun away at an angle she knew would make Lori let go. Lori screamed again and then looked up at Sadie with a stunned expression. Sadie could barely catch her breath as she stumbled away from Lori, who remained on the ground.

"Why are you helping him?" Lori rolled to her side and grabbed a rock to help her stand. Sadie kept her eyes trained on Lori's face as the rage drained from it, leaving an exhausted single mother of two, who was emotionally broken and mentally used up by everything that had happened in the last few days. Part of Sadie wanted to reassure Lori that everything would be okay and sympathize with the pain she was facing, but another part told her to run. When this was over, perhaps she would have a chance to explain herself and tell Lori that she understood why Lori felt the way she did, why her vision was skewed and her heart was aching so much she couldn't see straight.

But Sadie couldn't say those things right now. Lori wouldn't hear them. Sadie couldn't help her. She glanced at the Taser on the ground about five feet from Lori, but didn't dare go for it because it would take her closer to Lori and she wasn't sure she could wrestle her a second time.

"I'm so sorry," Sadie said as she took another step backward, holding the gun by the barrel in order to avoid touching the trigger. "You don't deserve everything that's happened to you, but I can't fix it." She then turned and did exactly what her instincts told her to—run as fast as she could.

She was halfway down the hill when the sound of loud voices brought her up short. A bright light shined in her face, blinding her. She put a hand up to shield her eyes, and she finally understood the words that were being shouted at her.

"Drop the weapon! Drop it now, or I'll shoot!"

CHAPTER 39

The hours between the moment Sadie found herself lying face down in the dirt and when she was told she could return to the hotel felt like days. Upon reaching her hotel in St. George, Sadie went into the bathroom and stripped off her clothes. She stepped under the water that she hoped would wash away all the ugliness of the last few hours. She winced at the sting of the water on the minor cuts on her hands and face and the head injury that hadn't yet healed.

Her brain was still reeling from the events of the evening, like a snow globe that was no longer being shaken but whose pieces of "snow" had not quite settled, either. She'd been able to speak with Officer Nielson on the phone. He'd been very gracious, and he regretted that things had become so intense. He said he'd had no idea when he asked for her help that he was asking for so much. She wondered if he'd really read her profile at all. For her part, Sadie would have been surprised if it *hadn't* ended this way.

The warm water relaxed her so much that it wasn't until Caro knocked on the hotel room door asking if she were all right that Sadie reoriented herself to where she was and finished her shower.

"You don't need to hover," Sadie said a few minutes later as Caro stood just behind her watching her comb her hair.

"You're sure you're okay?"

Sadie met Caro's eyes in the mirror and smiled. "I'm sure."

"I should have gone with you," Caro said. Was that the reason for her pained expression?

"If you hadn't called Officer Nielson, he'd have never been able to get the Rangers up there so quickly," Sadie assured her. "I don't know how I'd have gotten off that mountain if you hadn't done your part." By the time Sadie had arrived at the cabin clearing with her hands in cuffs behind her back and her mouth full of dirt, there were two SUVs and a truck there, Dr. Hendricks was being questioned, and Officer Nielson was on the phone with the ranger who was heading up the operation. It had wrapped up so quickly—that must be why she still felt unsettled.

"Do you mind if we pray before we go to bed?" Caro asked as Sadie pulled down the covers on her bed. "I prayed you'd be okay when I headed back to town, and then when I called Officer Nielson I prayed like crazy that he would know what to do. It seems like we should offer thanks for those prayers being answered."

"Absolutely," Sadie said. "Thanks are definitely in order." She also hoped that a prayer might help settle her thoughts.

They knelt beside their beds, and Caro offered a sweet prayer of gratitude. Sadie had never heard her pray like this, and she was struck by the humility of it. " . . . and help us to know of anything else yet undone and feel thy holy comfort and grace as we sleep this night. Amen."

They got into their beds, but Sadie kept thinking about the end of Caro's prayer. "Caro," she said after a full minute had passed.

Sadie could hear Caro sit up in the darkness. "Do you need something?"

"Why did you ask in your prayer for us to know of anything else that is still undone?"

Caro was quiet for a few seconds. "I'm sure it's just that I haven't dealt with this as often as you have."

"Something feels undone to you?"

"More like I just . . . feel unsettled. It's normal to feel this way, though, right? I mean when something so awful happens, something so unlike anything a person is used to, it's perfectly understandable that it would weigh on a person's mind, right?"

"Right," Sadie said, but she couldn't help but wonder if the unsettled feeling that Caro had was similar to her own unsettled feeling. What if what they were feeling weren't simply a result of the high emotions of the situation? What if it were more?

Though she was emotionally and physically exhausted, Sadie stared at the ceiling and tried to follow the threads of her thoughts and feelings to discover what, exactly, was causing such uneasiness.

"He ran right past me," she said out loud after what must have been several minutes. Caro's soft breathing had already given away the fact that she'd fallen asleep, so Sadie didn't expect an answer. She thought back to that moment when she disarmed Lori. Sadie was on the ground, and she fully expected Dr. Hendricks to help her hold Lori down—but instead he ran past her, leaving her there to fight for her own life after she'd just saved his.

Was that all? she asked her heart. She followed the feeling like a thread once again, and this time it took her to Jacob Waters. When she'd spoken to him at the office, he'd said he was talking to Anita at the church because he'd received the tax reports. Reports that Dr. Hendricks had received in previous years. Yet Dr. Hendricks had said he wasn't a business man, that doctors weren't known for their business sense. Why would the tax reports come to him if he didn't review them? Were they one more thing he simply signed without reading? He said that Anita took care of everything for the foundation—everything—so why would the tax documents come to him?

Sadie felt her heart rate increasing while she lay on the bed staring at the ceiling. Both trains of thought—Dr. Hendricks running past her in the mountains and Dr. Waters seeing mistakes that Dr. Hendricks apparently had not seen—fused together in Sadie's mind into a conclusion she didn't know exactly what to do with. Without Anita here to defend herself, would anyone consider any version of the story other than the version Dr. Hendricks told?

CHAPTER 40

The lights in the lobby of the Pine Valley Motel were some of the only lights on in the tiny town at three a.m. Sadie had chugged not one but two Mountain Dews and was in serious need of a restroom.

"I hope they leave the door unlocked," Caro said. She'd opted for coffee over soda, but she hadn't given Sadie a lecture on her choice of caffeine, which Sadie appreciated.

"Me, too," Sadie said. There were no other restrooms open, and she hadn't ever liked the idea of using shrubs and bushes. Sadie pulled up to the front of the motel, and they let themselves out of the car. They hadn't passed any other traffic since a few miles before the Pine Valley turnoff—the entire town seemed to be asleep. Sadie pulled on the front door and let out a breath of relief when it opened. She was only seconds away from embarrassing herself as she hurried toward the lobby restroom. When she returned to the lobby a minute later, she noticed that the night clerk wasn't at the desk. There was a sign on the counter that asked guests to ring a bell for service. The clerk must sleep at night. Sadie didn't ring the bell.

Caro was already sitting at the computer. "I found the history folder," Caro said, clicking the mouse. "And we should be able to look at daily histories . . . Yep, here they are. I'll open that first Wednesday."

Sadie leaned forward and forgot to breathe as she looked over the links listed under the first Wednesday following Dr. Hendricks's disappearance.

> www.grandcaymanrentals.com
> www.caymannationalbank.login/com
> www.hotmail.com

"Grand Cayman?" Caro read, sounding confused. "Maybe someone else was using this computer before he got on here."

"Maybe not," Sadie said. Her thoughts were swirling. "Isn't Grand Cayman one of the hotbeds for private banking and offshore trusts?"

"I don't know," Caro said, clicking on the link to Cayman National Bank. It took them to the login page.

"Click on that rental link," Sadie said, feeling increasingly anxious. That link took them to a rental house in Grand Cayman—a beautiful beach bungalow. What did that mean?

As they went through the entries for every Wednesday since Dr. Hendricks's disappearance, finding a pattern was easy. Every single week, he accessed the Grand Cayman banking site, as well as other sites focused on things such as moving money, hiding assets, processes for federal investigations of fraud, and precedent cases of non-profit owners facing prosecution. He had accessed Facebook, too, and the website for the local paper, and two weeks before, he'd gone to delta.com. Sadie was sure he'd accessed that because the URL was listed among numerous articles about moving money. Other websites were accessed, likely from guests at the motel, but the ones listed between 8:00 and 10:00 a.m. every Wednesday were similar to each other. The more she read, the heavier it all felt. Dr. Hendricks hadn't been sitting at a campsite recovering from depression. Something else was going on here.

After reviewing sites that were accessed each Wednesday morning since Dr. Hendricks had disappeared, Sadie pulled out her phone. She considered calling Officer Nielson, but she didn't think there was time to wait for the bureaucracy his help would automatically require. Instead, she called her son, Shawn. The call went to voice mail. She hung up and called again.

"He-hello?" answered a sleepy voice.

"I'm sorry to wake you up, sweetie," Sadie said, "but I need an extra set of hands right now. Can you help me with something? It's really important."

"Um, okay," he said, still not quite awake. Sadie felt terrible for interrupting his sleep, but she also knew he understood that investigative work didn't always take place during regular office hours. "What do you need?"

"I'm involved in a situation here in southern Utah."

"I'm so surprised to hear that," he said, yawning. She could hear him rustling around, and she assumed he was sitting up.

"Yeah, yeah, yeah," Sadie said, waving off his joke. "There's a man I think is hiding something, and I need you to do some fishing to make sure I'm on the right track before I take it to the police. You have better contacts than I do." He also had a knack for accessing information she couldn't dig into. She was careful not to ask him how he got this information, and he was careful not to tell her.

Sadie waited while Shawn yawned again. "Well, I love fishing at five o'clock in the morning. Where do I start?"

CHAPTER 41

Sadie pulled up to Dr. Hendricks's house around 10:00 a.m. and took a deep breath as her eyes scanned it side to side and up and down from the first to the third floor of the huge home. She couldn't help but wonder how much of this house was paid for out of foundation profits.

She automatically felt for the Taser in her pocket before remembering she'd left it in the dirt at the campsite. That was unfortunate—knowing what she now knew about this man, she could certainly use the Taser on Dr. Hendricks if she needed to.

Sadie took another deep breath and glanced in her rearview mirror. A dark SUV was parked out of sight, and two patrol cars were parked a block away. Caro was in one of the police cars, which made Sadie feel better, too. Working with the police was a surreal experience, and she couldn't deny that knowing they were there gave her more confidence. But the role she had to play for the next few minutes made her stomach tight and her head tingly. It was the best way to quickly resolve this case, and Sadie was the one who had suggested it, but Officer Nielson had told her what to say, how to act, and what kind of person she had to pretend to be. Even though whatever information Sadie collected wouldn't be admissible in court, it would at least allow the police to detain Dr. Hendricks and keep him from skipping the country—which, according to Shawn's research, seemed to be his plan.

Before getting out of the car, Sadie bowed her head over the steering wheel and waited until a sense of assurance settled upon her shoulders. Then she breathed deeply, let herself out of the car, and headed up the cobblestoned front walk. The Hendricks children had spent the night with their grandparents because both of their parents had been at the police station, each of them for a different reason. Sadie's heart ached for the mess their father had made of their lives.

Before ringing the doorbell, she said another prayer and took another deep breath, pulling together all of her confidence and trying not to think about how the people who loved Dr. Hendricks were about to have their hearts broken all over again.

A man opened the door, and Sadie had to look twice before she recognized Dr. Hendricks. In the hours since she'd last seen him, he'd shaved off the beard and trimmed his hair. Dressed in normal clothes, he looked like a different person, which only added to Sadie's understanding of the way he'd played her for a fool. All that vulnerability had been a ruse.

"Sadie," he said, and he stepped forward to give her a hug. She returned it as though she meant it. She hated touching him. When he pulled back, he smiled widely. "I didn't expect to see you again."

Sadie smiled politely back at him. Even if she hadn't known the truth, his comment and mood were completely inappropriate—his ex-wife was in jail right now, driven to the brink by his lies and manipulation, and his most recent wife was laid out on a slab in the medical examiner's office in Salt Lake City. Had he even seen his children yet? Did he care? Being angry helped solidify Sadie's determination. She could do this because it was the best way to ensure he got what he deserved.

"Um, could I talk to you for a few minutes?" she asked.

"Sure," he said, pulling the door open and waving her inside.

"How about out here?" she suggested, not wanting to go inside. The police had assured her that her microphone would work indoors, but she still felt better if she stayed outside. "It's such a nice day." Such a hot day was more like it. The temperature gauge in her car registered eighty-six degrees already at ten o'clock in the morning.

"Okay." He leaned back and grabbed the doorknob to pull the door shut. He motioned to one of the two wooden chairs on the porch—the same way he'd motioned to her to sit on a log the day before. He'd been anxious and unsure of himself back then. A completely different man from the confident doctor she was talking to now. And she'd fallen for that first act. She wouldn't make the same mistake again. She took the chair closest to the stairs and was grateful the porch was shaded, even though she was sweating anyway. The places where tape held the microphone wire in place beneath her shirt were starting to itch.

"So what can I do you for?" he asked, leaning his elbows on his knees and facing her with a smile. He really thought he had everything under control, didn't he? That was another boost for Sadie's confidence. If he thought he'd already won, he might not watch himself quite as carefully.

"How did things go at the station last night?" Sadie asked. She hadn't seen him after they were put in separate vehicles at the cabin.

"Boy," he said, letting out a breath and shaking his head. He leaned back in his chair and put his hands on his thighs. "Longest day of my life, I can tell you that. My attorney told me what I could and couldn't say, and I was home by one in the morning, so it all went pretty smoothly. They took the USB, and I'm hopeful things will work out. I can't thank you enough for helping me like you did. This turned out more positively than I ever imagined it would." He paused for a moment and then added, as though it were an afterthought, "And I'm so sorry for running like I did after you knocked Lori over—nice move, by the way. I've been operating on pure instinct for so long that I just went into 'fight or flight' mode. Apparently you can take care of yourself though—it was impressive." He reached over and tapped her arm, offering a smile with his compliment. She wanted nothing more than to punch him in the face.

Sadie hoped her own smile looked sincere as she nodded her acceptance of the thanks she no longer wanted. "And what's happening with Lori?" These questions weren't part of what she and Officer Nielson had discussed, but she wanted these answers as well, and she couldn't let the opportunity to get them pass her by.

"I hired the best attorney in the city to represent her," Dr. Hendricks said, his expression turning appropriately serious. "Not sure I'll ever get over all of that."

"All of what?" Did he mean the guilt of having cheated on Lori? The guilt of knowing Lori confronted Anita and that it resulted in Anita's death?

"It's not every day you find yourself looking down the barrel of a gun," he said. *Of course,* Sadie thought. He wouldn't be thinking of anyone but himself. "And to think of how hard I worked to help her with school and everything—my attorney during the divorce had told me not to be so generous, that it would come back to bite me. I had no idea." He paused to shake his head. "You just never really know people, do you?"

"I assume you'll be posting bond for her, though," Sadie said.

"Absolutely—it's the right thing to do. I've got a meeting with my lawyer later today. He'll advise me on the best way to go about that."

"And will the kids stay with her?"

"I'm not sure she's up to it right now, but I'm going to be so busy that I'm not sure I can put the time in at home that they would require from me. I need to determine what's in the best interest of the kids, of course. They've got to come first."

Every word grated on Sadie's ears. "You're going back to the clinic already?"

"Jake's been on call for two months, you know. Ironically, I think I came back just in the nick of time. I'm not sure how much longer he could have run it on his own."

"Especially with Anita gone."

He frowned appropriately and nodded his head, staring at his hands clasped in his lap. "It's overwhelming, to be sure. Hopefully I can keep us from losing any more ground. It's going to be a battle, though."

Sadie nodded and allowed the silence to stretch between them. She wondered how long he planned to stay before disappearing to Grand Cayman—a week? Two weeks? From the internet history she'd seen, she'd concluded that when he learned about the memorial service, he'd decided to leave the country. She wasn't yet sure why he hadn't left earlier, though, which was why she was here. The police needed more information to look for the proof they needed against him.

"You okay?" he said, gently touching her arm. She looked at him and took in the playful smile on his face. "You don't seem like a woman who just saved a man's life."

"I'm fine," Sadie said noncommittally as she sat up straighter, remembering the plan she and Officer Nielson had put together that morning. "I just had a couple of questions for you before I head home—I live out of state, ya know."

"Answering a few questions is the least I can do," he said with another charming smile.

"I'm curious as to where Anita put all that money she was taking from the foundation."

He leaned back and shrugged slightly. "I have no idea. A secret account, I guess."

"Offshore?"

He shrugged, but watched her closely.

"Three and a half million dollars is a lot of money. But I guess the feds will find it, huh?"

"I suppose," he said, but she noted a subtle shift in his expression. "I don't really know how that stuff works."

Liar. "Hmmm, it's a shame you don't have any way to access it."

She met his eyes and watched his expression as he tried to puzzle through her intent. She waited until he asked her a question she felt sure he couldn't resist asking. "And why is it a shame?"

"Because if you had access to the money, you might be able to keep me quiet about the things I've learned that I bet you'd rather the police didn't know."

He pulled back slightly and raised his eyebrows. "Excuse me?"

Sadie reached into her bag and pulled out the manila envelope she and Officer Nielson had put together. "They didn't take my statement last night," she began. "I go in later this afternoon, but there were a few things that didn't fit together." She undid the clasp and pulled out the stack of papers. "I did a little research and learned about the account in Grand Cayman you've been moving money to every Wednesday for the last two months."

His eyes widened ever so slightly, but Sadie continued as though she hadn't noticed. She showed him a printout of the bank's home page. Then she let him see a paper from the University of Utah. "I also learned that you minored in business as part of your under-graduate degree."

"I think you better go." He stood up, glaring at her while she carefully put the papers back into the envelope. She got to her feet as calmly as she could, keeping her expression neutral and her de-meanor calm despite the way her heart was racing. She could feel the heat in her chest and hoped it wouldn't spread to her neck and face too quickly and give her away.

"Sure," she said with a shrug, tucking the envelope back into her bag. "I haven't yet told them how you said that you're such a poor businessman, or how ignorant you pretended to be about the money you're now blaming Anita for having stolen—that's why I'm here." He continued to glare. "If I tell them some of the things you told me and then give them a few nudges in the right direction," she patted her bag, "they'll likely find the same things I've found. For instance, you've taken a few trips to Grand Cayman using your brother's pass-port, and on at least one occasion, your brother's wife posted pictures of him at his son's birthday party the same day he was supposedly out of the country."

She paused to let her words sink in, keeping a smile on her face the whole time. She gave him ample time to respond, but he re-mained quiet. "They don't even know to look for those things—un-less I tell them otherwise."

Fear mixed with anger on the doctor's face as she continued to hold his gaze. "You think you can blackmail me?" he said.

"You can't afford for me to take what I know to the police," Sadie reminded him. "Maybe Anita *did* set out to use the foundation to embezzle and scheme her way to wealth. Maybe you were a part of it, maybe you weren't. Somewhere along the way, however, you decided to be the one that benefited from it instead of her, and it's only fair that I get my share in order to protect your much larger portion, don't you think?"

He regarded her for a minute, his jaw tightening as he formulated a response.

"You're with the police," he said, watching her. "You're setting me up."

Sadie snorted. "You really think the police would let someone like me do this kind of thing? I'm a *private* investigator, and I cater to the highest bidder." She stopped to smile at him, not sure whether to be proud of herself, or disgusted, for playing this role so well. "For fifty thousand dollars, I'll corroborate any story you want me to, and then I'll go away. You won't hear from me again, and you can continue with your plan—because you most certainly have a plan, don't you, Dr. Hendricks?" She opened her purse again and removed an item wrapped in a plastic grocery sack. He tensed as she held it out to him, the bag falling to the sides of her hands as though it were a silk scarf.

"What's that?" he asked.

"The hard drive from the motel computer you've been using." Actually it was a hard drive from a fried computer stored in the back of the police department. The hard drive from the motel was currently being picked apart by a forensics team who expected to have Dr. Hendricks's bank account numbers and login information by the end of the day. She continued to hold it out to him. "It's yours right now if we can make an arrangement. Otherwise . . . "

His jaw tightened as he stared at the hard drive. She let him stare for nearly twenty seconds, and then she let out a disappointed breath as she rewrapped the hard drive and returned it to her purse. "Of course, if *you're* not worried about covering your tracks, then *I* have no reason to protect them." She turned toward the porch, trying not to panic at what seemed like the failure of their plan. Officer Nielson had told her that he'd have a plan B if this didn't work, but they both knew this was their only shot at a confession. Had she botched it? Had she not played this out the way she should have? Was it a mistake for them to trust her to pull this off? She went down the first step. Then the second.

"Wait," he said. Sadie closed her eyes briefly before she lifted her chin and turned around to look at him. He now towered above her, since she was standing two steps down from him. She didn't like the difference in their positions, and she stepped back up to the porch. "How do I know that's the motel computer's hard drive?"

A rush of adrenaline shot down Sadie's spine, but she was careful to hide her reaction. Officer Nielson had told her what to do if Dr. Hendricks took the bait. She pulled the hard drive out of her purse and extended it toward him again. He didn't take it. "Check it out for yourself," she said.

"Like I know how to do that," he said with the slightest growl of frustration in his voice.

She extended it closer to him—he had to take the hard drive from her to confirm that he knew there was something to hide. "Then find someone who can," Sadie said. "All I need from you is confirmation that you'll pay up—then I'll keep what I know to myself when I meet with the police later today."

He stared at the hard drive. She was careful to keep her breathing even as she watched his face.

Finally, he reached out for the hard drive, the plastic crinkling as he took hold of it. "I can't get to fifty thousand dollars right now," he said, his voice almost a whisper. "Not by a long shot."

"I know you have access to the money. You've been moving it for months."

He shook his head and looked at her. "I've been able to facilitate online transfers between numbered accounts in small enough batches that it doesn't tip off the feds. I can't get to any actual cash, especially right now. They'll be investigating the foundation, and we were careful enough to make sure they'll never find it as long as we don't lead them to it."

We? "So you and Anita set this up together?" Sadie asked. "I figured as much. Then, what? You decided you wanted it all for yourself?"

He didn't answer, and she shrugged as though she didn't care. "When can I get the fifty grand?"

"Do you think I'd have hung out in the woods and swept floors for tuna fish sandwiches if I could get my hands on that money? I've barely moved a third of what we siphoned off, and I won't be able to touch any of the rest for months—not until I know the police aren't watching me anymore."

"I can help them speed it up by painting the right picture. I want ten grand for the hard drive and a promise of forty more within the year. You in?"

"What about that?" he asked, nodding toward the top of the envelope sticking out of her bag.

"I'll give you that once you give me the first ten. When can you get it to me?"

"I can have ten grand by the end of next week."

Sadie nodded, and felt the tingling in her head again. She couldn't believe she was doing this. "I can live with that."

"Can you live with the fact that the next forty thousand will be dirty money? You're cool with where it came from?"

She sensed he was testing her, just as Officer Nielson had said he probably would. It was imperative that she handle this right. She recalled what Officer Nielson had told her to say if it became necessary. "What you took was peanuts compared to the 'free parking' that foundations bigger than yours land on every time someone wants to save the world with a twenty-dollar donation in exchange for a pink T-shirt, right?" She made a waving motion with her hand to emphasize how trivial the idea of stolen money was to her. "And dirty money funds trips to Europe just as well as a paycheck does."

A smile stretched across the doctor's face, which made Sadie feel even sicker than when she'd said those words out loud.

"People get to feel good about their philanthropy, and I get rich. And, now, you get rich too, of course."

"Well, I wouldn't say fifty thousand dollars is going to make me rich, but it can fly under the radar of my tax accountant." She adjusted the purse strap on her shoulder. "And what will you do now? The investigation is going to be in your way, like you said."

He shrugged his shoulders and looked past her at the red rock hills in the distance. "I'll keep up the practice for a while—try to reassure the community and all that—and then I'll retire to Grand Cayman—maybe claim post-traumatic stress or something to explain why I can't stay."

"Nice," Sadie said, but it was getting hard to play along with this. She felt physically ill. There had still been no mention of his children.

He smiled again. "And I've another Mrs. Hendricks to find, you know. There are some fine, fine women in the Caribbean. With or without my medical license, I can make a pretty nice life out there—stroke of luck, Anita hitting her head like that, don't you think? It's like it was meant to be. I couldn't have scripted it better myself." His smile was bigger than ever.

"Right, what luck," Sadie said. But she could feel her façade slipping. "Everything *is* happening just as though you scripted it. Could it have come together more perfectly?"

"I can't say it's been the best two months of my life or anything," he said, but his entire posture boasted pride and confidence. "But one of the most important skills you learn as a doctor is to think fast. You have people's lives in your hands, and you have to be able to react with skill and confidence—this isn't much different. I process through what's happening and instantly change course accordingly."

"So—you basically outsmart everybody," Sadie said. She wasn't smiling anymore, but he didn't seem to notice.

"And it's not as hard as you'd think—most people are idiots."

"And what about your children?" She couldn't help but say it, and his smile diminished slightly as he finally saw the change in her demeanor. "How are you going to explain all of this to them?"

"The kids will be fine." He stepped back toward his front door with the hard drive in his hand. "I'll let you know when I have that ten grand ready to go."

"I'll be waiting for that call," Sadie said. She pointed toward the hard drive in his hand. "Don't forget my show of good faith."

"I won't," he assured her as she turned and started down the steps.

When she reached the sidewalk, Sadie ducked her chin toward the microphone in her cleavage. "I'm going to throw up," she said to whoever was listening, feeling desperate to remind them that she was acting a part. She felt a hand grab her shoulder and spin her around.

Dr. Hendricks frowned at her. She'd been so intent on getting away that she hadn't realized he'd followed her down the steps.

"What did you say?" he asked, but he looked at the neckline of her shirt. He'd seen her talk into the microphone? Sadie lifted her hand to cover the opening of her shirt as though concerned over her modesty. He looked her in the eye. "What did you just say?"

Sadie heard the sound of a car engine behind her, and she lifted her chin so she could look straight back at him. "I said, 'I'm going to throw up.'"

He looked confused but also scared and angry. He'd just told her that his medical training prepared him to recalculate at a moment's notice, but she almost wished he'd hit her or do something that would cause the cops to pull their guns on him. He looked past her and backed up a step as Sadie heard tires squeal to a stop.

"You're a disgusting man, Dr. Hendricks," she said, taking a backward step herself. "And in your quest for riches, you've lost every treasure you ever had."

"Wh-what?"

A second police car pulled up behind the first. The drivers' doors flew open as the officers dropped behind them.

"Stay where you are! Hands where I can see them!" one of the policemen yelled. Sadie turned, lifting her hands above her head, and hurried toward the curb. Her adrenaline was rushing and her heart was racing now that it was all over.

"On the ground, both of you, legs spread and arms away from your body."

Sadie was the first to comply. She lay down on the hot sidewalk—the yard was xeriscaped, so there was no grass to offer a more comfortable landing spot. Dr. Hendricks took off running, and she turned her head to see one of the officers tackle him on the rocks of his beautifully landscaped yard. He started yelling and swearing, and Sadie turned her head away from the drama and forced herself to relax, take full, deep breaths, and accept that it was over.

The officers left her on the sidewalk while they dealt with Dr. Hendricks, and Sadie tried to pretend she wasn't as uncomfortable as she really was. She could hear Caro's voice but didn't tune in to it just yet.

She thought of Lori.

And Joey.

And Kenzie.

Dr. Hendricks's parents and brother and family and friends.

She thought of all the prayers offered on his behalf, all the hope stored up for his safe return, all the hearts that were soon to be broken again. *Mercy cannot rob justice*, she reminded herself. Sparing the tender feelings of all these people who loved Dr. Hendricks would only have delayed the heartache. It would have been only a matter of time before he'd have sacrificed them all over again. So much hurt, so much unfairness—and for what? Money? Stuff?

Another scripture came to mind as the officer helped her to her feet. "Be still and know that I am God."

Something as simple as that was sometimes the hardest thing to do.

CHAPTER 42

J ust wanted you to know that we've amended the charges against Lori Hendricks to misdemeanor attempted assault," Officer Nielson said into the phone Monday morning. "I'm hopeful the judge will limit her sentence to mandatory counseling. Dr. Hendricks's parents posted bail for her this morning, and I was able to talk with her before she left. She's doing better."

"I'm so glad to hear that," Sadie said as she looked around the hotel room she would be checking out of soon. Sadie was eager to start her trip home, but she was grateful that Officer Nielson had called her with an update. Despite the ugliness that had happened here, the city and its people had grown on her in the last few days. "And Dr. Hendricks?"

"The judge denied him bail due to the substantial flight risk with all the money at his disposal. Some federal investigators will be here in a few days—they'll take over most aspects of the case— although I'm trying like crazy to find something *we* can charge him with as well."

"Good," Sadie said. She hoped Dr. Hendricks's punishment

would at some point equate to all the pain he'd put his loved ones through, but she wasn't sure that was possible.

"We owe you a great deal for everything you did on this case," Officer Nielson said. "I spent the weekend going over your notes, and my estimation of you grew with every page."

Sadie was embarrassed by the praise. "Thank you," she said, looking at the carpet at her feet. She didn't know what else to say, and they sat there in silence for a few more seconds. The sound of a card-key in the door caused Sadie to look in that direction as Caro pushed the door open. She'd had breakfast with Tess this morning, and Sadie's eyes were immediately drawn to the aluminum foil pan in Caro's hands. Was that what she thought it was? She lifted her eyebrows as she looked at Caro's face.

"I did want to ask you something," Officer Nielson said, drawing Sadie's attention back to the phone call. "Did you feel God in this?"

The directness of his question startled her, and she took a few moments to review the last week and ponder his question. An answer didn't come readily to mind, so she hedged. "You know, Officer Nielson, I've never heard a police officer talk the way you do about God."

He chuckled. "Maybe the other ones didn't know Him like I do."

"No offense, but that's quite a statement to make," Sadie said, reflecting his boldness.

He chuckled again. "I don't mean to take anything away from anyone else's connection to Him, but neither will I apologize for the assurance I have of His hand in my life, my family, and my work. When I lost my legs, I gained something powerful that propels me more than tendons and joints ever did."

"You talk like a minister," Sadie said as Caro checked under the bed and in the drawers to be sure they hadn't forgotten anything.

Sadie had already checked, but since she was still talking, there was no reason to stop Caro from doing it, too.

"Thank you," he said with confidence. "But you haven't answered my question. Did you feel God in this?"

Sadie pondered the question again. It was simple and yet complex, and, try as she might to find an answer, she found herself stumbling through her thoughts. "Anita's dead," she said. "All of the people who mourned Dr. Hendricks are wrestling with even harder things than his death. The people who donated money to the foundation over the years, or purchased a Pink Posy Pin, have to come to terms with what their money was really used for. It's hard for me to look at those things and see God reflected back at me."

"It certainly is complex," Officer Nielson said with a humble but sincere voice. "But you still didn't answer my question. Did you feel God in this? Without trying to understand the esoteric ramifications of the things that happened, did you feel *Him*?"

Sadie remembered the times in this case that she knew what to do, when some little thing wouldn't rest easy in her mind, when she made a choice and saw it through to insight and understanding she hadn't expected at the outset. She could justify some of that as a result of the experience and knowledge she'd gained during the last few years, and yet, even with her logical side working overtime to make everything fit in that category, there were things that couldn't be explained away. As she pondered those things, her shoulders relaxed, her head felt less heavy, and her heart was lighter in her chest. Just as the stark white of the Mormon temple contrasted sharply with the red rock of the southern Utah landscape, there were stark moments of awareness that she couldn't ignore. The scripture that she'd been reminded of while Dr. Hendricks was being arrested stood out especially brightly. She'd felt calmness at that moment, a kind of salving of her concerns.

"Yes, Officer Nielson," she said into the phone, her voice quiet—reverent, almost. "I felt God in this." God's presence hadn't made everything better, but perhaps that wasn't the point. Perhaps perspective and patience and growth were the things He wanted His children to gain when bad things happened.

Sadie felt sure Officer Nielson was smiling on the other end of the line. "I'm very glad to hear that, Mrs. Hoffmiller." He didn't press her for details, and she realized he wanted her to simply acknowledge it, evaluate it, and learn from it. That wasn't a bad idea. If God were here, if He knew her and her gifts and wanted her to use them—where could that lead her?

They spoke for another minute or so about her trip home and the timeline for Dr. Hendricks's case—she would likely be expected to testify if he went to trial. By the time she hung up, Caro had rolled both of their suitcases to the door and was leaning against the wall sending a text message. When she finished, she looked up at Sadie with a smile. "He's a very interesting cop, that Officer Nielson."

Sadie nodded as she put her phone in her purse. "He certainly is."

"And Pete hasn't called?"

Sadie had worried about Pete's reaction all weekend, and yet at the same time she couldn't wait to tell him all about it. "Not yet. I imagine he'll get home and call me before he even checks his e-mail. It ought to be an interesting conversation."

Caro laughed at the understatement and then crossed to the dresser where she'd placed the aluminum pan she'd brought with her. "Tess wanted me to give you this—she remembered how much you said you liked Rocky Road fudge."

Sadie took the pan Caro cautiously held out to her and then looked up at Caro's face. "She also wrote you a note," Caro said, nodding at the envelope taped to the top of the pan.

Sadie looked at the note and wondered if she even wanted to read it, which made her feel bad. Sadie and Caro had finished out their girls' weekend without Tess, which had been fine with Sadie. There weren't many basically good people Sadie disliked, but Tess was on that short list.

"I'll head down and check out of the hotel," Caro said, inviting Sadie to read the note on her own. "Meet you in the lobby?"

"Sure."

When the door shut behind Caro, Sadie sat on the edge of one of the unmade beds and picked up the envelope. She turned it over and broke the seal. She couldn't imagine what Tess would want to say to her, but she felt a tendril of hope wrapping around the moment. It never felt comfortable to have bad feelings with someone, and if their relationship could be repaired, Sadie would certainly be open to that.

Sadie,

I hope you have a safe trip home.

Tess

Sadie laughed out loud. That's it? All that had happened, and this was Tess's version of . . . what? An apology? Not hardly. Sadie would bet a dozen doughnuts that Caro thought there was more to the letter than there really was. She put the letter beside her on the bed and turned her attention to the chocolate confection beneath the plastic lid. She'd always loved fudge—who didn't?—but Rocky Road was one of her favorites. Something about the smooth chocolate and the rough texture—the crunch of the nuts and the softness of the marshmallows made it a multi-sensory experience. And the fudge wasn't a bad commentary on what this week had been like—definitely a rocky road.

Sadie remembered seeing plastic spoons in the caddy of sugar and creamer next to the coffee pot. She walked over to get one. *Just a bite,* she thought. She removed the lid and used the spoon to carve through the chocolate, being sure to get a bite that included peanuts and a mini marshmallow, too. She put the spoonful on her tongue and closed her eyes to fully enjoy it as the chocolate melted on her tongue. Fudge could be tricky and she had to hand it to Tess—she'd done a great job with it. The texture was silky smooth, and the flavor was good. She savored the confection and allowed it to replace some of the negative feelings she felt toward Caro's cousin. At the same time, she smiled smugly at the certainty that although Tess's fudge was very good, Sadie's grandmother's recipe was better.

Granny Annie's Rocky Road Fudge

4½ cups sugar
1 (12-ounce) can evaporated milk
3½ cups mini marshmallows, divided (2 cups frozen, 1½ cups at
   room temperature)
1 stick butter, cut into tablespoon-size pieces
3½ cups (21 ounces) chocolate, such as chocolate chips or chopped
   candy bars*
1½ teaspoons vanilla
1 cup nuts (any type, but peanuts are traditional)

Put 2 cups of miniature marshmallows in the freezer. Butter a 9x13-inch pan.

In 4-quart saucepan (or larger—mixture will triple in size once it begins to boil) on medium heat, combine sugar and evaporated milk. Bring to a boil and boil for 7 minutes (to soft ball stage), stirring constantly. Remove from heat. Allow to cool 3 minutes. Do not stir mixture after removing it from heat or crystallization will occur.

While the sugar-milk mixture cools, mix together 1½ cups mini marshmallows, butter, chocolate, and vanilla in large bowl.

Pour sugar-milk mixture in bowl with chocolate-butter mixture (do not stir before pouring in sugar-milk mixture and do not scrape pan). Mix until smooth. Add nuts and pre-frozen marshmallows. Mix till combined. Pour mixture into prepared pan; smooth top. Allow to cool completely before cutting into 1-inch squares.

*Half milk chocolate and half semisweet chocolate makes a great combination.

Note: Fudge freezes well when wrapped tightly in plastic wrap or placed in an airtight container. Thaw before eating.

Acknowledgments

There are ten books in this series, and people still want to read about Sadie's adventures—that is the greatest compliment an author can ever have. Thank you to all who love Sadie, roll their eyes at her, and still root for her success. Without that investment on your part, gentle reader, she would not exist.

Thank you to Shadow Mountain for making Sadie come alive: Jana Erickson (product director), Lisa Mangum (editor and author of *After Hello*, Shadow Mountain 2012), Vicki Parry (interim editor), Malina Grigg (typographer), and Shauna Gibby (designer). Thanks to the marketing department and the board and thanks for the continual encouragement I get from every corner of Shadow Mountain. Kenny Hodges and Diane Dabczynki are responsible for giving a voice to Sadie through audio books, and I am so grateful for their talent and investment as well.

This book is dedicated to the test kitchen, and I thank them once again—they are the reason this entire project works, and I so much appreciate all they have done for this series. They also helped with the recipes in this book: Annie Funk provided the recipes for Barbacoa Pork, Tomatillo Ranch Dressing, Strawberry Pretzel Pie, and Granny Annie's Fudge; Whit Larsen provided the recipes for Funeral Potatoes and Maddox Rolls; Don Carey and his wife, Kara, who is known for this recipe, provided the Dream Cookies recipe; Danyelle Ferguson supplied the Lime-Cilantro Rice recipe; and Laree Ipson and her dad allowed us to use the recipes for Ol' Dad's Dutch Oven Chicken and Ol' Dad's Dutch Oven Potatoes. My love and admiration for these guys are beyond words. In addition to my fabulous test kitchen, my friend Jenny Moore allowed me to use the recipe for her wonderful Waffle Mania Waffles. I'm not sure I contributed any recipes to this book, but I sure did enjoy making them all ☺.

My writer's group once again stumbled with me through the creation of the story even though they didn't know the end—thank you, Becki Clayson, Jenny Moore, Jody Durfee (*Hadley, Hadley Benson*, Covenant 2013), Nancy Allen (Isabelle Webb series, Covenant 2009–2012), and Ronda Hinrichsen (*Trapped*, Walnut Springs 2010). The writing feedback is essential, but the emotional support and friendship is priceless.

Thank you to the Bear Lake Monsters writing retreat, which provided me the time to really get this story going, and the fabulous friends I came to love even more while we were there—Chris, Cory, Jenny, Krista, Marion, Margot, Nancy, and Rob. The energy of great writers is beyond measure, and I am so blessed to have many great writers within my sphere.

Thank you to my beta readers—Jenny Moore (yes, that's her fourth mention—the woman is amazing), Melanie Jacobson (*Second Chances*, Covenant 2013), and my sister Jenifer Johnson. You guys helped me see what I could no longer see correctly, and I thank you so much for your time and insight. Lisa Mangum also went through several brainstorming sessions to help me get the story just right. I very much appreciate her time and talents in helping this story shine.

And, of course, the beginning and the end of my experience with this book is my family. They are the ones who are there when the ideas aren't, who help me find the time I am certain I've lost, but who also remind me that there is more to life than fiction writing. I am grateful that my kids have accepted as normal the weirdness my writing brings into their lives, that they see in my accomplishments a reason to pursue their own gifts, and that they love me and encourage me and believe in my dreams. And above them all is my dear husband Lee, my best friend, my greatest cheerleader, the center I return to at the end of each day where I can be enfolded by his open arms, cheered by his easy smile, and reminded that I do not walk this path alone. I am grateful you are the people God gave to me for this life and beyond, and I love each of you so very much.

I am grateful for the grace of God in my life, and I thank Him for the greatness of it.

AUTHOR'S NOTE

Pine Valley is a real city in southern Utah, a true oasis when compared to the surrounding desert landscape. Should you find yourself in the area, Pine Valley is well worth a visit, but be aware that I took some fictional license in describing it. Though the Brandin' Iron is a fabulous steakhouse, the Pine Valley Motel does not exist, and as of this writing, the Pine Valley Lodge was closed. There is a beautiful campground near the lake, and the church tour is fascinating. There is an ice cream shop in the summer and a visitors center where you can learn about the region. I believe you can find cabin rentals online if you want to stay for a few days. I wouldn't blame you in the least.

Enjoy this sneak peek of

FORTUNE COOKIE

Coming February 2014

CHAPTER 1

Sadie Hoffmiller had always liked things to be just so. "A place for everything and everything in its place" was efficient, consistent, and reduced both stress and loss. Certainly the events of the last few years had shaken some of Sadie's confidence in being able to keep things as they should be, but for the most part, she felt the changes these disruptions had caused were for the better. She felt more capable of recovering from difficult circumstances, more aware of what went on around her, and increasingly confident in her ability to take life as it came and respond accordingly. Even a lingering threat on her life was something she had come to terms with, knowing she might one day face it but hoping that perhaps the threat had disappeared.

She still preferred order to chaos, of course, when she had any say in the matter—and of all the things Sadie should be able to have control of, her own wedding was it. Which is why the four-by-nine-inch envelope sitting in the middle of her kitchen table terrified her.

The wedding invitations she'd spent the last two days preparing were stacked on the entry table of her living room waiting for her to take them to the post office the next morning. They would soon be winging their way to her friends, family, and acquaintances all over the world—she was hoping the postal service would have a wedding-specific stamp that would be the perfect final touch. Even if the people living out of state couldn't be there, she wanted them to celebrate the occasion with her.

And yet the lone envelope on the table had been sent *to* her. Sadie had discovered it in her mailbox this afternoon, and she was trying to work up the courage to open it. Was it mocking her? Egging her on? Or simply staring back at her as a reminder that not everything in her life could be controlled and anticipated?

There was no name on the return address, just a P.O. box and the city, state, and zip code. But Sadie knew only one person who lived in San Francisco—her older sister Wendy, whom she hadn't seen for years. Did Wendy somehow already know about the upcoming wedding? Although the unexpected letter certainly triggered some of Sadie's overactive curiosity, it hadn't been enough to overcome her reluctance to invite her sister back into her life. Especially now.

Sadie pulled the final pan of jam bars from the oven—she'd managed to come up with a dozen tasks around the house to delay the inevitable opening of that envelope. She'd been trying not to bake after six o'clock in the evening—she had a size twelve wedding dress to fit into, after all, and at the age of fifty-eight, she couldn't simply eat salads for a week and expect to lose a couple of pounds like she'd been able to do in her twenties. But the letter had knocked her off the proverbial wagon. That Wendy had always hated their mother's jam bar recipe was purely coincidental.

The digital time display on her microwave read 9:44 p.m. Tomorrow would be a full day of more wedding preparations now that she was back home and sufficiently recovered from her vacation-turned-investigation in Utah the week before. The wedding was only three and a half weeks away, and she felt giddy every time she thought about it. *Mrs. Peter Cunningham*. Wow.

Her eyes strayed back to the envelope on the table, and she felt ridiculous for having put this off for the better part of the day. It was time to get it over with. She grabbed her letter opener from the drawer of the desk in her living room. She picked up the envelope. The handwriting looked different from what she expected—that is, if she had expected this at all, which she hadn't.

"Wendy," Sadie said out loud. Her sister's name sounded strange on her tongue. It was sad that they were so disconnected, and yet Sadie had little motivation to reach out to change what had always been a difficult relationship. Wendy was five years older than Sadie and the source of many frightening memories from Sadie's childhood, including broken and missing toys, dead spiders in her oatmeal, and, on one memorable occasion, being locked outside for hours while their parents were gone.

Wendy left home at seventeen, creating a void in the lives of Sadie's parents that was never remedied. Despite all the chaos and difficulty she'd brought into the family, she was still their daughter, and they'd always wanted to be a part of her life. Now and then, she'd popped in to ask for money or to throw a tantrum about one issue or another, but for the most part she stayed out of their lives completely.

Sadie hadn't seen Wendy since their mother's funeral almost fifteen years before. She'd stayed in town for four hours, long enough to put her rose on the casket and rifle through Mom's jewelry box. When their father died just four years ago, Sadie had tracked her sister down, only to have Wendy say she couldn't get away for the funeral but she'd send flowers. She didn't send any flowers, and Sadie and her brother, Jack, followed their father's casket from the church without even a whisper about Wendy's absence. After that, Sadie had stopped sending Christmas cards that were never reciprocated or marking Wendy's birthday on her calendar at the start of each new year, and each time she thought about her sister, she forced herself to think of something else. For all intents and purposes, she didn't have a sister and never really had. She hadn't even told Pete about her, other than admitting she existed.

Sadie inhaled deeply, hoping to control the growing anxiety that thoughts of Wendy induced. The scent of baking in the air didn't relax her like it usually did. No doubt she would eat a dozen bars herself before finally going to bed tonight. She'd faced off with murderers and crooks, but her sister could send her into a panic with just a simple letter.

Sadie took a breath, turned the envelope over, and carefully slid the letter opener into the open corner. The blade sliced smoothly through the paper with barely a sound. She pulled out a white sheet of paper that revealed a newspaper article folded inside of it. Intrigued yet hesitant, she unfolded the newsprint. She was a bit confused by the partial coupon for Fourth of July flower arrangements until she realized that must be the back side. She turned the article over and read the heading.

Woman Found Dead in Mission District Apartment

Sadie's heart rate increased as she read the opening lines about a badly decomposed body being found after an anonymous call to 911 about an apartment fire. Sadie squeezed her eyes shut tight. When she opened them, they wouldn't focus on the words of the article, as though they were unwilling to read more. Unable to process it, she put the article down and pushed it away from her, her head tingling.

After catching her breath, she turned her attention to the sheet of paper she still held in her shaky hand.

Ms. Hoffmiller,

My name is Ji Doang. My natural mother was your sister, Wendy Wright Penrose, and I found your address among her possessions. Her body was found in her apartment June 25th and I thought you would want to know. I am working to clear her apartment before the tenth of next month and determine what to do with her remains when the autopsy is complete. If you are available, I would appreciate your help as it is a big job and I am quite busy with family and work. If I don't hear from you, I will understand. I was not close with her either.

Sincerely,
Ji

Jam Bars

Crust
1½ cups flour
½ cup quick-cooking oats, uncooked
½ cup sugar
¾ cup butter or margarine, softened
½ teaspoon baking soda

Topping
¾ cup flaked coconut
¾ cup chopped walnuts

¼ cup flour
¼ cup packed brown sugar
2 tablespoons butter or margarine, softened
½ teaspoon cinnamon
1 cup strawberry or raspberry jam

Preheat oven to 350 degrees. For crust, in large mixer bowl, combine all crust ingredients. Beat at low speed, scraping bowl often, until mixture is crumbly, 1 to 2 minutes. Using hands, press mixture in bottom of greased 9x13-inch baking pan. Be sure to spray or grease sides of pan as well as bottom. Bake 18 to 20 minutes, or until edges are lightly browned.

For topping, in same mixer bowl, combine coconut, nuts, flour, brown sugar, butter, and cinnamon. Beat at low speed, scraping bowl often, until well mixed. Crumbling mixture with clean hands works well, too. Spread jam evenly on hot crust, almost to the edges. Sprinkle topping mixture over jam. Continue baking 18 to 20 minutes, or until edges are lightly browned. Cool completely in pan on wire rack. Cut into bars.

Makes 15 to 24 bars, depending on size cut. Serve warm with ice cream or cool with whipped topping.

ABOUT THE AUTHOR

J osi S. Kilpack began her first novel in 1998. Her seventh novel, *Sheep's Clothing*, won the 2007 Whitney Award for Mystery/Suspense. *Rocky Road* is Josi's nineteenth novel and the tenth book in the Sadie Hoffmiller Culinary Mystery Series.

Josi currently lives in Willard, Utah, with her husband and children.

For more information about Josi, you can visit her website at www.josiskilpack.com, read her blog at www.josikilpack.blogspot.com, or contact her via e-mail at Kilpack@gmail.com.

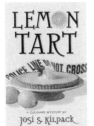